Cinderella in Spain

Cinderella in Spain

Variations of the Story as Socio-Ethical Texts

MAIA FERNÁNDEZ-LAMARQUE

Foreword by John Stephens

McFarland & Company, Inc., Publishers
Jefferson, North Carolina

LIBRARY OF CONGRESS CATALOGUING-IN-PUBLICATION DATA

Names: Fernández-Lamarque, Maia, author.
Title: Cinderella in Spain : variations of the story as socio-ethical texts / Maia Fernández-Lamarque ; Foreword by John Stephens.
Description: Jefferson, North Carolina : McFarland & Company, Inc., Publishers, 2019 | Includes bibliographical references and index.
Identifiers: LCCN 2019027225 | ISBN 9781476667829 (paperback) ∞ | ISBN 9781476637068 (ebook)
Subjects: LCSH: Cinderella (Legendary character) | Cinderella (Tale)—Adaptations. | Folklore—Social aspects—Spain. | Fairy tales—Social aspects—Spain. | Psychoanalysis and folklore—Spain.
Classification: LCC GR75.C4 F47 2019 | DDC 398.20946—dc23
LC record available at https://lccn.loc.gov/2019027225

BRITISH LIBRARY CATALOGUING DATA ARE AVAILABLE

ISBN (print) 978-1-4766-6782-9
ISBN (ebook) 978-1-4766-3706-8

© 2019 Maia Fernández-Lamarque. All rights reserved

No part of this book may be reproduced or transmitted in any form or by any means, electronic or mechanical, including photocopying or recording, or by any information storage and retrieval system, without permission in writing from the publisher.

Front cover image © 2019 Fer Gregory/Shutterstock

Printed in the United States of America

McFarland & Company, Inc., Publishers
 Box 611, Jefferson, North Carolina 28640
  www.mcfarlandpub.com

To all those who have been wronged and treated unjustly sometime in their life's journey, but have overcome obstacles shielded by strength, honor and courage.

Table of Contents

Acknowledgments   ix
Foreword by John Stephens   1
Prologue   5

1. "Estrellita de oro" and the Ritual of Branding   13
2. The Censored Version of *Cinderella* in Franco's Spain   26
3. Performance as a Mask in *La nueva Cenicienta*   41
4. The Notion of Otherness Through Synecdoche and Prosopopeia in *Sólo un pie descalzo*   54
5. Queer Cinderella: *Cenicienta en Chueca*   66
6. Cinderella as a "Chick" Protagonist in *Cenicienta siempre quiso un Wonderbra*   78
7. *La Cenicienta que no quería comer perdices*: A Cinderella Picture Book   94
8. Suicidal Cinderella: *Cenicienta en Pensilvania*   109
9. *Idiotizadas*: Comics, Folktales and Feminism in Spain   124
10. A Poetic Version: *Te cuento ... Cenicienta*   138
11. Versions of Cinderella in Spain: A Survey of Primary Texts   151

Chapter Notes   165
Bibliography   169
Index   183

Acknowledgments

The research for this book was possible thanks to several awards and grants from the following international and national entities: Program of Cultural Cooperation between the Spanish Ministry and U.S. Universities in 2007, Grant Award from the Ministry of Culture and Education in Spain, HISPANEX for research project: "Cinderella" *in Spain: The Other in Question* in 2014, two Faculty Development Research Grants from the Provost Office, Texas A&M University Commerce, 2006 and 2012 and a sabbatical (aka Faculty Development Leave). The Program of Cultural Cooperation between American Universities and the Ministry of Culture in Spain awarded me two grants to visit the Biblioteca Nacional in Madrid, Spain to gather versions of Cinderella not accessible in the United States. In 2014, HISPANEX and the Ministry of Culture in Spain also awarded me a grant to continue ancillary work on film and drama versions of the tale at the Biblioteca Nacional in Madrid. Texas A&M University–Commerce and Texas A&M University system awarded me the sabbatical in the fall of 2018 to finish this manuscript.

I would like to thank the librarians at University of Texas at Austin at the LLILAS Benson Latin American Studies and Collections Latin American Library for their help in finding one of the rare adaptations of the tale. My immense gratitude goes to the librarians at Texas A&M University—Commerce for their help finding books all over the world. In particular, my special thanks to Jake Pichnarcik, who made extra efforts to find the rarest books and seemly unreachable material for my research. Alkibla Publishers in Spain, Clemente Bernad and Carolina Martínez, are also acknowledged, who kindly provided a copy of one of the most poetic Cinderella versions found and motive of Chapter 10.

My graduate students in the seminar Cinderella around the world taught in the spring 2018: Reyna Conger, Alfonso Casares, Óscar Joya, Johanna Cáceres, Liliana Maldonado, Eunice Hernández; thanks for their insight and fantastic rapport in the class. It is worth mentioning two exceptional students for their help in my research, Jeannette Rivero for being a hardworking and dedicated assistant for part of this project, and my former research assistant in 2012, Michele Giltner for her dedication, professionalism and excellent job translating some of my work published in English.

Also my gratitude to colleagues and friends who contributed with their comments and suggestions: from Melissa Culver, Texas A&M University–Corpus Christi, to Joe Hayes author of "Little Golden Star," to my high school friend Irene Soler, for Dr. Nicola Darwood, the organizer of *All About Cinderella: retellings in a cultural imagination* in Bedfordshire, England, in the summer of 2017, where I presented the first chapter of this book and met scholars who gave me their insight on various themes on Cinderella from their particular fields: Dalila Forni from the Università degli Studi di Firenze and Tatjana Pilipoveca at the University of Tartu in Estonia.

A special thank you to two prominent scholars: Dr. John Stephens, emeritus professor at Macquarie University in Australia, who has honored me by writing the foreword to this book and by revising and editing the whole volume, improving it in both style and substance. Professor Stephens' guide, expertise and mentorship along my career as a scholar in children and adolescent literature have been priceless. And Dr. Jaime García Padrino, professor emeritus at the Universidad Complutense in Madrid, for his friendship, support and invaluable input on children's literature in Spain. Thank you to Kepa Osorio at La Casa del Lector in Madrid, who supported my research for HISPANEX grant; and to the Foundation Germán Sánchez Ruipérez, that helped me finding some of Antonio Robles' work at their site in Salamanca, and later in their location in Madrid.

My gratitude and respect to my friends and colleagues: Dr. Georgia Seminet, Dr. Ted Henken, Dr. José Antonio Giménez Micó, Dr. Jan Torres Po, Dr. Elena Grau-Llevería and Dr. Eleuterio Santiago-Díaz for their continuous professional support. I also wish to record my indebtness to the following individuals at the university: Dr. Edward Romero, Michele Vieira and Heidi Wright for their support in my tenure at the university as an associate professor and my gratitude to the dean of College of Humanities Social Sciences and Arts, Dr. William Kuracina for his support to my research.

Thank you to Mark Haslett who was a reader for part of the manuscript. Thanks to my best friends: The Fernández-Lamarque clan, and all my friends who have been or are part of my life: Ericka L. Mariela F., Noemi G., Juanpa O., Kaydy L., Norma B., Patricia B., Martha G., Blanca D., Maite M., María I. and all of those who have contributed with their actions of love and camaraderie to this book.

A special place in my heart is for my husband David and my son Luca for their presence and love, which sustained me in every path walked for this journey. Without them, this project would not have been possible.

Foreword
by John Stephens

The story of a young woman, of around marriageable age, who has been abandoned by a careless father to the charge of a second wife, is subsequently mistreated and reduced in social status, and unexpectedly becomes a queen, is told repeatedly in most parts of the world. She goes by many names, but in English is generally known as *Cinderella*, a name derived from *Cendrillon*, the protagonist of Charles Perrault's retelling of the tale in 1697. This name is so well-established that in English translations of the Brothers Grimm's version of the tale it has, since Margaret Hunt's 1884 translation of the *Household Tales*, commonly displaced *Aschenputtel* as the name of the protagonist.

In Spain she is known as *Cenicienta.* In this volume, Maia Fernández-Lamarque has gathered forty-four retellings of the story of Cenicienta, of various kinds in diverse genres, and has selected ten of these for extended discussion. This conception is unique, as scholarly approaches to such a globally retold tale are more apt to pursue a comparative agenda, as in the recent collection, *Cinderella Across Cultures: New Directions and Interdisciplinary Perspectives* (2016). Maia Fernández-Lamarque's study has not been concerned with retellings that are principally replications of Perrault's "Cendrillon" or the Grimms' "Aschenputtel," the two most common source texts. For example, Isabel Díaz' *Cenicienta* (2001) is a retelling of the Perrault version, but which also draws on the additions to Perrault made in the 1950 Disney animation: the stepmother and stepsisters destroy Cinderella's dress to stop her attending the ball, and Cinderella's mice friends help her escape when she is locked in the attic to prevent her trying on the shoe which is rightfully hers.

Such a retelling may not offer much that is intrinsically interesting, but it does demonstrate that the possible sources of even an uncomplicated retelling may be multiple and fluid, part of an extensive web of story. "Cenicienta" may hark back to Perrault or the Grimms, but as it flows across time other elements become embedded in it. In the modern era the number of text types used to tell the story has also multiplied, so that prose narrative has been joined by multimodal forms such as picture books, films, stage dramas, and so on, and a particular genre brings its own signifying strategies to the hypertext. Part of this web of story is the tale's relationship—explicit or implicit—with other tales it can be grouped with. In the Aarne-Thompson-Uther system, Cinderella is classified as *Tale Type 510A, Persecuted Heroine*. Consolidated recognition of a (sub-)genre referred to as the "Innocent Persecuted Heroine" genre was established by a special issue of *Western Folklore* in 1993. In his contribution, which defines the genre structurally and thematically, Steven Swann Jones identifies nineteen tales that belong to it, within which "Cinderella" is part of a sub-group of three (14–15). Of particular relevance to Maia Fernández-Lamarque's study are Jones' narrative paradigm and Cristina Bacchilega's comments on the social production of the feminine in the genre. Jones identifies a three-part structure: first, the protagonist's mistreatment in the home by hostile family members; second, her need to overcome various obstacles on her path to marriage; and third, the persecution she suffers in her husband's home after marriage (16). Versions of "Cenicienta" usually utilize only the first two parts of the paradigm, but the third remains a possibility. It is realized in the highly inventive picture book, *La Cenicienta que no quería comer perdices*, discussed here in Chapter 7. The "Innocent Persecuted Heroine" genre thus demonstrates links to a larger pattern of narratives, and this web of story imparts a significance to the specific story that makes it readily interpretable as a moral fable or allegory whose significance is shaped by its narrative affiliations and by its articulation within culture.

The misery endured by Cenicienta in her life with her abusive husband in *La Cenicienta que no quería comer perdices* resonates with Bacchilega's remarks on the production of the feminine in the genre. Bacchilega argues that the features of the Innocent Persecuted Heroine are shaped by ideological desires and constraints: that is, both her innocence and persecution/victimization are ideologically constructed (1–2). That "gender is understood within the frameworks of class and social order" (2) is a perception that recurs throughout Maia Fernández-Lamarque's analysis of how Cenicienta functions as a metonym for woman in Spanish society, and particularly (but not only) during the repressive era of masculinist, Francoist fascism, when women's life choices and even clothing choices were heavily regulated. Frameworks of class and social order are key elements which localize both the primary texts and the critical analysis, so that evident in both domains, especially in their combination, is a process that I and my colleagues characterize as an ethnopoetics. We argue that this process entails a focus on local practices and their dealings with embeddedness within a particular language context, flows of influence, glocalization (a dialogic blending of local and global), and preferred textualities (2). These elements, hard as it may be to describe them individually and in combination, are what make Maia Fernández-Lamarque's project to examine "Cinderella in Spain" so unique and so important. Comparative studies of a global phenomenon such as the "Cinderella" story can only have legitimacy if they are grounded in ethnopoetic studies which define how meaning is built up at national levels.

Those of us who work in folktale, fairy tale and children's literature studies can be woefully ignorant of what is produced in particular national domains, such as Spanish, and how the material is interpreted within that ethnopoetic domain. Maia Fernández-Lamarque draws upon a range of critical concepts which seem particularly pertinent to her focus texts, and which connect meaningfully with Spanish critical discourse. I feel unqualified to comment on what constitutes the "Spanishness" of the works discussed, but I apprehend that there is a local version of patriarchy disclosed in the discussion of *La Cenicienta que no quería comer perdices* and of the (surprisingly) raunchy *Cenicienta siempre quiso un Wonderbra* [Cinderella Always Wanted a Wonderbra], discussed in Chapter 6. Local retellings of "Cenicienta" appear in a wide range of genres and forms, and whether readers are more or less familiar with Spanish history, literature and culture they will be intrigued by the confronting interpretations of social assumptions and practices posed by these retellings. To understand the Cinderella story as a text of culture, we must begin with the kind of close national reading Maia Fernández-Lamarque has given us in this book.

John Stephens is professor emeritus of Macquarie University and editor of The Routledge Companion to International Children's Literature.

Works Cited

Bacchilega, Cristina. "An Introduction to the 'Innocent Persecuted Heroine' Fairy Tale," *Western Folklore* 52.1 (1993): 1–12.

Grimm, Jacob and Wilhelm. *Household Tales*. Margaret Hunt, translator. London: George Bell, 1884, 1892. 2 volumes.

Hennard Dutheil de la Rochere, Marine, Gillian Lathey and Monica Wozniak, editors. *Cinderella Across Cultures: New Directions and Interdisciplinary Perspectives*, Detroit: Wayne State UP, 2016.

Jones, Steven Swann. "The Innocent Persecuted Heroine Genre: An Analysis of Its Structure and Themes," *Western Folklore* 52.1 (1993): 13–41.

Stephens, John, with Celia Abicalil Belmiro, Alice Curry, Li Lifang and Yasmine S. Motawy. "Introduction" in *The Routledge Companion to International Children's Literature*. London and New York: Routledge, 2018.

Prologue

This book is the product of eleven years of research on Cinderella in Spain. I was awarded several external and internal grants for numerous stages of this project to travel to Spain to do ancillary work, publish my research, present at international conferences and, most recently, to finish the manuscript. This is the first study on Cinderella in Spain and is the first to examine the work as a text of socio-ethical and literary value in this part of the globe. Cinderella has walked with me through my scholarly career as an assistant professor, later as an associate professor, and as a full professor promoted in these past months at Texas A&M University—Commerce.

In the Perrault hypotext, a girl, orphaned by her mother's passing, lives with her father's second wife and her daughters. These new step-sisters treat her with disdain and force her to live as a servant, all the while denying her right to be part of the new family. They rename her "Cinderella" because she is always covered in soot and ash. Cinderella manages to attend a ball hosted by the prince by disguising herself as a princess (with the help of her fairy godmother in Perrault's version, and by a bird in the Brothers Grimm version). At midnight, Cinderella leaves the ball quickly, but in doing so loses one of her shoes. The prince is intrigued and falls in love with the beautiful woman, so he goes out in search of the one whose foot fits the shoe, so that he can make her his wife. At last, the prince finds Cinderella and he marries her, transforming her into a true princess.

As the most popular folktale around the world, Cinderella has captivated attention as the most rewritten fairy tale of all time. The idea of the undermined yet resilient girl has permeated the cultural imaginary across cultures and geographies. From the mythical story in Spain about Saint Teresa de Avila, who, according to the local fable left her shoes in the Four Posts in Avila, to the life of Peruvian writer José María Arguedas who was mistreated by his stepmother and stepbrother and was isolated to live with their servants, examples in Spanish fiction, art and history recounting the Cinderella plot and motifs abound. Studies of Cinderella have focused on various aspects of the tale and have attempted to classify the genesis, the themes, and the significance and meaning in the countless retellings and reinventions of the tale. Cinderella retellings produce a collage in which the various fragments united create a figure giving a distinctive configuration to a new version of the tale. In other words, Cinderella is produced as a metonymical figure from the dialogue between the syntagmatic (the relationship between the elements of the tale) and paradigmatic (the set of motifs or a motif pertaining to a specific aspect of the Cinderella story) dialogism functions of a text (Stephens *Language* 1992). Following Stephens' rationale, the idea of Cinderella is rooted within a socio-cultural code which inheres in any rewriting that appears. Cinderella in this volume is signified by the character, the tale's motifs and their relationships and multiple combinations among the elements. The character is a metonymic of female positioning within male-dominated social structures: she lacks both agency and a way to change her situation that is often tightly constrained by social expectation. Her metonymic nature persists over time because of the "overlapping" and continued flow among rewritings.

As a global and collective narrative, Cinderella is the most popular and well-known fairy tale in Western and Eastern cultures. Cinderella has been translated, adapted, and reinvented in innumerable versions not only in literature but also in music, theatre, film, and other arts. It has also been the object of extensive research: beginning with folklorist Marian Roalfe Cox's seminal compendium of several versions of Cinderella in the nineteenth century, and Anna Birgitta Rooth's study and Alan Dundes's 1982 compendium of twenty-one international versions of Cinderella. The most recent study of "Cinderella" is *Cinderella Across Cultures*, published in 2016, which, despite the title, does not include a single version from the Spanish-speaking world.

Folklorists have found hundreds of distinctive forms of Cinderella's plots and subtypes throughout the Western and Eastern worlds through analyzing the form, taxonomy, significance, and reflections of customs, including its diachronic and synchronic progression. Cinderella has been studied in a vast variety of fields such as anthropology, sociology, semiology, and psychology. For instance, extensive and now canonical psychoanalytical readings of the tale are found in Bruno Bettelheim's *The Uses of Enchantment* (1976) and Maria Tatar's *The Hard Facts of the Grimm's Fairy Tales* (1987).

The mainstream international research in the Cinderella story has been done mainly in the English language. However, while the majority of the research has focused on various international versions of the tale, the present book proposes to consider Cinderella in Spain as a metonymic product related to a culturally ingrained mentality that exposes the values, character, anxieties and disposition of our times. The study focuses on adaptations of Cinderella in Spain and its chains of textual evidence, although its associated ties coded by metonymy go beyond these borders. In other words, the focus of this book is Cinderella as a part of the phases and emotions inherent to individuals in society, while at the same time, more specifically, it examines a representative sample of the many Cinderellas that have inhabited the past and present of Spanish culture since medieval times, and what they represent in their various textual "cultural codings" (Stephens *Language* 22).

Cinderella portrays characteristics that are relatable not only to the narrow space of Spain, but also to human culture, rituals, values, and myths in their entirety. Cinderella is a social phenomenon and its characterization shows the significance of what we do in society. The repetition of the tale as the story of a victim and scapegoat that ends up redeemed after her suffering has acquired the fundamental characteristics of a ritual. Rites of institution, according to Bourdieu, are social rituals which "tend to consecrate or legitimate" (177) an arbitrary condition of marginality, delimitation and borders. The tale presents a human societal spirit as a reflection of our continuous limitations or our progresses, which are revitalized every time another reshaped adaptation of the tale arises. The story shows a world of ideas as every given recount expresses many aspects or qualities, which illuminate the common societal crises concentrated in one sole representation: Cinderella as "a signified that remains intact" in the words of Rice and Schofer's definition of metonymy (132).

The shoe, the ball, the prince, the fairy godmother, the stairs, and the metamorphoses aspects, among other motifs in the tale, create a sequential contiguity among versions, and make the story recognizable as they are stable units which enable uniformity and definition within the uncountable narratives about the famous folktale. The time, place, and details of the tale are connected and unified. Yet at the same time, they shape the montage of versions, in fragments, as depictions of societal rituals, crises, conventions and traditions and thus contribute to its metonymical anchoring. Cinderella as an imprint reveals the customary communal behaviors repeated boundlessly throughout the history of human cultures. Likewise, the tale discloses distinguishing marks in numerous layers and degrees: local, regional, societal, and global. The universals are displayed in the story, however, as societies across the world have created indigenous versions of the tale by glocalizing it to incorporate their way of life, ethos, social codes and habits—that is, as Anna Katrina Gutierrez expresses it, they produce hybrid forms "from the localization of global narratives" which remain recognizable across cultures (xvi).

Cinderella as described in this book is a chain of semantic associations (Eco cited by Schofer 129) and a trademark that uses Spain as the geographical niche. This study is the first in its field that critically examines Cinderella and its versions and representations from Spain. Carolina Fernández-Rodríguez' *Las re-escrituras contemporáneas de Cenicienta*, published in 1997, attempts to classify the variety of the tale's themes from a global perspective. *Las re-escrituras* does mention two "Cinderella" Spanish versions: Suárez Solís (1990–1991) and Lourdes Ortíz (1988) "Cinderella" rewritings listed and described in Chapter 11 of the present book. However, the study is not centered in the versions of the story produced in Spain.

Teresa Colomer, a Catalonian scholar of children's literature in Spain, has pointed out in her article "La evolución de la literatura infantil y juvenil en España" (3) that after the defeat of the II Republic by the fascist regime, arts and culture were stagnant for almost forty years in the country. This fact, along with the censorship of some literature written during the dictatorship, provides evidence to believe that research in the field was scarce. Today, international research in children's literature and folk tales in Spain is minimal compared to research done in other parts of Europe and is hardly known in the Anglophone world. This book attempts to contribute to the research in this field and the study of Cinderella as it is represented across Spanish rewritings.

The protagonist embodies the mark of the outsider, the other, the outlier, the different, the foreign but also the strong willed, tenacious, volatile, and flexible woman. Gender is part of her identity but not a stable one either, as demonstrated and developed in this study. In the more prevalent depiction of the character, she represents the perfect, ideal model of a woman or a culturally imagined creation of what a woman should be not only in Spain but universally. Going beyond this ordinary account, Cinderella is the actualization and reflection of a human values system. The combination of the constituent elements of the tale disseminated into single units are part of a larger and more complex narrative. The story aggregates and composes a new mimetic collage every time it is retold and also reproduces the universal marks of humanness. Cinderella as a flux remolds within the parameters or motifs that remain encrypted deeply within human nature. The main character as a mythical figure reminds us of our one characteristic that unites us as a group on a universal level as a perpetual and everlasting depiction of human ethos.

On the one hand, the volume recounts how the story represents some of the most historically significant moments of Spain. On the other hand, it analyzes the narratological structure and poetic aspects of the tale. Both approaches come together to form an intertextual and metonymic ensemble for the variety of themes gathered in the selected stories examined critically in this volume. Intertextuality in this sense reflects not only on the reference to other texts, but also on the dialogue between various societal aspects that repeat and reappear multiple times in the Cinderella stories. Spain is a microcosm that frames the ideas and values described in the studies that respond to, echo and emulate the worldliness of the story and its broader and deeper applications. Metonymy is the trope that unites and allows the cultural waves to synchronize the Cinderella character and motifs from single units or each of the forty-four versions found for this study into a larger and more complex semantic tapestry.

Chapter 1 studies the medieval version "Estrellita de oro" (Little Golden Star) recovered by A. R Almodóvar in *Cuentos a la luz de la lumbre* (1983). The story is the pretext to analyze Cinderella as the enemy and how she is created as such within the story. The chapter explains how the main character of the tale represents the plethora of individuals who are targeted and singled out while displacing the negativity inside a person or group onto them. The chapter establishes that the creation of the enemy is needed in every group in order to oppose "the other" that is dissimilar. Using the fictional and mythological character, the chapter projects this image in the relationships among Cinderella and her adversaries by following the stages of renaming, displacing and erasing as emblematic and fundamental in the creation of an enemy.

Chapter 2 is a critical reading of Antonio Robles' "Cinderella." His version of the tale was censored and banned from libraries and bookstores across Spain after the Civil War (1936–1939). The chapter establishes four key axes and exposes them as the disrupting factors that might have been the reason of its prohibition: politics, religion, gender, and race. The depiction of the main character as a progressive woman dissects the boundaries of politics by her rejection of the offer to become part of the monarchy. The text disrupts the limits imposed by religion by not ascribing any pious characteristics to the heroine. The normalization of androgynous characteristics in the main character disturbs the stable and fixed binarity of genders. The deletion of the white race as an attribute or value for Cinderella's appearance confronts the prototypical depiction of the character. These four principal angles are deconstructed and exposed theoretically in the narrative.

Chapter 3 addresses one of the few musical versions of Cinderella in Spain, *La nueva Cenicienta* (1964), starring the famous Spanish actress and singer Marisol as the protagonist. The theoretical ideas of Victor Turner on performance as a cultural conception are applied to the main character's performance as a mask. In the context of a family of performers, Marisol is the principal player and leader in the group. Her character takes up masks of various shapes throughout the film narrative. The *pícara* mask is the result of her indigent situation. Her mother-like mask dialogs with two fairy tale characters, Peter Pan's Wendy and Snow White, as Marisol protects, nourishes and takes care of the men in her charge. Her doll-like mask adheres to the social discourse expectations that she will be a submissive, ornamental, and beautiful doll without any agency. Freud's notion of the principles of pleasure and reality is the basis for considering her final mask, dance, which establishes her as an independent, resolute, and free individual in search of both the prince of pleasure and the prince of reality.

Chapter 4 is a study of Ana María Matute's *Sólo un pie descalzo* (1983) and its main character, Gabriela, as the Other in society. Using two main literary figures—synecdoche and prosopopeia—the analysis expounds how the Other as a social and cultural constructed concept is reflected in the narrative. Not only is the protagonist treated and perceived as the Other in the nuclear space, but the concept of otherness is inscribed in the story's structure and narrative. Synecdoche and prosopopeia connect with the thematic flow as they act as technical supports integrating the textual corpus as a cohesive critical whole.

Chapter 5 explores anxiety revolving around gender and ethnic identity in *Cenicienta en Chueca* (2003) by María Felícitas Jaime. The protagonist is a nameless woman who has moved to a foreign country in search of a better financial opportunity. In both geographical spaces, the indigenous and the adopted, her sexual identity is concealed in the private and public spheres. The space of freedom is the Chueca neighborhood in Madrid, where she can unfold her true sexual identity. However, as the analysis shows, she is still a minority in this "freedom space" and is continuously interpellated in a variety of forms. Cinderella is depicted as a foreigner and a lesbian without a name or a fixed place in the societal and fictional narrative.

Chapter 6 considers *Cenicienta siempre quiso un Wonderbra* (2009) by Noé Martínez as a representation of Cinderella as a protagonist of chick literature. The three Cinderellas depicted in the novel are economically independent and professional women in their thirties. Each character resembles one aspect of what culture has embraced and usually labels for women. Drawing upon Collette Downing's *The Cinderella Complex: Women's Hidden Fear of Independence* (1981), the chapter speculates on the stages of women as virgins, mothers, and lovers in a given culture as they fear emotional independence from men.

Chapter 7 is a study of an experimental picture book, *La Cenicienta no quería comer perdices* (2009) by Nunila López Salamero. The chapter draws upon Genette's theories to examine paratextual references and their significance as a medium to demonstrate the stages and various plateaus of meaning in the story. In this picture book retelling, the illustrations are a vehicle of meaning regarding women's freedom and right to equality in the social realm.

Chapter 8 deals with a suicidal Cinderella depicted in Cristina Cerrada's *Cenicienta en Pensilvania* (2010). Through a variety of modes—cinematic, musical, lyrical, and dramatic—the chronological order of events is disrupted as the story unfolds. Mary (the main character) and a variety of narrators in first, second, and third person tell the story through analepsis, digressions and shifts between these multiple narrative voices. Genette's categories of hypertextual descriptive and hypertextual intellectual are introduced to interpret the chronicle of actions in a story based on the protagonist's search for her absent mother.

Chapter 9 takes up the latest depiction of Cinderella as a comic character in *Idiotizadas* (2017) and, in the context of the history of feminism in Spain, studies the text as a parody. Zorricienta is Cinderella in this comic adaptation. Zorricienta's name is formed by the conjunction of *zorra* (female fox and slang for *whore* in Spain) and Cenicienta. The protagonist embraces the common sexually charged insult, *zorra*, and adopts it as her name. The story parodies the cultural double standard for men and women and its consequence that women are subjected to severe judgment in both the private and public arenas.

Chapter 10 explores another experimental version of the tale. *Te cuento ... Cenicienta* (2015), by Juan Carlos Monedero and Juan Carlos Mestre, is written as a long poem in which a variety of metaphors and allegories depict a history of humanity and fictional wrongdoings. Cinderella is placed at the center, where she embodies all women who have been victimized through time and space. The story's thread is a continuum with various thematic axes that depict and contrast the moral values in contemporary politics, society and culture. *Te cuento ... Cenicienta* is an honest reflection on human ethos.

Chapter 11 is a description of the forty-four versions of Cinderella found for this study. The chapter delineates and classifies the adaptations thematically: versions adapted from Perrault, versions adapted from the Grimms, drama versions, detective themed versions, fractured fairy tale versions, literary versions, picture book versions, musicals, film versions, versions in comics, and social and political issues versions.

The volume extracts the exemplary folk tale in its many varieties in Spain. Starting with the premise that culture is a flexible and kinetic entity, the Cinderella story and Cinderella character entail a continuous state of change and discovery. The multiple materializations of the story constitute a textual and metonymic ritual evident in the perpetual embodiment of its symbols and figures as "conventional extensions of meaning." Cinderella as a ritual is set in an organized, cyclical fashion and presents the conflicts inherent to society, while reflecting the social order and its performances, negotiations and common beliefs. At the same time, Cinderella as a ritual exhibits a spectacle of human capacities, awareness, affections, volition, and fears as it appears in a cyclical domain. The symbols in the story are the experience of social life in a conceptualization that illuminates our social reality as human beings. Cinderella in this book is not only a folk or fairy tale, it is a systematic insight into the context of human understanding and human values, or to put it simply: the condition of being a human.

Chapter 1

"Estrellita de oro" and the Ritual of Branding[1]

Many of the hundreds of medieval variations of "Cinderella" in Spain were recovered by Aurelio M. Espinosa. His compendium of Spanish folktales in *Cuentos populares españoles*, published in 1923, is the first volume on the theme of folktale tradition in this part of the Iberian Peninsula. In *Cuentos al amor de la lumbre* (1983), A. Rodríguez Almodóvar compiles and revisits some of the motives/characters in the Spanish oral tradition such as Blancaflor, Juan el Oso, the Enchanted Prince, the Enchanted Princess and other personages from the Spanish folktale tradition. Among the almost 80 folktales in this compilation, the adaptations of "Cinderella" are present under the section "La niña perseguida" (The Persecuted Girl). One of these numerous versions compiled by A. Rodríguez Almodóvar is the axis of this chapter, "Estrellita de oro" ("Little Gold Star").

As a tale from oral tradition, the story has an uncertain and unknown origin. However, because of the symbols and cultural references inferred from the story, it is very likely to have been of Persian origin. It is also possible that the story had entered the Spanish folklore oral tradition during the Moors' occupation of Spain during 711–1492 CE. As Aurelio Espinosa affirms, "Los árabes y los judíos vivieron y caminaron por muchos siglos en España y es de suponer [...] su cultura influyó poderosamente en la cultura hispano-cristiana..." [The Arabs and Jews lived and walked for many centuries in Spain. It is only natural that their culture had powerfully influenced the Hispanic-Christian culture] (13).

The heroine in "Estrellita de oro" is María, a very common Christian name that honors the Virgin Mary, mother of Jesus Christ in the Catholic tradition. The protagonist's name must have been Christianized or transformed from the Muslim version to be able to enter the Spanish folk tradition. It is usual that stories metamorphose or transform according to the culture that surrounds or adapts them, while often preserving their cultural and/or religious representations. In one of the Spanish American versions of this story translated into English, *Little Gold Star: A Spanish American Cinderella Tale* (2000) by Robert D. San Souci, in fact, the fairy godmother *is* indeed the Virgin Mary. In this case, the "Cinderella" tale is embedded in the story of Jesus Christ's birth in Bethlehem and a girl is the protagonist and heroine of the story. The plot is similar to many other known versions of "Cinderella" and it keeps several of the story's well-known motifs.

"Estrellita de oro" also shares similarities with other Spanish and English adaptations of "Cinderella," in particular with the Equatorial Guinean story "La señora del río" (1981) by Raquel del Pozo Epita (1938–1992), who used the pseudonym Raquel Ilombé, and also with Joe Hayes' bilingual version "Estrellita de oro" (2002)[2] and with another Spanish American version *Domitila* (Reinhart Coburn 2000). However, none of these versions show the extreme violence depicted in the tale compiled by Rodríguez Almodóvar. One commonality among all these adaptations of the story stands out: the present the maiden receives from her fairy godmother. Even though the personification or incarnation of the fairy is different in most of these versions,[3] the gift given to the girls is the same in all stories: a brand on her forehead. This chapter will analyze the depiction of branding as a physical and emotional phenomenon in "Estrellita de oro" and its relationship with the social fabrication of the enemy.

Marks have worked as both signs and symbols throughout history. Marking or branding has had a twofold meaning both historically and fictionally. For instance, in ancient Mesopotamia and Egypt, slaves were branded to determine who their owner was. Branding animals has also been common since the turn of the eighteenth century. Marking a particular group with a symbol has served to differentiate their members from others in society. During the reign of the Nazis in Germany, Jews were marked with the Star of David, symbol of their religion. In literature, placing a mark has been used as a representation of disgrace, dishonor and, in consequence, of isolation and differentiation from the rest of the group. In the classic American novel, *The Scarlet Letter* (Hawthorne 1850), the protagonist, Hester Prynne is forced to wear a garment with the letter "A" engraved as a symbol of adultery. In the Book of Genesis, Cain, the murderer of Abel, his brother, has a sign on his forehead.

In many literary or historical instances marking or branding depicts the same contrasting idea of the chosen and/or the damned as these marks are made or imposed on these individuals in several fashions. Angela Carter's protagonist in *The Bloody Chamber*, an adaptation of *Bluebeard* (Perrault 1697), has a red mark on her forehead. As she states about her blind husband: "No paint nor powder, no matter how thick or white, can mask that red mark on my forehead; I am glad he cannot see it—not for fear of his revulsion, since I know he sees me clearly with his heart—but because it spares my shame" (16). Consequently, branding carries the idea of possession, domination, and stigma but also that of selection and distinction.

In "Estrellita de oro," María is a girl who is the target of maltreatment and rejection. The tale follows the traditional "Cinderella" plot line about the orphan whose father marries an evil woman. The Italian version "La gatta Cenerentola" (1634–1636) by Basile holds some similarities with "Estrellita de oro" in terms of the plot. In both stories, a neighbor or housekeeper influences the girl to convince her father to marry the woman. In "La gatta Cenerentola" the persuasion goes further and beyond the act of enticement. In this Italian version, the girl's mother has died and her father has remarried. The housekeeper induces the girl to kill her stepmother, so she can marry the maiden's father. The woman's influence is such that the girl does kill her stepmother by the means she is advised. In the Spanish version, "Estrellita de oro," the episode in which the stepmother is murdered by Cenerentola is elided, but the collusion of the girl and her indignant neighbor is retained: "Oye, María, ¿por qué no vas y le dices a tu padre que se case conmigo? Así tú y mi hija serían buenas amigas y yo te daré sopita de miel […] [Hey, María, why don't you tell your father to marry me? You and my daughter will be friends and I will prepare honey soup for you]. The plot continues as the traditional storyline when María's father and his widowed neighbor indeed get married. In Joe Hayes' version the girl's name is Arcía and the stepmother makes promises to persuade the maiden: "I will give you something sweet to eat almost every day" (4). In San Souci's version, the girl, whose name is Teresa, does not intervene in her father's decision to marry the manipulative neighbor. Nevertheless, Teresa's father marries the widow by his own will and without his daughter's influence.

In "Estrellita de oro," soon after the father and widow's wedding, the maiden's father leaves the household for months to attend work-related duties. Immediately, the new stepmother's attitude changes towards the girl. María is constantly humiliated and ordered to do all the work at home and, even more, forced to accomplish impossible tasks. For instance, one day, her stepmother commands María to wash an enormous bag of dirty clothes giving her only a minuscule piece of soap to attain the goal. She also gives the girl a cup of soup to take as lunch, and commands her to return the cup still full. In other words, the stepmother ordered the girl to work hard, accomplish her duties with enormous difficulties and starve while completing these tasks. The girl, tired and dispirited arrives at the river, and knowing the impossibility of her stepmother's tasks, she sits by the shore and cries in frustration. At this very moment, a kind old lady appears and grants the girl three gifts: pearls, roses and money. These presents for the girl would appear in specific situations. Every time María would comb her hair, beautiful pearls would slide from her hair. Every time María would laugh, roses would come out of her mouth and when she would look into her pockets, she would always find money:

> Pues tú no te apures. Toma esta cesta y mete en ella la ropa y el jabón. Después te comes la sopa y después miras al cielo. Entonces te concederé tres gracias: que cuando te peines, caigan perlas; que, cuando te rías, caigan rosas, y que, cuando te metas la mano en el bolsillo, halles siempre dinero [231].
>
> You should not worry. Take this basket put the clothes and the soap in it. After that, you eat the soup, then look at the sky. Then, I will concede you three gifts: when you comb your hair, pearls will drop from it; when you laugh, roses will come out of your mouth, and, when you put your hand in your pocket, you will always find money.

One more gift was not mentioned to the girl. Nonetheless, when the girl looks at the sky, as instructed by the godmother, a star is placed on her forehead. María is marked with a golden star, a perennial brand on her brow after meeting the old lady. María's branding has contradictory meanings and contains both connotations of damnation and distinction as well. This surprising and shining gift would determine a shift in María's destiny as it will differentiate her from others. In Joe Hayes' version a hawk steals wool from the girl at the river and in exchange, it gives her the star.

> Arcía called out to the bird, "Señor Hawk, please give my wool back to me." And the hawk replied to her with human speech: "lift ... up ... your eyes.... Look ... where.... I ... fly-y-y." So she did what the bird had told her to do. She turned her head and looked up. When she looked up, down from the sky came a little gold star, and it fastened itself to her forehead [11].

In Sans-Souci's version, the Virgin Mary gives her the star as a reward for a good deed. The girl helps a father and child in need. It is later disclosed that they are Joseph and baby Jesus: "Teresa did not know it, but the woman was Blessed Mary. The old man was Saint Joseph, and the baby was the Holy Child, the baby Jesus" (n/p). The hawk that appears in Hayes version is the animal fairy, who is, according to the fairy tale tradition, a metamorphosed spirit (Alexander 33).

The animal fairies change their shape in numerous forms of wildlife. As they are considered guardians of nature, animal fairies appear as symbols of earth in many myths and legends throughout the world.[4] The fairy godmother takes multiple forms in the branded Cinderella versions: a bird of prey (a hawk), an old lady, a young lady and the Virgin Mary. According to the folklore tradition, the portrayal of the godmother/fairy in these Cinderella stories suits the classification of what Skye Alexander defines as a "hag" (30). These kinds of fairies are often interchangeably called witches/spirits, because they grant wishes to humans and are represented as elderly women. They are also attributed with the capacity to cast spells, curses or incantations on humans. In fact, more than any other motif in the tale, the fairy godmother has been adapted to every specific cultural context in which the story appears.

The godmother figure is germane to the climax of the story. The mark given to the girl by the godmother will set her apart from her stepsister and stepmother, which will trigger more envy and, naturally, a major disgrace for her. Upon the girl's return home, her stepmother and stepsister find out about how María obtained her new shining appearance. Therefore, María's stepsister is sent by her mother to the river the next day, hoping her daughter would also be given this rare and desirable gift. The stepsister repeats the same path that María walked to the river, as she is advised, expecting the same glorious fate. Indeed, she finds the old lady by the river walk. As a result, like María, the sister returns home with something on her brow. In this case, when the girl looked at the sky, it is not a golden star that was given by the old lady, but a donkey's' tail is branded on her forehead.

The hag's ambiguity and twofold characteristics and capacities to either damn or distinguish humans are notable in "Estrellita de oro." On one hand, the fairy offers the luminosity, brilliance, and fame of a star to María. The golden star is given as a sign of dignity, honor, and prestige as well; on the other hand, she gives María's stepsister a donkey's tail as a present. The fairy's present to the stepsister is a synecdoche that carries the connotation of unimportance and insignificance. The tail is the part farthest from the animal's head, considered the most predominant external body part. A tail also suggests male sexuality seen in other versions of the tale discussed later in this chapter. The two gifts from the fairy are thus counterposed: stars are far from our human physical existence as they are unreachable, whereas a donkey is part of a world that humans dominate.

Humans subjugate, use, domesticate and have power over animals. María's symbol on her forehead, a star, elevates her to a higher stratum away from a mundane existence. As for her stepsister, the animal symbol lessens and reduces her human attributes, degrading her to the level of an animal. None of these matter to María's cohorts, nonetheless, as the star symbol in María's case is a reason to belittle and mock her.

The mark given to María's stepsister on her forehead carries a double meaning, nevertheless. Donkeys are symbols of stubbornness and dumbness as they are known in popular culture. In Portuguese, Spanish, English and other languages calling somebody a "donkey" or *burro* is an insult that implies lack of understanding, stupidity, and/or ignorance. However, in some of the folktale tradition, donkeys are also a symbol of authority. The donkey has an important function in two popular folktales published by the brothers Grimm in *Children and Household Tales* (1812): in "The Donkey," a prince is born in a donkey's body and in "Donkey Skin" a princess escaping from an abusive and dysfunctional father hides in the skin of a donkey.[5] In both tales, the heroine and hero use the donkey as a "second skin," a temporary and transitional state. Concealment within the donkey acts as a protective womb, which will release a noble and kind human being. Notwithstanding, in "Estrellita de oro," the stepsister is scorned and vilified with the nickname "rabo de burro" (donkey's tail), due to the branding given by the fairy on her forehead. In this instance, there is only one side to the donkey symbol: the one of scorn and contempt.

Previous scholars of Cinderella (Cox, Birgitta Rooth) have not mentioned a European version with the branding variant. In Alan Dundes', *Cinderella: A Casebook* (1982), however, Margaret A. Mills' article "A Cinderella Variant in the Context of a Muslim Women's Ritual" discusses a version of "Cinderella" which is, not surprisingly, similar to the Spanish tale. Mills examines the motifs in this variation in relation to the culture that permeates it. In particular, Mills studies how the Muslim rituals are represented in the tale and its signification. This Middle Eastern version shows a heroine very similar to the others as the story follows the same pattern with one variation. The girl is also given a star as a gift and it is also imprinted on her forehead, but the stepsister obtains another quite unusual mark, a "donkey's penis" (187) not a donkey's tail. In addition, in the Muslim version the heroine is given a "moon on her chin" and the stepsister a "snake on her chin." According to Mills, the donkey and snake symbols are in reference to male genitalia: "She is marked with sexual stigmata as a direct result of her and her mother's attempted exploitation of other females..." (190). Mills' article was published in 1982 but its resonance has had an impact in global studies of Cinderella until today. In the latest publication on this topic edited by Marine Hennard Dutheil de la Rochère, Gillian Lathey and Monika Woźniak, *Cinderella Across Cultures* (2016) Mills essay is mentioned in the foreword. Cristina Bacchilega highlights "the insightful [sic] and boldness" (xii) of the article regarding her critical feminist and cultural analysis regarding Muslim culture.

Branding as a complex phenomenon operates as a multidimensional aspect in the tale. After the stepmother realizes that her daughter is not the one that is "positively branded" she is infuriated. The tension only increases when the prince wants to marry the girl with the star on her forehead. Once the prince leaves the stepmother's house to make the expected wedding arrangements, the stepmother enraged by the devastating news, decides to kill the girl: "-A ésta la matamos" [We will kill this one] (234). The women beat María fiercely, cutting her tongue and pulling her eyes out. The girl is left in the middle of the forest unconscious and in excruciating pain. As studied by Roalfe Cox and reviewed by Sidney Hartland in "Notes on Cinderella" (1982), the typology of the tale has not shown the motif of "branding" and/or mutilation. In her studies, both folklorists dissect the motifs of Cinderella and its variants in various geographical regions. In their revisions, the origins of the motifs are traced and quantified in a meta-analysis. The variant of murder is present in most of the versions studied tracing back from the ninth century version from China. As in the hundreds of versions examined in parts of Europe, the order to kill the girl is a constant as well. This demand is followed by a request to bring proof that the girl is in fact dead. In all of these adaptations including two from Spain (Basque country and Oviedo) the proof of death is offered by showing an animal's blood, heart, eyes, tongue indicating that these organs belong to the victim. Another proof is given by showing the heroine's garment soaked in dog's blood (Hartland 61). Animals are sacrificed and mutilated to convince the girls' enemies that she has been killed; the girl's mutilation does not appear in any of these studies, however. In "Estrellita de oro," unlike some of the other rewritings with a similar plot line, the stepmother does not order Cinderella's murder; instead, she and her daughter proceed to attack and harm María themselves. As well as in the other adaptations mentioned before, this variation is not present in any of the versions studied by these researchers either. The reason for the mutilation is the prince's preference for the girl and his desire to marry her. As the star represents guidance and luminosity, for the protagonist, it is a sign that also triggers pain and suffering.

Through oral tales, cultures fix and insert models, myths and ideas.

Folktales act as social vehicles as they represent the voice of the society that sustains them. By the same token, and as societies change, folktales are the epitomes of transformation. The branding as a form of change is implanted in these versions of "Cinderella." Throughout these adaptations, the mark given and the fairy godmother has varied according to the societal narrative. For instance, in Sans-Souci's version, the girl is branded by the Virgin Mary herself. As a transcultural tale, "Estrellita de oro" in the Spanish-American world in the U.S. has evolved to a Catholic tale. In this instance, the mark on the girl replicates the mark in the cultures that create the tale.

Creating the Enemy

In *Costruire il Nemico* (2011), Umberto Eco speculates on the meaning of an enemy. Eco describes the phenomenology of a created foe throughout history. According to the renowned semiotician, an enemy is shaped due to a number of perceptions related but not restricted to religion, ethnicity, culture, race, and politics, among other motives. Eco affirms that the existence of an enemy is extremely important not only to define one's own identity but also to measure one's value as a human being (10–11). Even when an enemy does not exist or is not perceived in the surroundings, explains Eco, it is paramount that he or she be created.

The act of displacing our fears, rejections, ugliness, and imperfections onto somebody else is crucial for the affirmation of the human self. In this manner, one distances oneself from the darkest sides of one's being. This action creates the illusion that these obscure characteristics do not exist in ourselves. Transposing the unwanted elements, detaching and placing them far away in somebody else seems to relieve the negative emotions caused by them. This mechanism creates an artifice that makes the "enemy" the carrier of our own failures and pettiness. The responsibility for the void in ourselves is symbolically transferred onto this "other." In the story of "Cinderella" the construction of the enemy is also the reaffirmation of the deepest values and identity of María's stepmother and sisters. Throughout the story, the process of demonization and production of the enemy called María unfolds. As it is known throughout history, the creation of an enemy constitutes a ritual. Gian Antonio Stella affirms that there is indeed a pattern of human conduct and its animosity toward "the other" created culturally that resembles a ritual (Negri 2009).

Rituals are present in cultures as they represent their landmarks and deepest values. They play an indispensable part in society as they express codified thoughts and beliefs. The creation of an enemy establishes a symbolic and often necessary ritual in humanity, as it has been represented in the story of "Cinderella" for centuries. Anthropologist Bronislaw Malinowski suggests that humans are "more likely to turn to rituals when they face situations where the outcome is important, uncertain and beyond their control" (*Magic, Science, Religion* 32). As rituals are known as series of actions performed according to a prescribed order, in the case of the "Cinderella" ritual there are three clear stages. In the ritual of the creation of the enemy are distinguished and are made explicit in "Estrellita de oro" these three phases: renaming, replacing and erasing as a gradual process.

Stripping and removing the name originally given to an individual is the first step to make the enemy disappear. Naming has the power of appropriation and colonization and has an enormous impact in the rupture of an identity. In the fifteenth century, European conquistadores in America and other parts of the world renamed cities, sacred sites, objects, natives, symbols, etc., as part of the annexation and invasion of territories. Along with occupying the physical terrain, the invader erases and eliminates the original individuality by giving it a complete, new and enforced mask. The collective palimpsest or rewriting tends to minimize the original name or identity and force a new one imposed by the group, or individual in power. The human target of our own misguided projections needs to be renamed, causing him/her a double blurry image of his/her identity. The imposer has distorted the enemy's initial image and is providing a new altered one. This change serves the purpose of forming the outcast and rejected individual with a new and acceptable identity for the dominant group or individual in charge. The different recreated persona is the one that pleases the group as it diminishes and belittles this hated other. In contrast, the group that fabricates this unedited enemy seems more powerful, greater and cleaner; the darkest sides of themselves have been deposited into the "enemy." As for the "enemy," his/her own identity has been also blurred for herself causing, in many cases, a dislocation.

In the story of "Estrellita de oro" the changes appear shortly after María is branded with the star on her forehead. María's father, ignoring the abuses that his daughter is subjected to, leaves the house on another work-related trip and almost blames the girl for her disgrace: "Ya te lo decía yo, que primero te daría sopita de miel y después sopita de hiel" (231) [I told you that first I would give you soup and honey; and later, soup and gall]. María loses her place in the household as part of the family and is treated as a servant. She is exiled as not only are her spatial limits circumscribed to the kitchen and cinders but also her ability to be part of the family and part of the group. Soon after she is branded with the star on her forehead, not only the physical and emotional isolation takes place but also her name is replaced with "Estrellita de oro." Ripping off the name of another reimagines and disperses the individual as it is replaced as a caricature of herself. In Sans Souci's version this is clearly expressed: "Because Teresa bore a gold star while her stepsisters wore hideous horns and ears, they taunted her even more. They called her 'Estrellita de Oro,' 'Little Gold Star,' turning the words into a cruel joke." Once the enemy has been stripped of her given name and has been displaced physically and emotionally, the third stage of this ritual follows: the erasure.

Human societies have created rituals of various kinds. Social, political, religious rituals abound around the orb, as they reflect on communal values and ideals. Victor Turner studies rituals across cultures and defines them as follows:

> Rituals reveal values at their deepest level [...] men express in rituals what moves them most, and since the form of expressions is conventionalized and obligatory, it is the values of the group that are revealed. I see in the study of rituals the way to an understanding of the essential constitution of human societies [*The Ritual* 241].

The production of an enemy is ingrained in cultural rituals as it is represented in "Estrellita de oro." As noted by Claude Lévi-Strauss, rituals are processed by sophisticated cognitive mechanisms and they are not at all intellectually primitive. In *L'Pensée Savage* (1962) he explains how the application of abstract and analogical thinking results in rituals: "Mythical thought is therefore a kind of intellectual bricolage [...] like bricolage on the technical plane, mythical reflection can reach brilliant unforeseen results on the intellectual plane." (17). In other words, myths and rituals are the result of extraneous observation and experimentation with the natural and societal surroundings in hand. Social rituals are generated from a historical human experience with the encompassing world. The result of this examination, inspection and consideration is the plethora of ancient myths and customs that have been inherited through history in cultures.

In "Estrellita de oro," the physical ritual follows the intangible ritual of delineating the enemy: María. Once the stepmother and stepsister learn about the prince's predilection for the girl, they attack her and mutilate her eyes and tongue: "La cogieron y se la llevaron al campo arrastrando y allí sobre una piedra, la golpearon hasta que la creyeron muerta. Luego le sacaron los ojos y la lengua y la abandonaron" (234) [They grabbed her and dragged her to the fields. There on a rock, they beat her until they thought she was dead. Afterwards, they plucked her eyes out and cut her tongue off and left her there]. As it has already been recorded by Richard M. Dorson in his study of folktales around the world (2016), this motif is also found in the oral tradition in Egypt and Canada (587–88). Also Dan Ben Amos in, *Jews from Arab Lands* (2011), records the mutilation of arms and eyes performed upon the encountered enemies (487). In the folktales tradition, it is one of the recurrent practices. Kate Bernheimer makes a statement based on her finding about violence and its forms and consequences in fairy tales: "Fairy tales contain secrets in images. The images have rapturously ambivalent effects." (72).

As in many so called "primitive" societies as the *jíbaros* in the Amazonian jungle, the enemies are also treated in a similar fashion. In the *jibaro* culture, once an enemy is captured, defeated and killed, he/she undergoes the last step in the process of disappearance and erasure. The enemy, though dead, is still dangerous until the ritual is completed. Similar to what happens to the protagonist in "Estrellita de oro," whose eyes and tongue are removed, the *jibaros* shut off the enemies' eyes and sew their lips to finalize the ritual. In the *jibaro* tradition, this ceremony prevents their enemies from recounting what happened in the other world and/or inform who the perpetrator of such action was. Strictly speaking, their enemies' last vision will not be reproduced in the afterlife; therefore, the deed made upon them will not be chastised or even acknowledged by others, or as they believe, the superior powers will not punish them for their crime.

As the eyes comprise an opening to the world, the window to experience the external stimuli, the act of blinding somebody is in itself an act of murder. The eyes are connected to the ability to see, the incoming light is received and perceived through them; thus, removing the eyes is symbolic of disappearance as well. Being in the dark carries the perception of being unseen, invisible as a reflection of what has been removed from the individual, thus giving them a living death. In this sense, the enemy is not only prevented from seeing but also is made invisible to the others' eyes. The erasure happens simultaneously within the private and collective realm as the enemy is unrooted from the society and from their own relationship with the world. The wound inflicted is embedded in the individual in a permanent fashion. As the word trauma in Greek means wound, in "Estrellita de oro," the physical damage made upon the girl reveals and exposes the fear of the possible strength and power of the enemy (María). The bodily parts that have been wounded and removed are emblematic. As seen in several cultures bodily parts represent symbolic meanings. In

"Estrellita de oro," María's tongue is also removed. As in the Indian pantheon, in the goddess Kali, the tongue signifies not only a mobile, muscular organ, but also the characteristic of nurturing and absorbing the forces of life (ARAS *The Book of Symbols*, 372). With such a loss, María is removed from her contact with her surroundings in a physical, symbolic and metaphysical sense. The removal of her communicative organ makes her a mute as human beings express with speech and the tongue is the organ that allows speech to be produced. Not only the tongue is imbedded in the buccal cavity, but also it is where language originates.

Communication is possible through language and language is possible through the existence of a tongue.[6] In Inca society, for instance, where the moral code was extremely strict, the tongue was removed from liars as a punishment according to their four laws of truth.[7] In various ancient cultures, muteness as a form of bodily and social mutilation is imposed upon the enemy, so it cannot use language (lingua) as a medium of expression. In her study of myths, Clarissa Pinkola Estes mentions the punishment for those who intend to break or modify the social status quo: "mutilation, incapacitation or death" (53). Symbolically the enemy is detached from his/her right to appear or act through voice. A disadvantaged enemy is the goal to be attained. In the case of María, the creator of the enemy can speak in her place, and only one voice will be heard. This is particularly relevant in the social and political arena. A voiceless enemy is the road to his/her ultimate death, since the power to destroy or create is made through communication as well.

Another example of this cultural rite is the Byzantine Empire, where enemies were disfigured and/or mutilated. One of the most vivid examples in this culture history was Martina, empress successor of Heraclius, the Elder (6th Century). The Senate and populace disapproved of the power bestowed on her by her late husband. Martina was mutilated as her tongue was cut off. To that end, mutilation serves as an effective way of social disappearance, as the person who is disfigured is not seen as a threat anymore. Once María is muted and blinded, her stepmother and stepsister take her tongue and eyes as symbols of their victory.

According to Victor Turner who has studied rituals in various ethnic groups in Africa, rituals often appear in critical situations. Societies develop their own set of rites to convey their fear, preoccupations and morale. In "Estrellita de oro" a society symbolic ritual is developed as allusive rituals are shaped parallel to the society that englobes them and nourishes them. The German word *Schadenfreude* is charged with the semantic power to describe this negative sentiment. Ironically, the pleasure in the other's misfortune is inherent to humans despite the various religious or moral traditions that censure this negative emotion. Clarissa Pinkola Estes who has studied rites, legends and myths around the world calls it the "internal predator" (52). According to the renowned psychoanalyst, this sentiment of predation is intrinsic to humans and it should be suppressed by consciously embracing compassion.

The end of the story has a typical "fairytale ending." After the attack, María is found by a shepherd who takes care of her. Soon after, the girl recovers in the peasant's hut and her three gifts given by the godmother reappear spontaneously: pearls, roses and money. Using gestures to communicate, María asks the shepherd to exchange the roses and pearls for a tongue and eyes, while he can keep the money. Finally, María recovers the capacity to see and communicate when her organs are restored through a magic ritual: "Varita de virtud, por la gracia que tú tienes, que me pongas mis ojos como los tenía antes." (235) (Magic wand, for the power that you possess, put my eyes back as they were). She is found by the prince and the narrative ends with their wedding and the stepmother's and stepsisters' punishment.

All and all, this version, possibly from Medieval times in Spain, shows the symbolic and physical branding of an enemy as a ritual, as a process and as a human strategy. Bestowing a name, displacing and erasing are the three tactics in the Michel de Certeau sense of survival. Poor human relationships are depicted in this folk tale and the creation of an enemy who is resilient, in the case of Estrellita de oro, appears. Jean Paul Sartre's famous phrase "L'enfer sont l'autre" (*Huis Clos* 1944) exemplifies clearly the constant need for an enemy reflected in the story of Cinderella historically. In his famous play, where this phrase is found, the three characters, Garcin, Inez and Stelle are trapped together in a room arguing and making each other suffer, while they are awaiting their punishment in hell. After a while and realizing they are not going anywhere, they come to the conclusion that *they* are the actual hell.

CHAPTER 2

The Censored Version of *Cinderella* in Franco's Spain[1]

During the government of the Second Spanish Republic (1931–39), the country found itself bitterly divided between two opposing ideological camps. In 1936, the Spanish Civil War broke out, pitting the two factions against each other in a conflict that lasted for three years, and tinged the country with blood. It is in this same year that Antonio Robles (1895–1983) wrote his version of "Cinderella," based on the Perrault version (1697). Antonio Robles' version was censored by Franco's government and, as a consequence, it was scarcely distributed. This chapter focuses on a study of the symbols and omissions with respect to the elements of class, race, gender and religion that are evident in this version, and that were possibly the cause of its censorship for showing opposition and/or questioning the ideology of the regime. Although Francoism did not exist as such in 1936, the publication date of Antoniorrobles' "Cinderella," the Spanish Falange indeed did. Its ideology would later form part of the fundamental base of Franco's dictatorship.[2] *Textos de doctrina política* (1964) includes a collection of the discourse and philosophies of the founder of the Falange, José Antonio Primo de Rivera. Primo de Rivera's clearly delineated ideology in *Textos* is in obvious contrast to the axis of Antoniorrobles' version of "Cinderella," which dismantles the story with respect to class, race, gender and religion and was thus considered subversive during the Franco regime. At the time of his death, José Antonio Primo de Rivera was converted into a symbol of Francoism and as the "Great Absentee" following the victory of the Nationalists.[3]

Antonio Robles always penned his works using his pseudonym, Antoniorrobles, his first name and last names blended into one word. He is considered a pioneer of children's literature in Spain, in addition to being one of the representatives of the writers known as the "Other generation of '27."[4] His representation of subjects as diverse entities, rebels who have their own voice and refuse to adjust to the roles culturally assigned to them, constitutes a rupture with the themes and representations of Perrault and the Brothers Grimm. These authors served as the icons of canonical literature for children throughout Europe at the time, and were a natural reference for any writer in the genre. Naturally, Perrault and Grimm served as models for any artist of popular narrative. As has already been discussed profusely in previous studies of children's literature worldwide (Zipes, 1983; Tatar, 1987; Soliño, 2002), the stories of Perrault and the Brothers Grimm tend to reaffirm the ideology of their time. Perrault was in charge of distracting the public and avoiding the dissemination of any ideology that might be contrary to that of Louis XIV, King of France. In his writings, Perrault worked to stylize and provide the culture that was acceptable for the King (Soliño 14–15). In the nineteenth century in the Kingdom of Prussia, the stories of Jakob and Wilhelm Grimm did not differ in their intentions from those of Perrault. The Brothers Grimm wrote as part of a movement by the government to promote Prussian nationalism. In fact, the Empire needed an entire canon in order to establish its cultural legitimacy. The Brothers Grimm were at the service of the King of Prussia, who, during this period, instituted and centralized a secular school system, including *Nursery and Household Tales* (1812) as part of the educational curriculum. Such an act gave the work instantaneous status as part of Germany's cultural canon. As is widely known, the stories by the Brothers Grimm are along with Perrault's the most popular adaptations of folktale in the Western world.

By contrast, in Spain in the 1930s, the work of Antoniorrobles was designed to entertain and instruct Spanish children by offering them unorthodox versions of traditional fairy tales. Antoniorrobles published hundreds of children's stories[5] and essays about children's literature. He illustrated his own stories and also wrote versions of seven famous fairy tales, which he adapted to modern times. In the decade of the 30s, part of his work was also translated into English by his great admirer and friend, Edward Huberman. Stepping away from the typical versions that were so common amongst these traditional tales, Antoniorrobles strove to find a space within the balance of "good" and "bad," and consequently the dichotomy between these two extremes was diluted. In an interview with the Spanish journalist and writer Víctor Claudín, the author underscores the importance of representing "a better world" in children's literature:

"Hemos de ver al niño como la semilla que contiene el fruto maduro de la paz universal" (50) [We should raise a child as the seed that contains the potential fruit of universal peace].

The defeat of the Republic at the end of the Civil War forced Antoniorrobles to go into exile and his books disappeared from the Spanish libraries and bookstores, depriving the children of his literary talent. He went to Mexico, where he continued to write, but for the Spanish people his name was practically erased from memory during Franco's dictatorship. In the years after Franco, his work was still not promoted, with the exception of a few isolated cases. Upon his return to Spain, Carmen Martín Gaite did an interview with him, which was published in *La búsqueda de interlocutor y otras búsquedas* (1973), where he laments, among other things, the lack of distribution of his work. In 1979, the National Center for Theater (CNINAT) paid homage to him under the title *Fiesta del teatro de Antoniorrobles*, in which they dramatized several of his pieces (Torres 1983). Concerning the investigation of his work, the most recent publication on his life and work is *Nuestro Antoniorrobles* (1996) by Jaime García Padrino. A few of his books have gone back to the editors for publication, but in general, in today's Spain, the author's work is rarely recognized and his magnificent literary legacy has been mostly ignored. In fact, his folk tale rewritings of the "Ugly Duckling," "Little Red Riding Hood," "The Musicians of Bremen," "Puss in Boots," "Ali Baba and the Forty Thieves" and "Tom Thumb" are hardly known in Spain.

Antoniorrobles was one of the writers of his generation who remained steadfast in his political commitment, and who continued to live with it throughout Franco's dictatorship. Many of his contemporaries, like Elena Fortún, even though they did not show enthusiasm for the new political situation, opted for a prudent retirement or adapted their talent to a new cause. Antoniorrobles, on the other hand, was always faithful to his ideals of equality and liberty and portrayed these values in his work for children. At the beginning of the war, Antoniorrobles wrote his version of "Cinderella." In his version, the text puts into question ideas that would become fundamental to Francoism—concerning class, by making reference to the recently abolished monarchy in Spain[6]; about gender, by making reference to the position of the woman in society; and finally, regarding the Catholic religion and the Spanish race, by omitting that for the regime these were values and a stronghold fundamental to the new Spanish state.

Social Class

In the version by Antoniorrobles, the concept of social class and noble hierarchies that are present in the canonical versions of the stories are subverted. At the same time, the figure of the monarch, nobility and kingship, of which Franco was an avid supporter, is eroded. Also, communist ideals are promoted in the story but were emphatically rejected by the Francoist paradigm. This part of the chapter analyzes the monarchy as a symbol of power, which is repudiated in the story and replaced by a defense of egalitarian society without social hierarchies.

In this version, Cinderella's father is administrator of a factory called the Dukes of the Seven Chimneys. Upon the Duke's death, the Duchess forces John Littleclock, the administrator, to marry her. The step-sisters, Ramona y Romana, together with the step-mother, make fun of the girl and force her to do all the worst household tasks. While the Duchesses of the Seven Chimneys[7] attend the ball sponsored by the prince, Flora, the Duchess' cook, offers to help Cinderella so that she may attend the ball: "Escucha una cosa: los trabajadores de todas clases, hartos ya de que los poderosos abusen por la fuerza y por el dinero, vamos haciendo sociedades secretas, que cuando sean fuertes serán las que gobiernan el mundo. Yo iré a mi sociedad y te proporcionaré de todo, porque son buena gente" (3) [Listen to me: workers from all over the world are fed up with the abuse from the people in power, we are creating secret groups that one day will become stronger and will govern the world. I will go to my group and will ask them to help. They are good people].[8] In this version, magic does not intervene to convert Cinderella from a servant to a noble woman. In Perrault's original version, the fairy godmother, with her magic wand, transforms the rats into footmen and the pumpkin into a carriage. In Antoniorrobles' version, the discourse of the cook, who acts as the fairy, serves as a parallel to Marx's ideas on social classes. It also echoes Lenin's 1917 revolution motto: "Every cook can govern" meaning that the change in society should come from the lower classes. Like the cook, Marxism conceives of the reach of progress as the result of the fight among social classes. These differences are based on communal property and the means of production, distribution and exchange. This theme is repeated throughout Antoniorrobles' story, making clear his rupture with the ideas of the recent monarch[9] and the divisions of classes and hierarchies. For example, towards the end, and just like the versions of Perrault and the Brothers Grimm, when the prince discovers that Cinderella is the woman that he has been looking for, he proposes marriage. She asks Flora, the cook, to respond to the prince's Messenger by saying: "No me casaré con ningún príncipe ni con ningún personaje de clase privilegiada. Soy trabajadora, y si no lo fuera no tendría la conciencia tranquila y no sería feliz" (7) [I will not marry any prince or anybody in a privileged class. I am a worker and if I would not be, I would not have a peaceful conscience and I would not be happy]. The prince, upon receiving this news, decides to change his name, abdicate the throne to his younger brother, open a business and work for the first time in his life in order to be a decent man for Cinderella. This version by Antoniorrobles shows a diametric change from the official versions of the story. In the versions of the seventeenth and nineteenth centuries by Perrault and the Brothers Grimm, respectively, Cinderella is converted into a member of royalty, leaving the proletariat altogether. The story retold by Antoniorrobles promotes social change and raises the Communist flag, enemy of the Francoist ideals, by breaking and opposing, on a textual level, the social foundations as defined by the new regime.

In addition to Marxism, also anarchism, freemasonry and the liberal parties of the left were in opposition to the ideology of the Falange. Franco's regime pursued these groups until the end of the war, promoting a "Law of Political Responsibilities" that established the rules for prosecution (Payne, *El régimen* 234). Antoniorrobles' story touches on a delicate thread in proposing equality in society and rejecting the hierarchical model. By opposing the idea that Cinderella is converted into a princess, and pressing instead for the change in social status of the prince, the story also contradicts the model stipulated by the Franco regime. The symbols of the king and of the prince, which represent the monarchy and the endless hierarchies of power, seem diminished by Cinderella's rejection of the privilege of being a princess. Cinderella opposes the favoritisms of the monarch and supports a society without such hierarchies of nobility: "Además como esta aventura tan bella se la debo a los trabajadores, no quiero abandonarles e irme a ningún palacio" (7) [Besides, because I owe this beautiful adventure to the workers, I will not abandon them by going to a palace].

Gender

Another aspect that stands out in this version is its representation of gender, which centers itself on a vision opposed to that proposed by the Falange through the Sección Femenina. This part of the essay will be supported by the exhaustive study by Carmen Martín Gaite on the uses and customs of the Spanish post-war period, which analyzes in detail the position and role of the woman in Spain during that era. In addition, the symbolic aspect of the dress and the carnival will be examined under the lens of the theories of Jacques Lacan and Umberto Eco, all the while continuing the comparative dialog between the present version and those of Perrault and the Brothers Grimm.

Within the Franco regime, women were conditioned for the private sphere and confined to a mold of restricted behavior. Women formed part of the ideological tenets as a support to the man, with pre-established parameters and limits. "La mujer muy mujer" [The woman, the real woman] that Pilar Primo de Rivera describes, who would later become the founder of Obligatory Social Service, synthesizes the assigned place for the woman according to Franco's ideology in an official diary of the era as: "enamorarse. Que es una de las tres únicas cosas serias que puede hacer una mujer. Las otras dos, ya sabéis, son coser la ropa de su marido y darle todos los hijos que se ofrezcan" (Martín Gaite, *Los usos* 71) [falling in love. Which is one of the only three important things that a woman can do. The other two, as you know, are sewing your husband's clothes and giving him all the children you can] (Jones 67). With the diffusion and promotion of the ideology of the Social Service, the advances achieved by women during the Second Republic disappeared. In 1931, women had been given the right to vote and the equality of rights was established. In this era, new possibilities arose for women in the areas of politics, the arts, sciences, and knowledge in general. The climate of the Republican period nurtured these social changes for women, and in addition, urged their involvement as political subjects. The foundation of the Patronage of Pedagogical Missions[10] and the promotion of cultural development during this time also coincided with the opening of possibilities for social advancement for women. Generally speaking, the mark of the Republicans gave great importance to the promotion of reading as a vehicle for the formation of cultured individuals: "[L]a difusión y exaltación de la lectura eran consideradas como una de las fuentes de la España por venir. El crear lectores era el ojetivo de los hombres de la República" (Franco 267) [The promotion and exaltation of Reading were considered one of the main foundational sources of modernity in Spain. The creation of readers was the objective of the men of the Republic]. Another of the organizations that promoted education for women as a crucial part of their development was the Lyceum Feminine Club founded in 1926, the first Spanish cultural association created by women. It was directed by María de Maeztu, and it had as its headquarters the House of the Seven Chimneys in Madrid. This association grouped women together exclusively from the middle and upper classes, and offered educational activities for them. In the story, the factory of the Duke and Duchess is called "Seven Chimneys," which is the same name of the building in which the Lyceum was housed. The story makes reference to the elitist character of this organization.

In addition, during this era names of Republican intellectuals like Margarita Nelken, La Pasionaria and Victoria Kent stood out for their intellectual efforts concerning rights and equality for Spanish women. Nelken, as a representative of the Popular Front during the war, deals with social themes concerning the position of women. She champions the working woman and, in fact, led the first women workers' strike in Madrid. For Nelken, women have been raised assuming attributes falsely considered "feminine," which for her, serve as a tool of submission. The parameters and models assigned and labeled as part of "being a woman" constituted a delay in progress, which she aimed to shed.

In the version of Cinderella by Antoniorrobles, the characteristics that are supposedly essential and later promoted by Francoism are completely discredited. One of the aspects that symbolizes the rupture with these postulates in the story is the dress of the protagonist. In Franco's Spain, and under the supervision of the Feminine Section, certain attributes were made to stand out and were reinforced as to what all Spanish women should attempt to show. One of these was "decency" and "femininity" in dress. "[L]a decencia en el vestir se interpretaba como síntoma de españolidad" (Martín Gaite, *Los usos* 20) [modesty in clothing was interpreted as an indication of Spanishness] (Jones 21). Any hint of a sense of "liberality" in dress was overseen and immediately corrected. Clothing marked a line of behavior and signaled the values of the woman in Francoist society. In fact, Lacan affirms that clothes are an essential element of identity: the clothing that one wears defines them, determines who they are, and categorizes them: "Clothes promise debauchery (ça promet la ménade), when one takes them off … when there are no more clothes it leaves intact the question of what makes the One, that is, the question of identification" (6). For Lacan, clothing is a garb that constitutes the mask with which the subject regulates him or herself, and rises to meet what her exterior demands: On the one hand, the clothes/habit functions as a costume or a set of distinctive characteristics that repeat themselves, and in this way they reinforce the attire that one wears. On the other hand, the habit presents itself as the clothing that priests wear, as an emblem of an ideology that frames them. In this sense, the clothing in Franco's Spain served to define women and determined their "moral" values and behavior. However, in this version of "Cinderella," the clothing that the young girl wears to the ball forms part of a discourse that not only fails to reinforce, but rather rejects completely, on a textual level, the "feminine" attributes and values of the Francoist ideology.

The dress of Cinderella in the canonical versions of the story extols the "femininity" of the young girl and shows her temporary change in social status: from servant to nobility. In Perrault's version, the protagonist, with the help of her fairy godmother, goes to the ball in a ball-gown adorned with jewels: "Her godmother just touched her with her wand and at once her clothes turned into a ball dress covered with jewels" (Perrault 14). In the version of the Brothers Grimm, it is not a fairy who helps Cinderella, but rather a bird, that also provides a dress to the girl: "The bird threw a gold and silver dress down to her, and slippers embroidered with silk and silver" (124). However, in the version by Antoniorrobles, Cinderella does not receive help from any sort of fantastical or magical character,[11] but rather from a tangible entity—real, material, and probably not so glamorous—the cook that works in her home. She provides Cinderella with rather uncommon attire that does not correspond to or contain an element of "femininity" and opulence (social status) which is implied in the dress of gold, silver and jewels that corresponds to versions of Perrault and the Brothers Grimm: "En efecto, el dependiente de una casa de modas le dejó un vestido de 'Pierrot' de seda blanco con botones negros; y una antifaz" (7) [In fact, a clerk in a fashion store gave her a white silk Pierrot's dress with black buttons and a mask]. This change in the young woman's dress is contrary to the gender roles and also to the social status that is connoted in the traditional versions of the story. The Pierrot costume originally belongs to a mime character from the *Commedia dell'Arte italiana*. The character represents the sad clown, who yearns for the love of Colombina, who rejects him and leaves him for Harlequin instead. Pierrot is a masculine character who is generally represented dressed in a loose, white tunic. Pierrot's baggy clothing counters the tailored dresses that the step-sisters wear in the traditional versions of the story: "They [the stepsisters] broke more than twelve laces in pulling in their corsets to make their waists look smaller" (Perrault 8). One of the most distinctive characteristics of Pierrot's personality is his naiveté. He is also presented as distant and far-removed from the reality that surrounds him—he is owner and creator of his own reality. Antoniorrobles' Cinderella dresses as Pierrot and also creates her own reality, adopting an alternative to the expected dress of a woman in the public sphere. On the other hand, Pierrot's costume is diametrically opposed to the postulates and principles of the Franconian "morals" on various levels. First, because the woman should be, in all of her modalities and in her dress, eminently "feminine," it is in the pants that were tailored for her and in her use of girdle as a popular extreme [*sic*]. The famous "pololos" (traditional knickers) were the obligatory garment that women in the Social Service wore for their physical education class. These garments were uncomfortable and constituted the paradigm of oppression not only on a physical level, but emotional as well: "El uniforme reglamentario ... para aquellos ejercicios era tan incómodo y tan feo que convertía en sacrificio lo que hubiera podido ser placer. Estorbaba. Embarazaba" (61) [The uniform got in the way and hampered movement ... it was a burdensome hindrance imposed on a body that had not experienced the pleasure of freedom] (Jones 59). In contrast, the attire of Pierrot does not accentuate the contour of the feminine body, nor does it carry any vestige of "femininity." Secondly, Pierrot is a masculine character and Cinderella is a woman dressed as a man. The funny and or dramatic characteristic of Pierrot, in this sense, serves as a metaphor concerning the strict division of genders in the era. This variation of Cinderella's dress involves a change in the codes of gender performance, which are extrapolated by the mention of Pierrot's mask as part of Cinderella's attire, and at the same time, reflects an integration or break with gender boundaries. Cinderella dresses herself in clothes of the opposite sex, generating a conjunction of the "masculine" nature of the clothes and the "femininity" of who is wearing them. Third, the dress or disguise of Pierrot evokes the carnival party, which in addition to opposing what would be "adequate" in dress for a woman, also evokes the so-called "paganism" of this deep-rooted tradition in Spain, which Franco prohibited. The carnival in Franco's era acquired a subversive character, just like Cinderella's dress in this particular version. The traditional carnival party in Spain was prohibited from 1939 to 1981, when it once again re-emerged in the streets and it recovered its validity, leaving behind its clandestine aspect. The work of Antoniorrobles was also prohibited for his polemic and rebellious nature. For Eco, the simple idea of the carnivalesque evokes the breaking of rules and the idea of transgression. Is it for this that during Franco's regime, the carnival was considered a harmful element that would promote breaking away from what was permitted under the regime. In this case, by breaking social rules and laws dictated by the imaginary collective, it gave rise to the gender issue in terms of what a woman "should" do. This carnival, which in its essence is temporary, establishes a series of masks, also temporary, that create a space of power. Cinderella, in this version, accesses this space temporarily and creates a sense of fluidity regarding gender norms in terms of her creation and stripping of a preconceived identity.

As a consequence, a scene takes place that establishes a sort of "upside down world." Being Cinderella is the epitome of "femininity" within the imaginary collective, and upon dressing like Pierrot (masculine), the Cinderella of the text answers to and proposes an evolution within the hierarchies of the "feminine" versus the "masculine." Ideologically, Cinderella integrates the opposing forces marked by Francoist discourse and dissolves the rigid vision imposed by the regime. In addition, the androgynous element of dressing Cinderella in the clothing of a Pierrot accomplishes an effect that integrates the two genders. This image reforms the idea of Cinderella as a "feminized" subject and transforms it in response to the strict constitutions of masculine and feminine set forth under the mark of Franco's regime.

Religion

Yet another thematic thread that the censors probably considered subversive is the omission of any religious element whatsoever in Antoniorrobles' version of "Cinderella." This part of the essay will analyze the lack of religious allusions in the story, in light of the theory of Antonio Gramsci concerning political and civil society.

Religion constituted one of the insurmountable bastions that drove Francoist morality in the public, as well as in the private, sphere. For the Nationalists under the order of Franco, the Catholic religion was one of the fundamental causes of the war in defense of Spanish culture and tradition. The ideologies of the Falange insisted on affirming that the new policies were intimately tied to the Catholic religion: "Spanish fascism must be supported, in its form, on an historical Catholic-traditional essence.... Spanish fascism will be ... the religion of religion" (Penmartín 69). In this sense, Franco's ideology imposed upon civil society the rules of a political society, as defined by Gramsci. Gramsci makes a careful analytical distinction between civil and political society, the first being formed by voluntary groups, not coerced or controlled by force, and the second integrated by the army, the police, the bureaucracy, that is to say, the governing components that impart a particular code of social behavior. Franco's ideology regulated civil society in this way under the behavior of a political society. Martín Gaite relates the collision between politics and religion in this way: "[D]e la misma manera había que mirar a Franco y al Papa. Encadenados uno al otro, apoyándose mutuamente en aquella cruzada del espíritu contra la materia" (*Los usos*, 21) [You have to look at Franco and the Pope in the same way: chained to one another, supporting each other in the crusade of spirit versus matter] (23).[12] Once the Civil War was over, the efforts to "re–Christianize" and "Spanish-ize" the people began in the schools: "Initial decrees abolished co-education, reinstated the teaching of religion and sacred history, and mandated a purge of teachers, textbooks and school libraries to eliminate the 'aesthetic' and 'materialistic' doctrines" (Boyd 94). In this way, books for children's audiences were revised by the censors to ensure that they contained, disseminated, and emphasized the religious paradigms of the regime.

In the context of this religious crusade within the civil life of the country, another subversive aspect in Antoniorrobles' story is the lack of any mention of religion, which is present in both canonical versions of the story, and in the children's literature that was accepted by the regime, as is the case with the stories of Celia by Elena Fortún. For example, in *Celia novelista* (1939), published towards the end of the Civil War and later promoted and distributed by the regime, Celia attends a religious school and makes repeated mention of religion and Catholic rituals. The chapters "En Belén con los pastores," "El paraíso" and "La puerta del cielo" tell how Celia finds herself with Saint Peter, with the Wise Men and with the lions at the gates of Paradise respectively. Just as much in these stories by Fortún as in others, the religious references abound in relation to the education and formation of Celia as a good Christian, respectful of the Catholic dogma.

In the version by Perrault, Cinderella's godmother is the one who helps by means of magic to grant her wish of going to the ball. The word 'godmother' implies a connection with religion, since, by definition, the "godmother" is the woman who presents the one receiving the Baptism, a sacrament of the Christian faith. When a woman becomes a "godmother" she also become bound by the obligation of serving as a spiritual parent to the baptized child. This figure acts as a protector of Cinderella and, through the use of magic, manages to transform her and converts her into a princess with the goal of helping her attend the ball. In the original version, there are repeated mentions of being "good," but the characteristic of devotion that occasionally appears in the version by the Brothers Grimm is not present. In the Perrault version, the Christian religion is expressly mentioned and in various instances, the name of God is invoked. For example, at the beginning of the story, from her deathbed, Cinderella's mother asks her: "Dear child, be good and pious, and then the good God will always protect you" (121). Cinderella cries over her misfortune and prays at the foot of a tree that grows from the branches that she herself planted: "Thrice a day Cinderella went and sat beneath it, and wept and prayed." (122). In this scene where her savior appears to her in the form of a little white bird, "and a little white bird always came on the tree, and if Cinderella expressed a wish, the bird threw down to her what she had wished for" (122). The white bird of the Brothers Grimm is a substitute for the godmother, connoting clear religious symbolism, since the white bird evokes the representation of the Holy Spirit in Christian imagery. From this moment on, God protects Cinderella in both versions, and this divine presence works as a primordial element in the success of Cinderella's ascendancy and the positive resolution of the story.

On the other hand, in Antoniorrobles' version, religion is not mentioned. It is implied that being pious or devout will not determine the fortune of the protagonist, but rather that it is determined by being a just and fair individual. Cinderella promotes the equality of human rights and rejects the ties with royalty and the privileges that come with it. The morality of Cinderella in this version does not have any reference to Christianity, as is present in the canonical versions, but rather a more humanitarian focus in its interpretation of the world and the wish for the common good without any religious support. The "communist atheism" was one of the most ferocious criticisms launched against the ideas that were contrary to Francoism: "Leading Catholic bishops were soon referring to the war as a sacred crusade, a new Reconquest to rid the nation of atheism, communism and other imported heresies" (Boyd 93). Franco imposed the Catholic religion as a fundamental element of Spanish society, designating religious individuals as educators within his government. In this way, Catholicism acted as part of what Louis Althusser terms the "Ideological Apparatuses of the State" that were in charge of the formation of children and Spanish adolescents. Any form of agnosticism or atheism was condemned as something "pagan" or "irreverent." For this reason, the version of Antoniorrobles resulted in being highly problematic within the Francoist parameters by not supporting or even alluding to the Catholic religion, which formed the base of cultural and social values for the regime. While this version did not adhere to any religious belief, it did indeed propose a range of values based on kindness, peace and harmony. Tejero Robledo comments thus on the values of the author: "Lo que sorprende de Antoniorrobles es que en tiempos de confrotación pasional fue capaz de avanzar en un campo minado con un ideario de paz, de conciliación y de valores universales" (346) [What surprises the most about Antoniorrobles is that in times of passionate confrontation, he was able to move forward through a minefield with his ideals of peace, conciliation and universal values].

Race

By omitting any allusion to the ethnicity of the protagonist, the story subverts the thematic thread of race. This part of the chapter will be a comparative analysis of Terdiman's theories on counter-discourse and Antoniorrobles' version, alongside those by Perrault and the Brothers Grimm, and also *Celia novelista* by Elena Fortún, whose work was accepted and disseminated by the regime. For Franco, the definition of "Spanishness" depended on the exclusion of any ethnicity that was not Castilian: "Spanishness was defined explicitly in the public sphere with significant absences ... such as the ethnocultural disappearance of the Moors and the Jews" (Hertzberger 14). Franco's ideal race was the Aryan race, and this was to be represented in the literature that was accepted by the regime as well. Elena Fortún's books about Celia faithfully reproduced these patterns of race. It is for this reason that her work was not censored as was the work of Antoniorrobles. On the contrary, her works were widely distributed to children's audiences. Her name is known today and her work has been edited and published repeatedly, even adapted into a television series in the 1990s.

Children's stories, as meaningful representations, function by making associations between the images they present and the reality inhabited by readers. This associative logic is what reinforces stereotypes about race, class and gender that is underscored in the media of mass communication, such as film and television, but also in literature. In the version of the Brothers Grimm of Cinderella, the ideal of the white race is clearly stipulated: "The woman had brought with her into the house two daughters, who were beautiful and fair of face, but vile and black of heart" (121). In Perrault's version, the reader is informed of the blond hair of Cinderella: "Cinderella had beautiful blond hair, which she took from her mother" (16).

In contrast, the version by Antoniorrobles is free of this typical reinforcement with respect to race, since in his story, any mention of the color of Cinderella's skin is notably absent, as is that of any other character in the story. The hegemonic representation of Cinderella as blond and fair-skinned is destroyed by not making any reference to her appearance, and by limiting itself to the simple affirmation that: "Cenicienta era una chica muy linda" (1) [Cinderella was a beautiful girl] and that upon seeing her enter the ball dressed as Pierrot, the crowd exclaimed: "¡Qué bonita! ¡Qué distinguida! ¡Qué alegre!" [How pretty! How distinguished! How jolly!] (4).

Franco's government characterized itself by emphasizing the Spanish "race" as a standard of value and pride. "Spanishness" was based on one ethnicity only, which excluded any other group that differed from the Francoist fundamentals of "true Spaniards," and that did not highlight the characteristics proposed by Franco of the "Spaniard."[13] In the version by Antoniorrobles, the idealized stereotypes of race are eliminated, which are present in other children's texts from Spain of the same period, like those of Elena Fortún,[14] creator of the character, Celia. Fortún represents the protagonist in a series of adventures, in what Juan Cervera classifies as "literatura instrumentalizada." (18) In this type of children's text, the same character appears in diverse situations in which, according to this Spanish theorist, a "didactic intention" predominates. In *Celia lo que dice* (1932), the narrator describes the protagonist: "Celia es rubia y tiene los ojos claros" (48) [Celia is blond and has green eyes] emphasizing here the race of the girl. Celso Medina also presents an argument on this topic: "Franco exalta una raza, en una clara coincidencia con el sentimiento racista que acompaño a unos de los movimientos ideológicos que le fue muy afecto: el nazismo. Su raza es una estirpe histórica, vinculada al origen de la España castellano-leonesa" [Franco exalts one race in a clear nexus with the racist ideology that he supported: Nazism, His race is a historical lineage, linked to the origin of Castilian-Leonese Spain]. This idea of the purity of lineage can be clearly observed in the film *Raza*,[15] the script of which was allegedly written by General Franco. The famous singer, Marisol, illustrious popular icon, portrayed the preoccupation with race by dyeing her hair platinum blond and thus transforming herself to the racial ideal of Spanish popular culture of the 1960s. In this way, a girl from Malaga of humble origins becomes the "novia de España" and the national symbol of the "prototipo idílico rubio y con ojos azules" (Aguilar 14)[16] [the idyllic prototype of the blond, blue-eyed person].

Richard Terdiman's study, *Discourse-Counter Discourse* (1985),[17] explains how two discourses, in particular the cultural forms of bourgeois domination and resistance movements that contest it, exist in opposition to one another by showing and proposing different social and political models. The writings of Fortún and Antoniorrobles represent such an opposition: the dominant hegemony asserts its power to monopolize the formation and expression of social attitudes in the text of Celia, while the discourse of Antoniorrobles' "Cinderella" operates as a "symbolic resistance" to the political and cultural models promoted by the Falange. Celia embodies the stereotypes of the dominant class that are incorporated in her discourse (Celia is white, blond, her domain is the house, she adheres to the mandates of the church, etc.), while Antoniorrobles resists integrating and subverting those relationships of power in his text. Celia complies with what the hegemonic discourse supports and finds favorable: "The dominant is the discourse whose presence is defined by the social impossibility of its absence" (24). On the other hand, the discourse found in a children's story like Antoniorrobles' "Cinderella" counters the discourse established by Franco by questioning it on a textual level but also, as the absence of religious reference attests, by striving to exclude the dominant discourse.

Conclusion

The intellectual, according to Santos Juliá, forms a large part of the individual debate, "libres de servidumbres corporativas o de lazos de patronazgo eclesiásticos o nobilarios" (10) [Free of any corporative servility or bonds of ecclesiastical or aristocratic power]. The "especialista en el trato con los bienes simbólicos" (2) [Specialist in dealing with symbolic goods], as Pierre Boudieu defines it, poses that ideas are her unique tools for work, and her position links it to the defense of universal values and of the common good. In the text of Antoniorrobles, one can perceive this profile of the intellectual who delivers a literary product that possesses "esta infinita y plástica ambigüedad" [this infinite and plastic ambiguity] (Borges 127); he rids it of cultural supports and at the same time invites freedom of interpretation. This analysis, in addition to dissecting the political, social and cultural axes of the Francoist ideals, also proves the contrary quality of this text. The story by Antoniorrobles re-writes society, leveling out the different social classes and political, gender, and racial hierarchies, while trying to eliminate the dogmatic precepts of traditional Catholicism. The text reiterates the power of literature, as an intangible asset, which has the resources to penetrate all dogma and all laws. This reading grants the text a voice and a purpose, perhaps utopian, of liberty and equality, that urges its child readers to contemplate the world from a shade of gray, where black and white are diluted, in order to create a vision of the world that is more egalitarian, and as a result, more peaceful.

Chapter 3

Performance as a Mask in *La nueva Cenicienta*

In 1964 the film *La nueva Cenicienta* (*The New Cinderella*) appeared featuring Spain's sweetheart of the sixties, the charismatic, dancer, actress and singer, Marisol (1948–   ). In this musical adaptation of "Cinderella," the protagonist is the leader in a group of artists. Marisol, who bears her stage name in the fiction (her birth name is Josefa Flores or "Pepa Flores"), lives with her father (played by famous Spanish actor Fernando Rey), five other men and a chimpanzee, named Miguel. They all live at a pension-like house in Madrid. Marisol thus has a family, rather peculiar but a family indeed, as the concept of family implies not only the consanguine ties and sharing of the household, but also that each of them cares for the well-being of each of the others. Every member of this unorthodox family occupies their own room in the pension, except for Fernando, who shares his bedroom with the chimpanzee. The six men and Marisol share the same passion and love for art, music, dance as they also have the same profession: performers. This chapter analyzes performance as a mask in the main character, Marisol/Cinderella, and how it operates in the evolution of the protagonist as a pícara (rascal), a mother, a doll, and an independent woman.

Performance is central to the narrative thematically and hermeneutically. As all members of the family perform a different role—a magician, a pianist, an acrobat, a composer, a showman, an animal trainer—in the same way, the theoretical concept of performance originates from diverse fields: sociology, anthropology, literary theory, philosophy, theater, and dance, among others. Associated mostly with the ideas of Victor Turner (1988) and Richard Schechner (1985), Performance Theory studies individuals as performers in society and as acting a specific character played and ruled by a certain code of behavior framed by culture. Erving Goffman also affirms that performance is a form of social conduct "to fit into the understanding and expectations of a society" (*The Presentation* 35). Theorists like Butler in *Excitable Speech* (1993) and Derrida in *Limited Inc* (1990) state that performances bolster and reveal our identities in society. Therefore, societies in various contexts, are examined through the way each group and individual reveal themselves through myriad performances.

The main and more multifaceted performer of the family is Marisol. The film's establishment shot begins with an apostrophe narrator stating, "Entremos a la película sin miedo" [Let's enter the movie without fear], and a high angle camera shot that descends to the town and then to the pension showing a zenithal shot of the house, living room, kitchen and stairs that take the viewer to each of the rooms where all the men are sleeping. The chimpanzee, Miguel, is the first of the males to get up, at 9:15 a.m. When the alarm clock goes off, Miguel rushes to the next bed and wakes up Fernando. Immediately after that scene, another shot shows Marisol riding a bike with a big smile on her face and entering a neighborhood store in search of food to feed the family. However, she does not have money to buy the groceries needed, and the family already owes the store owner 1,300 pesetas. In spite of her family's debt, she expects to obtain the groceries. The owner, however, refuses to allow her more credit and, loudly and rudely, tells her to leave the premises. Despite the uncomfortable and certainly humiliating situation, Marisol keeps the same smile and positive attitude and even sings for them. She tells the couple, keeping her smile, that the family will just need to hold on one more day without eating, as they are all already used to starving quite often. With this recourse, finally, the grocery store owner and his wife feel pity for the girl and let her have the groceries needed and requested by Marisol. In exchange, the couple asks Marisol to promise to sing for them the next musical composition written by her father.

Performance theory considers that everyone in society plays a part or acts a performance in their micro and macro cosmos. As for the heroine of *La nueva Cenicienta*, she puts on four different performances throughout the film as a tool of survival in her society. Her first performance is that of a *pícara* as a means to contest her challenging economic situation. Through performance, Marisol exercises resistance as part of her daily actions common to the marginal societal group to which she belongs. In fact, performance in the film functions both as a theme and an act of creation and reaction embodied in the figure of Marisol/Cinderella at various stages.

Marisol plays the part of a poor starving girl, knowing that this performance will trigger the couple's compassion and clemency. In this scene and others at the beginning of the film, Marisol seems to perform a character from the picaresque genre: a low-class heroine rogue with charisma who, through her wit and inventiveness, obtains favors and survives her poverty. This aspect of the heroine is shown also when she and Tino, one of her friends, steal groceries from the customers at a street market. Tino is the seller and Marisol approaches the stand pretending to be a regular buyer while Tino duplicates the customers' grocery list, and gives the extra items to Marisol while concealing this action from the customer's view. Her performance as a *pícara* is also notable, when she twice brings Miguel, the chimpanzee, to scare their debtors away. With this stratagem, Marisol avoids paying the bills that she and her family owe. Her wit and quick mind are celebrated by her father and friends, lauding her for being so fast and clever.

As performance is central to human understanding, in this particular example Marisol reveals her highly ritualized routine and elaborated performances displayed in the grocery store, in the street market, and outside her house, as the outside is the constant space for her various displays of her *pícara* performances. As a traditional *pícara* character, her economic situation is precarious as she and her family do not have the minimum resources to feed themselves every day. In spite of this circumstance, she endures the disgraceful situation with humor, imagination, and savviness. In *Búsqueme a esa chica* (1964), Marisol is also a *pícara* along with her father who pretends to be blind in order to obtain money from tourists. In both films, Marisol as the motherless orphan heroine plays the role of a picaresque beautiful princess who fights the injustices of poverty with her dancing, singing, positive attitude and trickster persuasiveness as tools to survive.

Performance as a subversive concept is charged with a transformative force and is considered a zone of "contest and struggle" (Conquerwood 137). The narrator describes these combative and powerful characteristics represented in Marisol: "esta chica espanta brujas y ogros" [this girl scares away witches and ogres], making a reference to her force, strong will and the centrifugal power that she represents culturally. On the other hand, the phrase alludes to the fairy tale tradition that the story and the title echoe. On a superficial level, the Cinderella allusion is made through the plot, the characters and the motifs. For instance, as it has been mentioned, Marisol's mother is absent in the story, and she, the girl, seems to have occupied the place of a traditional mother in her relationship with her cohabitants and friends. She is not only the person in charge of feeding them and taking care of the house, but she also resembles a mother-like figure to all the grown-up men. This aspect of the story line echoes another famous fairy tale story, J.M Barrie's *Peter Pan* (1911). All grown-up men in the Neverland pension seem childish as they act as small children, forgetful and irresponsible. They do not live a life of adult maturity, for example, holding a job to contribute to the household, and even though they are adults, do not seem concerned with acting as such. None of them, including Marisol's father, pay attention to the appointment time for a job interview that Marisol has secured on her meeting with the famous actor Bob Conrad. The elderly men seem to live in a Neverland-like place, where they will never grow up and accept responsibility. As in the film *Tómbola* (1962), Marisol becomes the "little woman" image created by Francoism in school books such as *La niña instruida* (1945) and mentioned by Sarah Wright in her book *The Child in Spanish Cinema* (2013). Marisol is the Wendy, or little woman, of the Peter Pan story, cooking for the males, protecting them and searching for work possibilities. Their condition of indigence does not seem to preoccupy the men whatsoever. Unlike Wendy, there is no father figure for the "lost grownups." Marisol's father frowns upon the idea of Arturo finding a job cleaning windows at high rises. Don Etérri perceives this change of profession as downgrading, because Arturo is an artist, an acrobat and not a laborer, as he states: "Esto es inaceptable" "This is unacceptable." Marisol, although the youngest of all, carries all the responsibility and burden of finding food for the group, but her father nor anybody else in the family seems to acknowledge that. Marisol's father is the Peter Pan of the story and Wendy/Marisol his companion. As in Peter Pan, the relationship between them is also filial.

"Snow White" (Grimms 1812) is another fairy tale tangentially embedded in the story. Marisol/Snow White lives with six men and a chimpanzee. She is also in charge of all the domestic labors and each of the men has a trait that frames their behavior in parallel with the characters of Snow White's seven dwarfs. The pianist of the group of artists, Ramón, resembles "Doc"; Tino is "Bashful," as he blushes when Marisol kisses him on the cheek; "Grumpy" is Don Echérri, as he scorns and chastises the members of the group; "Sleepy" is Fernando (Miguel's owner); and "Happy" is Rafael, the dancer who seems to be always in a good mood. Miguel, the chimpanzee is "Dopey" as he is clumsy, while "Sneezy" is Arturo, who seems to be always on the verge of exploding or falling. Marisol is not poisoned and later "saved" by a prince's kiss like the traditional "Snow White" story recounts. As in her film *Tómbola*, Marisol is also the beatific figure who looks after a group of men, in this case, swindlers. The intertextuality with "Snow White" is seen by the family of seven males and Marisol and the fact that she takes care of them and how those in the group look after each other.

In the story, the intertext with the "Cinderella" tale has, as expected, more axes of conjunction than with "Snow White." The major goal of Marisol/Cinderella is to be a dancer and not, as in the traditional story, to attend the ball to meet the prince. She is the agent of her decisions as she defines the most important goal in life: "Lo más importante es trabajar en lo que te gusta" [the most important thing is to work in what you love], and she is determined to find jobs in the performance arts field for her friends. The idea of performance is referenced at various levels in the narrative as Marisol/Cinderella transforms the protagonist paradigm of the tale. In contrast to Snow White and Cinderella, who are both passive, mistreated and the target of female jealousy, Marisol is the engine that makes the family go forward and is not a passive subject that is abandoned and neglected. The absence of other female characters in the movie is notable and it makes impossible the jealousy factor that is predominant in the majority of the Cinderella versions and in Snow White. Marisol's major enemy at this stage is poverty not jealousy, as for Cinderella and/or Snow White.

Another form of performance in the film is made evident in the dancing and singing numbers. The concept of performance and dance in the narrative shapes how Marisol acts in and reacts to her society and situates herself within the cultural realm. In her study of the music in Spanish film in relation to women's identities in the sixties, Virginia Sánchez-Rodríguez observes that Marisol's identity in *La nueva cenicienta,* as in other movies, is that of a traditional woman in her classic interpretations of the Hollywood-like musical numbers. However, to some extent it also shows a modern part of her identity (497). "De acuerdo con nuestro estudio, Marisol representa la imagen de mujer tradicional con el argumento y con la interpretación de números populares musicales aflamencados, pero también aparece próxima a temas más modernos que quieren mostrar una imagen más actual" [According to our study, Marisol represents the image of a traditional woman with the plot and interpretation of musical numbers of popular and folk songs, but also she seems to approach more modern themes, that seek to portray a more up-to-date image of a woman].

Sánchez-Rodríguez' study approaches the relationship between Marisol and her identity as traditional and/or modern woman. However, the author does not mention the multiple performances or personae that Marisol represents through these musical numbers and the transformations that are intrinsic to these performances that this chapter discusses.

Dance as discourse and performance emphasizes the inability of words and language to resist certain societal constraints or to assist individuals in their opposition to those constraints. Through the number of dances, Marisol creates and shifts the performance, in Victor Turner's conception of the term, from mimesis to poesis. Her second performance is that of a homemaker and caregiver. In the first phase, Marisol seems to adjust to the representation of women culturally as the caretaker and "mother" like figure. In the second phase, and Marisol's third performance, she changes to a more creative and thus free and resolute version of herself. In other words, Marisol's performance changes from representational mirror-like (mimesis) to poetical or driven by the force of creation/re-creation of her cultural self (poesis).

This notion is shown through Marisol's several dancing and singing numbers in the movie. Unlike Cinderella and Snow White, her fairy tale counterparts, who only dance with a partner, Marisol dances by herself and in various places. The fairy tale heroines aforementioned either dance with the prince or with the dwarfs in the ball scenes of the filmic Walt Disney popular adaptations of "Cinderella" and "Snow White" respectively. Marisol on the contrary does not have a dancing partner in the first musical numbers that she interprets. Marisol dances and performs everywhere as dance is a way for her to live, communicate and create her own version of Cinderella (poesis) rejecting at the same time the traditional Cinderella attributes (mimesis) of a passive subject and realizing these transformations in kinesis.

Kinesis as movement, motion, and fluidity as "restless energies that transgress boundaries" (Conquerwood 138) are configured in Marisol's several dancing scenes. She dances on the streets of Madrid. In the first two dancing scenes, she does not have a dancing partner, as it has been stated before, showing her independence despite her apparent traditional position in the household. In these two instances, Marisol is in the private sphere, her stage is the house. More specifically, the two spaces depicted in these two dances scenes are the kitchen and the bedroom. Those two spaces limit the possibilities of Marisol/Cinderella to the domestic sphere, mimicking the Cinderella character that she represents. Performance in these two internal locations is reserved to specific private activities that constrain Marisol's movement and allow her mobility only within a certain perimeter. Dancing as performance is the spine of the tale and the center of Marisol's equilibrium. Marisol expresses herself through dance and communicates through movement. The protagonist is not only a dancer, but she also feels the act of dancing in her core as the axis of her life. As dancing is both a way to communicate and also the expression of the "human soul," according to Graham (96), Marisol reveals her inner self through her various dances in the film. In other words, dance in *La nueva Cenicienta* is charged with the protagonist's emotional and personal force expressing the kinetic characteristic of performance in society.

The first dance is in the kitchen at the pension/house. This performance reveals the first mimesis and the Cinderella mask that she wears; that of domesticity and conformity to the ideology. She dances and sings the tune that her father has composed for her. In other words, the Lacanian Father through the Symbolic Order and through "the father" figure gives her the societal score to follow. The Francoist ideology is patent as Marisol adheres to it and sings the music composed for her by her father/patriarchal society. The title of the song, though, is emblematic and related to the many facets which Marisol portrays in the film as Cinderella. The song composed by her father, entitled "Máscara," (Mask), paradoxically unveils and anticipates the layers of the film. In "Máscara," Marisol's first dance and song routine in the movie, she is in the kitchen with the chimpanzee. She moves through the kitchen island, to the windows, to the stove, drying the dishes and using the kitchen towels as handkerchiefs, waving them while she dances. She sings about wearing the mask and being happy. The song lyrics make clear reference to the ambivalent depiction of Marisol/Cinderella as an independent woman, but with the mask of a submissive, traditional and domestic caregiver. Her first space is the kitchen and Marisol shares it with Miguel, while he washes clothes in the kitchen sink. The dancing space is experienced as a continuum to the spectator coming from the interior of the house to the exterior, and within the limits of the kitchen space. Marisol opens the window and looks out, although viewers are not shown what she sees. On the contrary, she is momentarily out of sight behind the window emphasizing her domestic confinement. Marisol leaves a trail between the outside and inside spaces through her dance allowing the narrative to flow between dance numbers. As the filmic narrative flows from one space to the other, women's roles in Franco's society, here personified in Marisol, also flow within this restricted space to reach the next performance.

As a dancer/performer Marisol articulates space but also disarticulates it or undoes it. The sign of dance acquires multiple signifiers in the film. In this first dance number, the gender space is deployed for her and Miguel. Her leadership and authority in the household is to lead the "lost grown-ups" and provide for them but it also excludes and prevents the (human) male characters from performing traditional "female roles." She also sings about everything being fantastic, while you wear the mask, which refers to the roles that she plays in the house but hides her real role as a leader, a provider and a modern woman who looks for a professional opportunity. The song reveals the attitudes and projections of a society and the imposition of roles on women as a mask that needs to be worn at all times.

The second dance is in her bedroom. Marisol comes in her private space at the house, her bedroom, after chatting with the men in her family about how much money they have, and about the need for everybody to find a job to contribute to the family support. Somewhat disappointed with the few resources at hand for the family, she retires to her bedroom. Upon opening the door, she looks at her doll and stares at it. The close-up showing the features, the hair and the doll's dress resembling that of Marisol seems to compare the two. The doll as a little version of Marisol or a mini Marisol is the passive object and merely the representation of herself without any movement (kinesis). As Simone de Beauvoir puts it: "While the boy seeks himself in his penis as an autonomous subject, the little girl pampers her doll and dresses her as she dreams of being dressed and pampered; inversely, she thinks of herself as a marvelous doll" (*The Second* 293). In fact, in the sixties, a Marisol doll was made as a marketing tool and it was a miniature version of the actress (Wright 62). The advertisement for the Marisol doll was "!Y como tal actúa, habla, piensa y ama!" (Anon 1969) [And like Marisol, she performs, talks, thinks and loves!]. The doll in the movie also mimics Marisol as an alter ego pointing out and anticipating Marisol's next performance. This scene foreshadows what is to come as it acts as a preamble to the next performative space/stage; Marisol as the doll-like incarnates her new role or a role assigned to her. There is a sudden change in the camera vision from the doll, to Marisol to Marisol looking at herself in the mirror. The film narrative exposes a conundrum for Marisol's identity and role in her next vital scene. It also seems to pose a question regarding Marisol's cultural options as a static woman-doll or as a woman with agency looking at her reflection in the mirror. The spectator is part of the scene and part of her vital panorama. At that moment, she starts her performance looking her reflection and singing: "Yo sé que muy pronto, encontraré un amor para toda la vida, ese amor que ya nunca se olvida" [I know that very soon, I will find a love for my whole life, that love that one never forgets] and walks outside her balcony singing "No sé quién será o dónde irá, pero sé que algún día llegará"

3. Performance as a Mask in La nueva Cenicienta

[I do not know who would that be, or where he would go, but I know one day he will arrive]. At that very moment the camera shows an oblique angle placing Marisol smaller and smaller, suggesting a transition of performances while she looks at the sky, the noise and the image of a plane crosses it. On that plane, the prince charming, Bob Conrad, is about to land in the city. The plane flying and landing on this scene resembles the transitional stage of the actors, performers and the transitional stage of Marisol, who is constantly moving from scene to scene, performance to performance, stage to stage, dance to dance. As individuals and their many performances in life, Marisol/Cinderella is ready to perform a new role, while she prepares her road to independence. From the pícara, to mother-like, to the maid, to the doll-like woman are some of the performances that lead to the path to becoming and transforming her identity.

The prince charming is another character paradigmatic of the Cinderella story. In *La nueva Cenicienta*, the notion of the prince is constructed within two Freudian concepts: pleasure and reality. Marisol's priority is aligned with the social moment in Spain of the sixties. Realistic and resolute, Marisol/Cinderella searches for a job, as her goals are related to survival. There is not much time for play and leisure for her. Marisol looks for a tangible, practical, and realistic goal. The prince charming figure in the story, therefore, expresses this notion, as there are two princes charming: the provider of pleasure and the provider of work. In an impoverished Spain of the sixties, the counter discourse of Marisol's goals challenges the ultimate desire of women in this epoch: to become wives and, as a result, mothers. Franco's society would award a pension as incentive for women to stay home, take care of the children and husband as part of their "duty" as females according to Franco's ideology. Marisol, on the other hand, represents the opposite. Even though she appears with the mask of a sweet caregiver, taking care of the household along with Miguel, the chimpanzee, in her inner self she is looking for economic independence and to be able to work, prohibited to women at the time. The notion of wearing a "mask" or performance is ingrained in the first song that she delivers in the kitchen. The subtle Francoist discourse about women is stated in the film through the song praising the "mask," that everybody should wear to be "happy."

Marisol's situation in the family is very clear. In the pension/house, the only two members who cook and clean are Marisol and the chimpanzee, Miguel. Arturo, the owner of Miguel, when asked for his share and contribution to the household, says: "No tengo dinero, ni trabajo, pero contribuyo con la chacha y ya saben que hoy en día lo difícil que es encontrar una" [I do not have money but I contribute with the maid, and you all know that nowadays it is hard to find one]. Marisol is equated to the primate, and with a maid, as the only two individuals capable of cooking, which seems a clear reference to the patriarchal vision of Franco's regime concerning the role of women. A primate is put at the same level as the only woman in the household. Like Marisol, Miguel also wears an apron and his space is the house or that of a caregiver. Nevertheless, the dynamic in the household is contradictory and twofold. Marisol/Cenicienta is restricted to the kitchen but she is the voice of the group and the one who makes the decisions and organizes the family.

The third dance is on the street. Marisol has moved from mimesis (stagnant) to kinesis (mobility). In fact, on the street is where the famous flamenco dancer, Antonio, spots Marisol dancing, chases her and in her attempt to escape his pursuit she loses one of her shoes. After that episode, Antonio keeps the shoe and is obsessed with finding the great dancer who is the owner of it. Antonio, though, is not a prince but a dancer. Marisol transforms into a flamenco dancer by looking at Antonio's poster while he comes alive by her side in her imagination. She is wearing an elegant flamenco dancer light green dress; her hair is pulled up in a typical flamenco bun adorned with a bouquet of pink roses. Her shoes are also pink and the lyrics are: "la luna es un pozo chico, las flores no valen nada, lo que vale son tus brazos cuando de noche me abrazas las manos de mi cariño te están bordando una capa" [The moon is a small well, the flowers are worth nothing, what has value are your arms which hug me at night, my sweetheart's hands are embroidering a cloak]. They dance to the flamenco tune as Marisol sings. When the song finishes, Antonio disappears and through his shape on the door, Marisol enters another dimension or room. On the other side behind the billboard, there is a stage and it is completely dark. Antonio is seated on a chair in the center of the stage and there are other musicians and dancers. Marisol sings and Antonio dances to the song. It is a lively song, a *bulería*. Marisol repeats the lyrics and dances with Antonio this time. It is a lively melody with strong forceful steps of flamenco, where the male dancer, Antonio, takes the lead as Marisol, Cinderella, joins him. This dance number in Marisol's imagination sets the ambience for her reaching the goal of reality: a job.

The famous American actor and singer from the sixties, Robert "Bob" Conrad, is the prince charming in the story and the prince of reality. The American movie star, like Marisol, keeps his real stage name in the fiction. Bob arrives in Madrid for a performance with the famous flamenco dancer, Antonio. He spends his first day in Madrid visiting tourist sites and taking

3. Performance as a Mask in La nueva Cenicienta

pictures of the city, when he accidently photographs Marisol standing by the promotional billboard of Antonio's flamenco performance. After a number of events, the prince charming, Bob, realizes that the girl in the photo that he took is the same girl dancer that he has met at the studio looking for a job for her father and fellow artists. The princes charming, Antonio and Bob, are the emblematic presence of reality and pleasure. One provides a job to Marisol and her family/friends the artists and the other one offers her or provides her with, it is implied, a romance.

At the end of the movie, Both Marisol and Bob are reunited on the stage singing "Me conformo" [I conform] for the second and last time. The first time they sing the song "Me conformo" is on the way to Marisol's house, one more time on the street. While accompanying Marisol and her father after having dinner, Bob Conrad stops at a construction site and starts singing to Marisol. They both dance and sing in unison, until they end up sitting and staring at each other. Marisol, then, arrives home glowing with happiness. The site for this first "Me conformo" tune is a place under construction full of tools, a ladder, remnants of building materials and construction signs. This atmosphere frames the emotional situation of the couple as they start building a relationship from scratch, just like the place where they are situated.

The plot reaches its problematic peak when the performers, Marisol's friends, ruin the worldwide broadcast of Bob Conrad's international appearance on television. After the problem is solved and Bob forgives and forgets the incident the couple meet again on stage. The romantic lyrics suggest that they will reconcile and overcome their former differences and misunderstandings. The tone is mellow and the music seems to tell their mutual sentiments. Both Marisol and Bob sing the song expressing their devotion to each other in a very romantic and folktale Walt Disney–esque ending. Nevertheless, in this case both Cinderella and the Prince are professional partners and equals in this arena. The duality of princes, Bob and Antonio, and their roles is expressed clearly at the end of the film in this scene.

After Marisol sings "Me conformo" with Bob Conrad, Antonio comes onto the stage and takes Marisol's hand as her dance partner, while Bob disappears from the scene. The second part of the lyrics, though, indicates a subtle comment on the remaining challenges that they face as individuals. The anaphoric ending repeating the chorus at unison suggests a mutual understanding and acceptance of the present situation. Political, societal or emotional, the song "I Conform" as a colophon gives an open-ended and ambiguous technical closure to Marisol's performance.

At the end of the musical number, Marisol/Cinderella is invited to have dinner with Bob. As she rushes to change her outfit for the dinner date, she loses a shoe on the stairs. This time she wears a beautiful light blue dress embroidered with diamonds and a tiara. Marisol resembles the transformed Cinderella in the traditional story. The light blue shoe also shines, as it is made of satin. Unlike the first time she loses a shoe to Antonio, this shoe is delicate, bright and shiny. Marisol is glamorous, fancy, elegant; her hair is adorned and pulled up in a very classy style. The first event is quite different: Marisol has her hair down, has little or no make-up, her dress is modest and the colors are a sober and serious brown and beige. Her shoe is an opaque brown color and looks like it has been used and worn. The prince of reality/work receives the shoe representing the responsibility, obligation and quotidian. The prince of pleasure/party receives the shoe representing light, debauchery, joy.

The two princes portray reality and pleasure markedly. In a dialog with his boss, Antonio's assistant mentions "responsabilidad y trabajo" [responsibility and work] or "lo que los alemanes hacen" [what Germans do] delineating a clear reference to the diligence and hard work attributes of the German culture. This implication posits hard work versus leisure and marks the bilateral directions of Marisol's needs and priorities: work and responsibility in the first place and leisure and romance in the second. The relationship between these two concepts is demarcated in the two princes. In fact, Marisol obtains her ultimate goal, a job as a dancer through the influence and help of Bob Conrad, who brings her to the studio. As Spain received help to boost its economy from the United States, when its economic structure in the sixties left behind the autarchy economic model imposed by Franco's regime and turned towards a more free-market economy.[1] At this time, Spain entered a new cycle of prosperity not known after the end of the Spanish Civil War in 1939. The emergent economy was in part driven by the foreign investment of the United States and European countries such as Germany. As already noticed by Camporesi, the inclusion of Bob Conrad in the film was a sign of "Americanization" (2007b). One other factor that dialogs with the appearance of the American actor Bob Conrad is that more than 40 percent of the foreign investment in Spain came from the United States and almost 17 percent came from West Germany. During the economic boom of the 1960s, tourism was central to this improvement. The common motto "Spain is different" served to publicize the country overseas with flamenco dancers and bullfighters as emblems of Spanish culture. Catholic conservatism had to water down the strict rules about how Spain was portrayed in order to draw more tourism and dividends from this source. A certain level of tolerance to the eyes of overseas allies benefited Spain's economy, and a relatively liberal development of tourism introduced foreign influence into the country. The correlation between the contribution made to Spanish finances by external visitors correlates with Bob Conrad's visit and pivotal offer of a job opportunity to Marisol. The permissiveness in Spain's external economic influences was also revealed in cinema production between the sixties and seventies, before the death of Franco in 1975. A similar plot about Marisol and a foreigner offering her employment opportunities is depicted in *Búsqueme a esa chica* (1964). Marisol as an icon in the sixties in Spain was the representation of the emergent Spain as explained by Javier Barreiro: "los filmes de Marisol querrán dar la imagen de la España emergente a la que la llamada tecnocracia en el poder aspiró como modelo" (Marisol frente 25) [Marisol's films would want to offer the image of a modern Spain, which was the desired model for the technocrats in power].

Performance entails a dual structure of functioning in the movie: on the one hand, it may function as a mask or multiple masks adopted by members of a society in response to society's constraints, but it can also be a vehicle of resistance. Indeed, the marginal space of performance has constantly been its historical nature. For instance, theatre in medieval European cities was peripheral and situated at the city limits. The marginal condition of Marisol and her family can be understood as a *mise en abyme* within the film, mirroring a larger theme. Historically, oppressive regimes often put restrictions on performances, and in Franco's Spain carnivals were banned by his government, as the core force of performance is the potential ability of disseminating and promote rebellion, as Odai argues (2000). The preponderance of the carnivalesque over the traditional is a danger to society, according to the traditional conservatism. In *La nueva Cenicienta* the carnivalesque predominates as a cultural practice in the theme, the characters, and the protagonist's various performances and the core of the movie. Contrary to Virginia Sánchez Rodríguez' argument that *La nueva Cenicienta* is a film focused mainly on the musical numbers and not on the character interpretation, I argue that the narrative through music creates and deconstructs Marisol's/Cinderella's identity formation through the film. At the same time, the film installs Marisol's performance of her various identities as a *pícara,* as a mother, as a doll based on Franco's ideological system for women and as an independent woman. Performance as identity is ingrained in the main character as a political discourse and as a countercultural stance.

Chapter 4

The Notion of Otherness Through Synecdoche and Prosopopeia in *Sólo un pie descalzo*

Ana María Matute (Barcelona, 1925–2014) is a contemporary Spanish author and part of a group of women writers that appeared in the forties and fifties in post–civil war Spain (1936–1939). Matute belongs to a generation of mainly writers of fiction, whose work represented Spanish society under Franco's regime. Along with Carmen Laforet, Carmen Martín Gaite, Josefina Aldecoa and other women artists, Matute wrote from and within this social and political devastating experience. The famous writer's novels have been translated into multiple languages and her work has been studied extensively in hundreds of academic articles, dissertations, books, etc. However, the Catalonian artist is best known for her novels and short stories written for an adult audience, since the author's work for children has not drawn the same attention as the rest of her extensive *oeuvre*. In 1985, Geraldine Nichols observed that the academic reception of Matute's work in this field, considered for many a "Cinderella discipline" (Bachilega 2), deserves greater critical attention (125).

Matute's novel *Sólo un pie descalzo* (1983) (*Only One Bare Foot*) studied in this chapter as a version of "Cinderella" won the Premio Nacional de Literatura Infantil y Juvenil (National Award for Children and Adolescent Literature) in 1984. In spite of this achievement of her literature written for children and adolescents, Matute's work for this audience remains in almost complete obscurity. My analysis of *Sólo un pie descalzo* and its representation of otherness is framed by two literary devices: prosopopeia and synecdoche.

As argued by Margaret Jones (*The Literary* 1970), Matute's motifs and characters in her novels and short stories are recurrent. In general, children in her novels are the voice of a society in a state of division and rupture due to the Spanish Civil War. Matute depicts child heroes and heroines who are often orphans and who are usually in conflict with their surroundings. The political turbulence of the post–civil war years in Spain is represented in her fiction as a fractured society in pain and divided by two opposed ideologies; on one hand, Francoism as the conservative winner of the civil war; on the other, the defeated republicans. Matute's protagonists suffer and echo this division and isolation as well. For instance, in "Caballito loco" (1976), *Paulina* (1976), as in her novels *Primera memoria* (1959), *Historias de la Artámila* (1961), *Fiesta al noroeste* (1952), among others, Matute represents this unique universe in narratives in which the relationship between the world of the adults and the world of the children is in constant tension and consequently children are usually left alone and frustrated. According to Janet Díaz, Noël Valis and Geraldine Nichols, in Matute's work there are certain consistencies regarding techniques, themes, characters, and motifs that make her work a mosaic with similar patterns. The protagonists in her fiction are generally children impacted by an unsettled world.

In *Sólo un pie descalzo*, the protagonist Gabriela is depicted as a distressed and abandoned girl, even though, unlike many of Matute's main protagonists she is not an orphan. Unlike the intertextual counterpart, Cinderella, in her many versions, Gabriela has a biological family: a father, a mother and siblings, differing from the typical story of the tale. Gabriela's family has a privileged status as a high-middle-class household: The family has in-house servants (Micaela, the cleaning maid; Tomasa, the cook; and Elisa, the handmaid), and two state properties, one in the city and another in the countryside. There are no economic constraints for this protagonist and she is not obliged to perform any housework or sit by the cinders. The reference to Cinderella is mainly highlighted by the emotional state of the protagonist as a consequence of her condition of otherness. A synecdochal image of a bare foot and the finding of a shoe by an occasional "prince" is also another leit motiv evoking the fairy tale web (Bacchilega 2013, 18) which encompasses the socioeconomic and geopolitical frames and the intertextual dialogs in which "Cinderella" and other texts examined in this chapter are enmeshed.

The most salient initial reference to the story is the family dynamic in the protagonist's household. Gabriela finds herself often marginalized by the members of her family, and her relationship with her parents is estranged and alienated: her mother is distant from her, as she finds Gabriela, "different" to the rest of her children; and her father is absent most of the time and she scarcely interacts with him. Her two sisters and cousin, Fifita, constantly set her aside because of her "awkwardness" as Gabriela seems to be quite often out of place. She is the absent-minded girl who loses one of her shoes repeatedly, which makes her the target of constant disdain. She is scolded by her mother and mocked by her siblings, because of her peculiar behavior, and she is thus considered "weird." "Esta niña, la pequeña, es muy rara" (Matute 53) [This girl, the little one, is very weird]. Even Tomasa, the cook, does not consider Gabriela fit for inclusion in the "ceremonia de la *croqueta*" (ceremony of the *croqueta*) as she gathers the other children to receive the delicious treat. Gabriela is not even acknowledged in the cook's daily, almost rite-like custom. Her father, nevertheless, does not set Gabriela apart like the others in the house, but he is hardly at home: "Papá era el único de la familia que no la apartaba, pero por desgracia lo veía poco" [Dad was the only one in the family who did not set her apart, but, unfortunately, she saw very little of him]. The physical and emotional absence of Gabriela's father is also reminiscent of the lack of the father's presence in the many versions of "Cinderella."

As already stated, the shoe, but particularly the repeatedly lost shoe, is a constant in Gabriela's behavior and a reference to the Cinderella story as well. Differently from the many Cinderella versions, in *Sólo un pie descalzo*, Gabriela loses her shoe repeatedly and constantly, and the lost shoe becomes a recurrent symbol throughout the novel. In many versions of the tale the shoe is made of crystal, gold, cloth, diamonds, among other materials, and is the symbol of encounter, engagement, realization or union. In Bettelheim's analysis, the shoe is a symbol of the female genitalia, as the foot is of the male; therefore, the trying on the shoe represents a sexual encounter between Cinderella and the prince. Shoes as a synecdoche have attracted mainly men to the point of fetishism and power. In the literary realm, for instance, in *Madame Bovary* Emma's husband Charles is infatuated by her shoes, as in Henry Miller's fiction shoes are an object of sexual desire. In Manet's *Olympia* her shoes, as a highly erotic object, are the only garment that covers her body; on the other hand, the feet of saints' statues are kissed all around the Catholic world as a gesture of adoration. Shoes are also linked to the filthiness of the world, and sacred sites prohibit entrance while wearing shoes. In many cultures, shoes and feet are given an important place in their traditions. The ancient Egyptian custom of writing the name of their enemies on their soles represents a profound scorn towards those enemies, represented by the dirty condition of the shoes. In *Sólo un pie descalzo,* the lost shoe is central to the story and expresses the esthetic climate of the novel as well as marking the beginning and end of the narrative.

The first time Gabriela loses her shoe is at the river, while swimming with her siblings, echoing one of the many oriental versions of the tale. In the Egyptian version of the story, Rodophis, an Egyptian-Greek courtesan, loses her shoe while bathing at the Nile river when a hawk snatches and drops it in the Egyptian prince's lap. This version was first registered by the Roman historian Strabo in the first century BCE (Anderson 27–29). The historical fact surrounding this story is that a Greek slave girl named Rhodophis married Pharaoh Amasis (Dynasty XXVI, 570–536 BCE). However, Fay Beauchamp argues that the origin of the "Yexian" story is Asian and that eurocentrism has attributed the story as Greek: "The Yexian story reflects Tang Dynasty Zhuang creativity, culture, and interaction with other Asian cultures" (3). Beauchamp argues that the contact might have been with other South or East Asian ethnic groups (Java, Vietnam, Tibet, India) as reflected also in the symbols of Hinduism and Buddhism apparent in the Yexian tale. Contact between two or more ethnic groups is a constant in both the Western and Asian hypothesis of Cinderella's origin. The story of a poor foreign beautiful girl marrying a prince seems to have inspired the many versions and adaptations of "Cinderella." The otherness of Cinderella makes her also, as Rhodophis or the Asian Yexian, from an ethnic group different to that of the prince she marries, and a foreigner, an outsider, and in the case of Gabriela, the other that is rejected from her own kin.

The idea of *otherness* is pivotal in the story of "Cinderella." *Otherness* has been defined and studied in sociological, cultural and literary analyses (Edward Said, Tzvetan Todorov, Judith Butler, Michael Foucault, Adrienne Rich, Pierre Bourdieu and most recently Zuleyka Zevallos). This notion determines how majority and minority identities are defined and constructed within the social realm. Sociologists have studied the concept of *otherness* seeking to set a critical view on the many forms in which identities are constructed. The above-mentioned critics and theorists agree that the representation of different groups in a particular society is depicted, in general, by the groups that have greater power. Gabriela becomes a target of judgment and rejection because she is the only one in the family who breaks the mold and who has a divergent personality. One of her most salient personality features is that she is creative. Gabriela is an avid reader, who is constantly abstracted from her surroundings and exercising her imagination.

Identities in the past were often assumed to be innate; however, since postmodern theories emerged in the nineties this view of the essential character of identity has been challenged as a theoretical argument. Pierre Bourdieu, for example, has questioned the learned and taken-for-granted aspect of cultural behavior (108) and argues that the meanings and values used to maintain boundaries between groups and individuals constitute what he calls "symbolic power" (164). Bourdieu demonstrates that these culturally constructed identities are not innate but learned and practiced. In other words, the choices that individuals make in trivial everyday actions unite them in a group. By extension, this group excludes another and creates the differences and/or similarities with a certain community. Elliot Weininger explains this concept: "Through the minutiae of everyday consumption each individual continuously classifies him- or herself and, simultaneously, all others as alike or different." (141)

According to these insights about culture, identities project how and through which terms individuals and groups internalize established categories within their societal group. Cultural (or ethnic), racial, gender, class identities, and so on are built in the cultural space that surrounds them. These many categories shape ideas about identity, about interrelationships, and about how we want to be or perceive we are seen by others. This perception also molds the idea of the societal groups to which we belong or think we belong. As Gabriela feels isolated, rejected and singled out for her "conflicting" behavior, she perceives herself as out of place within her own family and school environment, but her development as "the other" leads her to build a world where she is accepted and welcomed.

One afternoon while in the Cuarto de Estudio (Study Room), she finds a doll whose leg is missing: "A pesar de que no era la primera vez que curioseaba su interior, encontró algo que antes no había visto: un muñequito de madera, al que le faltaba una pierna" (Matute 54) [Even though it was not the first time that she had browsed in the room, this time she found something she had never seen before: a little wooden doll that was missing a leg]. This encounter helps her, as the doll appears as a mirror image of herself. Gabriela builds a home for the doll using a variety of objects; for instance, a cigarette pack serves to build a stove; and with matches she builds the furniture, dishes, buttons and other house items for the doll. The world for the handicapped doll is a space where it can live without feeling alone and abandoned anymore. In this fabricated world, the doll can thrive and be itself and relax in

4. The Notion of Otherness in Sólo un pie descalzo

the dwelling built for her. By shaping this world of freedom and comfort for the doll, Gabriela starts the process of liberating herself from the stigma of being "the other."

Even though the doll is inanimate at first, later it becomes human-like in *El País del Pie Descalzo*, and builds a strong connection with Gabriela. The reflection and perception of who Gabriela thinks she is, begins to be transformed by these ongoing social exchanges with the doll and the objects in *El País del Pie Descalzo*. Gabriela's contact with the world outside is hostile and her exchanges come mainly in the form of acute criticism, mockery and spite. The world becomes foreign to her as she does not understand the reason why she is the odd one: "También a ella le parecían raros *los demás*. Sobre todo cuando la rechazaban sin motivo [...]" (Matute 57) [Also for her *the others* seemed weird. Even more when they rejected her without a reason]. On the contrary, her relationship with the doll is rich, committed and caring. Gabriela finds herself accepted and embraces her new group with joy and hope.

The ideas of sameness or otherness are pivotal to the vision in which one achieves a sense of identity and social affiliation. As such, in the case of Gabriela, she cannot belong to any group unless "they" (other people, her family, siblings, teacher, classmates) accept her as part of it. The awareness of certain exclusivity or the belonging or not to a group is part of the formation of an identity. Gabriela does not fulfill the tacit criteria needed to be part of the group, whose standards are made by the collectivity she is supposed to belong to. In Gabriela's microcosm, the otherness goes beyond ethnicity or culture to include psychological states.

In *Mind, Self and Society* (1967), Herbert Mead shows how identities are produced through agreement, disagreement, and negotiation with other people. Individuals adjust their comportment and their persona based upon interactions and self-reflections which are products of reciprocal communication. By building a world for the doll, Gabriela starts to self-reflect upon the need to find a place and space for herself as well, as she has done for the doll. In the process of constructing a physical place for the handicapped and, for that reason, rejected doll, Gabriela becomes aware of her void, as she seems to be "handicapped" or not suited for the outside world as well, but she discovers that is also possible to fill her lack with a pleasant place build by her fantasy and with a companion.

One afternoon, after recovering from a long sickness, Gabriela sneaks into her father's personal library and finds a magical book. Hugging her new friend, she runs to her bedroom holding the book and not only reads but also hears the title: "El País del Pie Descalzo" [The Barefoot Country]. "Gabriela no sólo leyó, sino que oyó: 'El País del Pie Descalzo'" (Matute 66). This encounter opens a new world for Gabriela physically, symbolically and emotionally.

When Gabriela stares at the first pages of the book, she notices that a dense fog comes out from the pages and, within the haze, words are floating. Although the book is written in a foreign language, at least foreign to her, she finds colorful illustrations visible through the fog on the pages and a light coming through it with changing colors. Gabriela enters the *El País del Pie Descalzo* or a metaphor for a space for all the odd and weird, foreign ones that do not correspond to the "normalcy" of the world. The magical aspect of Gabriela's encounter resembles Alice's entrance into Wonderland and her experiences upon falling into the hole.

In the book, Gabriela finds the "Viejo roble" [the Old Oak Tree], which also opens up within the book recently found. The once unintelligible words become clearer as she hears: "'Has entrado en el *País del Pie Descalzo* ¡Bienvenida! Desde ahora nadie—salvo tú misma- podrá expulsarte de él'" (Matute 69) [You have entered the City of the Barefoot, Welcome! From now on nobody—except for yourself—could expel you from here]. This encounter resembles Ofelia in *Pan's Labyrinth* (2006), who enters a new universe through an oak tree to accomplish several tasks and save her baby brother.

Finally, Gabriela finds a place for her liberty and comfort, where her exchanges with her surroundings become pleasant and safe. As the public/external space, her family and school become more invisible and she immerses herself in this new realm of peace and joy. Gabriela finds a physical route to escape, through the book she "finds" in her father's library. The book and the Old Oak Tree make it possible for her to become aware and in contact with her emotional inner world. This situation enables Gabriela to traverse between her displacement as a family member (external world) and the voluntary placement of her in *El País del Pie Descalzo*.

In her newly created family in the Old Oak there are no humans, but only objects and animals that talk, love and care about and for her. Homolumbú, becomes alive and humanized, as it is the name of the one-legged doll, who introduces himself and guides Gabriela in the Country of the Barefoot. Through the oak tree and holding Homolumbú's hand, Gabriela enters this new imaginary place. The first place that she visits is La Región de las Alacenas (The Pantry Region) in the kitchen. Once, the girl accepts that the cook, Tomasa, is also part of those who reject her, she immediately finds a means to transform this lack. Tomasa's many cooking tools acquire voice and life, making Gabriela's private space a pleasant one. For Gabriela the main interaction with the world is now through the kitchen tools as she molds a new imaginary space for herself. Therefore, the inanimate objects which acquire human traits as a figure of speech highlight the narrative structure in *Solo un pie descalzo*.

Prosopopeia

Personification as a literary trope is a recurrent technical device in Matute's narratives. Berta Savariego explains that this lack of communication in the social world for the protagonist is compensated by interfusion with the landscape either natural or artificial (65). Used and forgotten kitchen utensils like a kettle, a milk jar, a pot, a sugar bowl (*azucarera*), spoons, forks and even food remains, as the half-croqueta, become alive before Gabriela's imaginative eyes, resembling the talking kettle and cup, Mrs. Potts and Chip, from the *Beauty and the Beast* (1991). Each one of them tells their story of abandonment and forgetfulness as they have been replaced for new and shiny ones. Discovering humanized objects that feel and have the same experience helps Gabriela deal with her own situation of otherness. This new society for Gabriela shares the same values and faces the same issues. The protagonist finds a group to which to belong, as common ground and similar approaches is what unites individuals and motivates their getting together. Therefore, collective ideas congeal and usually determine who gets to belong to one group or another. Groups/societies historically have had a set of principles/ideology and mind sets to determine which types of people are seen as different or become the outsiders from their own group. Gabriela finds a group to be part of, and although it is imaginary it is real for her as she delves into their stories and shares compassion and joy with them.

Prosopopeia as a literary device aids the protagonist to survive and engage with others. At the same time, this figure brings light to a broader meaning in the story. According to Rifaterre "prosopopeia finally becomes a figure of truth" (123). In fact, as a technical literary device, prosopopeia gives a mask to concealed emotions, ideas, feelings and at the same time offers, paradoxically, a visage to faceless entities. As a consequence, the poetic function of prosopopeia enables a voice to speak and bear the truth, as Rifaterre puts it. Gabriela's talking objects give materiality to her feeling of isolation and offer authority to her own state of otherness, felt exclusively by her as nobody is aware or conscious of it. The lack of relationship with her cohorts is made patent when inanimate objects become human-like and thus make her solitude explicit while creating her own world of fantasy as a survival tool. The asymmetry within Gabriela's world of solitude is balanced by her imaginary world in the *País del Pie Descalzo*.

Gabriela becomes the leader of the group as the only human in her Prosopopeian world. Prosopopeia is invested with the power to reveal ideas as an embodied presence within the human world in the narrative. Entering this space, Gabriela articulates and resolves the tension between being the other within her world and how she perceives herself. As Denver puts in in her study of the protagonist of Charles Dicken's *Bleak House*, "As she talks to her doll, she talks with herself, and by talking to the doll, she constitutes herself" (48). As Gabriela gives life to her inanimate friends, she develops authority as the creator of this world and as the main voice bestowing identity and power upon her. The rhetorical condition (prosopopeia) is equivalent to the condition of its main character, Gabriela, who becomes the rhetorical vehicle the novel employs to first unveil and later overcome Gabriela's otherness.

The title of the novel, *Sólo un pie descalzo*, contains another main literary trope; synecdoche. Gabriela thinks that losing a shoe is what triggers the rejection of her surroundings. She felt as "una 'niña aparte'" [a girl apart from the group], "'fastidio'" [an annoyance], "'insoportable'" [a burden]. Gabriela's fear of making more mistakes by, for example, repeatedly losing a shoe, forces her to be quiet and timid in order to appear invisible to the others. Despite her efforts, she acts clumsily and is immediately castigated by her relatives, peers and even her teacher, and labeled with such names or attributes such as "'distraída y desidiosa'" [distracted and indecisive] (Matute 12). Gabriela is clueless as to what is the reason for her exclusion and why her behavior annoys the rest of the world so much. The narrator gives a key reason for the separation of Gabriela from the rest of her siblings:

> Cuando Gabriela nació había, además de Rafael, dos niñas en la casa. Y quién sabe por qué, Mamá [...] esperaba que en lugar de una niña nacería un niño. [...] En aquel momento llegó hasta su corazón un feo insecto llamado Resentimiento, se posó en él y tardó mucho tiempo en abandonarlo [Matute 13].
>
> When Gabriela was born, besides Rafael, there were two girls in the house. Who knows why, Mother [...] expected to have a boy instead of a girl. [...] At that moment an ugly insect called Resentment reached her heart, she was with him for very long and it took a long time to get rid of it.

Gabriela thus becomes the undesired baby girl for her mother, and she is despised by her two sisters who tell her how ashamed they are for what

Gabriela is: "La mayor había encontrado su zapato y lo traía en la cartera. Se lo tiró a los pies y gritó con rabia: -¡Eres idiota y nos avergüenzas! ¡Procura que nadie se entere que eres nuestra hermana...!" [The oldest sister had found her shoe and she was bringing it in her suitcase. She threw it at Gabriela's feet and yelled in anger: "You are an idiot and you make us ashamed! Make sure nobody knows that you are our sister!"] (49). As Gabriela experiences, the notion of "otherness" puts emphasis on how the societal group (her sisters, for example) create a sense of adherence or rejection as it strengthens being part or not of a determined group. Gabriela displays the opposite characteristics of the cohesive family group, and therefore since birth she is positioned as the other in the family, the person who was expected that she is not. This sense of belonging or not belonging nourishes Gabriela's identity and status by constructing several categories as opposites in her family group. For this reason, she grows constantly apart from the collectivity to which she is supposed to belong.

Synecdoche

Synecdoche is a literary trope whose history, taxonomy and philosophical development have evolved from a quasi Cinderella-status to what, according to Brigitte Nerlich, is a trope "that speaks the truth" (299). Tzvetan Todorov adduced a similar folktale connection in "Synecdoques" (1970):

> Just as in the fairy tales or in *King Lear,* where the third daughter, long despised, is revealed as the most beautiful and intelligent, so Synecdoche, long neglected and even forgotten because of her elders Metaphor and Metonymy, seems to be nowadays the most central figure of speech [30].

The notion of the other also functions as a synecdoche, because, technically, the other is a part of a whole that exists by virtue of inclusion in this whole. *Otherness* is a fundamental category of human thought as it is through this concept that humans understand and elaborate their own position in the world. *Sólo un pie descalzo* is synecdochal in various levels, starting from the noun in the title: *pie* "foot." This common noun refers to the foot as part of the general human body, but an incomplete body because two feet are needed to have symmetry and balance. Further, it is not only singular but also a bare foot—unprotected, natural, without affectation or anything accessorial.

Gabriela not only loses a shoe on purpose to attract the attention of her parents, siblings and peers, but her shoe incarnates the motive of her abandonment and rejection. Gabriela's shoe is synecdochal as the object of Gabriela's semantization as Cinderella: "Cuando se sentía triste, empezó a tomar la costumbre de quitarse un zapato y esconderlo" (Matute 53) [When Gabriela felt sad, she started the habit of taking off a shoe and hiding it]. Seto affirms that synecdoche is characterized by an inclusion in the semantic sense as a "relationship between a more comprehensive category and a less comprehensive category" (4). Following this idea, Gabriela and her bare foot delineates through the synecdoche the idea of otherness and incompleteness but also reinstates Gabriela in the family realm as well as in the story of "Cinderella" to complete the otherness and place Gabriela back in her family and in the fictional narrative. The reference to shoes leads to the obscured, concealed or hidden according to Cristina Morozzi's introduction to *Cinderella's Revenge* (Mazza 1994) as shoes contain the semantic dichotomy of the sacred and the impure. For Gabriela, this ambiguity is also established in the narrative as the main motive of contempt/disappearance is centered on the shoe. At the same time, the shoe gives the protagonist an appearance and reinstatement in the family narrative at the end.

In fact, synecdoche according to another theorist of literary tropes, Seto, (1995) establishes the "cognitive triangle" consisting of metaphor, metonymy and synecdoche. He determines that the poetic function of metaphor and metonymy is established by a relationship of similarity and contiguity respectively. As for synecdoche, Seto finds that this trope or change "calls for inclusion" (311) or what is a semantic inclusion. Gabriela struggles to be part of the group through calling their attention to her by deliberately and repeatedly losing one of her shoes. The shoe is used as a catalyst and thread with which to connect with and be included in the social arena, even if it as a negative inclusion or attention. At the same time, losing a shoe is the initial cause and origin of her ostracism from the family. However, this action is twofold since it also determines Gabriela's inclusion in the primary narrative and the social narrative. At the end of the novel, a new character is introduced: Gabriel. A neighbor finds Gabriela's shoe by the river and helps Gabriela put it on: "Tomasa los miraba. ¡Dijo como hablando consigo misma"-! ¡Quién lo hubiera dicho! Como la Cenicienta y el Príncipe.... En fin, la historia se repite, los niños crecen... (249) [Tomasa looked at them. She said it was like talking to herself. Who would have said! Just like Cinderella and the prince.... Anyway, the story is retold, children grow up...]. That Gabriel shares his name with the protagonist is a form of a complement for her. By finding the shoe, Gabriel becomes the prince and Gabriela's companion; at the same time. Gabriela gets reinstated in the family narrative through the finding of the shoe.

Another significance of the lost shoe for Gabriela is that it represents the avoidance of barriers that constrict movement. She dissolves at least one of the symbolic obstacles which constitute her as the other, the strange, the one that everybody points a finger at. At the deliberate loss of one shoe transforms the synecdoche into a metaphor, as Samuele Mazza has observed: "They (shoes) are a perfect metaphor for the continual opposition between life and form that has obsessed great philosophers over the ages" (25). The inclusive nature of synecdoche instigates the yearning to find her peers, or, in other words, others like her. As Gabriela becomes the leader of the synecdochal world, her peers realize the positive side of being an outsider: "¡Dejad ya tantos lamentos inútiles! ¿No os dais cuenta de que esta noche tenemos la suerte de que haya venido Gabriela, a demostrarnos qué cosa tan buena puede ser (al contrario de lo que creen los necios) ir por el mundo con sólo un pie descalzo?" (85) [Leave off all this useless lamenting! Don't you realize that tonight we are lucky that Gabriela is here, to show us what a good thing it can be (despite what fools think) to go through the world with only one bare foot?]

Otherness turns into a positive trait and becomes a link to a community or group, that shares the same experience. Gabriela does not change to a point that she is like the group. She is still "the other" but it does not affect her, as she has embraced and understands the value of being different. Through the lost shoe that was the object and vehicle of condemnation and punishment, she finds a human friend, Gabriel. After all her tribulations and sufferings, she has entered a new facet in her life. She is still Gabriela and still loses a shoe, but now has a companion who accepts and receives her "otherness" as a positive aspect of her character.

Gabriela as the incarnation of Cinderella depicts the characteristic of otherness, which is intrinsic to the protagonist. This version unveils the topic of otherness not only as a theme in the well-known folktale, but also as a literary device operating the concept of otherness throughout the novel using prosopopeia and synecdoche as vehicles of meaning.

Chapter 5

Queer Cinderella: *Cenicienta en Chueca*

After Franco's death in 1975, Spain experienced a massive cultural explosion, with Madrid as the epicenter. Almost forty years of tight traditional invisible and visible social laws imposed by an oppressive regime had created sociocultural phenomena that erupted in many areas of artistic expressions. These years produced the well-known countercultural movement called La Movida. The film *El Calentito* (2005), for instance, develops the political and cultural moment very effectively through the story of a teenage girl coming of age in these transitional years. The film's protagonists are women in a punk music group, whose open sexualities and gender identities represent the spirit of the moment. *El Calentito* is set specifically during the famous February 23, 1981 *coup d'état*, when Francoist forces unsuccessfully attempt to overthrow the recent democratic government.

The sexual identity of the protagonist of *Cenicienta en Chueca* echoes this *madrileño* subversive movement that appeared in the eighties. The protagonist embodies two cultural and demographic spaces: her native Lima and her adopted city, Madrid. The novel seems to be set at the time when Peruvian society was attacked by terrorist groups that slaughtered entire rural communities. In the late eighties and early nineties, the leading terrorist groups Sendero Luminoso and Movimiento Túpac Amaru reached the capital, Lima, creating a time of unrest, hopelessness and fear. The protagonist flees this social turmoil in her native Peru and travels to Madrid in hope for a better future. Both spaces, Lima and Madrid, have experienced changes. In the South American country, the changes have caused chaos, disruption and instability; in Spain, the societal transformation has also produced these same phenomena, but in a postmodern fashion characterized by individuality and freedom.

In particular, La Movida disrupted many of the traditional and heteronormative conditions spread and reinforced by Franco's regime, particularly his ideology on gender roles. This countercultural initiative culminated in the approval of gay marriage in March 2005 in Spain. *Cenicienta en Chueca* coincidentally was published in 2003. In order to examine how women's non-traditional sexual identities have been made visible in and through literature after Francoism, this chapter analyzes a lesbian version of the Cinderella character, *Cenicienta en Chueca,* by María Felícitas Jaime. I explore the depiction of Queer Cinderella as the immigrant other, the sexualized non-normative other and the marginalized faceless other.

In general, the representation of lesbianism in Spanish literature has been extremely scarce. Jill Robbins mentions Esther Tusquets's *Siete miradas en un mismo paisaje* (1981), Ana María Moix's *Julia* (1970) and *Las virtudes peligrosas* (1998) and Beatriz Gimeno's *Su cuerpo era su gozo* (2005), among others, as representations of lesbianism in modern Spanish fiction. Robbins, though, observes that the portrayal of lesbianism in these narratives is not always explicit. Carmen Laforet's *Nada* (1942) is a novel in which the protagonist, Andrea, and her friend Ena are perceived by some critics as lesbians (Barry Jordan 96, Samuel Amago 66), and for other critics as androgynous (Fernández-Babineaux 335). Non-traditional gender identities in Spanish narrative are elusive and not explicit in most if not all cases. However, more recent texts, such as *Sexutopías* (2006), a short story collection by Sofía Ruíz, is one of the few works of fiction in Spain depicting female homosexuality. In the twenty-first century, representation of lesbianism has been almost limited to *Egales* and *Odisea*, which publish LGBT fiction and are centered in this genre. In other words, instead of being categorized within general literature, fiction with lesbian protagonists is the province of specific publishing companies. In fact, *Cenicienta en Chueca*'s publisher is Odisea.

Of forty-four versions of Cinderella in Spain identified for this book project, only one represents Cinderella as a lesbian. Not only is this population underrepresented in Spanish versions of the tale but the author of the lesbian Cinderella in *Cenicienta en Chueca* was not born in the Iberian Peninsula. Thus the only representation of "Cinderella" with an alternative gender identity comes from a foreign writer, just as the representation of women as non-heterosexuals in Spain is foreign. Felícitas Jaime, the author, lives in Madrid and calls it "her adoptive city," but her birth origin is Argentina.

Jill Robbins has examined the short stories in *Cenicienta en Chueca* through the various plateaus of relationships between Latin American and Spanish cultures. In "Cyberspace and the Cyberdildo: Dislocations in Cenicienta en Chueca" (2006) she analyzes the dependence and interdependence of domination and power in the sexual and social realm. Colonialism and Postcolonial theories are expressed as the foundation of the relationships among individuals from these two regions. Critical studies of LGBT culture in Spain have arisen only within the last two decades or so (for example, the work of Smith, Llamas, Pérez-Sánchez and Pertursa, among others). Retellings such as Emma Donoghue's *Kissing the Witch: Old Tales in New Skins* (1997) or the most recent one, Julie Law's *Cinderella* (2016)[1] are English versions which represent Cinderella´s sexual identity as non-normative. Books such as the *Sappho's Fables* series (2012) rewrite folktales portraying the female protagonists in homosexual relationships showing a modern and contemporary sexual identity prism, although the "Cinderella" tale itself is not included among these adaptations. *Ash* (2010) by Melinda Lo and a novel with the same title by Mel McIntyre (2018) use the same name for the protagonist but diverge in their take on Cinderella's sexual identity. In fact, the heroine in Lo's *Ash* is infatuated by the King's huntress, Kaisa, and becomes her lover. In McIntyre's novel, Ash is a heterosexual secretary working at a publishing company.

A very scarce body of work has appeared since the end of the twentieth century representing Cinderella as a lesbian. In contrast, the popularity of male Cinderella's in LGBT tradition has grown considerably since the nineties. The latest collection of studies on Cinderella, *Cinderella Across Cultures: New Directions and Interdisciplinary Perspectives* (2016), includes six articles in a section titled "Regendering Cinderella," all of which develop analyses of the gender inversion of Cinderella as a male. None of the eighteen chapters in the volume mentions a lesbian Cinderella adaptation. In his contribution Jack Zipes does notice the emblematic inverse gendered representation in Jerry Lewis's *Cinderfella* (1960), a figure he refers to as a "stupid misogynist" (379).

It is important to observe that the portrayal of women's queer sexual identities, homosexual desire, homoeroticism and/or queer subjectivity does not abound in Spanish-speaking fiction and is only recently emerging in its English counterpart. This lack is patent in Spain as versions of a gay Cinderella have not proliferated over the years, in spite of the many progressive political and social changes attained in the country. It is not a surprise, as this thematic void resonates with the 1971 Social Dangers Law which proposed methods and measures for the "rehabilitation" of homosexuals, both men and women. In *Confessions of the Letter Closet* (2005), Patrick Paul Garlinger argues that the story of queer desire in Spain is not a narrative in which sexuality was first repressed then liberated after the death of Franco, but that the works explored in his study demonstrate a persistence of the social homophobia and psychic ambivalences around sexuality and identity that were foundational in the emergence of homosexuality as a category (xv).

As narrow-minded, restrictive and dogmatic politics pervade the social realm, so fictional discourses of homoeroticism have proved elusive in the literary panorama. In Spain, with some exceptions such as the work in film by director Pedro Almodóvar, there are very few works bold enough to represent women's nontraditional sexual identities. Almodóvar's work is no doubt seminal for the representation of queer identities in Spain. Lesbians abound in his film universe. For instance, *Pepi, Lucy y Bom* (1980), with the famous singer Alaska as the protagonist, is the first movie to depict a lesbian. The popular "golden shower" scene scandalized Spain at its release. Other Almodóvar lesbian characters such as the nun in *Entre tinieblas* (1983), Suzanna "the untamed" in *Tacones lejanos* (1991), Juana in *Kika* (1993) are some of the characterizations of lesbians through his genial comic and tragicomic film narratives. On the topic of folktales, Almodóvar has rewritten the folk tale *Sleeping Beauty* in his film *Hable con ella (*2003), according to various critics, who see an intertextual reference to the famous popular tale (Adriana Novoa, Rebecca Naughten, Carla Marcantonio, Despina Kakoudaki and Fernández-Lamarque).

Many critics concur in affirming that representation of women's homoerotic desire in fiction has been pervasively concealed, erased or muted. According to Patrick Paul Garlinger, who offers examinations of contemporary Spanish writers such as Carmen Martín Gaite and Carmen Riera, women's homosexuality is hidden or non-existent in the work of these authors, thus replicating the social realm of Spain after Franco´s regime. A prestigious scholar in contemporary peninsular literature, Brad Epps, has also noticed the absence of lesbian sexuality and describes it using Carmen Riera's lesbian protagonist in "Te deix, amor, la mar com a penyora" [I leave you, my love, the sea as a token]: "It is along these lines that the letters of Riera's text point to what is at stake, both ethically and politically, in consigning the lesbian subject to a state of virtuality, where nothing can ever be" (317) in modern fiction that represents sexually queer (non-normative, homosexual) characters.

The title of the collection *Cenicienta en Chueca*, resonates with and evokes the queerness inherent to this famous neighborhood. Chueca in Madrid is the center of queerness in the Spanish capital. Even though Chueca expresses the image of openness and freedom, the population is predominantly male. Not only in the literary space but in the queer space par excellence, the Chueca neighborhood excludes female queerness, according to Robbins. It is thus reasonable to say that the female gay community has been confined within the spaces of freedom created for non-traditional identities in Spain. For this reason, *Cenicienta en Chueca* is a unique depiction not only of the representation of lesbianism but also of Cinderella's character as a concealed and camouflaged caste.

Cenicienta en Chueca is one of the short stories contained in the book by María Felícitas Jaime. The nameless protagonist is a Peruvian immigrant in Madrid. She has left her native Lima searching for better employment opportunities and a more suitable future for herself and her family. She has left her girlfriend, Susana, back in Peru, hoping to reunite with her later in Madrid. The story starts with the protagonist's analepsis about her first encounter with Susana, and her memories of their relationship in Lima. She recounts and describes how their relationship was concealed because of the pervasive social pressure which would not accept a homosexual relationship. She states:

> Ella y Susana hacían una vida normal, como se estila en aquellas tierras; vivían con sus padres, participaban de los almuerzos maratónicos que incluían abuelos, primos, tíos lejanos y un sinfín de parientes; trabajaban en la misma tienda como dependientas, iban a la universidad; luego solas, en un apartamento alquilado en las afueras de la capital, transgredían las normas y se descubrían mutuamente... [178].
>
> She and Susana had a normal life, as it is the standard in those places; they lived with their parents, they participated in the huge and extensive family gatherings; they work at the same department store as sellers, they went to the same university; and when they were alone, in a rented flat in the periphery of the capital, they would transgress the norms and mutually discover their bodies....

Both women in the story keep their sexual identity concealed from family, friends and co-workers or as Sedgwick puts it "in the closet." Eve Sedgwick explains in *The Epistemology of the Closet* (1985) that gay identities are forced to keep part of their individuality concealed in the metaphorical closeted space. Both of the lovers in the story are constantly under scrutiny about their lives and bombarded with questions about their private affairs. They are encircled by a society that is heterosexist and projects this as the norm. According to Sedgwick, "the closet" is in general a permanent presence for a gay individual. In the case of the unnamed protagonist and Susana, this closed space is their fundamental feature and it is epitomized by the apartment outside the city where they meet for their amorous encounters. Susana and the protagonist are hidden in the closet as they are forced to keep their sexual identity a secret. As they are not acquainted with the lesbian community in their native city, it is hard to even know, as they state, if there are any more lesbians in Lima. If there are more women who share their same identity, they see it is difficult to find out who and where they are, as it is customary to keep this part of life in secrecy. The protagonist's sexual initiation is with Susana, who becomes her lover and with whom she realizes and discovers her queer sexual identity.

Despite local and society restrictions and judgment, Susana and the protagonist engage in a passionate relationship. Because of the nature of their transgression, their relationship evolves intimately at a rented apartment. Not only are their sexual encounters performed exclusively in the outskirts of the city as a resource to be free, but the apartment also reflects the physical space (closet) hidden within the city as the closet is a closed space inside a house. The apartment is located in the periphery of the city, which places it tangentially on the limits of society and of Lima. The nameless protagonist echoes Lord Alfred Douglas' 1894 poem "Two Loves" in which the Irish poet possibly alludes to his relationship with Oscar Wilde: "l am the Love that dare not speak its name" (1894). On the same token, the protagonist does not bear a name and is not described physically ever in the story, and thus parallels the thought of Douglas' poem. The lesbian closed space is a quiet space represented as their lack of recognition as lesbians in the public arena and the covertness of their identity.

As the story unfolds, the first person narrator recounts her decision to emigrate to Spain without Susana: "Lima era un infierno, el Perú y toda Latinoamérica, un polvorín que empujaba al exilio" (182) [Lima was an inferno, Peru and all Latin America was a real war battle that pushed one to exile]. The protagonist finds herself forced to emigrate and with the aid of her professional training hopes to find a place in Madrid to work and live. Upon arriving in Madrid and without Susana, she is lost and lonely in this new environment, where she feels isolated: "¡Qué idiota se sentía! ¡Haber creído que todo era posible! ¡Haber pensado que Susana estaría con ella en unos meses! ¡España, la madre patria, sentía una cierta fobia contra los peruanos!" (182) [She felt like an idiot believing that everything was possible! She had thought that Susana would be with her in a few months! Spain, "the so called motherland" had a phobia against Peruvians!].

The protagonist is not only an outsider as an immigrant but also feels she is an outsider in the profession she practices in Madrid. Having paid for the accreditation of her Peruvian professional nurse title, she finds the contrary of what she had expected, that there was not a single possibility to work as a nurse in Spain. Finally, in Madrid she ends up accepting a job as an in-house maid for an older woman named Doña Carmen. The intertextual reference is clearer in this part of the novel, when the protagonist refers to herself as being enslaved by her boss. Doña Carmen's restrictive midnight curfew and her hard work for long hours are another reference to the hypotext, "Cinderella." The relationship between the new maid and Doña Carmen is hostile and vertical, while the *patrona* is demanding and often yells at her servant. The cultural gap between the two women is made patent and present frequently in racist remarks about Latin Americans. Doña Carmen asserts that Spanish gastronomy is the best and disdains, for this reason, the protagonist's cooking and cooking style from her country of origin. This dichotomy represents what the dominant culture usually perceives as natural or pure and unnatural or impure, which is prevalent in the vertical relationship between the two women. The natural is seen as the norm, or such as is perceived by Doña Carmen from her Spanish origin persona, and the unnatural and foreign, the Peruvian. As a foreigner in Madrid, the protagonist feels stripped from her identity in a third level. She is constantly interpellated by Doña Carmen and even by Charo, Doña Carmen's granddaughter, who frequently remarks upon her origin.

Discontented with her life, lonely and sad, the nameless and undescribed protagonist's only hope is to find more women who share her romantic interests: "Si en Lima no había lesbianas, en Madrid era imposible que no las hubiera: una ciudad cosmopolita, sin prejuicios, abierta a todo el mundo, tenía que tener mujeres que amaran a mujeres" (183) [If in Lima there were no lesbians, in Madrid it was impossible not to find them: Madrid is a cosmopolitan city, with no prejudices, open to everybody, it must have women who love women]. Finally, in one of her Thursdays off, the heroine discovers a place where she can find women who share her sexual interests. The Chueca neighborhood is where the nameless protagonist finds a collectivity where she can belong. Chueca is what "urban sociologists" call "a transitory occupation of low-rent districts by cultural and sexual dissidents, who recast the neighborhood in their image… " (Chisholm 196) and the bohemian district in Madrid. The protagonist feels relieved to share a space where communities like her gather. Chueca, she feels, is a place of freedom where she does not need to perform her phony heterosexual role and can unleash her inner identity in the public/closeted space of the gay bar.

In relation to the space-construction of binary identities, one in the public and the other in private, Judith Butler talks about the performative condition of gender. Society interpellates individuals and constricts their identities to one space, the heteronormative. The protagonist is interpellated on two levels. On one hand, she is a lesbian who is expected to be heterosexual and, in Madrid she is a maid and works as one, even though she is a professional nurse. The protagonist performs and acts two faces and identities that do not pertain to her personal or professional persona. Her sexual identity is not heterosexual and she has adopted a new professional role. Her life in Madrid disguises her professional identity, as she finds herself employed below her skill level as a house helper. As for her life in Lima, it demands that her sexual identity is masked in the social and familiar realm.

The protagonist's romantic life takes a sudden change when Doña Carmen's granddaughter comes to visit her from London. First, she resists the idea of having one more person to serve in the house. Later, when meeting Charo, she becomes attracted to a woman for the first time in Madrid. Doña Carmen's granddaughter visits the house every Thursday and the protagonist becomes more and more infatuated by her. The sexual desire grows as she looks for relief in the bars of Chueca. In one of her days off, she finds a "manly woman" with whom she leaves the club:

> Una mujer masculina, con gafas, leía el diario en la barra. Se sentó junto a ella y cuando la otra levantó la vista, la miró con todo el potencial de seducción dormido que llevaba dentro [...] y a las tres horas estaban en su cama follando... [185].
>
> A manly woman wearing glasses was reading the paper at the bar. She sat by her and when the woman raised her eyes, she stared at her with all the seductive potential that she carried inside [...] three hours later they were in her bed fucking....

Yearning for sexual contact, the protagonist sees the woman every Thursday religiously for her sexual encounters. In their intimate moments, she pictures Charo instead of the woman, displacing in this manner her sexual desire from the occasional lover to Charo and growing in carnal desire for her bosses' granddaughter. The crude sexual language describing their encounters reaches a point of pornography as it recounts in detail the couple's intimacy. In general, unless it is a pornographic version of "Cinderella," the sexuality of the folktale's main character is not described in such carnal details. The protagonist comes alive in the narrative through the vivid account of her sexual encounters. Through sexuality, the nameless protagonist acquires a voice and an image in the narrative. In both instances, with the description of sexual encounters with Susana, her first lover, and with the "manly woman" in the club, Cinderella suddenly materializes. Her socially uncategorized identity becomes visibly in control of the very eroticism described in detail, authorizing her and liberating her, at least in her sexual encounters. Butler asks, though, how "can sexuality even remain sexuality once it submits to a criterion of transparency and disclosure, or does it perhaps cease to be sexuality precisely when the semblance of full explicitness is achieved?" (1708). In other words, if sexuality becomes raw and on stage of any kind, becoming a pornographic object, it is turned into a public and exposed affair that limits its appropriation as an intimate act. As Butler explains, the explicitness creates a counter discourse and makes sexuality a stage matter and for that reason, a less valid one. In the sexual act that discloses the true and full contents of that "I" lesbian, according to Butler, "a certain radical concealment is thereby produced" (1709). Salmon and Symons in their study of slash fiction also argue that pornography or the portrayal of pornographic acts "falsifies" relationships (96) making them appear invalid. In all these levels, the lesbian subject is made artificial and camouflaged. The interpellation of the protagonist happens at a level, as it has been already mentioned, where she is never described to the reader physically or has a name. The mask that constant interpellation produces covers her narratological status as the main character at the level of the agency she is given as well as through sex, but is also taken away. This depiction concurs with Butler's description of the disappearance of the lesbian subject:

> The "you" to whom I come out now has access to a different region of opacity. [...] We are out of the closet but into what?? What new unbounded spatiality? The room, the den, the attic, the basement, the house, the bar, the university, some new enclosure whose door, like Kafka's door, produces the expectation of a fresh air and a light of illumination that never arrives? [1709]

In *Cenicienta en Chueca*, the protagonist is not disrupting the social order, though, because she hides in anonymity. Not only is her name never uttered by her lovers but the narrative entirely elides any mention of a first name assigned to her. Instead, she is only addressed by a demonym as "la peruanita," which highlights her origin. She is still in the closet, lives in it and gets out of it only in Chueca or in private. Chueca is the quintessential place of performance, and the only place where the protagonist can "appear" as a persona, but then, "disappear" in the explicitness of her sexual recount. The omission of a proper name for the protagonist is not the only factor that leads to concealment in the closeted space. The protagonist is never described by the third person narrator that intercalates the narrative with the first person narrator, and readers only tangentially find out some information about the character of this Cinderella. However, nothing precise is said about her personality other than her predilection for women instead of men. Her place as a lesbian is one of ambiguity, contradiction and struggle. As Butler puts it:

> If it is already true that lesbians and gay men have been traditionally designated as impossible identities, errors of classification, unnatural disasters within juridical-medical discourses, or what perhaps amounts to the same, the very paradigm of what calls to be classified, regulated, and controlled [1709].

The sexual innuendo is tied to mentioning the shoe motive in *Cenicienta en Chueca*. Thursday after Thursday in her meetings with her lover at the bar, she is commanded to leave before midnight. Doña Carmen's curfew establishes that her maid must be home no later than 12 o'clock. However, their explosive passion makes her and her lover forget the time. The protagonist mentions "the lost shoe" as a metaphor of her unleashed sexuality with the woman in the bar. She loses "the shoe" as she loses the tightness or encapsulation of this object and gets herself not only lost but loose in her passions:

> Exhausta, la peruanita miró la hora. Casi la una de la mañana. Se vistió de prisa ante la mirada suplicante de la mujer de la barra. -Quédate a dormir…. Hay muchas horas y muchos folles hasta que amanezca…! ¡Vamos, ven aquí! -Uf…, me encantaría, pero a estas horas ya perdí el zapatito y corro muchos riesgos… [188].
>
> Exhausted, *la peruanita* looked at her watch. Almost one in the morning. She dressed rapidly while the woman stared at her with a supplicant gesture…. -Come on, come here! -I would love to, but at this hour I already lost the shoe and I am taking too many risks….

The ball motive appears at the end of the novel as a colophon resembling the Cinderella dance with the prince. This time, the ball is at a gay discotheque. The protagonist finally obtains permission to have her day off on a Saturday instead of on Thursday. At the discotheque, she finds Charo, and fears immediately that Doña Carmen has sent her as a spy: "De golpe toda su timidez se le vino encima. La vieja la había mandado para espiarla, adiós al trabajo, adiós a enviar dinero el próximo mes, adiós a la homologación del título…" (190) [All of a sudden, her shyness has invaded her: the old lady has sent her, I will kiss goodbye to my job, to the possibility of sending money next month, to my nurse diploma certification…]. Later, she learns that Charo is at the gay bar because of her own sexual preferences. Charo is attracted to her and invites the protagonist to dance with her:

> -¿Yo…? Balbuceó, -Y yo… -¿Bailamos? -Y yo… -¿Bailamos o no? -No sé, creo que ya tengo que irme, La Señora…-¿Qué señora, nena? -Su abuela…-Estará durmiendo a estas horas…-Eso, la hora, tengo que irme… -Déjalo por favor, hace un par de meses que te tiro ideas y pensé que lo habías captado … en vez de dormir con mi abuela, podrías dormir en mi casa…" [190].

-Me...? She gasped -And me...? -Shall we dance? -And me...? -Shall we dance or not? -I do not know, I think I need to go, the madam... -What madam, darling? -Your grandmother... -She must be sleeping at these hours... -That is why, it is time to go... -Forget about it, it has been a couple of months that I am trying to get your attention and I thought you realized it ... instead of sleeping with my grandmother, you could sleep in my house....

The novel closes with a fairy tale-sque ending: the protagonist moves to an apartment closer to Charo's, she finds a job as a nurse and they live happily ever after. However, the interpellation prevails as the protagonist does not move in with her lover, but continues in the closeted space. The only difference is that the space has moved to the center and is no longer on the outskirts of the city. The inhabitants' physical proximity to each other implies that the two women's situations have changed. Nonetheless, lesbian identity is still hidden in the corners and only comes to life in sex and in the Chueca neighborhood for the protagonist. As Butler puts it:

> If I claim to be a lesbian, I "come out" only to produce a new and different "closet." Curiously, it is the figure of the closet that produces this expectation, and which guarantees its dissatisfaction. For being "out" always depends to some extent on being "in"; it gains its meaning only within that polarity [1709].

For Butler the fact that the subject is "out" by force will generate other closets to keep the person in this state of "outness." In this sense, outness solely produces a new social perimeter; and the closet seem to entail a vow or commitment of promise of an acknowledgment that can, by definition, never come. The expected visibility, exposure or assertion within the outness of the protagonist does not happen. On the contrary, the elision at the level of the protagonist's name and the protagonist's appearance is present in the narrative. She wanders the story without a proper name and a defined identity. At the cultural level, the lesbian Cinderella is also absent as the quintessential representation of a woman. In the literary representation this absence is also noticed and creates an insoluble contradiction of reasoning, an aporia. According to Butler, it is always finally unclear what is meant by invoking the lesbian-signifier, since its significance is always to some degree out of one's control, but also because its specificity can only be demarcated by exclusions that return to disrupt its claim to coherence. Pugh agrees that Queer and Lesbian identities constitute a disruption of cultural norms, which they deconstruct "as they relate to intersecting forms of desire and control" (217). Lesbian identity is similar to Queer identity because both are fluid, difficult to define in the outside world as it is in the case of the protagonist. "What, if anything can lesbians be said to share?" (1709) asks Butler. To answer Butler's rhetorical question, the protagonist of Cinderella in Chueca emotionally shares the anonymity, closure and invisibility of an individual that is condemned to live in the closet. Physically, she is also placed in the urban space of "freedom" per excellence, Chueca, which is also an enclosed space within the city. Geographically, she is displaced from her country of origin as well. The Cinderella in this version is a nameless woman, a lesbian, a foreigner, a maid; in other words, an outsider archetype having to conceal herself in society and lie hidden in the pages of a unique representation of the Cinderella character.

Chapter 6

Cinderella as a "Chick" Protagonist in *Cenicienta siempre quiso un Wonderbra*

In 1994 the Wonderbra, a brassiere designed to enhance a woman's bust by pushing it up with underwire material and padded cloth adding more volume to the natural breasts, was introduced in the U.S. market, where it gained immediate success. The garment had originated in Canada and made its way to Europe in the 1960s. Noé Martínez' novel, *Cinderella siempre quiso un Wonderbra* (2009) *(Cinderella Always Wanted a Wonderbra)* combines the elements of the popular underwear garment and the Cinderella character and motifs into a metaphor that discloses a number of issues related to women's bodies and women's sexuality in society. The Wonderbra epitomizes the figurative and physical prosthetics used by women to make an illusionary and fictive image of their bodies and themselves to fit the created beauty standard in society.

In this loose adaptation of the tale, there are three female protagonists, who are named Paulina, Olvido and Coro. Each at some point in the narrative incarnates a type of "Cinderella," or a plastic one, defined by their tastes, values and goals. The novel is catalogued as "chick literature" on the distributor's list of works. The precursor of the chick lit genre is considered to be Helen Fielding's successful novel *Bridget Jones' Diary* (1996) (Rowntree et al. 124: 2012), made into a blockbuster movie starring Renée Zellweger, Colin Firth and Hugh Grant in 2001. Chick lit is broadly seen as fiction written by women, for a female readership, and depicting protagonists who are middle-class professionals and whose story-lines revolve around friendship, romance and career. Chick lit mainly depicts white women in their quotidian lives and daily amorous and job crises (Whelehan [2002], Ferris and Young [2006] and Harmer [2005], all cited in Rowntree et al.). These protagonists challenge images of docile femininity, but at the close of their journeys have settled into heterosexual monogamous relationships. The stereotypical classification of the novel aligns perfectly with the culturally oversimplified and contradictory depiction of its female characters. Margaret Rowntree, Nicole Moulding and Lia Bryant (2012) argue that chick novels have originated an ongoing debate about the cultural representation of women and its depiction of empowerment and liberation through sexually graphic descriptions. They conclude that, as postfeminists premise, the chick lit genre also holds contradictory trends.[1]

In Spain, chick literature has become increasingly popular in the new millennium. Some of the Spanish writers in this genre are: Megan Maxwell with *Los príncipes azules también destiñen* (2012) [Prince Charming Also Fades], Miriam Lavilla Muñoz, *Aceptamos marido como animal de compañía* [We Accept Husbands as a Companion Animal], Regina Roman's *Del suelo al cielo* (2011) [From Floor to Sky], Rebeca Rus *Ginebra para dos*, (2013) [Gin for Two] and Emma Reveter, *Citas en Manhattan* (2008) [Dates in Manhattan]. This chapter will analyze the representation of Cinderella as the stereotypical woman or "chick" as embodied in the three Cinderella characters in Martínez' novel. The three women incarnate sometimes individually and sometimes collectively, the representation of different motifs and episodes in the traditional Cinderella story in some of its multiple versions.

Colette Dowling applies the "Cinderella Complex" to a woman's incapacity to socially survive without a man and the difficulties she finds in embracing independence. Downing's rethinking of the Cinderella folktale gives insight about how women's psychology has been permeated with the idea of dependency and a wish to be saved (1–4). She contends that women's avoidance of independence becomes more potent with age. All three main characters in *Cinderella Always Wanted a Wonderbra* are in their early thirties. They are single and/or are involved in unhappy sentimental relations. They constantly complain about their unfortunate relationships and the lack of a committed male companion. The constant commentary from the three protagonists about their misery makes it appear as they are incomplete despite their successful careers and economic independence. In many instances in the narrative, the protagonists express their sadness and anger at being single. The most visible factor that contributes to the lack of fulfillment in the lives of these women, as expressed in Dowling's argument, is their lack of emotional independence.

In *Cinderella Always Wanted a Wonderbra* there is not one but three Cinderellas. The narrative develops around the lives of the three friends, who live in Madrid. Olvido, Paulina and Coro are frustrated with their amorous relationships and roam the city looking for the right man. Their behavior resembles the famous sitcom *Sex and the City* (1998–2004), and the story unfolds centering on the topic of "looking for the right man." In a sitcom, the plot structure and the characters become familiar and predictable, and likewise all characters in *Cinderella Always Wanted a Wonderbra* are similarly flat. Equally, men and women show little or no subjectivity as their behavior is easily predictable and a reader can easily foresee their demeanors. The plot is unsurprisingly simple as well and without much substance or depth. This characteristic permeates the esthetic aspect of the narrative. The light literary weight of the characters depicts the aporia entangled within the textual threads and motifs of Cinderella as a metanarrative for the novel.

The story of Paulina, Coro and Olvido frames the narrative. Paulina (Cinderella 1) is a very successful attorney who works for Alejandro, her boss and lover. Alejo, as she calls him, is married and has maintained this parallel sentimental association with Paulina for almost two years. Paulina tries to end the relationship with Alejandro many times, but she fails in her attempt to battle her deep feelings for him. Alejo promises Paulina to divorce his wife but also fails to follow through and honor his word numerous times. Olvido (Cinderella 2) is a pharmacist and has recently divorced Francisco. She is also struggling to cope with her new life as a single woman. Moreover, since her ex-husband abandoned her for someone else, she feels worthless and angry at him. The ex-couple keep a pseudo amicable relationship, as they still communicate with each other. Francisco visits and calls her sporadically and they talk as friends. However, Olvido's inner self has not pardoned him and is still extremely depressed and hurt. Coro (Cinderella 3) works at a bank and is deeply enamored with Eugenio, an ophthalmologist's assistant. She meets him at the doctor's office and falls immediately in love. For Coro that was love at first sight, as she recalls the encounter: "Ella decía que se había enamorado de Eugenio a primera vista, y no había sido tarea fácil: acababan de dilatarle las pupilas para comprobar el estado de suma y sigue [*sic*] irreversible de su miopía" (25) [Coro said that she fell in love with Eugenio at first sight, even though it was not easy: her pupils had just been dilated at that moment to check the state of her irreversible myopia]. Eugenio, nevertheless, does not give her the attention and sense of security that Coro yearns for and demands.

All three women express their discontent with men but feel empty and incomplete without them. Each feels isolated, abandoned and incapable of finding her "prince." The representation of the body and sexuality as depicted in the novel creates a cultural dialog with the fairy tale genre and some of its motifs as they relate to the social vision of women.

Cinderella and the Body

The story is recounted by a third person heterodiegetic narrator. The focus of the narrative oscillates between the narrator and the dialogs between the characters. The narrator and the protagonists are described directly and indirectly through their language and, in the case of the characters, through their personality traits. The three Cinderellas are, as stated before, professional women; the language they use throughout the novel is somewhat ordinary, very lively, exhilarating, at times crude with an abundance of sexual references. The esthetic of the narrative echoes a very informal and private space, where readers seem to be observing a quite intimate side of the characters' personalities and the interactions among them. As Rowntree et al. suggest about the chick genre in general, "the reader feels as though she gets to know the protagonist well by gaining intimate insight into her mind in its various states of mental health" (124). In *Cenicienta siempre quiso un Wonderbra*, in fact, the reader seems to enter the women's inner circle in a relaxed environment, where the three women express their feelings openly and frankly and, at times, even very immaturely. Paulina, Olvido and Coro convey and recount to each other confidential feelings and events about their daily lives. There is no substance or reflection in their mindsets, so that at times they resemble a group of very young teenagers. Their ways of expressing astonishment, protestation, rage and sadness are very similar to one another, and reveal their standards of value.

The triviality and superficiality in the characters is constantly depicted through the multiple mentions of costly clothes brands, shoes, furniture and, among other things, expensive automobiles. This characteristic echoes Brett Easton Ellis' thriller novel, *American Psycho* (1991), in which the protagonist, Patrick Bateman, is a young and successful banker during the day but slips through Manhattan luring his victims during the night. Bateman's mentions of expensive restaurants, clothing and exclusive clubs in his conversations with fellow bankers resonates with his banal personality. Similarly, the three friends constantly refer to their expensive and luxurious tastes with descriptive images of their daily habits. As Bateman in *American Psycho*, all three women are extremely concerned about their appearance and offer numerous details of their massages, beauty salons, nail salons, constant shopping in expensive stores, make-up and body enhancement routines, and so on. The perception of their bodies and how they look and hold themselves is germane to the characters in both novels.

In filmic adaptations of fairy tales, the depiction of the body of the female protagonist is very distinctive and homogeneous. In the case of the Disney "Cinderella" versions of 1950 (film animation) and 2015 (live action starring Lily James), separated by sixty-five years, the heroine is depicted with the same slim figure. In the written versions, however, there are no specific descriptions of their bodies. The most popular representation of fairy tale heroines is Walt Disney's movies and filmic adaptations of this genre. Disney's conception of the bodies of princesses has in general led to portrayals of them as curvaceous but slim. Rapunzel, Cinderella, Sleeping Beauty, Bella, Snow White, Ariel (above the waist) to give just some examples, are represented as slim young women. Even though, the issue of race has been addressed in Disney by showing more racially variegated heroines like Jasmine, Tiana, Mulan and, most recently, Moana as a beautiful Polynesian girl, in the case of body depiction or dimensions there is still a pervasive characterization of the bodies of princesses as both slender and curvaceous.

Olvido and her obsession with her body is an example of the adherence to this cultural representation of women's body in fairy tales, and the struggle to fit this model. The narration of the preparations for her wedding begins by tweaking the familiar fairy tale classic opening: "Érase que se era... (40)" [Once upon a time or, in this case, there was one time]. This phrase marks the description of Olvido's hydro massage treatment. She tells her girlfriends of the need for "el culo perfecto" (the perfect ass) in her effort to have a more desirable body for her wedding with Francisco. The soon-to-be-married woman undergoes a special procedure that leaves her bruised and in pain in order to fit into her tiny wedding dress and display a "culo redondo y firme de JLo" [the round and firm ass of JLo (Jennifer Lopez)] (41). In this aspect Olvido is more similar to the characters of the stepsisters in "Aschenputtel" (1812), the Grimms' version, who mutilate their feet in the hope of obtaining the prince's favor. Olvido cries in distress when she realizes that her arms are so tight inside the dress that she cannot lift or move them. In an attempt to raise her friend's spirits, Paulina again recalls the Grimms' version (and modern jokes) and says in a humorous tone: "¿Quién necesita levantar los dos brazos al mismo tiempo el día de su boda? [...] ¿Y Blanca Nieves, necesitó ella las dos manos para empiltrarse con los siete enanitos?" (58) [Who needs both arms at the same time the day of her wedding? (...) and "Snow White," did she need her two hands to have sex with the seven dwarfs?]. In "Cinderella" the women's bodies have a distinctive role. These bodies are represented as moldable and/or as an obstacle to the attainment of a goal: the prince charming. Thus in "Aschenputtel," the stepmother demands that her daughters mutilate their feet to fit into Cinderella's shoe: "Then her mother gave her a knife and said, 'Cut off your toe. When you are queen you will no longer have to go on foot.'" (Grimm 4). Therefore, Paulina's joke with Olvido about not needing mobility after finding a prince, rich husband or good sexual companion is grounded on the objectification of women.

After her body surgery, Paulina and Coro help Olvido fit into the wedding dress: "A seis manos, se consiguió embutir (literalmente) el torso de la novia en un elaborado sujetador de cuerpo entero, profuso de blondas, finos encajes y lazos tornasolados" (54) [Six hands could squeeze (literally) the bride's torso in a body shaper and cincher corset with laces, fine lingerie and colorful bows]. Olvido's goal is to attain the perfect derriere to be liked by her husband and to obtain her desirable objective; she, like the stepsisters of Aschenputtel, is ready to maltreat her physique in order to obtain the precious prize. Olvido imagines that Francisco will be thrilled with his bride's appearance: "Ese culito, cariño mío, me recuerda al de alguien, pero ahora no caigo. Deja que piense..." (41) [That little ass, my darling, reminds me of the one of someone else, but I do not recall now. Let me think..."]. As the characters in Cinderella's most famous versions, the women are preparing their bodies to be accepted.

Despite all the sacrifices made to reach the goal of an ideal body, something goes awry with the treatment. Olvido's body transformation is extremely painful and leaves her skin extremely damaged. Despite her poor condition as a result of the treatment and her friend's comments on how brutally bruised her body looks, Olvido persists in undergoing the procedure again and again to reach that dream body. In the end, however, Olvido's marriage with Francisco, her prince charming, has a very short life. After one year, Francisco leaves her for another woman. Olvido is even more hurt when she learns from her ex-husband that he will soon become a father.

It is shown in *Cinderella Always Wanted a Wonderbra* that bodies are central and paramount to the protagonists' lives. The excessive focus on their bodies seems to limit their capacity for enjoyment. The "ideal body," the protagonists believe, will make them happy and fulfilled. Coro also has a problematic relationship with her body image. She tries to minimize and confront Eugenio's indifference by eating sweets and carbs in her anger and pain. She chastises and stresses her body as well by eating unhealthy foods only later to regret doing so. This behavior is connected by Clarissa Pinkola Estés with the restrictions society places upon women through fairy tales and myths, and she explains how the dynamic body-women can be restrictive or focused on one "model" or one way of behavior: "Women are sometimes discussed as though only a certain temperament, only a certain restrained appetite, is acceptable" (217). In *Women Who Run with the Wolves* (1992), she explains how women's physicality is framed in one single model. The idea of a beautiful body is constrained by a specific paradigm propagated by media, films, and popular culture that praise a certain desired shape for women. Most fairy tale heroines depicted by Disney are svelte, one of the elements satirized in Dreamworks *Shrek*, which depicts an anti-prince and anti-princess (as Jaime J. Weinman observes, "The *Shrek* movies are basically grotesque comic parodies of fairy tales, and therefore of traditional animated movies in general") or shows a subversive image of women as Mínguez López affirms (257). This satiric position resonates with Estés argument that moral goodness or badness is attributed to women according to whether a woman's size, height, gait, and shape conform to a singular or exclusionary idea (127).

In *Cinderella Always Wanted a Wonderbra* this ideal representation of women in fairy tales resonates in the character of Olvido. Her body beautician, Soraya, appears often in the narrative as Olvido goes back and forth from her office to undertake several body treatments to get rid of fat excess. Olvido's obsession with the "perfect body" seems to rule her behavior as she expects to look more desirable and similar to the bodies displayed in popular culture artists and in her alter-ego Cinderella.

Olvido deals with an unfaithful ex-husband whom she does not seem to be able to forget. It enrages her to learn that he is happy and stable with his new love and seems to have completely forgotten her. Olvido's name echoes the feeling that she experiences, as Olvido means "forgotten," or in her case, the one forgotten by her ex-husband, Francisco. Olvido yearns to attain a body of flawless appearance, and many times asserts her professional achievement or having a "trabajo perfecto" [perfect job], but laments the lack of the ideal figure as a paramount aspect in her life fulfillment. As with her friend, Paulina, Olvido's body is an adaptable mold that can be modified through minor or major surgeries or food ingestion. Olvido is the quintessential woman who is tied to societal restrictions and the cultural expectations regarding appearance. Olvido's idiosyncrasy reveals her conformity to the Cinderella Complex defined by Dowling and her submission to the archetype of woman in search of a man. As Pinkola Estés puts it: "When women are relegated to moods, mannerisms, and contours that conform to a single ideal of beauty and behavior, they are captured in both body and soul, and are no longer free" (213).

Not only are their bodies the vehicle to attain their goal—the prince— but also the locus of projection of their ideal image either symbolically or physically. Every time Olvido feels unhappy or lonely because of Francisco's abandonment, she compensates for the void or lack of happiness by shopping uncontrollably:

> Olvido iba de compras muy a menudo y regresaba invariablemente de sus excursiones con un alijo inverosímil de prendas que, una de tres, o no eran de su talla [ni lo serían nunca] o eran tan atrevidas que sólo se las pondría en casa [99].
>
> Olvido went shopping very often and returned home from her mall excursions with an incredible amount of clothes that, one out of three, did not fit her (and never will) or they were so provocative that she will only wear them at home.

Shopping for clothes that would fit her ideal body is pointless and only creates frustration and despair for Olvido.

Coro, the third woman in the group of Cinderellas, works at a bank and also proclaims that she has "the perfect job." She is successful professionally but, as perceived by her peers, her economic independence is not sufficient to make her feel "happy." Coro has a relationship that she calls "no-relación" [no-relationship] with Eugenio. Coro complains that Eugenio does not give her any attention and hardly sees her or talks to her. Nevertheless, she is still infatuated with him. Coro complains about her multiple failed relationships with men and is also worried about her body shape and weight. She demonstrates a problematic relationship with her body image as she insults herself by saying: "va a ser que esta báscula está escoñada. ¿Quién coño pesa sesenta quilos [sic], cerda-asquerosa-desagradecida?" (37) [it might turn out that this scale is fucked-up. Who the hell weighs 130 pounds, filthy unthankful pig?]. Coro's self-belittling concurs with the observation by Rowntree et al. that in chick lit soliloquies are common as the protagonists use humor to deprecate themselves (124). Coro relates her privileged economic status to the ability to maintain a slimmer figure and insults herself in frustration for not accomplishing that desired goal.

Paulina is also obsessed with shopping as she constantly comments that a (Visa) credit card is what every woman needs: "Lo que Cenicienta quería era un Wonderbra y una Visa!!!!" [What Cinderella wanted the most was a Wonderbra and a credit card!!!] (150). Showing financial solvency is also another vehicle to enhance their diminished image in their attempts to project a bigger and stronger image that does not seem to exist.

Cinderella and the Ball

Paulina, Coro and Olvido decide to forget temporarily their supposedly miserable life without the "perfect body" and a "perfect man" and attend a costume party. Olvido convinces her two friends to put their costumes on and go to the party. The three women attend the ball dressed-up as what they call "Faith, Hope and Charity" [Fe, Esperanza y Caridad], the three Theological Virtues. However, in the novel, the three friends' outfits resemble more the three Greek or Latin Graces because of the emphasis on their bodies. In most depictions, The Graces are represented nude or wear transparent or satin-like tunics that show the shape of their curves, nipples and genitals. Olvido gives a very descriptive image of her friends and judges their appearance: "tetas prácticamente al aire, minifaldas CA (Chichi al Aire) y zapatos de supertaconazo, debían de ser sus amigas, aunque, a simple vista, Olvido no tenía ante sí más que un par de putones..." (90) [tits almost fully exposed, miniskirts showing the coochie, and super high heels, these girls must be her friends, even though at one glance they seemed to Olvido more like a couple of hookers].

Unlike the Cinderella story, these princesses are dressed in a very provocative way. The three virtues Hope, Charity and Faith, supposedly the bastion of Catholic values, are mocked as the women in the novel subvert the spirituality contained in them with a sensual and carnal image of women, or as Greek goddesses. The costume party epitomizes the carnival and the outfits incarnate transgression itself. As stated by Weldt-Basson, dressing up reveals a form of social justice as it equates all individuals in the same terrain (Masquerade 11). In the case of Paulina, Olvido and Coro, they are masked as "virtues" mocking the values that they represent, emblematic of the archetypical Cinderella character, and finally placing purity and sensuality in the same plane.

In Catholic tradition, the three theological virtues (Faith, Hope and Charity) are gifts of God through grace, instilled in human will and intelligence, and are habits that are strengthened through practice. Because of the women's appearance, they seem rather to personify the three graces, in that their sensual outfits revealing their bare bodies are paradigmatic of the archetypical women as they appear in representations of Greek and

Latin mythology. These three theological virtues get ready for the party (or the Ball) by wearing excessive make-up, tiny short skirts and high heels. The Three Graces incarnate a more diverse representation, identified with chastity, beauty and love. In various art depictions from the Renaissance to the eighteen century (Raphael, Vincenzo Livi, Rubens, Canova), the Three Graces are portrayed as youthful women embracing each other, holding fruit in their hands or wearing it on their heads (Raphael, Lucas Cranach) or sensually touching each other's' bodies or breasts (Vincenzo Livi, Lucas Cranach, Raphael). Paulina selected costumes that would create a parallelism between the personalities of the three friends and the goddess/virtues they actually seem to represent. As E.M. Berens relates: "They [the Graces] not only possessed the most perfect beauty themselves, but also conferred this gift upon others…. And whenever joy or pleasure, grace and gaiety reigned, there they were supposed to be present" (146).

In the novel, the Graces are assumed to represent three stages of women: the virgin, the wife and the lover. Thalia, Euphrosyne and Aglaia, the three Graces, are the personification of "flowering, joy and radiance" respectively and they are usually "depicted in joyous dances celebrating the bounties of nature" (Daly 61:1992). Plato also names the Graces as "viridity, gladnesse and splendor" as Thalia is "viridity" (youth, freshness, innocence) Euphrosyne, "gladnesse" (rapture, pleasure) and Aglaia, "splendour" (dignity, glory) (Pico della Mirandolla 35: 1914). Therefore, Thalia, the virgin is Coro waiting for Eugenio, Aglaia, the (ex-)wife is Olvido, and Paulina, Euphrosyne, is the lover. This blend between the personages of the Greek pantheon related to fertility, conception, pleasure and eroticism, and the virtues in the Catholic tradition in the images of women are paradoxical. As the novel portrays the collusion between godly/pure (typical Cinderella) and its profane representations of women, it also parallels the common characterization and construction of women in society as either saints or whores.[2]

Fairy tales are the paradigm of a culture's representation and in them women are depicted as evil witches or as innocent, even saintly, maidens. In most versions of "Cinderella" around the world, there is always an evil stepmother and/or stepsister(s) that conspire against the poor beautiful girl. Because they are symbolic representations of society, the antithesis between the sweet, innocent and kind protagonist and her evil counterparts appears in most versions of the tale, through the Muslim, Russian, Hebrew, Chinese, African adaptations to the Western retellings (France, Germany, Italy, Poland, Spain). For Nicolaisen, for instance, the "innocent, persecuted heroine" tale-type informs its audience about the disruption and subsequent reinstallation of social order and the need to maintain the cultural norm.³

At the party, Olvido finds Marco her high school literature teacher. She remembers her old infatuation for Marco and tries to seduce him at the party, but he leaves the ball/party before midnight, thus reenacting the Cinderella story with reversed gender roles. Olvido expresses it:

> ¿En serio os vais a [sic] ahora? -Olvido no podía creerse lo que estaba oyendo. ¿A qué venía esa huida en plena vorágine? ¿Era él, acaso, la versión masculina de Cenicienta? [123].
>
> Are you serious, are you really leaving? -Olvido could not believe what she just heard. Why would he want to flee at that precise convoluted moment? Was he the masculine version of Cinderella?

As Cinderella, Marco also leaves a trace. It is not a shoe as it is in most versions of the tale, but a piece of napkin with his phone number written on it for Olvido. Unfortunately, inadvertently, her friend Paulina uses it to wipe some blood on Olvido's nose and Olvido thus loses Marco's trace and thinks it would be almost impossible to find him again. In this episode, Olvido/Faith is the incarnation of Cinderella more vividly than her other two friends.

Cinderella and Sexuality

In her study of Cinderella and its representations, Susan Lochrie Graham argues that the Cinderella character is related to beauty, joy, and life and her power comes from inner goodness and innocence (83). Specifically, Adessa Towbin et al detail four themes found in Walt Disney adaptations of fairy tales: "(a) A woman's appearance is valued more than her intellect; (b) Women are helpless and in need of protection; (c) Women are domestic and likely to marry; (d) Overweight women are ugly, unpleasant, and unmarried" (30). A woman's physical appearance is a value which determines how she is represented as an individual in fairy tales. In Cinderella, in particular, purity, chastity and innocence are paramount and inherent to her character, whereas her sexuality and/or her sexual activity or arousal is not a theme in most of the traditional adaptations of the tale.

In *Cinderella Always Wanted a Wonderbra*, sexual innuendos and sexual references are one of the characteristics of the main characters' discourse. This version contradicts and transgresses the typical portrayal of Cinderella as an innocent and asexual young woman. Cinderella has been identified as the object of desire for the prince but hardly ever has she herself been depicted as sexually active and nor have her sexual needs been expressed either overtly or implicitly. A sexual Cinderella has been rare and uncommon in versions of the story. In *Cinderella Test: Would You Really Want the Shoe to Fit?* (2009) Vera Sonja Maas affirms that, "We can be sure that the fairy-tale Cinderella was a virgin until the prince found her" (86). In fact, in the many versions of the tale in Spain, Cinderella's sexuality is not an aspect mentioned or depicted, except for the underground comic and porno version by Nazario listed in Chapter 11 and the twenty-first century versions analysed in chapters 5, 8 and 9. It is implied that Cinderella will initiate her sexual life after her marriage with the prince.

The traditional "good female character" of Cinderella is replaced by its diametrical opposite in the novel, where the three women are open to sexual encounters and are not shy to express their libido. At the costume party, Olvido flirts with Marco, her prince and former high school teacher: "¿Te imaginas qué pasaría si te tomara en serio y te confesase mis fantasías quinceañeras y la de veces que soñé con perder mi virginidad contigo, profesor?" (118) [What would happen if I were to take you seriously and confess to you my teenage fantasies and the so many times that I dreamed about losing my virginity with you, teacher?]. Olvido is candid, flirtatious and voices her sexual needs, a social taboo in general for women and a complete reversal of the representation of a heroine such as Cinderella in the folk tale. Paulina also expresses her sexual physical excitement in her encounter with Lorenzo at the party:

> Paulina sintió que algo se licuaba en su entrepierna. No tenía ni idea de cuál era la temperatura de combustión del algodón finamente tejido de su ropa interior, pero su pubis la había alcanzado sin necesidad de brasero [105].
>
> Paulina felt that something was wet in her crotch. She had no idea what was the combustion temperature of her fine cotton underwear, but her pubis had already reached it without the need of a brazier.

It is made evident that these Cinderellas feel the need to be protected and cared for. Even though the pursuit of pleasure is a sign of liberation, it is not sufficient to free them as individuals/women. Paulina's words denote the yearning for that external salvation and it is suggested that it will not come from within themselves and/or from the self-development of a sense of well-being as an individual but from an external and magical force called "the prince." When Paulina, Olvido and Coro feel rejected by men and not recognized as the "chosen one" (Cinderella), they are displaced as the objects of desire and lose the means for salvation and sexual satisfaction. The three Theological Virtues that they represent are charged with the metonymic value of Cinderella's virtues as a feminine object, which they subconsciously struggle to portray but without success.

The Fairy Godmother

The narrative function of magical helper performed by the fairy godmother in Perrault's (and subsequently Disney's) "Cinderella" has appeared in many shapes throughout cultures and places. Where the magical helper is a fairy it is humanized, animalized, hybridized; there are dancing and singing fairies, invisible, flying ones and many other forms. In the Chinese version of the tale, *Ye Shian*, the helper is incarnated in a fish, very emblematic of Chinese culture. In "Aschenputtel," the helper is a white dove representing the holy spirit. In the German version, the doves are the magical entities that help Aschenputtel and also are those who punish the stepsisters by plucking their eyes out. In the Egyptian version an eagle helper acts as the mediator that aids Rhodophis to be found by the pharaoh.

In *Cinderella Always Wanted a Wonderbra,* the fairy godmother as a main motif in the Cinderella adaptations, seem to appear for only two of the characters; Paulina and Olvido. After breaking up with Alejo, her married boss, Paulina initiates the search for a boyfriend. After various attempts, she decides to search the internet chats. The first night Paulina enters a group chat, she meets "Rhett" with whom she converses through this popular medium. Paulina uses the pseudonym "Cibeles," the Phrygian Goddess of nature and fertility, whose worship is related to euphoria, pleasure and raptured states. In the case of Paulina, the aid, vehicle or medium through which her finds her prince charming is a modern device: the internet. After a number of meetings on the chat and multiple conversations about their personal lives, they both discovered that they have been abandoned by their respective romantic ex-companions. Rhett and Cibeles finally meet in person at "Il Bocaccio" bar.[4] Paulina wonders before the encounter how such a wonderful prince can be real and speculates about his appearance: "Que tal si el tal Rhett resultaba ser un Cuasimodo, un elefante con dos cabezas o una niña de quince años que se hace pasar por el hombre ideal..." (220) [What if Rhett is a Cuasimodo, or an elephant with two heads or a fifteen-year-old girl who pretends to be the ideal man...]. Again, the focus of Paulina's concerns is on superficial values and cultural standards of beauty.

Soraya is the fairy Godmother for Olvido, who transforms her into the perfect bride. Instead of giving her a makeover, centered on a beautiful dress, and help to get her to the ball and find the prince, Olvido's transformation comes from Soraya's body sculpting techniques to give her a new body and a new appearance. The transformation is not superficial as in the "Cinderella" story and does not imply only a temporary change as wrought by luxurious clothing, but a permanent change in her body.

In the case of Paulina, it is through the vehicle of the internet that she finds her "prince," whose real name is Sergio. On the second date, Sergio visits Paulina's apartment and it all end with a Disney fairy tale resolution. They find each other perfect and it is assumed they start a relationship. Coro also finds her prince but without the help of a fairy or other medium. Only her patience and tenacity to wait for and pursue Eugenio is the vehicle to obtain his love. At the end of the novel, Eugenio appears unexpectedly at Coro's door and declares his love: "-Que te quiero, Coro..." (260). (That I love you, Coro). Coro's first response shows her personality: "-Cabrón... -Beso. 'Gilipollas...' -Beso *again*. 'Lárgate de mi vida de una puta vez... -Otro beso'" (259) (Jerk ... kiss ... Asshole ... kiss again. Get out of my fucking life already ... another kiss).

This modern adaptation of Cinderella has a fairy tale ending for all three women. Rhett/Sergio, the man whom Paulina meets on a chat discloses his identity. Paulina/Cibeles does likewise and they both fall immediately in love with each other. At Paulina's apartment, she listens to a voice message from her ex-lover Alejandro while Sergio is there. Alejandro's messages show regret and desire to recover her. The story ends as Sergio is about to leave the apartment to allow Paulina to reflect on her emotions, but instead she deletes Alejandro's voice mail, symbolically erasing at the same time the old relationship with him, while embracing her new one with Sergio. It is insinuated that they will spend the night at her apartment and start their own love story. As for Olvido, Marco finds her and shows up at her door:

> Puerta abierta de par en par. Un Marco con barba incipiente y una sonrisa de esas que lo habían coronado como el profeta más sexy allá por la adolescente época del instituto, se abalanzó sobre Olvido... [241].
>
> Door wide open. Marco slightly unshaven and with a smile that had crowned him as the sexiest prophet in the high school era, threw himself upon Olvido....

All three Cinderellas end their misery finding a new love and embracing a new beginning for their amorous lives. In the case of Paulina, Rhett/Sergio is somebody in the same situation, which creates solidarity between them. Her prince has also been rejected and has had a broken heart like her. For Olvido and Coro, their princes are men they already knew. Olvido reencounters Marco and an old passion is revitalized. Coro, thanks to her patience, recovers Eugenio who finally demonstrates his love for her.

Conclusion

The Wonderbra is an undergarment designed not to be functional but to enhance the wearer's appearance by creating an illusion of firm, voluptuous breasts. The goal of the garment is to push the breasts up and together, while a plunge at the front center of the bra exposes and emphasizes the elevated cleavage so produced. An absence of volume is thus compensated for by external elements (underwire, padding) built into the bra that display the breasts as something they are not.

The emphasis that the protagonists place upon the body is epitomized by the specially designed garment, the Wonderbra, and manifests the importance of physical appearance. This is made clear when Paulina tells her newly encountered chat prince "Rhett" that Cinderella probably only wanted a Wonderbra and a credit card:

> Cibeles: <lo que en realidad quería ella no era un príncipe y un castillo. Cibeles: <lo que quería era un buen escote. Cibeles: <lo que Cenicienta quería era un Wonderbra y una Visa!!!" [151]
>
> Cibeles: <what she (Cinderella) really wanted was not a prince or a castle. Cibeles: <what she wanted was a good cleavage. Cibeles: <what Cinderella wanted was a Wonderbra and a Visa.

The idea that Cinderella wants to be sexy, provocative and capable of spending money is the ideal for a woman, according to Paulina. The intimate desire of the successful lawyer is uncovered. In other words, physical appearance and economic capacity are the most relevant characteristics and personal values of these chick Cinderellas. As a metaphor, the Wonderbra entails a deeper meaning to the story as it is the symbol for the prosthetic and plastic depiction of Cinderella as a chick. The underwear garment serves to project a bigger and stronger image creating the volume and density that does not seem to exist.

As represented in the novel, the women's almost obsessive mentioning of expensive clothes brands and body enhancement treatments aids to appease their fragile self-esteem and diminish their constant self-conscious state. The Wonderbra as a substitution for a supposed lack serves to enhance their inner world and not reveal what is missing. The recurrent references to their big and successful jobs appear also as a mask to hide

6. *Cinderella in* Cenicienta siempre quiso un Wonderbra

their bigger concerns: an unsuccessful love life and a brittle ego. Their costume for the ball as the three Theological Virtues disguises the true inspiration for their outfits: The Greek Graces. Their sexual language and blunt expression of their sexuality seem to camouflage their feelings of the Cinderella Complex, as explained by Dowling. The Cinderella syndrome is also unmasked in this chick version of the tale, when in the twenty-first century, professional independent women are still fearing life without "a prince charming."

CHAPTER 7
=========

La Cenicienta que no quería comer perdices: A Cinderella Picture Book
----

Modern picture books have acquired more and more popularity lately around the world. Although picture books have existed for decades, they have only recently been conceptualized as such. The eighties could be considered as a watershed decade for picture book conceptualization, with the publication of Perry Nodelman's *Words About Pictures*, Joseph and Chava Schwarcz's *The Picture Book Comes of Age* and William Moebius's "Introduction to picturebook codes," *Word & Image* (1986). The closest relatives to picture books are comics and manga, as they all have in common the combination of images and words. This genre is characterized by having a narrative with a succession of pictures that illustrate the story.

Since the 1960s, picture books have been popularized around the world and have been the successor of another current and trendy genre: manga.[1] They are delineated with the combination of images and texts in various formats, as both words and pictures support each other and create the balance for one another. Manga, since the 1960s have become the most popular of picture books adding its own particularities to the genre. Picture books in this decade started to use some of the features of manga and comics, according to Bettina Kümmerling-Meibauer, but she also contends that although these genres are very similar, they have an aspect that differentiates them: the targeted audience. However, with globalization and other cultural shifts, picture books have gone beyond the borders and limits of having a unique audience since the seventies. In fact, English author/illustrator Raymond Briggs was making picture books for adults from the 1970s: *Fungus the Bogeyman* (1977), *When the Wind Blows* (1982), and *The Tin-Pot Foreign General and the Old Iron Woman* (1984, a satire about the Falklands War) are examples of his work. Currently picture books globally also target teenagers and adults and have popularized a variety of themes and topics.

Many theorists have used a number of metaphors from various disciplines to develop a set of premises about picture books. The first ideas that are common to these attempts in conceptualization are the relationship between the text and the image. Education teachers have written about the prominence and popularity of picture books for children, and its advantages for instructors and students. Renaissance educator Jan Amos Comenius (1592–1670), known as the precursors of picture books, thinks that education should pose attractive content to children. Education, he argues, should be a gymnasium not only for the mind but also for the moral and spiritual aspects of its formation (Hendrich 13). Lawrence Sipe summarizes how various critics such as Cech, Pullman, Ward and Fox, Ahlberg, Miller and Moebius have used Music, Geology and/or Wave Theory to describe the tie between the visual and the written aspect of picture books. Sipe indicates how Goldman creates a taxonomy of relationships between picture and words, its domain and power interdependence, and how Nodelman contends that there is more a transaction type of association between the two. Sipe draws upon the term synergy as well to define the link between the two and elaborates a theory from a cognitive perspective and describes the idea of how image and words connect together at the abstract thinking level. From the pedagogical field, Sipe notes that Keith Schoch has set up the advantages of using picture books in the school curriculum. Among other benefits, Schoch argues, the use of picture books aids with teaching critical thinking skills as students see abstract concepts in concrete forms (Sipe 98–99). Similarly, *From Picture Book to Literary Theory* (Stephens 1994) employs picture books to teach literary theory to high school students.

In Latin America, the codices from Mesoamerican cultures could be considered roughly as precursors of the picture books in this part of the world. The codices were artifacts that had pictures and hieroglyphs depicting various aspects of Mesoamerican cultures. For instance, Mayan texts not only included information about their calendar, but also about their complex cosmovision and their history. There are around 700 Mayan *glifos* but only a partial amount of them have been deciphered. These codices are based on a mixture of pictures, logograms and syllabic glyphs. Indigenous books such as the Maya sacred book, the *Popol Vuh*, have been rewritten, translated and studied for decades. The *Popol Vuh* is very ancient: fragments survive as carved panels from about 300 BCE, but it presumably existed in oral form long before, and is then recorded in Mayan hieroglyphics in K'iche', the Mayan language.[2] The *Popol Vuh* is probably the most important text produced by an indigenous culture; it tells about the creation of the Mayas and their cosmovision. In modern times, the *Popol Vuh* and other indigenous texts are often commercialized as picture books and marketed for children.[3] Currently in the Spanish speaking world, picture books have also acquired immense popularity, mostly among young adults. The corpus abounds in themes drawn from folktales, historical events, and cultural practices, and in translations of English picture books. As Bettina Kuemmerling-Meibauer states, picture books, comics and manga "are highly intertextual with their artists drawing on diverse sources from the arts to popular media" (100). Picture books have also been used to promote and defend certain ideologies or lines of thought. Since the late eighties and nineties picture books have been studied as mediums to express societal beliefs and dogmas. In "Picturebooks and Ideology" (2018) John Stephens mentions a number of scholars who have studied picture books as ideological apparatuses; they affirm that picture books have created the framework for certain paradigms of identity, forms of behavior, race, and multiculturalism, among others (Picturebooks 138).

This ideological impulse is evident in the work which is the focus of this chapter. In *La Cenicienta que no quería comer perdices* (2009) [The Cinderella Who Did Not Want to Eat Partridges], a Cinderella adaptation picture book in Spanish by Nunila López Salamero, illustrated by Myriam Cameros Sierra, the traditional Cinderella story is transformed into a highly charged ideologically tale on the topic of women and their position in society. Nunila López Salamero combines the recreation of the popular and mythical story of a girl who is mistreated by her environment with the feminist ideology encircling it. In fact, her version has served as a source for public debates on social issues, such as Claudia Carrasco Aguilar and María Julia Baltar de Andrade's article "Chilean Public Policies on Female Labour and Sexual Education: Because One Day We Were Told That We Were Going to Be Princesses" (2013), where quotations from the story are used as an epigraph to center the discussion of policies concerning women in Chile. Aguilar and Andrade examine how political institutions have promoted inequality between men and women in modern history. The authors conclude that Public Policies do not have gender consciousness in the case of women and/or men. (90–100) Fernando José Azevedo (2015) examines the relationship of the story with cultural ideology and proposes that it is an example of emancipating forces escaping stagnant traditional patriarchal thought (126). Eduardo Encabo Fernández and Isabel Jerez Martínez (2011), on the other hand, argue that the protagonist constitutes a rupture with former paradigms of the Cinderella character and question if it is possible to educate with this heterodoxical and culturally different text (1). Laura Molina Molina in *Un cuento de hadas en Educación Infantil* [A Fairy Tale in Children's Education] (2016) compares *La Cenicienta no quería comer perdices* with canonical versions of the tale starting with Charles Perrault and finishing with the latest Disney Cinderella version of the tale. She proposes that the picture book can be used in the classroom to further a number of cognitive skills and ethical reasoning for children that could be developed using this text (25–43). In all of these studies, *La Cenicienta que no quería comer perdices* is approached through a discussion of gender issues and an analysis of story content. None, however, has analyzed the integration of gender and picture book discourse to explore the social issues depicted in this Cinderella story.

The Contribution of the Paratext

Topics taken up by the above scholars have already been anticipated within *La Cenicienta que no quería comer perdices* by its paratexts, which connect the story and its ideological core. According to Gérard Genette (*Paratexts* 1987) paratexts are what make a published work possible. Genette contends that paratexts not only present the text to the public but also make it present in the world (1). This literary device enables the *ouvre* to exist physically and as a source of knowledge as well. Initially, paratexts reveal the general reader envisioned by the publisher. In the case of children's literature this reader is twofold: an adult who acts as a vehicle of mediation between the book and the child, and the child her/himself. The external elements of the paratext such as commercial catalogs, online reviews, and publicity are part of the paratextual realm. In the current era we might also add author web pages and blogs, and, in the case of *La Cenicienta que no quería comer perdices*, a radio performance which adds a narrator and dramatic music and whose text often differs from the picture book text. Nonetheless, the size and shape of the book, the number of pages, the paper quality, the font type(s), endpapers, and the prologue are all internal paratextual elements or are what is more specifically referred to as *peritextual* elements (see Higonnet 1990).

The three-page prologue by Maruja Torres, as an internal paratextual aspect in *La Cenicienta que no quería comer perdices*, substantiates the meaning of the picture book. The prologue is an invocation to readers. In the first paragraph, Torres talks about the transition of the Cinderella story from an online character to the short story. Cinderella is held up as an example of a woman who finally says "NO" and the short story as, "un libro que debería de entrar obligatoriamente en los programas de los colegios" [A book that should be mandatory in all schools]. Torres proposes what John Stephens has called "the polyphony of discourse" (*Language and Ideology* vii) in the social realm or the variety of positions in a particular theme or area.

The prologue in this manner urges upon readers the need to interrogate the subjectivities and to challenge the conventions of fairy tales as they are traditionally known. Torres advocacy that readers should disseminate the idea of a free Cinderella is the main point of the prologue. It also reflects on the notion of the already won battles of women in politics and society. However, Torres implies that there are still a plethora of challenges and that every woman should be prepared to fight: "Nuestra Cenicienta, sin ceniza en la frente y con la cabeza muy alta, nos avisa, que cada generación, cada mujer, tiene que volver a empezar" [Our Cinderella, without cinders on her forehead, and with head held high, warns us, that each generation, every woman, needs to start again]. The prologue describes the collaboration of the writer and illustrator as a couple who procreated a "newborn child" as the book/product of their union. Torres insists on the concepts of women's self-rebirth and self-recreation through the reading of this duo's picture book. The continuum and solidarity of womanhood is highlighted by Torres as a must among women—"vivas o muertas" [dead or alive]—as is the need to open the narrow social horizons and gender restrictions not only for girls but also for boys around the world. As a paratextual element the prologue shapes the reception of *La Cenicienta que no quería comer perdices* to a target audience. Torres affirms that women of many generations are entitled to dispose of the inherited negative "mirrors and examples."

All in all, Torres' prologue is a cultural Manifesto that proposes awareness and aroused activism in relation to societal change concerning women. Torres uses the boat as a metaphor for women sailing on the ocean with the same envisioned end and goal; women coming together searching with the same purpose. She reiterates the significance of this book for all children around the world and its reach that should be as wide as the ocean: "Un rumbo que sería mucho más ancho si este cuento tramado con verdades pudieran leerlo todos los niños y niñas del mundo, en todos los días de su vida, para que no lo olvidaran jamás" [A route that would be much wider if this tale, woven with truth, could be read by the girls and boys of the world every day of their lives, so they will never forget it]. The importance of the paratextual in *La Cenicienta que no quería comer perdices* increases and defines the insightful idea of women and agency ingrained in this work.

The sketches of Paula Seré which appear on the interior book jacket flap and the endpapers are a second key paratextual element that throws light on the narrative. Seré's drawings of the crystal shoe, which fill the endpapers, are all upside down or set at oblique angles. Only one of the crystal shoes is shown as if it were ready to be worn. The rest of the shoes are scattered, seemingly thrown into the space, where they appear to be flying out of place. There is only one crystal shoe on the front cover slip and it is also unbalanced like the others, and it is the same shoe that appears on the front of the hardcover in the right bottom corner, while on the back, seven crystal shoes are in the center of the page, apparently moving with a centripetal force.

The abundance of shoes in the paratextual realm of the story is paramount to the narrative. As the crystal shoe is one of the three motifs recast in this version, it is also the epicenter of Cenicienta's threshold life between being single and married. The shoe is also the entrance to the new life with a different status and at the same time it is also the shoes (high heels) that constitute Cinderella's major constraint and hassle of her new condition as a wife. The social demand her marriage makes upon her to wear high heels that oppressed her feet is the ultimate and bigger burden of Cinderella's married life. The shoe/s are dual charged as they are both the door that opens the beginning of her misery, but also the exit from it, as Cinderella's liberation is made through the shoes.

Overthrowing the Cinderella Stereotype

In *La Cenicienta que no quería comer perdices*, the protagonist, unlike other traditional versions of "Cinderella," does not have a given name, besides "Cinderella." She is plainly called "La Cenicienta" (The Cinderella). The use of a determinate article gives an idea of precision but also that of the opposite, vagueness, as the protagonist is "the" Cinderella amongst the multiplicity of other given Cinderellas as a social paradigm. The story thus evokes the commonness of Cinderella as the stereotypical image that culture has nurtured. Nonetheless, this version contradicts the archetypical girl who pursues the dream of marrying a prince. Unlike most adaptations, this story starts where most traditional Cinderella folktales end: the ball. Another adaptation by Julia Massip, *Cenicienta tiene un mal sueño* [Cinderella Has a Bad Dream] (2012) mentioned below in Chapter 11 uses the same chronological order of events, starting where most adaptations end.

Readers are not given any back story about the motives, obstacles or various situations that the girl has endured previous to attending the ball, nor does the plot supply any details about a previous encounter between the girl and the prince. Readers only learn some of Cinderella's past history after the story climax and the resolution:

> Primero empezó llorando por el príncipe, por tantas perdices muertas y por los zapatos. Luego siguió llorando al recordar que su madrastra la maltrataba, que su padre la trataba peor y que sus hermanas casi se mueren por querer usar una 38 de Zahara.
>
> First, she cried for the prince, for so many dead partridges and for the shoes. Then, she continued crying when she remembered that her stepmother had mistreated her and her father had mistreated her even more and that her sisters had almost died trying to fit into a size 4 Zahara shoe.

In most Cinderella stories the social status factor is stated explicitly or implicitly. Cinderella is usually a girl who has become poor or who is poor. In this version, the reader might assume that the heroine is not rich because of the illustrations of her housing. The very colloquial language used by her is indicative of her tone; for instance, when she tries on the shoe brought by the two men, she states: "pero apretó y apretó hasta que le "cabió," y metió la pata" [she tried and tried, pushed and shoved until it fit in]. Cinderella's language and diction are rather colloquial and her register is one used in very familiar environments, including slang words and nonstandard or erroneous use of verb conjugations. This aspect is not in itself a distinctive sign of social status; nevertheless, it could be an indication of having or not having had access to formal education. On the other hand, it could also be a means to portray Cinderella's rebellious nature, in that she does not adhere to the strictness of standard language. For instance, when the fairy godmother appears in the story, she is addressed as "la hada" and not "el hada." The latter is the normal and grammatically correct form of the article for the noun "hada" in Spanish. However, it is stated in the story that the masculine article is rejected, and the feminine article is substituted. There is a legend in the text that explains this purposely changing of articles: "No es una falta de ortografía. Ponemos 'la' en vez de 'el' porque no nos parece bien tanto artículo machista en la lengua castellana" [It is not an orthographic error. We are placing "la" instead of "el" because we do not find it fair to have so many words with a sexist article in the Spanish language].

The story opens with an illustration of the girl hanging from a building of what seems to be a public housing area. The text says: "La Cenicienta tenía tantas ganas de ir a la fiesta ... que al final lo consiguió" (s/n) [The Cinderella wanted so badly to attend the ball ... that she finally got to go]. The next page immediately shows that Cinderella did indeed go to the ball, but she is not able to recall anything that happened there. The day following the great event, she wakes up with a blurry image about the previous evening. It is stated that she was so anxious that this state prevented her to be conscious of her surroundings. The girl arrived home from the ball at 12, but noon the next day, not at midnight as the popular story tells. The illustrations show Cinderella drinking, dancing, enamored (showing hearts in her eyes) and vomiting. It is implied that Cinderella partied very hard at the ball and passed out losing consciousness. There is even a traffic sign with an exclamation mark saying: ¡Cuidado! Es peligroso llegar a estos estados de inconsciencia [Warning! It is dangerous to reach these states of unconsciousness]. Whatever specific happened at the ball is uncertain, but the narrator states that the day following the party: "Pero ahí estaban esos dos señores, con el zapato de cristal de tacón de palmo y de punta... " (s/n) [But there, there were those two men with the high-heeled crystal shoe waiting for her to try it on].

Immediately after the classical episode of the shoe test, the narrative jumps to depict a married Cinderella who is already having issues about her husband's temperament and constant demands about his food and its preparation. Cinderella is a vegetarian or o "vegatariana" [*sic*] but her newlywed husband devours and yearns to eat meat, more specifically, partridge. Partridge is *perdiz* in Spanish and is used, as in the title of the story, to imply happiness as in the popular saying: "vivieron felices y comieron perdices" [they lived happily eating partridges]. In Spanish there is a rhyme in the popular saying between "felices" and "perdices," which is lost in the English translation. In other words, the husband's liking of partridge as his favorite dish contains the sense of marriage tied to happiness embedded in the popular saying. Cinderella cooks her husband's favorite meat dish in many different forms: "Se las cocinaba al horno, rellenitas, fritas" [She cooks them (the partridges) grilled, baked, stuffed and fried]. In spite of this, the "prince"/husband frequently complains about her cooking by screaming and saying that the partridges taste badly and are constantly either salty, raw or burned.

On these successive pages, Cinderella's domestic misery is juxtaposed with her husband's unattractive boorishness. Cinderella is framed by the image of the house and trapped by the shoes (the prince) and the cooking. The rays of light surrounding the shoes suggest a double meaning, as in popular visual art this can signify two things: on the one hand it is an aura expressing value, but on the other it signifies violence and pain, as from a blow. Her mouth is in the conventional comics shape that signifies pain and suffering. The left foreground is occupied by an overturned cup whose contents spill off the page, indicating that Cinderella's "cup is empty." The cup handle establishes a vector that flows diagonally to Cinderella in anguish. The same vector is repeated in the contrasting image, now flowing from the yellow object in the foreground to the wine bottle, taking in the overturned table, dead partridge, the prince's fat hairy belly and his general untidiness. In a move possibly borrowed from manga, the prince's face is deformed by his huge, wide-open mouth, expressing his rage. The little crown has flown off his head, marking both who he is and what he isn't—a prince a girl might dream of. Overall, the image is borrowed from the conventional image of a man who makes a woman unhappy: untidy, lazy, drunken and violent.

The marriage to the prince is thus shown to be a burden for Cinderella very early in the story. The shoe motive present in all versions is also highlighted in *La Cenicienta que no quería comer perdices* but portrays a reverse meaning. In the traditional story, Cinderella is found by the prince due to the shoe, which translates into finding love and happiness ever after. In *La Cenicienta que no quería comer perdices,* the shoe episode only opens Cinderella's unhappiness, discomfort and depression for her. The shoe is an element that brings the opposite effect of what happens in the traditional story, since shoes bring for Cinderella, in *La Cenicienta que no quería comer perdices,* only burden and hardships. Not only are the shoes a negative component in the figurative sense, but also the quotidian one. Wearing high heels every day is damaging to the heroine's feet as she reports that she feels trapped in those extremely high heels she is expected to wear in her daily activities and all the time. The shoe/s that once was/were the vehicle of finding happiness are now the cage that oppresses her, and one of the main reasons of her discomfort. Her feet and spine are affected by the constant walking on those uncomfortable shoes. As the spine is the center of the human body, her core is affected by Cinderella's obligation to wear high heels.

Cinderella is "sick, depressed and lost" in her newlywed life. She is miserable and lonely, and finally decides to open up about her marital situation and confide her private life details to acquaintances and family members. When she proceeds to confide her hardships, Cinderella receives a variety of advice from different kinds of people. The opinions of her associates puzzle and confuse Cinderella even more. All of them: her friend, "a modern neighbor" and "a queen mother" advise Cinderella not to complain about the life she has with the prince, as it is a good, desirable life. After receiving this dumbfounding feedback, she then decides to be quiet and endure her situation in silence. Befuddled and depressed, and after several years of living with the prince, Cinderella realizes that no prince will change her situation: "Después de años viviendo con uno, se dio cuenta de que los príncipes no te salvan ... tampoco los camioneros, ni los disc-jockeys, ni las pasteleras" [After many years of living with one (prince), she realizes that princes do not save you ... or truck drivers, or disc-jockeys, or bakers].

Cinderella suddenly has a vivid epiphany: nobody will be able to save her but only HERSELF. For the first time depicted in the illustrations, Cinderella's face looks symmetrical, her eyes, nose, hair, mouth, and ears are finally brought into balance and show a sense of equilibrium. The fact that the two pages are in the center of the book also offers the idea of stability and steadiness. On the second page Cinderella is on a magical swing suspended from the moon. The scars and wounds inflicted on both of her feet by the destructive high heels are still visible, but so too is her underwear, a subtle reference to a new sexual freedom counterposing the shackles imposed formerly by the high heels. On the other page, the phrase in capital letters "eres TÚ MISMA" following the previous page as in "la única que te puede salvar..." [the only one who would be able to save you is ... Yourself]. Cinderella here appears to be alone in the universe, as the background is the sky with stars surrounding her. It appears at this stage that Cinderella is embracing and creating her own figurative world away from the constraints of marriage. Breaking with this idea of "happiness" is symbolic of rupturing the idea that women's ultimate goal is marriage, as represented in Cinderella and other folktales. For this reason, *La Cenicienta que no quería comer perdices* is considered a feminist adaptation of the tale.

Folktales and Feminism

The topic of folktales and feminism has been studied extensively since the 1970s, when critics initiated a discussion on the patriarchal representation of women in fairy tales. Margaret Atwood's fictional work—in particular *The Edible Woman* (1965), a version of "Cinderella"—is considered proto feminist by Fiona Tolan and it is recognized as one of the first works to subvert the traditional image of passivity engrained in the Perrault and Grimm versions of the story. Haase and Joosen have discussed the embedding of images of stereotypical women in society through fairy tales. The seminal work of Jack Zipes, published in 1986, *Don't Bet on the Prince* offers in the introduction an insight central to this issue:

> Recent feminist criticism and feminist fairy tales in America and England have sought to confront the "real problem" which lies *beyond* and *around* fairy tales. At the very least, feminists endeavor to alter our gaze and challenge our perspective with regard to literature and society [1].

According to Zipes the "real problem" in fairy tales is the mutual repression in society both from moralists against its sexual depictions and liberals who defend their existence.

Also, in her groundbreaking article "Fertility Control and the Birth of the Modern European Fairy-Tale Heroine" (2004), Ruth Bottigheimer recounts the history of the transformation of the fairy tale heroine from sexually independent women to submissive, abused and controlled ones. John Stephens' has coined the term "metaethic" to define the phenomenon that traditional stories have predetermined horizons of expectations already molded by a particular cultural narrative (Retelling 6). Ideology and children's literature and folktales are no doubt a topic of discussion. In *Cinderella Across Cultures* (2016), the theme of feminism, ideology and the tale is discussed in Chapters 7 and 8. Ronna May-Ron's analysis of Margaret Atwood's *The Edible Woman* draws attention to the revolutionary nature of the story and concludes that some of the motifs that reinforce Cinderella's passivity in some versions function in exactly an opposite way in Atwood's retelling. Hennard Dutheil de la Rochère examines how the Perrault and Grimm versions of the tale were inverted by Angela Carter's unorthodox adaptations of Cinderella in *The Bloody Chamber* (1979) and *The Mother Ghost* (1987). Dutheil de la Rochère draws attention to how Carter's rewritings of the tales develop a social commentary which portrays the relationship between women as positive rather than conflicting and destructive as in the traditional versions. The topic of gender relations in Cinderella rewritings has resulted in a variety of studies, not only discussing feminism but also other gender related representations.

These examinations of folktales and gender have been scarce in the Spanish-speaking world, however. In 2004, for instance, Patricia Anne Odber de Baubeta states in "The Fairy-Tale Intertext" that at that time there were only a very few studies that intersect the topic of fairy tale intertextuality and feminism in "Latin American or Iberian women's writing" (129). A few scholars, such as Carolina Fernández-Rodríguez, have also studied global Cinderella versions from a feminist approach (1997). Most recently in 2017, I have discussed elsewhere the intertextuality with Almodóvar's *Hable con ella* (2003) and *Sleeping Beauty* in the context of comparative cultural studies and cinema from a feminist perspective.

Even though most studies have not been focused on intertextual relationships between Latin American or Iberian texts and fairy-tales, scholars have recently produced a handful of stories from manga, the genre cousin of picture books, which replicate the Cinderella tale. One of the most popular Cinderella rewritings in manga, a version entitled *Fukigen Cinderella* (Morose/Grumpy Cinderella, Murayama 2010) has a gender identity theme dealing with transvestism, androgyny and culturally ascribed gender roles. Because of the popularity enjoyed by this Manga, *Fukigen Cinderella* is one of the few Cinderella Manga versions that has been translated from the original Japanese into Spanish. Kanna Haruhiko is a male protagonist who is by magical forces transformed into a girl in twelve-hour cycles, becoming female at midday and returning to his male self at midnight. The alternation of his male and female personas is a curse imposed as punishment for his sexist attitudes, and he consequently must struggle with the socio-cultural aspects of communicating and experiencing female identity. This Manga shows how the social construction of genres is often detrimental to individuals living under gender categorizations. In particular, it develops this notion with regard to female characters, and demonstrates how female and male are apt to be seen and treated in a particular and distinctive manner because of their gender identity.

The Cinderella motifs embedded identify it as a version, adaptation or rewriting of the tale. R.D Jameson's taxonomy of "Cinderella" is based on the events that are frequently found in the story (Dundes 81). According to this classification, *La Cenicienta no quería comer perdices* would belong to the D1 and E typology, as "She is identified by the shoe test" (Dundes 82) and E, "She marries the prince." Category C corresponds to "She meets the prince" and the sub-categorizations offer details of this encounter. Nevertheless, in López Salamero's story no details of the meeting between the couple are offered, and therefore it is impossible to give this adaptation a category C. The clear motifs of the Cinderella story in *La Cenicienta no quería comer perdices* are only the shoe and the marriage to the prince. An allusion to the Cinderella tale, besides the already mentioned subtexts and motifs classified by Jameson, is also made obvious by the title, and so the traditional versions are evoked by the missing or altered elements. The plotline diverges from the "happily ever after" stories and inverts the story order, starting near the end of the traditional story with the ball. The organization of the story as picture book panels enables the sequence of events to be presented clearly and quickly. From the start, a change in the Cinderella character is evident. The illustration shows the girl with a broom and a bucket cleaning. In her face and eyes is depicted the illusion and ingenuity that continues through the following pages. The girl's features are distorted more and more showing six various stages of Cenicienta at the ball, until she passes out and ends up on the floor with her tongue sticking out.

Cinderella's lapse into unconsciousness is a liminal state from which she awakens to the shoe fitting test and thence passes into domestic servitude symbolized by the shoes, which invest the tale with a sustained allegorical logic. As Max Barnish et al report in their review of research into the impacts of high heels (2), fashion operates by capitalizing on concepts of social compliance and conformity and the expectation to perform normalized gender roles. Because standards of beauty define dimensions of physical freedom, footwear can become a form of gendered violence when it disables its wearer. Like many modern women, Cinderella's high heel wear is due mainly to social expectation rather than her own free choice, and the consequences, as the picture book perceptively details, are those common to women who wear these shoes: injury to the spine, hips, and knees, and various foot disorders and injuries. The shoes have a literal presence in the tale, but also a physical impact and a symbolic significance, especially in expressing the dire consequences of gender conformity. To have freed herself from the shoes and to walk barefoot is the second major transition in Cinderella's life.

Once Cinderella says "STOP" the fairy appears or what she calls "La Hada" [sic]. The "chubby, hairy, dark-skinned fairy" embraces her and Cinderella feels her support. "En cuanto el hada vio a la Cenicienta la abrazó y la estrujó, y la Cenicienta en el momento en que se sintió recogida, se puso a llorar" [As soon as the fairy saw her, she hugged her strongly and Cinderella at the moment, when she felt understood, started crying]. The first stage of Cinderella's recuperation is to release all the fear and sadness stored and hidden inside her for all these years. She cried and cried about all the bad family situations in the remote past, when she was a little girl. Cinderella even cried because at birth she was separated from her mother at the hospital. Cinderella's catharsis leads to emptiness or the state reached in meditation. Calm and empty from the past, she starts a new life, her life in the present. Her first action is to leave the prince, then get rid of the shoes and then the partridges, in that order. Once alone, she decides to enjoy her body that was so mistreated all these years.

The Rebirth of Cinderella

Cinderella's next stage after leaving her past life behind is to regroup and recreate herself. Her first step of this new self is the discovery of her body, getting rid of the old clothes as a representation of their habits and former customs and manners to operate in the world. The nakedness of her body in the illustration shows her desire to expel everything that covers her culturally and that was imposed on her. Nude and free, Cinderella starts a new beginning as a child born nude and free of all cultural constraints and chains. As Nietzsche proposes in *Thus Spoke Zarathustra* (1891), the metamorphoses of the spirit is to become a child who represents a new beginning. Secondly, she discovers dance as part of the rebirth of her body. Movement as the opposite of rigidity, stiffness, unyieldingness unleashes the woman inside against the coercive forces, which are then left behind. Cinderella states that dance is for every woman no matter the age or shape. As she discovers the movement of her body with dance, Cinderella frees herself also metaphorically and unleashes her true inner self for so long captured and chained. The notion of flexibility ingrained in dance and body opens for Cinderella a flowing momentum with her new persona encountered through the freedom and joy of movement. Corporeal flexibility is possible at this stage allowing the protagonist to loosen up and emphasizing the mobility of her body in the social realm as well. Cinderella is not anymore framed in the narrow space of her old, married, unhappy life, she has broadened her body and mind to another stage of consciousness.

The Cinderella story implies the theme of transformation. The girl in the canonical versions of the tale derived from Perrault and Grimm, by the power of her fairy godmother goes through a metamorphosis along with the elements and animals that aid her in her plan to attend the ball. Her appearance changes "from rags to riches" as the popular phrase expresses it. Her dress, shoes, make-up, hairdo and accessories magically appear to change a peasant girl into a beautiful and rich looking princess. In *this* picture book version, the girl undergoes a transformation as well. This time the transformation entails not the physical appearance or the clothes and shoes that she wears, that allow her to attend the prince's ball.

Cinderella's transformation comes from a deeper level that will not fade away at midnight. Her garments are not mentioned except for the shoes that she disposes of after leaving the "prince." Her alteration and change is at the core level. Metamorphosis in this story operates in a much more meaningful way, when she faces her life without the "Cinderella Complex."

In her path of change and transformation, Cinderella encounters a number of other fairy tale characters in the same situation. Among them, she finds Sleeping Beauty, Snow White, Little Red Riding Hood, and Pinocchio. These fairy tale characters have also transformed themselves. For instance, both Sleeping Beauty and Snow White are finally awakening and recovering from their constant intoxication with "Prozac" alluding to their perpetual state of somnolence even when they are awake. Little Red Riding Hood is now conscious of the situation with the hunter who saved her, but who turned out to be violent. In this comment alluding to the Brothers Grimm version of the tale, there is an implication that Little Red Riding Hood and the hunter who saves her and the grandmother have an amorous relationship. Pinocchio has also transformed himself by finally finding his true self and becoming honest.

All these fairy tale heroes and heroines hold hands and embrace their transformation into individuals with a new and renewed facet in their lives. The transformation is illustrated not only in their individual actions and change, but in their appearance. Snow White, for example, is not the paradigmatic white-skinned girl with beautiful black hair. Snow White has been transformed and Sleeping Beauty has an olive complexion and black hair. The physiognomy of the characters indicates the changes have operated from the inside to the outside. The new and refreshing ideas of freedom and liberation have permeated not only the core of these characters, but are also reflected in their exterior.

In conclusion, picture books as a dialogic genre composed of illustrations and text have propelled new ideas and new concepts about women's representation in fairy tales around the world. The Spanish picture book version of Cinderella, *La Cenicienta que no quería comer perdices,* is an example of how a new paradigm of women portrayed in fairy tales can demand a rupture with the stagnant myths about women's cultural roles and expectations within society.

Chapter 8

Suicidal Cinderella:
Cenicienta en Pensilvania

Cinderella as the main character of the most popular folk tale of all times has become the source of studies, theories, paradigms and ideas based and construed around her fictional persona, from Colette Downing's well-known *The Cinderella Complex* (1981) mentioned earlier in this study to the various interpretations surrounding the paradigmatic depiction of the character throughout global history. Cinderella, as the quintessential scapegoat, is also often seen as the incarnation of pain and hurt. In some versions of the tale, the pain is physical and torture is part of Cinderella's punishment (see Chapter 1). Other levels of pain are inflicted upon the protagonist as emotional and mental distress that hurt and pursue Cinderella in her lifetime. Pain as a human notion is shown in this version of Cinderella as the main axis of the protagonist's life. Approaching Cristina Cerrada's *Cenicienta en Pensilvania* (2010) through its self-conscious emulation of cinematic technique, this chapter analyzes pain as an aspect of Cinderella's vital experience.

Cenicienta en Pensilvania tells the story of Mary, a young actress struggling to cope with adverse personal circumstances. The story opens with a New Year's party at which Mary loses a shoe. The objective focalization of the narrative walks the reader through a detailed description of the festive atmosphere and the traces left in a mansion, describing everything with the camera approaching the scene: "La cámara se acerca entonces a la gran terraza de la mansión, al pie de cuyas escaleras, abandonado, se descubre un zapato de mujer" (13) [The camera approaches the mansion's terrace, at the foot of whose stairs, abandoned, a woman's shoe is shown]. Three of the various Cinderella's motifs, the shoe, the stairs and the ball, appear immediately at the beginning, opening the story with a clear reference to a "Cinderella" hypotext. Genette proposes two kinds of hypertextual reference: "the derivation can be of a descriptive or intellectual kind." (5). *Cenicienta en Pensilvania* employs both kinds of literary allusion intertwined within the text: the hypertextual descriptive and the hypertextual intellectual in relation to the "Cinderella" stories-adaptations. The loss of the shoe placed at the beginning of the novel in the context of a New Year's Eve dance will initiate the palimpsestic nature of this Cinderella rewriting.

Hypertextuality is a text in "a second degree" or a text derived from a pre-existing text (Palimpsests 5). This derivation can be descriptive, which implies the co-existence among texts through concrete objects or material tangential elements that both share. As I understand it, the intellectual kind refers to the self-reflexion within the text where a metatext "speaks" itself (5). The intellectual kind implies also an abstract process to reach and unite the textual threads to find the derivation and co-relation among them and the ability to critically analyze by dissecting the structure and components of the text.

Immediately in the first paragraph the hypertextual descriptive is patent in the story. The narrator makes a clear reference to the shoe motif when introducing Mary, a beautiful, famous and glamorous actress who proclaims that she wears her shoes one size too small to keep her arch high and, in consequence, her feet smaller:

> También calzaba un número de mocasines más pequeño. Siempre nos decía que, cuando se pusiera tacones, su empeine resultaría más arqueado de lo normal por haberlo llevado apretado así [...] no hay sin duda otra actriz que pueda ponerse sus zapatos de pequeños que son [16].
>
> She also wore a smaller size of shoe. She used to say that when she would wear high heels, her feet would be more arched than normal, because of the tightness of her shoes[...]. It was certain that no other actress could wear her tiny shoes.

The other form of hypertextuality, the hypertextual intellectual, appears in relation to Mary's discomfort. The uneasiness which is a constant attribute of Mary's life is present in the first pages of the novel as embodied in the mention of the constraining shoes, but, further, she also complains about other physical and emotional restraints that has been imposed upon her, mostly by her environment. The opening scene at the aftermath of the New Year's Eve party, which displays Mary as the epicenter, describes two feelings of discomfort: one is the physical constraint of the hair style she has endured during the night for the sake of her looks, and the other is emotional, her search for her lost mother. The hypertextual description continues as camera-like in the first pages of the novel: "La sirvienta no está allí. La mesa está llena de migas de pan, hay una lata vacía de fiambre sobre el horno, un cuchillo clavado en la tabla de mesa de cortar" (14) [The maid is not there. The table is full of bread crumbs, there is an empty meat can on the oven, a knife embedded in the cutting table]. There are two main hypertextual axes in the novel: the first is the various intersections with versions of Cinderella, as Margaret Atwood's contemporary version *The Edible Woman* (1969) and others. Second, there is another clear hypotext evoked in the novel and intertwined with the multiple Cinderella stories, which is a resemblance between Mary's life and the life of Hollywood icon Marilyn Monroe. There are several elements which make up the Cinderella/ Mary/ Marilyn triangle. As Genette affirms about the hypertext: "whereas the hypertext is almost always fictional—its fiction derives from another fiction or from the narrative of a real event" (397).

The protagonist is Mary/Marilyn and thus shares a name, and she is a Hollywood actress who was abandoned by her mother as an infant and did not know who her father was. Some writers, such as those who contributed to McDonough's *All the Available Light* essay collection (Clare Boothe Luce, Marge Piercy, Molly Haskell) have drawn a comparison between the movie star and Cinderella based on the schema of the bullied and ill-treated girl. Of her life in an orphanage, Luce wrote: "The fairytale Cinderella, sweeping ashes from the hearth, lived a normal, protected, happy life compared with that of this rootless little orphan of the City of the Angels" (91). Like Marilyn, Mary was in foster care and endured sexual abuse in her childhood as well. There are many references to the protagonist's childhood, depressive episodes, yearning for love, solitude and abusive events against her during her life. For instance, the camera-like narrator approaches and highlights the mentioning of a knife on the table, and places extreme importance on this detail. As it is known, an event in Marilyn Monroe's life involving a knife affected the actress's fate as a child. Monroe, born as Norma Jean Baker, was taken away from her mother, Gladys Baker, because in a mental crisis, Gladys attacked Marilyn's caretaker and Gladys' close friend, Grace McKee, throwing a knife at her. This situation was the turning point for removing the two-week old baby from her disturbed biological mother (Banner 26). This is a clear example of how a cinematic narrative technique—in this example, a dolly in—is used to remark and approach objects exactly as if in a movie, where this technical resource bestows significance upon defined targets.

Immediately after this symbolic moment in the story of Mary's personal life appears one of the novel's leitmotivs and another source of pain for the protagonist: the relationship with her mother. As in almost every "Cinderella" story, the death of the protagonist's biological mother is the catalyst for her struggle. In most versions, the stepmother takes the place of the protagonist's mother, abusing and mistreating the girl unjustly. Cinderella's father is constantly absent in these versions as he ignores or chooses not to acknowledge his daughter's situation. In some versions, the father also suffers the abuse of his new wife (Grimm; *Zolushka* [1947]) or he disregards the situation altogether and rejects his daughter even advising the prince not to marry her (Basile's version). A further element of the hypertextual intellectual mode unveiled in *Cenicienta en Pensilvania* is that Mary's mother is also absent emotionally and physically. At the beginning of the novel, Mary finds out that her mother has disappeared, making her void clearer and very present. After the party, she looks for her, but fails to find her. Mary, then, is determined to search for her mother, who has only left a note alleging to have gone to the city of Mazatlán in Mexico.

The camera-like description continues to offer dynamism to the scene leading the reader to focus on the details and apprehend their relevance. It contributes to the hypertextual nature of the story as well. As Kotecki explains: "Hypertext need not only apply to literary theory and computer science. As a medium where the auditory and visual channels already run alongside the narrative, film's multitrack and multiformat structure allows for the possibility of conflicting and layered messages to be presented simultaneously in something akin to hypertext" (241). The quasi-cinematic technique yields a close-up view of certain elements that later will be part of the story's significance. This feature also attempts to create objectivity as the narrator/camera purports to show the elements as they are. The visual effect organizes the narrative as a film and numerous times mentions the mechanical object, the camera, that is directing the recount of events as if a reader was actually seeing them.

Unlike the traditional Cinderella traditional story, Mary has three siblings; nevertheless, unlike most known versions of the hypotext, they are half-sisters (named Tina, Lucy and Coral). The sisters do not show concern about their mother's disappearance as Mary does, showing lack of empathy and love for their biological mother. In contrast, Mary is obsessed with finding her and constantly blames herself for her mother's disappearance. After the party and her realization that her mother is suddenly absent, she searches for help and requests the company of one of her ex-lovers: Goran Gradovich. The narrative is centered in the trip that Goran and Mary make together towards the town "El Cajón" in Mazatlán, Mexico, in search of Mary's mother. This narrative thread is interrupted several times with numerous digressions and change of narrators adding complexity to the recount of events.

The self-reflexive strategy of setting the novel as a film integrates the thematic core into the narrative. According to Elaine Scarry in *The Body in Pain* (1985), the systematic production of pain in history through torture has been generated as a stage performance. For instance, oppressive regimes in the Philippines, Chile and South Vietnam named their sites of torture with stage metaphors: Production room, Blue Hit Stage and Cinema Room respectively (28). The stage/film narration is the setting of the protagonist's life performance and her road of constant pain and solitude. Pain as the center of Mary's life is clearly stated as the camera shows the reader every detail of the events in her personal circumstances. The alternation of narrators and the switch to second person narrator also includes the reader as a witness of the protagonist's emotional precarious situation. For this reason, the camera also acts as one of the narrators in the story. However, there are several and diverse narrators.

The first part of the story is told by an omniscient third person narrator without character focalization (that is, in Genette's terms, it is zero focalized). This mode emphasizes that the narrator knows more about the protagonist than the main character herself. The narrative is framed in three dimensions/directions and modes: one is the frequent analepses that flow in the text and take readers from Mary's past with numerous flashbacks from her childhood and adulthood to Mary's present, when she is looking for her estranged mother. Second, is the change of narrators from a first person to a third person to a second person narrator, transposing the focalization from one perspective to the other without any transition. The third is the cinematic frame within the narrative, which conveys the impression that a film is being projected within the story or that the story itself is a film. Again, the esthetic of pain is integrated in the constant camera recording of the production of pain in the life of the protagonist at various levels. As in film montage, the narrative alters the setting as it changes from one scene to another. The only textual flagging of these various changes of narrators or digressions are the extra spaces left between certain paragraphs. In the case of the camera, the mechanical device is mentioned and in this manner its presence is established very clearly and positions readers as spectators of a film in progress.

The hypertextual descriptive is also made patent with the inclusion of films in the narrative or references to particular movies in which Monroe/Mary is the star. For instance, resonances of Marilyn Monroe's life are made evident through the mention of her films and or historical events related to the famous sex symbol. There are various references to Marilyn Monroe's movies, in particular *The Prince and the Showgirl* (1957, *El principe y la corista* in the Spanish-dubbed version), which precisely makes allusion to the Cinderella story. The film stars Laurence Olivier as the Prince of Carpathia and Marilyn Monroe as a cabaret singer in London. Coincidentally, *Cenicienta en Pensilvania* also shows Mary's life with her lover Mardon, the film director who takes her to Europe where she begins her career as an actress. The connection between this novel and the city of Pennsylvania in its title is made clear at the end of the movie. Pennsylvania makes reference to Glenn Miller's popular song *Pennsylvania 6–5000* (1940), which is mentioned several times in the narrative and is played at the end of the movie *The Prince and the Showgirl*. The third person narrator states while the song is playing at the end: "it has a happy ending, as it should be." The irony is clear as the ending of Cerrada's version culminates in Mary's suicide paralleling Marilyn Monroe's death.

Another aspect of the spectrum of diverse narrators is the remarkable second person narrator, who appears to tell the plot of a movie where the protagonist is called Cinderella: "A ella comienzan a llamarla Cenicienta, ya sabe, por el cuento y durante un tiempo todos son felices y están contentos..." (38) [Everybody starts calling her Cinderella, you know, as in the tale, and for a while everybody is happy and content...]. This same narrator also establishes the links to some films as part of the hypertextual descriptive. For example, *Trapeze* (1956) is mentioned by the narrator to refer to Mary's acrophobia as she recalls how she acquired it. This movie, starring Burt Lancaster and Gina Lollobrigida, is the frame and vehicle to present one of Mary's most salient fears. The narrator attributes the cause of Mary's phobia to her memory of being held in the air on a ferris wheel with her father. Nevertheless, it also states at the same time that Mary never met her father. There is thus an ironical link between the fictional nature of the film and the fiction created by Mary that she has had a father.

The second film hypertextual descriptive is the mention of *The Cop and the Anthem* (1952) in which Monroe has a brief appearance. The allusion to this film is made as a digression, again from a second person narrator, immediately after an episode in which Mary feels nausea after a number of sexual encounters. In this film, Marilyn Monroe plays a prostitute. Parallel to Mary's feeling of abhorrence for sex, the streetwalker character played by Monroe expresses joy after one potential client calls her "a lady" and gives her a present without having any intimate contact with her. The prostitute explodes in joy for being treated as a person and for not having any sexual contact with the man on the street.

8. *Suicidal Cinderella:* Cenicienta en Pensilvania

The third aspect in the narrative is the constant digression that abruptly interrupts the focal theme of the fiction and shifts to the analepsis mode. The multiple digressions vary from Mary's memories of her childhood to recent past events. In one of the story diversions, the narrator describes Mary engaged in what seems to be an orgy. The somnolent protagonist is entrapped in a state of semi consciousness, but surrounded by nude women and men:

> Otros brazos femeninos se agarraron a sus caderas, con firmeza, con una tremenda sensualidad. Después, ante su cara, unas nalgas apolíneas, pálidas, marmóreas, y luego un pubis rasurado, y la mano de él ensortijándose, [...] penetrando despacio en el coño de labios sonrosados, casi grises, y su cuerpo aprisionado entre las piernas de una mujer de color, y la sensación infinita de placer, lacerante, monstruosa, y el olor a sexo, a asco, a sudor.
>
> Other female arms hold her hips firmly and sensually. Then, before her face, Apollonian buttocks, pale, marmoreal, and then a shaved pubic part and his hand twirling [...] penetrating slowly in the vagina with pink labia, almost gray, and her body imprisoned between the legs of a woman of color, and the infinite sensation of pleasure, lacerating, monstrous, and the odor of sex, repugnant, filthy.

Mary's disgust for sexual activity is evident and repeatedly expressed as discomfort to the point of either apathy or rejection. Her sexual encounters appear to be one sided as she lies like a doll with no desire, as described by the third person narrator in a shift to zero focalization: "Después de cenar faisán frío fueron al dormitorio, y ni siquiera fue consciente de cuanto el hombre hizo con ella" (145) [After dining on cold pheasant, they went to the bedroom, and she was not even aware of what the man did to her]. As in zero focalization, the narrator has taken the lead and knows more than the character herself, who does not focalize. It implies that Mary's body is taken over as she is not conscious of what is happening with her as if she was being ostracized from the sexual act. As another source of psychological pain, sex is not a source of pleasure and union with her lover but a site of abuse and sense of repulsion toward it.

Mary often experiences nausea, that repeats and echoes Antoine's constant sensation of filth in Sartre's *Nausea*: (1938) "Then the Nausea seized me, I dropped to a seat, I no longer knew where I was; I saw the colors spin slowly around me, I wanted to vomit. And since that time, the Nausea has not left me, it holds me" (7). Mary strives with disgust and the sensation of wanting to vomit constantly appears after an unpleasant experience or an emotionally shocking episode. Like Sartre's protagonist, Mary feels contempt for her experiences in the world and her surroundings.

One of the third person narrator's digressions in the story recounts the day that Mary's mother left her at a summer camp in the mountains.

After the camp was over, her mother failed to pick Mary up. A stranger picked her up and she was raped and then abducted by this unknown man, who pretended to be a relative. After the rape episode Mary vomits, expressing her disgust not only emotionally but physically, her whole body reacting to the molestation suffered as a child. The sensation of expelling the bad elements from her body has been a recurrent aspect in her life since she has had memory: "Vomitar. Vomitaba ya antes de hablar, si lo piensa. Oye el distante rumor de un tren que surca en la distancia. Vomitar comiese o no, es su recurso" (42) [Vomiting. She vomited even before she learned how to talk, if she realizes it. She hears the distant rumble of a train in the distance. She vomited even when she had not eaten, that is her recourse]. In the same token in Margaret Atwood's novel *The Edible Woman* (1969) the protagonist Marian McAlpin suffers from this same condition when adjusting to her societal "woman role." Later, when she liberates herself from the myths of being a "woman," she recovers her appetite and can eat again without her stomach revolting. Mary, on the other hand, never adjusts to her situation of loneliness and abuse and continues to vomit throughout the novel. Her physical revulsion at the end turns upon herself, when she commits suicide.

The third person narrator also serves to represent what the protagonist feels in an indirect stream of consciousness fashion about her actual mental state. The description of the Winter afternoons that precede the night and how they turn into lighter evenings in the Spring shows the flow of the narrator's consciousness and the flow of the time, day and cyclic pattern of it. Mary's feelings of sadness and disgust for the world are expressed by the narrator as he or she continues to retell the sentiment of imprisonment and monotony of her life: "El sol intensifica sus colores, aportándoles palidez, restándoles importancia y trascendencia, son cosas que están ahí, un árbol seguido de una cerca seguida de una puerta seguida de un cielo seguido de un sol" (40) [The sun intensifies the colors, giving them paleness, reducing their importance and transcendence, they are things that are there, a tree followed by a fence followed by a door followed by a sky followed by a sun].

The mother figure in this Cinderella version is as in the traditional rewritings central to the protagonist's life. In *Cenicienta en Pensilvania*, the figure is a biological mother not a stepmother who prefers her own daughters over the stepdaughter as in the well-known versions such as Perrault, Grimm and others. In *Cenicienta en Pensilvania*, Mary's maternal relationship is conflictive. As in the Cinderella story, the mother is a pivotal element that causes Mary's pain because she seemingly acts like the paradigmatic stepmother of the story. She abandons, ignores and does not acknowledge her daughter as she is invisible to her: "Mamá se murió en el parto que la trajo a ella a este mundo. Mamá parió un fantasma y después ella misma se convirtió en un fantasma también" (65). [Mama died in the childbirth that brought her into this world. Mama gave birth to a ghost and after that she herself turned into a ghost as well]. Mary´s mother is absent, distant and this is one of the causes of Mary's struggles with her experiences in life. Mary's mother has a mental illness that seems to prevent her from taking care of her daughter as a child. Mary directs a rhetorical question to her now lost mother: "Mamá, ¿por qué no me quieres, no estoy muerta, estoy aquí?" (29) [Mom, why don't you love me? I am not dead; I am here]. The resemblance to the sex symbol and Hollywood icon Marilyn Monroe is patent. Monroe also was not raised by her mother because of her mental disability: schizophrenia. According to her biographer J.R Taraborelli:

> Norma Jean was a helpless infant who had entered this world without any form of welcome. There was no freshly furnished nursery awaiting her, no tiny wardrobe, and in fact no one on earth whose future plans included her. She spent the first few days of her life simply being sustained, not nurtured [18].

Monroe was a burden for her mother, one that needed to be unloaded, and the lack of mother care and love haunted Monroe all her life. The hypotext reference is clear and the search for her mother in the story resounds not only physically but also metaphorically in the impact of their abandonment upon Monroe and upon the fictional protagonist, Mary.

Mary's mother commits suicide in Mazatlán, as is stated by the second person narrator speaking directly to the reader, when describing her fate and her relationship with her sisters: "Murió poco después, se arrojó a las vías del tren en un pequeño pueblo de México. Después supe que, tras su muerte, ella les dejó la tienda a sus hermanas. La historia de Cenicienta, ¿no le parece?" (115) [She died shortly after; she threw herself on the train tracks in a little town in Mexico. After that, I learned, as her mother died, she left the shop to her sisters. The story of Cinderella, don't you think?]. The street and town names related to Mary's mother suggest a further comment on the relationship between mother and daughter. They lived in Union Street and the town in Mexico was allegedly named El cajón (the box) which is a slang word for casket. The name Unión speaks for itself, as Mary and her mother were always apart.

There are two princes in this version of Cinderella: the aforementioned

Goran Granovich and Mardon. Mardon is Mary's ex-lover, who is driving her in the search for her mother. Mardon is of Slavic origin and often comments on his experience as an outsider in conversations with Mary, with whom he shares this same sentiment: "-Cuando uno no tiene familia puede sentirse muy solo en estas fechas—le dice a Mardon. [...] -Créeme, uno puede sentirse muy solo en Navidad" (44). [When one does not have a family one can feel very lonely during the holidays—Mardon says (...)— Believe me, one can feel very lonely at Christmas]. Both share the feeling of solitude, Mardon for his condition of foreignness and Mary feels also she is an outsider, a solitary person since she was born. Mary sometimes uses alternative name to refer to these two "princes": Goran and Mardon are sometimes called Guy, Phillip or Felipe. Goran is a film director who discovers Mary as an actress as a teenager and takes her with him to Rome. They become lovers and Mary initiates her successful career as a film star. Goran is an intellectual, and Mary's relationship with him is mainly superficial. He treats her like a beautiful doll, as a sexual object with no will. As a successful and famous film director, he is pursued by many women and the narrator states: "acudían a él en manadas, las más mundanas, también las más sumisas y recatadas, y por supuesto las más ignorantes, cuanto más ignorantes mejor" (20) [women would come to him in droves, the most mundane, and the most submissive and demure, and of course the most ignorant, the more ignorant, the better].

Goran appreciates when Mary does not oppose or question any of his demands and/or requests and expresses it repeatedly. In contrast, Mardon is a technician whom she meets in the film studios. Mardon, according to Mary, is brutish and has no manners but is sincere and blunt. She describes both men as being violent but in a different way, and for this reason she is afraid of both. At some point in the story, however, Mary suggests that Mardon has been invented by her. It remains an open question whether Mardon has been produced by Mary's imagination in order to have a companion in her mother's search, or if he actually exists. Mardon and Goran are often mentioned interchangeably, as if they were one. The narrator says:

> Tal vez es así porque ese Mardon de rostro esculpido a hachazos que conduce concentrado en la carretera lo ha inventado ella. O quizás sea al otro, quizás es el Mardon inocente y puro al que ha inventado y este otro, el Mardon cruel, hambriento y despiadado es real [93].
>
> Perhaps that is the way it is because that Mardon, with the aquiline face who drives focused on the road has been invented by her. Or perhaps it is the other, maybe the innocent Mardon is the one she invented, and this one, the cruel, hungry and ruthless Mardon, is real.

8. *Suicidal Cinderella:* Cenicienta en Pensilvania

Mardon is the prince that appears more often and active in the narrative but the question remains whether he is nonexistent and created by her desire to have a companion. Another prince, Guy, is mentioned and emerges only once in the narrative in a conversation between Mary and Rita, a friend who asks Mary about her relationship with Guy. According to this encounter, Guy, it is suggested, is a married man and cannot formalize his relationship with Mary. It is implied that Guy is another name for Mardon. This ambiguity shows that any of Mary's lovers are one or none since the impact they have on her emotional state is almost the same.

Solitude is another source of pain and an emotion that Mary attempts to combat without success. She recounts how loneliness has been part of her life since she was a baby. Going from one foster home to another, while seeing her mother occasionally and intermittently, has molded her character. Mary is surrounded by a multitude of fans, colleagues, acquaintances and admirers but her loneliness is immense. As her solitude embraces her, she tries to fight the sentiment to no avail and even tries a strategy to have company. Mary constantly expresses her fear of being alone and jokingly says that she colors her hair from red to blonde with the purpose of not being in solitude: "Pero Mary era así, dijo que se proponía ser rubia porque siendo rubia no había la menor posibilidad de estar sola" (16) [But Mary was like that. She was determined to be blonde, because being blonde would eliminate the possibility of ever being alone]. Ironically, her hair color change does not prevent her from being solitary and sad. The Hollywood sex symbol is treated as an object with no agency or will and is constantly asked to just "try to be sexy" (Bowyer 140) just as Monroe was in her lifetime. According to Justin Bowyer's recount, British actor and Monroe's co-star, Laurence Olivier, publicly humiliated Monroe by also uttering the same command.

Her loneliness and the silence that it produces horrifies Mary, who finds that lack of sound extremely agonizing: "sola, en su apartamento, la cabeza le retumba de tanta calma" (140) [Alone in her apartment, her head resounds with so much calm]. Solitude and quietness are fearful sentiments for Mary. She is terrorized by this "música macabra" (140) (macabre music) as the narrator poetically calls absolute silence. She yearns for a conversation with somebody as the quietness of her apartment invades her more and more with the implication that death is also surrounded by silence and seclusion. On the last day of her life, she desperately calls one of her lovers, Phillip, and offers to be "alegre, muy alegre […] prometiste que si me portaba bien y no lloraba, vendrías hoy. Y no estoy llorando. No lloro. ¿Lo ves? Te prometo que si vienes estaré alegre y desenfadada" (143) [happy, very happy (...) you promised you would come if I behaved and did not cry, that you would come today. I am not crying. I do not cry. You see it? I promise you that if you come I will be happy and carefree]. However, Phillip never comes and she is left alone and at the edge at which she feels that there is no other way out but death.

Mary herself identifies with being weak both mentally and emotionally. Goran repeatedly calls Mary "La princesa del guisante" and even Mary herself identifies with this name. La princesa del guisante alludes to *The Princess and the Pea* (1846), a famous folk tale by Hans Christian Andersen, which depicts extreme delicacy and sensitivity as the main quality of a princess. According to the story, the prince is searching for a "real princess" and his bride will be the most sensitive and delicate girl. The selected bride would be the girl who can feel a pea at the bottom of twenty mattresses. This physical reaction will prove her fragility as the pea will bruise her body.

Mary on the other hand has suffered and faced hardships in her life but is ironically compared to a princess who is wounded by a pea or a feather (Italian version of the tale). In her second and this time successful suicide attempt, Mary looks at herself in the mirror after swallowing various sleeping pills and says: "-¿Sabes lo que te digo? Se dirigió al espejo con desdén. -¡Adiós, princesa del guisante!" [You know what I tell you? She glanced at the mirror with disdain. Bye, Pea Princess!]. In other words, Mary perceives that the suicidal act is her final abandonment of herself and for this reason her surrender and final act of weakness.

The flight of Cinderella from the ball at midnight is also present in this story. In the traditional versions, the flight is done for fear of the reverse transformation into her poor garments in front of the prince. The metamorphosis from a beautiful noble aristocratic dame to a poor peasant is the central motive that the protagonist in most versions tries to prevent. In *Cenicienta en Pensilvania,* Mary's connection with midnight is made while she is in the car with Mardon looking for her mother. The clock at midnight will indicate the advent of a new year. The physical transformation of Cinderella/Mary is also made patent in that year, as she foresees her destiny in an internal focalization and stream of consciousness while she looks through the car window: "Se imagina el año nuevo como un obsceno monstruo bíblico, una masa de músculos brillante y roja, oculto tras la siguiente curva, agazapado en la oscuridad y listo para saltar sobre ellos y lanzarse a su persecución" (94) [She imagines the New Year as an obscene biblical monster, a mass of shiny and red muscles, hidden behind the next curve, lurking in the darkness, ready to jump on them and to pursue them]. The monster that she foresees is evidently the approaching end of her young life.

Mary flees as well. As her alter ego, Marilyn Monroe, Mary also puts an end to her own existence. She experiences, as in the traditional versions, a physical transformation but this time a permanent one. A personified death is waiting for her that year. In contrast to all Cinderella versions around the world, this protagonist's transformation is final and without any more alteration. The doctor who helps Mary to have an abortion notices her sudden change: "Aunque poseía esa hermosura que uno contempla en dos, a lo sumo, en tres ocasiones a lo largo de su vida, su rostro, su organismo entero, parecía haber sufrido una profunda transformación. Era como si se hubiese marchitado" (77) [Even though she possessed that beauty that one only sees on two or at the most three occasions in your life, her face, her entire organism, seems to have suffered a profound transformation. It was like if she had wilted]. The transformation is abrupt and terminal with no regression to the original self, when Mary commits suicide just like her mother did. Cinderella flees toward her final destiny.

Mary's suicide would fall into Durkheim's category of egotistic suicide, which suicide results from the "lack of integration of the individual in society" (14). The poor support and void in Mary's family circle leads to and promotes her perception that she lacks validity as a person. In her case is not only a period in her life but it is pervasive and a continuum from birth to adulthood. Durkheim claims that society also tends to regulate individuals and impose invisible demands on them. In the case of Mary, she is constrained to one single role: the ornamental woman who needs to smile and agree to the needs of others. The correlation between the social phenomena and the personal is decisive for an individual/group inclination to suicide. In the case of Mary/Marilyn Monroe the two areas, the personal and the collective, align in what is "expected in a given type of society" (16). According to Durkheim, suicide discloses a profound crisis in a modern society and its inability to integrate individuals in a personal and collective realm. Mary as a child is only intermittently assimilated to a family as a foster child of many families. As an adult, Mary is required to perform a role not only as an actress but as a woman. She is subject to the demands of her career as the sex symbol that she is and that is the only role she is required to perform. In the private realm, Mary also performs her acting persona by pleasing lovers and agreeing to their requests or demands. The narrator says about Mary: "Al final solo la arrastran con ellos por un largo túnel de oscuridad y vértigo, retorciendo sus muñecas y atrayéndola y alejándola de sí, depreciando su cuerpo una vez satisfechos, arrastrándolo por el largo y tenebroso túnel negro del que luego es tan difícil salir" (50). [At the end, they (men) only drag her through a long dark tunnel causing her vertigo, twisting her wrists, pulling and pushing her, depreciating her body once they are satisfied, dragging her body through the long dark somber tunnel from which it is so difficult to get out].

The ending of the novel implies Mary's suicide, after the third person omniscient narrator relates how Mary feels in her last moments: "Siente en sus muslos un lamento, un vértigo, una pena. Hay un cielo de plomo, y por encima de su cabeza, un zumbido, un sonido como de cientos de cables de alta tensión sonando a la vez" (147). [She feels a lament, a vertigo, a sorrow in her legs. There is a sky of lead, and over her head, a buzzing sound, a sound as if hundreds of high voltage cables were sounding at the same time]. Again the focalization is taken away from her, which is part of her experience in life. Right after Mary's death, the story turns into the dramatic-cinematic genre mode as in the beginning of the novel. It describes the environment in the Cathedral of Our Mother (Catedral Nuestra Señora), the doors are opened and there is a multitude waiting for the bride and groom. The metanarrative esthetic continues and makes itself clear: "La música sube y la voz del cantante va superponiéndose despacio al sonido de la película, mientras el título *The End* aparece en sobreimpresión" (148) [The music is louder and the singer's voice is subtly superimposed on the sound of the film, while the title The End appears on the screen]. The transcription of the song indicates and summarizes Mary's life metaphorically. It refers to her solitude surrounded by many followers/fans and her final destiny. The ending lines of the lyrics state: "Y cuando el campanario dice: 'Buenas noches, duerme bien,' nosotros le damos las gracias al pequeño y maravilloso hotel" (149) [And when the bells say: Good night, sleep well, we give thanks to the small and marvelous hotel].

The last paragraph goes back to the movie-narration film/recount and the beginning of the story: "Coincidiendo con los últimos acordes, travelling de la cámara desciende hasta situarse tras los novios. Primer plano de los pies de ella. Como la princesa del cuento, calza un zapato caro de tacón en uno de sus pies. El otro, está descalzo" (149). [Coinciding with the last music chords, the tracking camera descends to show the groom and bride. Close up of the bride's feet. Like the princess in the fairy tales, she wears an expensive high heeled shoe on one of her feet. The other one is bare]. This last segment attempts to give the image of a woman (Mary and her alter ego Monroe) and of many others, who are surrounded by people at some stage of their lives. However, they are only actors (literally and allegorically) whose lives are engulfed by a huge void. The lost shoe at the beginning and ending of the story creates the idea of continuation and circular motion in the context of the Cinderella story. This gap and lack is constant and recurrent suggesting that the folktale happy ending resounds another culturally created image, which is nevertheless false.

This singular portrayal of the Cinderella character presents the limitations and a darker but inevitable and inexorable side of life. In contrast to the happy ending of many rewritings, *Cenicienta en Pensilvania* depicts the pain and suffering to the limits in the protagonist. This suicidal Cinderella version uses film esthetic and rhetorical mechanical devices to express the feelings of emptiness and bareness as one more aspect of Cinderella's vital experience.

CHAPTER 9

Idiotizadas: Comics, Folktales and Feminism in Spain

Comics as a form of text offer the reader another style of narrative. Similar to picture books, the images and illustrations are central to this medium. As Scott McCloud, among others, observes, the iconography (the images used to represent people, places, things or ideas) which is an essential part of this genre enables a more fluid communication between the reader and the text (26–31). For this reason, the popularity of comics has grown over the years, captivating audiences that find more appeal in a story told with visuals. Unlike solely written narratives, in comics, image and word are linked automatically in the text and without much need of a complicated cognitive process or abstraction that some literature demands. It is perhaps for this reason that comics were highly controversial in the fifties, when their popularity arose. In some extreme cases in the United States and Europe, the depiction of violence and horror in comics was accused of being the cause of "juvenile delinquency" (Barker 14). Nowadays this argument might appear absurd, but every epoch and era has had a similar contention. Video games are now identified as the promoters of violence at a point that it became unlawful in California to sell certain video games to minors without parental supervision (Xiaolu Zhang 2011). However, when the law was challenged in the Supreme court it was declared unconstitutional because it breached the First Constitutional Amendment.

On one side of a discussion about the negative impact of comics is an assumption that comics are triggers of immediate emotions and affective reactions. As such, they could also cause eruptive and uncontrolled rage in adolescents and youngsters and thus lead them to violent acts. On the other side stands an argument that the comic's genre is, on the contrary, a sophisticated form of art. Eisner, for example, affirms that the pictography equals language and for this reason "should be considered literature" (5). Erin La Cour, on the other hand, attempts to establish that comics should be considered "minor literature" and escape from the literary scholarly realm by establishing its own textual niche (79–89). However, La Cour only bases her discussion on three works that fit Deleuze and Guattari's principles of "minor literature." I would like to argue that since the general definition of literature implies the use of words in a work, in this sense comics and other texts (written) are literature but they are not necessarily and not in all cases literary works.

The ongoing debate about the literariness of comics and the aesthetic quality of the genre is global. In fact, in the prologue of *Tebeos: los primeros 100 años* (1996) Antonio Lara, the chief of the Comic's History Exhibit at the National Library in Madrid, anticipates the possible public reaction to the exhibition. Lara states:

> Es posible que algunos visitantes de esta exposición se pregunten con cierta extrañeza, cómo es posible que la Biblioteca Nacional de España, símbolo del sistema bibliotecario español y médula del saber de nuestro pueblo, se atreva a ofrecer una muestra sobre el centenario de los humildes tebeos [19].
>
> It is possible that some visitors would wonder how it is possible that the National Library in Spain, the symbol of the library system and the axis of the knowledge of our people would dare to offer a showcase on the one hundred years of this humble genre.

Nevertheless, literariness weighs on the complexity and "poetic aspect" of the text and by implication its capacity and richness for analysis and study. Any form of art that is prone or permeable to multiple or multilayered readings is in fact poetic. *Idiotizadas*, by Moderna de Pueblo (pen name of Raquel Córcoles), which is the main text of analysis in this chapter, belongs to the comic book genre and is susceptible to deep tiers of analysis. One aspect that stands out and is the reason for choosing it as part of this volume is its polyvocality in relation to its depiction of folktale heroines. This sole condition of hypertextuality makes it possible to have a thread of study and critical analysis in any text. The most important aspect for an analysis of *Idiotizadas* is indeed this condition which brings it into dialog and coexistence with other texts, and in particular its allusions to "Cinderella" in order to parody certain societal structures.

In Spain, the comic's tradition dates from the eighteenth century when images with text were carved on wooden-sheets. The most important cities that published Comics were Barcelona and Madrid. Valencia was a third center, but, according to Antonio Martín, it mainly published: "literatura de cordel, aleluyas y todos aquellos impresos provenientes de la estampería tradicional" (12). [string literature, hallelujahs and all these texts derived from the traditional print shop]. Later on, comics were printed in newspapers and popular magazines, as the famous *TBO, Macaco, Pocholo, Chiquitín*, among others, and were mainly directed to a juvenile audience. Other comics in newsweekly publications in Barcelona were the popular *Patufet*, also for children. *La Rondalla del Dijous*, for instance, was a "comic" that printed short stories from Spanish and foreign authors, among them the stories of European and Latin American authors such as the Russian Leon Tolstoi, the Danish Hans Christian Andersen or the Chilean Gabriela Mistral.[1]

According to Antonio Martín, the first example of "historieta" or a comic published in Spanish newspapers was "Un drama desconocido" ["An unknown drama"], which appeared in *Los Niños* magazine in January of 1875 by an unknown author. The themes of the first comics in Spain varied from political satires, short stories, historical events, folk traditions to children's stories and others. One of the most renowned and popular comics' artists of nineteenth century Spain was the Barcelonian Apeles Mestres. His surreal and deep illustrations and comics were published in newspapers. An example of his work is the publication "Cuento lúgubre," which is characteristically charged with his ideological position, satirizing the Catholic church and using a very subtle and complex style depicting the Zeitgeist of his time.

Another prominent figure in the Spanish comics tradition was Eduardo Sáenz Hermúa, who published under the pseudonym Mecachis. In 1884 Sáenz was the director and founder of the newsweekly *La Caricatura*. Like Mestres, Mecachis used sophisticated techniques for his illustrations and experimented with various shot frames that subjectivized the narrative. For instance, his well-known comic strip, "El día de la boda" [The Wedding Day] is a visceral and intelligent criticism of the Spanish bourgeois customs and traditions of the epoch. In Spain, during the Civil War, comics engaged in the conflict by taking the side of the Nationalists or Republicans. The Comic strip "El pueblo en armas" appeared in the magazine *Pocholo* (n/p), which depicted republicans as heroes but without simplistic identification of good and bad sides. After the war, the comic "Las aventuras milicianas del terrible Paco Lara" would depict the defeated group as dirty, lazy, cowardly and/or stupid (Martín 276). Such examples of ideology ingrained in comics might be compared with the renowned work of Art Spiegelman in the eighties. His groundbreaking Comic *Maus* depicts mice as Jews and cats as Germans as a historical revision of World War II. For his outstanding work, Spiegelman was the first Comic artist to be awarded the Pulitzer Prize in 1992.

Critics such as De Vos and Ana Merino affirm that background cultural knowledge affects how readers understand comics. They also state that the genre constitutes a reflection of modernity. For this reason, audiences find comics based on folktales easier to understand. The stories told in these narratives are part of a traditional literary background and employ as a foundation and main reference a well-known and world-wide recognized story.

Folktale tradition has grown increasingly in importance for anthropologists, sociologists and cultural analysts because they convey the particularity of the populace from which they originate. Comics based on folktale tradition are a cultural trace and imprint of their social space. According to De Vos, folktales and comics have much in common:, "both the comic book and the oral tale depend on dialogue and tone of voice, body language and gestures, and timing for an effective experience for the audience" (1). Vos' connection clearly shows the origin of fairy tales, which come *per excellence* from the oral tradition, which is one of the reasons why there is no original version of the ancient, globally known fairy tales such as "Cinderella," "Little Red Riding Hood," "Sleeping Beauty" and others. Folklorists have identified numerous versions, but despite speculation it is impossible to determine a specific hypotext. The implication for adaptation of a folktale in the comics genre is that as the oral tradition evolves from one version to another each version adds its own local, regional, philosophical and, in many instances, personal imprints, situations and experiences to the new retelling.

The history of comics in Spain took a new turn in the seventies, eighties and nineties after the death of Franco and the subsequent democratization of the country. Only then and in the incipient democracy it became possible for new themes to emerge in comics that broke with old schemes and ideological messages. The representation of feminist concerns in comics, for instance, was scarce at this time. María Antonia Díez Balda describes in her article on Comics and Feminism the null portrayal of strong women in this genre. Diez Balda, however, highlights and mentions that Nuria Pompeia was one of the few artists to denounced the patriarchal system in their work. Her comics are considered precursors in the defense of women's liberties and denouncers of sexism in Spain in the early seventies (2).

With the newly acquired liberty, comics authors started experimenting with innovative formulas and began to explore not only political and cultural satire but also the historically banned theme of erotism and sexuality (Lara, *Tebeos Catálogo de la Biblioteca Nacional* 49). One of the most famous collections of Spanish erotica in comics was *Lola, el más gracioso personaje sexy del cómic* [Lola, the funniest and sexiest comic character] by Íñigo. Coincidentally, at that time the Italian porno-comics were popular also in Spain as they depicted classic folktale characters such as Cinderella, Snow White and Pinocchio but altered the traditional stories to give them a humorous sexual innuendo (Lara 144).

Idiotizadas[2] is the most recent depiction of Cinderella and another three main characters in the folktale tradition in Spanish: "Snow White," "Sleeping Beauty," and Andersen's *The Little Mermaid*. The book belongs to the comics genre and parodies the popular stories that have been told and ingrained in societal behaviors historically. Most traditional versions around the world depict submissive, passive and vulnerable protagonists. The title *Idiotizadas* is a play on words in Spanish; instead of "Encantadas" [Enchanted] used in the fairy tale convention, it replaces, and parodies, the past participle by changing it to "Idiotizadas" [Idioticized]. Parody plays a central role in this depiction of Cinderella and the other fairy tale characters in relation to the context of Feminism in Spain.

Idiotizadas is divided into eight sections and one introductory chapter. The introductory part offers an overview-commentary on the mores and morals of Spanish society in the fifties and sixties. Each one of the following chapters contains and describes a "Hechizo" [Spell] or a cultural fable turned into a spell with particular application to women. In other words, the text connects a "Spell" to each of the myths about female and male behavior that have permeated society through the fairy tale stories and characters.

The first folktale character and protagonist, who sets the story in motion, is Sleeping Beauty, who has left her home town to live in the big city, presumably Madrid. She is tired of her life in the provinces and wishes to escape from their people's narrow idiosyncratic mind frames. Looking for adventure and "modernity," as she calls it, she establishes herself in the urban section. In the city, she meets other women, including Cinderella, who becomes her roommate and friend. These encounters among the fairytale characters unfold the story of each women and is the medium to show how their personal situations reflect a certain "Spell" or a specific aspect entrenched, internalized and repeated culturally in society.

The part of the book dedicated to Cinderella covers the "Hechizo #3"

[Spell 3] which reads: "¡Si dejas tu cuerpo tocar, en zorra te convertirás!" ["If you let your body be touched, into a hooker you will turn"]. The spell encompasses the common theme of a double standard that the social environment has created and has imposed upon men and women. Hechizo 3 is better understood in the context of the introductory chapter, in which the story of another fairytale character and her mother is told. Sleeping Beauty begins the narration of the story of her family with the opening formula conventional in fairy tale: "Érase una vez..." [Once upon a time]. She recounts the experience of her recently divorced mother and her hardships as she learns how to cope with the life-change situation of a divorcee.

The timeframe of the story indicates that her mother was born in the fifties or sixties during Franco's regime. Her societal background, a legal system assembled within a patriarchal order, placed extreme restrictions upon women. Arbitrary and partial laws were created to restrict women's liberties. For example, according to the Spanish law of the time, the legal age for a woman to be a responsible adult was 25. Before this age, a woman was under the strict rule of her father and then, when married, under the supervision of her husband. Women were not allowed to inherit property and the rules on social conduct were even more rigid. Adultery by women was penalized as a crime but laws were much more relaxed for men who would commit adultery. There were a number of restrictions under the Spanish penal code and punitive laws were created, supported and promoted against women's rights (Caballé 236).

It is already particularly striking for a woman who was raised during Franco's regime to be divorced, when the stigma of a divorced woman was present. In Franco's era, Carmen Martín Gaite recalls, "el divorcio no existía, era cosa de rojos" (*Courtship Customs* 23) [divorce did not exist; it was something for the reds (progressivists)]. After the victory of Franco in 1939, divorce was abolished, and was only restored in 1981 by Law 30 of the Spanish Penal Code. Legally a woman could divorce her husband in the eighties but the shadow of contempt was still present. This initial story subtly depicts the Francoist era model for women and subsequent generations in which women's only goal and source of economic independence from their parental household was marriage.

The narrator, Sleeping Beauty, states how her mother was raised and how she, in turn, raised her. Cleaning, sewing, cooking were the essential activities for women. It was common practice to criticize and shame women who would not follow these and other invisible but present rules. That getting married was the only goal in life for a woman was the tradition in these years, and folktales clearly echo this paradigm. Women's roles were so constrained especially in the versions and adaptations of the popular folktales between the sixteenth century and the fin-de-siècle. The well-known versions of Perrault, the Grimms and others represent female protagonists who are constantly saved by a male prince, suitor, hunter or lover. For instance, the ultimate goal of Cinderella's sisters and Cinderella herself is to attend the ball and have the opportunity to meet and perhaps marry the prince. In Franco's era, this parameter and expectation for women was constant and palpable. In *Usos amorosos de la posguerra española* [Courtship Customs], Carmen Martín Gaite explains:

> Even before the war had ended, a 1938 ministerial order let it be known that the program of family restoration was based mainly on young Spanish women's giving up their silly notions about emancipation. It proclaimed "the intention of the new State [is] for women to devote their attention to the home and leave their jobs" [50].

Contrary to the expectations and mores within which she was raised, Sleeping Beauty's mother finds herself divorced and struggling to survive without the economic support of a husband. She, then, becomes conscious of her unequal upbringing and how her male siblings were raised under completely different approaches and advantages. Sleeping Beauty's mother realizes a decisive factor about her family background and questions her parents with a rhetorical inquiry: "¿Por qué a nuestros hermanos les pagaron unos buenos estudios y les ayudaron a montar un negocio y a nosotras ¡Nada! ¡A casarnos y ya!" (s/n) [Why did they pay for a good education for our brothers and help them to set up a business and to us, (women) nothing! Get married and that's it!].

According to Pilar Folguera, it is only recently that autonomy and independence for women in Spain is founded upon a solid academic background. This change of attitude was only developed recently within the three past decades in the 1990s and twenty-first century (188). In Folguera's study, Spanish women in the current century link their economic independence to their professional career and capacity to support themselves. Sleeping Beauty's mother belongs to a generation of women whose role in society was limited to the private sphere as caregivers, homemakers, and child-bearers, because professional education for women was seen as an unattractive attribute. As the popular Spanish saying went: "mujer que sabe latín, no encuentra marido ni tiene buen fin" [a woman who knows Latin will not find a husband or have a good end]. This popular aphorism is used as a title in an Anthology of essays by Mexican writer Rosario Castellanos, who represents in it the patriarchal sentiment toward education and women.

Not only the restrictions of education and legal equality for women

9. Idiotizadas: Comics, Folktales and Feminism in Spain 131

were immense obstacles for their development in society, there were also highly restrictive expectations regarding women's sexual conduct. Sleeping Beauty's mother was born during the heyday of Franco's regime, whose morals put a strong emphasis on purity and chastity. The regime was linked to the Catholic church and the morals and dogmas about women's sexuality created a highly sexually oppressive environment.

Sleeping Beauty raised by her conservative mother is also taught to be pure as the paradigm of the Virgin Mary was the one to follow. Especially under Franco, the example of the Christian virgin mother (even though it might be seen as an oxymoron) and its role as a reproductive agent without sexuality was the standard. Sleeping Beauty is told by her mother to make herself respectable and "respected" (respetada) by men and commands her to emulate her own conduct by waiting until marriage to experience her sexuality. Being "pure" until marriage was the social mandate. Her mother, consequently and logically, was a virgin when she married. Paradoxically, affirms Ana Caballé, this ideology encouraged hypocrisy and double moral standard that promoted and tolerated prostitution as a clear consequence. The very popular and frequented brothels were euphemistically called "Casas de tolerancia" [Tolerance houses] (240). In relation to this fact, one of the most important rules was indeed to avoid being called a *puta* [whore] and/or to maintain a profile and conduct that would never attract that horrific, morally charged label: "algo nada fácil para una mujer" [something not easy for a woman], retorts Sleeping Beauty.

Contrary to all odds, even though Sleeping Beauty's behavior adhered to the morals demanded as part of her upbringing as a young girl, she recalls being called a whore for the first time when she was a freshman in high school. What triggered this crushing insult was that she received a present from two boys for Valentine's Day. Each of her two classmates gave her a rose as a gift. For this reason, the girls in her classroom spread the rumor that she was a "puta" (whore) because she received this unexpected double Valentine present. She was petrified and upset and did not understand the reason why she was being insulted and bullied. In any case, even though she did not comprehend the logic of it, she determined from that day on to do everything in her power to adjust to the morality of the group, whether she found it just or not. From that episode forward, Sleeping Beauty made every effort to avoid being called that feared and diminishing name again. In any case, she remembers sadly, men would always find a way to call her some other derogatory term related to her sexual performance. For instance, she recalls being labeled with the very vulgar term "calienta-pollas" [cock-teaser] because she avoids having intercourse with her occasional dates.

She was very cautious about her reputation as she was growing up, and when she reached her adolescent years Sleeping Beauty decided to only have sexual relationships for the first time at the acceptable age of seventeen and with a boyfriend who she had been dating for at least a year. That was the common societal rule for a "good girl" of her generation, an advance from what her mother had lived, but still restricted only to women's behavior. The fear of being called derogatory names was the central motive in her decision to follow the demanded practice in society. In this way, she would avoid being judged and/or criticized according to her conduct. Because of these standards, it was known that men expected women to be shy, sweet and inexperienced in sex related themes. Sleeping Beauty wants to follow that common assumption and decides that, with the boys she dates, she will pretend to be ignorant about issues related to sex. Especially and in particular, she stresses this practice with the boyfriend with whom she plans to "lose her virginity." Sleeping Beauty recalls telling her boyfriend that she was "naive" about sex and knew nothing about it. Therefore, the suitor would never think she was a "loose girl" or "guarra" [dirty]. She falsely performed the act of being innocent and pure complying with the expectations of a woman in society.

The name-calling for women is used, as depicted in the story, as a weapon to restrain women's liberty and keep them scared to be judged by society. Sleeping Beauty evokes the day she moves to the city and meets her roommate Cinderella (Zorricienta) seven years ago. Zorricienta works at a radio station and has her own radio show with an emblematic and auto referential name: "Empoderhada Madrina" [Empowered fairy godmother]. Her show consists of receiving phone calls from the audience who consult her about their relationships and personal issues, as she comments and reflects on the particular situation of each of her callers. She is a modern, liberal woman with an open mind about life and her role in it as a person with autonomy and freedom. As Zorricienta and Sleeping Beauty become closer, Zorricienta tells her roommate the story about how she turned herself into a woman who rebels against conventions and false moral preconceptions.

When Zorricienta was sixteen and still named Cenicienta, she was invited to a party. As the story goes, the girl does not have the proper garments to attend the festive event. A mouse in the house advices her about a website on YouTube called Fashion-Hada [Fairy Godmother Fashion], that she can use to obtain her outfit for the night. In seconds, the Fashion-Hada through a spell gives Cenicienta a new outfit and hair style and through

9. Idiotizadas: Comics, Folktales and Feminism in Spain 133

tele transportation sends her to the prince's ball. Once at the party, Cenicienta is approached by the most handsome guy in the high school or "El buenorro del insti" [The hottie of the high school]. She spends time chatting with him even though she finds him extremely stupid, but sexy. "En menos de media hora ya se estaban comiendo la pista. Y al poco rato ya se estaban comiendo los morros" [In less than an hour, they were the hottest couple on the dance floor and a little later they were devouring each other kissing]. As happens in the traditional "Cinderella" version, a transformation takes place at midnight. This time it was not "Cinderella's" clothes and carriage but the attitude of the crowd at the party that changed and turned into a group of judgmental men and women. Both alike and in unison they call Cinderella derogatory names as "Zorra" [Whore]. Cenicienta was perplexed and starts sobbing in front of them, sad, embarrassed and in despair. When she is about to leave the party, ashamed and confused, she goes back to another room within the ball's facilities and is surprised to see "the prince" surrounded by men and women. The same crowd that was insulting and calling her names is around the "prince" in a state of devotion. He is sitting in a throne-like chair with the name "Fucker" inscribed on the chair and above his head as he proudly smiles to the crowd of admirers.

The prince is praised, lauded and applauded because of his romantic encounter and the recent "scoring" with Cinderella at the ballroom. Cinderella observes carefully the situation as she wipes the tears from her eyes; she enters the room and looking at all of them says in an exclamatory tone: "Así que yo soy un putón, pero él es un triunfador" [So, I am a big whore while he is a winner]. She has an epiphany and realizes at that precise moment that she does not want to marry "the/a prince, she wants to be like him!!" as Cenicienta yells humorously.

Cinderella becomes Zorricienta by playing with the words Zorra and Cenicienta and appropriating the derogatory name used to diminish her. She takes the name and uses it in a way to redeem it. Zorra in Spain and other Spanish speaking countries connote women's promiscuity and sexual lewdness. It is a negative marker which labels and judges women's sexual performance and at the same time classifies them. On the other hand, *zorra*, or female fox, in English slang indicates an extremely attractive, cunning and untrustworthy woman. A fox is a small but wild animal with a reddish fur and "amber eyes" (ARAS *The Book* 278) that possesses an elusive nature. Comparing both meanings of the word, the English connotation of fox is also negative but is not related to women's sexuality and performance in particular.

The fox is a canine known for its ability to erase its own footprints to misguide predators (Caspari 111). According to popular legends, foxes ambush their victims by imitating the sounds of other animals to attract them and kill them. The connection with the insult for women is obvious as they are perceived as a shrewd predator of men. Nevertheless, along with these characteristics, foxes are also distinguished by their dexterity to break barriers and survive. In this context, the name Zorricienta not only connotes the negativity attributed in society to a concupiscent woman but it also entails the connotation of a fighter who confronts her environment. After this eye-opening episode at the ball, Zorricienta reflects upon her attitude towards the "rules" applied to male-female relationships and changes, evolving into a free person. She tells Sleeping Beauty that after having fun with all the boys in the town, she leaves and goes on to live her life in the city. The party scene exposes the extremely sexist and patriarchal basis of the sexual model, which triggers the protagonist to confront it and change.

In adopting the pen name "Moderna de Pueblo," Raquel Córcoles exploits the adjective "moderna" [modern] to reflect the change which occurred in the early twentieth century in the situation of women in Spanish society. As Susan Kirkpatrick points out, "la Mujer Moderna independiente e intrépida, quien, con su cabello a lo garçon y su falda corta, se negaba a aceptar las restricciones tradicionales que mantenían a la mujer española fuera de las universidades, las profesiones, y los espacios públicos" (9) [The modern woman independent and daring, wearing a garçon style and a mini skirt, would reject accepting the traditional restrictions that kept Spanish women away from the universities and professional spaces].

This modern transformation of the Cinderella character parodies the components of the tale. The comic as the genre used for this version is in the words of Bakthin the "hero of the parody" (51) as it breaks the mold of the known source and instantiates a new one. Simon Dentith (2000), Linda Hutcheon (1985) and Margaret Rose (1993) have conceptualized parody as a form that intervenes in forming a new inflection to a work. Hutcheon perceives parody as an ironic inversion of any work of art which always takes a "critical distance" (7) in "revisiting, replaying, inverting and trans-contextualizing previous works" (11). In an innovative and current engagement with the actual discourse of women, this version parodies the tale and invests a new meaning, a new objective into the story. The comic uses the motifs of the shoe, the ball and the prince to invert and convolute the paradigm of the princess in search of husband. Zorricienta, the pejorative epithet she adopts and appropriates, stands for what the protagonist believes. The elements of the story are preserved but are turned upside down to depict the current digital era which combines the modernity of media (internet) and the antiquity of ideologies regarding women's sexuality and performance as sexual beings. In this comic's rewritings, the text reuses the main plot but uproots its foundations in a jocose and comedic recount.

Since parody's function is to connote irony or satire, the story of Zorricienta is a comprehensive picture of a woman's creation of a new self-freed from stigmas and constructed roles. This formula produces a comic with a "comic" effect as among various humorous changes to the traditional story it transforms the fairy godmother into "Fashion-Hada," the prince into a mediocre Don Juan, and the hosts of the ball into ordinary gossipers. The fairy godmother, for instance, appears on the screen from a subscription to a YouTube channel. Once Zorricienta is registered and connected, the godmother "Fashion-Hada" offers her a spell to change her clothes, shoes, hair and makeup:

> ¡Para un buen outfit llevar, de mí te debe fiar, fuera esos harapos que solo atraen sapos, un vestidazo que te dé rollazo ... mejor botín bajo que taconazo. Pasada de cuchilla, medias de rejilla ... y un poco de blush en la mejilla. Labio rojo, rabillo en el ojo y solo con verte me mojo!
>
> For a good outfit, you should trust me, get rid of those rags that only attract rats, a striking dress and better boots than high heels, sexy stockings and a little color in the face, a line in the eye and only by looking at you I am already moist!

The distortion of the text has a satirical effect and subsumes the comic as a genre and the comic tone of the story. The mice do not transform into horses in this version but are her advisors and helpers in finding sources to accomplish Cinderella's goal and desire to attend the ball. The encounter with the prince is a straight hit off romance where they start kissing almost immediately after meeting at the party. The ideological travesty of the role of the girl results in the figurative extirpation of an ingrown cultural practice through a playful transformation of the story into a serious and current matter: women's equality and women's freedom.

Transformation is one of the vital aspects of the Cinderella story. In many versions the changes are radical (even death, as discussed above in chap. 8), while in others it reflects the psyche of the protagonist and the encounter with herself and her own identitarian phases. In *Idiotizadas*, the change of Zorricienta implies the notion of finding liberation as unity of being reflected in the internal and external form of her persona as a metamorphosis which in *The Book of Symbols* is defined as "coming about through an intense incubation and release of libido" (ARAS *The Book of Symbols* 774).

Zorricienta defines her own personal and sexual identity for what she is and not for what she represents for these men and women at the party. As Pilar Folguera remarks, twentieth-century women face the persistence of old conventions regarding women's performance of sexuality: "En contexto formalmente igualitario, las mujeres jóvenes deben enfrentarse a la pervivencia de estereotipos sexuales que se reproducen en numerosas facetas de su vida diaria" (189) [In a current context formally egalitarian, young women still face the continuation of sexual stereotypes that are reproduced in various facets of daily life]. The depiction of this constant interpellation in the story reveals the double standard as a chronic and endemic symptom in society even in the twentieth-first century and, naturally, not exclusively in Spain.

The dichotomy between the town mentality and urban progressivist mentality is patent in the story. All four fairy tale characters leave their home town to live in the city. Cinderella, Sleeping Beauty, Little Red Riding Hood and the Little Mermaid decide to escape from the town or "pueblo" as the site of narrowness and provincial discursive reason. Traditionally, progress has not reached into the small towns and for this reason the Pueblo seems to remain untouched and unevolved. In *Idiotizadas, el pueblo* is a space of mental backwardness in contrast to the city as a place where many forms of advance have found their niche. The author's pseudonym reflects the change, as "Modern" displays the advances in her own penself from a rural persona into a mindful independent woman. The town or pueblo shows the wilderness or primitivism within human beings and the small perimeter constricts the space not only physically but mentally. The city is a destination of possibilities, reorientation and remaking. The city in the comic has no name, as this story could happen in any progressive city: "Y aquí estaba ahora, después de 10 años en una gran ciudad *random*" [And there she was now, after ten years in a big random city]. The group of friends move downtown, which is the axis of the city, as the center configures the dwelling place in which to attain another level of consciousness for Cinderella, Sleeping Beauty, and the others, and a centrifugal force for the group of women.

The end of the book shows the four folktale characters: Cinderella [Zorricienta], Snow White [*Gordinieves*/Fat Snow White], The Little Mermaid [*La Sirenita Pescada*/The Caught Little Mermaid], Sleeping Beauty [*La Bella Durmiente—con el reloj biológico* (Sleeping Beauty but with a Dormant Biological Clock)] who have chosen various paths in life based

9. Idiotizadas: Comics, Folktales and Feminism in Spain 137

on their experiences. They have become assertive, independent and free from old myths about women as individuals and sexual beings.

The final illustrations show all women changed and evolved, as the fairytale main protagonists are at the pool spending time together as usual. They have aged as it is shown by their gray hair, and bodies in swimsuits. They are having drinks and are joking about getting old and its normal processes and consequences. One of them, a more matured Zorricienta, asks rhetorically: "¿Quién crees que la palmará primero?" [Who do you guys think will die first?]. Gordinieves in her unequivocal sense of raw and dark humor retorts: "Espero que seas tú, así me quedo con la habitación grande" [I hope it's you, so I can take the bigger bedroom]. This final scene shows that as the characters have matured, they have not changed their happy, defiant and playful attitude towards life.

Provocative and highly disruptive, *Idiotizadas* as a parody blurs the traditional story and creates a more actual and anomalous irreverent version of the folktale. *Idiotizadas* manages to reinvent and dismantle everything that has been written in any version of Cinderella in the Spanish language. The comic presents a refreshing portrayal of the character of Cinderella and the other folktale heroines by imbuing them with progressive structures. Most importantly, the narrative asserts and advocates the unveiling and revelation of a radical transformation in women's self-made destiny as persons and as autonomous individuals in the twenty-first century.

CHAPTER 10

A Poetic Version: *Te cuento ... Cenicienta*

A poet and an ex-politician and professor, Juan Carlos Mestre and Juan Carlos Monedero, are the authors of the 2015 adaptation of Cinderella entitled *Te cuento ... Cenicienta*. This book is part of a collection of fairy tale rewritings by several authors. As Emilio Silva affirms in the presentation of the book in Madrid, these adaptations of famous stories are an attempt to clear away the myths and sempiternal social narratives stagnant in culture and create new ones, different from the "official story." In the words of Mestre, this series aims at "correcting the tale," playing with the double meaning of "cuento" in Spanish to signify both "a tale" and "a made-up story, a lie." The story opens a new discussion and does not reproduce schemas which depend upon old ideas contained in the "official" versions of the tale.

Specifically, the notion of demolishing the well-known story in order to create another more real and current is perceived in this reworking. The tale recounts the Cinderella story by mentioning the protagonist's name in the title and by showing some of the main motifs of the Cinderella story in bits and pieces within a larger narrative. The persecuted girl motif studied by Nicolaisen is evident in the text and the three structural questions he poses are answered, but within a global perspective.[1] The tale is retold almost as digressions and/or as a chorus of a lyrical composition. Cinderella, the stepmother, the father, the ball, the shoe and the prince are recognized in the avalanche of poetry that comes with this highly metaphorical adaptation of the tale. The text consists of two parallel discourses, the graphic (as photographs) and the written, with the effect that fiction and reality are intertwined. *Te cuento ... Cenicienta* is an excellent

10. A Poetic Version: Te cuento ... Cenicienta   139

work with which to conclude this study, as it contains all the concepts and ideas explored in previous chapters.

Remembering versus forgetting, natural vs. man-made structures, hope versus despair are some of the antithetical concepts developed in the first part of the narrative. The genre of the text is charged with ambiguity, but it would possibly be most accurately described as a poetic essay, because it displays themes, ideas and concepts of various kinds in a highly poetic manner. Cinderella incarnates the myriad women around the world, of whom a great variety of examples are mentioned. For instance, Ana de Peralta is reported fighting for the rights of indigenous women in Ecuador, Mouna represents Muslim women, Niara represents Hindi women, or Sharik represents Russian women's struggle—all are involved in contesting what their environments have imposed upon them (9). The lives of women who have been enslaved, victimized, silenced, or rendered invisible intersect throughout the book. Cinderella is not only any women treated unjustly at a particular time but the narrative highlights Cinderella's ubiquity in time and space. Either during the Chinese Empire in the twelfth century, or in a bombarded Berlin in World War II, or an occupied Poland, Cinderellas are present and their voices are muffled historically amongst the hundreds of unknown women who suffered in these historical events.

Cinderella amalgamates a variety of women in strenuous difficulties and experiences. For instance, Cinderella in the story is in the middle of a war and is depicted as a refugee escaping her death by crossing a border from Africa to Europe in the midst of political debates deciding her fate. At the same time, the description of snow falling in Vallecas, an underprivileged neighborhood in Madrid, falling on "la vergüenza de los vivos y la sonrisa inmaculada de los muertos durante la guerra" (8) [the shame of the living and on the immaculate smile of the dead during the war] depicts the cynicism of the war and the final liberation of the victims following their death. It also refers specifically to all the victims who were murdered and buried in a common grave during times of political conflict that tainted Spain and other countries with blood, such as represented in the photographs of Clemente Bernard in the book.[2] The cold and whiteness of the imaged snow described in the narrative seems to touch and dirty everything as it falls onto the ground, which is the landscape inhabited by the multiple Cinderellas in these moments and times.

Nature is the witness in this version of Cinderella. In the face of the devastation caused by wars impacting the women of the world, nature is the only entity that keeps hope and faith for them, even if it is as an illusion. Confrontation among humans is used in the narrative with the metaphor of the Genesis story of Cain and Abel implying the brotherhood of humans and the endlessly destructive relationship of hate among them. Nature is the only voice that emerges in the war and its cruel devastation. A nightingale [el ruiseñor] is the embodiment of the earthly wisdom of nature and its sense of equilibrium in contrast to the societal struggles. The nightingale in the story not only appears in the middle of a catastrophe but also lightens the spirits of rich and poor equally because it makes no distinction between them: "Solo el ruiseñor no teme cantar en las rosaledas del rey ni en los espinos del carbonero" (9) [Only the nightingale does not fear to sing in the king's gardens or in the thorny fields of the charcoal burner]. It thus resembles Hans Christian Andersen's "Nightingale" (1844) whose singing delighted everybody from all walks of life who heard it, and who revived a dying emperor. Clearly the hope for the Cinderellas and humans of the world is centered in the wisdom and clarity of nature, according to the first-person narrator. This is expressed in the various metaphorical images: "Cada árbol es un caballo de madera que se levanta temprano para ir a lavarse en la fuente" [Every tree is a wooden horse that wakes up early to wash in the fountain]. The readiness and diligence of the natural world is defined by its ability to move along with the earth's flow.

As shown in the narrative, the protagonist is not only part of a smaller group, but a human being with value, strength and courage who defies the odds against her. This idea is expressed in a mixture of rhetorical figures within the story. The use of an abundance of hyperboles, antitheses and synesthesias are the literary resources that support this notion. Cinderella's universal nature is detailed with hyperboles: "y cuando llora el agua de todos los afluentes del mundo desembocan en sus ojos" [and when (she) cries, the water of all rivers in the world ends up in her eyes]. She is the epitome and representation of all suffering around lands, mountains and forests as a universal character. Her incarnation of freedom and courage is defined by synesthetic images: "La libertad huele al cielo de un día de verano, al coral rojo y los panecillos de aceite cubiertos de canela" (26) [Freedom smells like the sky on a summer day, red coral and oil bread covered with cinnamon]. "Volar, desobedecer la costumbre, repartir panfletos contra la pena de muerte y el sí a la misericordia, el no a la explotación de las libélulas por las libélulas" (27) [Fly, rebel against the tradition, distribute pamphlets against the death penalty and say yes to compassion, oppose exploitation of fireflies by fireflies]. Synaesthesia as a figure depicting perceptions denotes a revolutionary tone. This trope constantly mixes sensations to create new products or as Kevin Dann puts it: "Synaesthesia is forever inventing the world anew, (and) militates against conventionalism" (122).

10. A Poetic Version: Te cuento ... Cenicienta

The Underworld or Hell is a recurrent theme in the narrative. The Greek mythical river in the underworld is often referred to without being named, although Lethe is the obvious allusion made to the river in the Underworld, which causes anybody who drinks from it forget all the past. Cinderella is an observer and a protagonist who reflects on social injustice and inequality in the world and thereby parallels the idea of being in Hell:

> Y el corazón blanco de los negros y el corazón negro de los blancos se ponen a latir porque ya ha pasado la medianoche [...] los jóvenes del MIR desaparecidos en Chile, las muchachas con rosquillas de miel y agua de manzanilla asesinadas en Ciudad Juárez, las chicas musulmanas bajo los cipreses de Bosnia, los adolescentes violentados en los Reformatorios de Tegucigalpa y Nueva Inglaterra [20].
>
> And the white heart of blacks and the black heart of whites beat because it is past midnight [...] the youngsters of MIR disappeared in Chile, girls carrying honey cookies and chamomile water killed in Ciudad Juárez, Muslim girls underneath the cypresses of Bosnia, the adolescents molested in the prisons in Tegucigalpa and New England.

As part of the hellish panorama, dictatorships and their victims appear in this part of the story. However, the story suggests that dissidents against the regime were not only persecuted and killed during dictatorships. According to Monedero, between 1976 and 1981, which was the idyllic period of transition, about 580 people were murdered in Spain due to political reasons. In the story, art and music are part of this scene as representing a victimized and resistance group. The music of Leonard Cohen celebrates the poetry of Federico García Lorca, assassinated by Nationalists in 1936. Iconic singer-songwriter Víctor Jara was murdered by the oppressive regime in Chile in 1973. Through references to artists such as Chilean composer, singer, and political activist Violeta Parra, a fierce defender of the disenfranchised, the story places artists in high strata as metaphors for oppositional forces in a world that Cinderella inhabits and recognizes with despair. Cinderella is the metonym of all victims and targets in society as is expressed in the multiplicity of images of herself recurrently and obsessively appearing in physical mirrors that all reflect a different being: "Cenicienta se mira en los espejos de la semejanza y en ninguno se ve a sí misma, siempre es otra, una brizna entre los pajonales de arroz, una rosa con siete manos, una beduina besada en las axilas por los hombres azules" (26) [Cinderella looks at herself in the similarity mirrors but does not see herself in any of them, she is always somebody else, a fragment in the rice crop, a rose with seven hands, a Bedouin woman kissed in the armpits by the blue men]. She is fragile and ephemeral, or delicate but proactive and powerful, or a powerful woman in a matriarchal nomadic ethnic group. Similarly, the photographs in the book depict specular figures portraying a multitude of women and their experiences: prostitutes, evicted women, volunteers, refugees' camps, exhumed bodies, mothers with children, etc., all of them united in one character.

The name of Cinderella is mentioned a handful of times and arises only as sparks in the narrative. The first time that a reference to Cinderella is made overt appears in the book's fourth page in a dialog between Cinderella and an unidentified person who is mistreating her verbally.

> ¡Cenizosa! ¡Ven aquí inmediatamente!
> ¡¡No me llamo Cenizosa! ¡Me llamo Cenicienta!
> ¡¡Te llamarás como yo quiera! ¡Tú no eres de aquí y te callas! [9–10]

> ¡Cinderolla! Come here immediately!
> ¡My name is not Cinderolla! My name is Cinderella!
> ¡You will be named as I choose! You are not from here and should shut up!

The reader's first encounter with the main character as a singular persona depicts her condition of strangeness, foreignness, otherness, which is one of the main conditions of being a Cinderella in society and developed in the previous chapters. Cinderella's interlocutor is nevertheless not defined. For this reason, it is everybody or anybody around her at a given time in history. The depiction of mistreatment represents the stepmothers of the tale, or the abusive in power who look down on the underprivileged. The figure of control is the stepmother, who is projected into many other characters in Cinderella's environment. The stepmother's power is accessible symbolically through negative forces (government, politicians, fundamentalists) that come united against the minorities and abused—represented as Cinderella. The orphan girl as in many myths of creation concerns the bearer of some calamity but destined to a greater realization.

Imposition and violence is reflected clearly in the stages of creation of an enemy, which appears in this version vividly. Cinderella as the protagonist comes into view in the narrative through a reprise of the dialog on page 4, now with another interlocutor but which again annuls her and makes her invisible:

> ¡Cenitonta! ¡Ven aquí inmediatamente!
> ¡¡Que no me llamo Cenitonta! ¡Que me llamo Cenicienta!
> ¡¡Te llamarás como a mí me apetezca! ¡Tú no tienes dinero y te callas! [30]

> ¡Cindermoron! Come here immediately!
> ¡My name is not Cindermoron! My name is Cinderella!
> ¡You will be called as I please! You are poor and should shut up!

Cinderella's underprivileged economic status makes her an object of possession as her unidentified interlocutor places her again as socially undetectable and not worthy. Subjected to a mimicry of a political discourse of oppression and hatred, Cinderella becomes an emblem of the disadvantaged and is forced or expected to be voiceless. Renaming as part of the creation of the enemy is clearly displayed in this version. In three instances within the narrative, the protagonist is addressed with a made-up name as a form of eliciting and calling for her disappearance as an individual. The refusal to call Cinderella by her given name is an attempt to erase her persona as it is and create a new one. The imposition of a new name on the protagonist diminishes and mocks her by replacing her original characteristics with a corroded version of herself. The renaming is not only an attempt to depreciate and minimize this Other as a person, but it also allows the agent of the imposition to become empowered and thrive. Symbolically, the displacement of the enemy through renaming cripples her and inevitably activates the challenging notion that she is the disabled, the strange, the different. In another adaptation of the tale ("Estrellita de oro"), discussed in Chapter 1, the protagonist is physically muted and blinded, which expresses the limitations that characterize Cinderella as an object of hatred and animosity. Once the imposed name erases the other and dehumanizes him/her, then it is easy to step on and destroy what is now perceived to be a non-human creature.

Cinderella in this rewriting, nevertheless, reacts and counterattacks, correcting her abuser and not allowing the imposition of a new diminishing name to be left unchallenged. In other versions, the characters remain silent and accept their fate sadly and passively. In *Te cuento ... Cenicienta*, the story gives a rebellious nature to the main character, who does not accept the attacks docilely. As a modern version of the tale and following the progress made towards women's equal treatment, Cinderella is no longer willing to acquiesce to the abuse, but retorts immediately to the invectives against her in the form of renaming. Her combative nature is revealed as the narrator indirectly describes Cinderella's character: "Cenicienta piensa en lo que no se puede pensar si se está de rodillas, si se trabaja de rodillas, si se piensa de rodillas" (30) [Cinderella thinks about what it is impossible to think if you are on your knees, or if you work on your knees, or if you think on your knees].

In the story, an agent is manifested as the promoter of hostility. In most versions of the story, the stepmother demonstrates the stronger position of power over the disadvantaged alien Cinderella. As in the traditional story, Cinderella's dead mother is a source of energy for her, that keeps and guides her motivations. The powers are divided into the beneficial and positive versus the evil powers. In many versions of the story, the stepmother and stepsisters are eliminated either symbolically or physically as a form of rejecting the "evil." In *Te cuento ... Cenicienta*, the protagonist is in constant contact with the evil and oftentimes invisible forces. The stepmother as the paradigm of evil exercises her power on the social level as she communicates and reflects the constant alienation of and control over Cinderella. This figure of power ramifies in the story as it projects many other powers that oppress women and other minorities in the world.

However, the negative aspects of humanity are not all that this version displays. The story has a positive turn as well, which is shown through the ability of movement and state of freedom when Cinderella dances. Nevertheless, she does not attend the emblematic royal ball or dance with the prince. Instead, Cinderella dances by herself. In various instances, the protagonist dances with the underdogs. For example, the narrator recounts that Cinderella dances and enjoys the tunes of an orchestra that experts say "tocan horrible" [plays horribly] (51). The heroine dances with those who dare and confronts the authorities when they are abusive; she also chooses to dance with those who are unpopular or unattractive. The story makes a reference to Frankenstein, the emblematic figure of what humans are capable of creating as a duplication of their own defective inner self. Ugliness as described in the narrative is a sentiment of character, an internal personality portrayal and/or a reproduction of what society has formed, nurtured and modeled. At a point in this whirlpool of ideas in the narrative, Cinderella stops and dialogs with another interlocutor, who recognizes her by her name for the first time.

> -Hola ... dijo Cenicienta sorprendida y tímida. -¿Por qué sabes cómo me llamo? ¿Quién eres? ¿Acaso te estaba esperando? [52]
>
> "Hi..." said Cinderella surprised and shy. "Why do you know my name? Who are you? Perhaps I was waiting for you?"

This new character interrupts her dancing and for the first time in the story gives her hope, kindness and guidance. The newcomer tells Cinderella that her parents have sent him/her with an announcement. The gender of the messenger is not revealed and the ambiguity denotes the universality and neutrality of this being. The bearer announces that the purpose of the visit is to offer Cinderella a magic word ("palabra mágica") conveyed by her parents to the messenger. "Me han pedido que te dé una palabra mágica para que no estés nunca sola y te hagas valer mientras el mundo se adecenta. Pronúnciala cuando te haga falta, después de decirte a ti misma tu nombre, en silencio, como haces por las noches, y los sueños se te harán realidad" (52) [They have asked me to give you a magic word to accompany you and make you brave while you tidy up the world. Pronounce it when you need it, after telling yourself your own name, in silence, like you do at night, and your dreams will come true].

As dance has been seen as a political tool historically, dance is also for Cinderella an act of liberty and a confrontation of the external world. There are many instances in history where dance has offered a comparable outlet for rebellion and defiance. After the invasion of the Inca Empire, a movement called *Taki Unkuy* appeared as an insurrection against the Spaniards. During 1564–1572, Andean people's dance was inspired by their gods who would embody them to reject the Christian god imposed by the Westerners. Andeans would dance for long hours while Europeans at first did not know what to repress. Over time the movement was brutally suppressed by the invaders once they understood that dance performed a political function to move the minds and spirits of the indigenous people. In other latitudes, dance has been suppressed and artists have been designated as rebels and enemies of dictatorial governments. In China during Mao Zedong's regime (1949–1975) the Cultural Revolution (1966) initiated by him persecuted civilians and artists. In particular, *Jingju* or Peking opera performers were targeted as criminals. Many of the artists, dancers and singers were tortured, disappeared or murdered by the regime. In Cambodia the brutal rule of the Khmer Rouge in 1975 "murdered ninety percent of Cambodia's professional artists, musicians and dancers" (Leigh Beaman 67). Dance is not only linked to the aristocracy and elites but is also ritualistically performed since ancient times to link the terrestrial with the outer world or spiritual and inaccessible realm. In *Te cuento ... Cenicienta*, the narrator highlights the importance of art as the language of truth and a depiction of humanity's capacity for resistance. Once she begins to dance, Cinderella is not afraid of marble palaces, or hierarchies, or of dreaming of a better world.

The magic and supernatural is expressed in character of the messenger who appears to Cinderella. In general, an information bearer who reveals some sort of truth to the recipient potentially embodies a rescuer. This emissary of ideas is the agent of guidance in Cinderella's chaotic environment. The messenger leads the girl to a revelation and manifests notions of intellectual power to her. For the first time in the story, the protagonist interacts with someone who does not despise, annul or mistreat her. In contrast to the former visitors or interlocutors, this newcomer instills in the girl wisdom and his/her proclamations are reflective and deep. The fairy godmother in this story is incarnated in this character, since it bestows the protagonist the premises to change. The endowment of this fairy godmother is not tangential or involve clothes and/or physical transformations. The messenger gives Cinderella through language, words of strength and guidance to follow her life enduring the difficult paths ahead. As a magical spirit, this character gives access to dreams, visions and a meditative frame of mind to see clearly in the darkness of the world.

> Y cuídate de los príncipes que son príncipes sin haber hecho nada para merecerlo. Y cuídate de los que tienen demasiados miedos, precisamente por no ser curiosos. Y cuídate de los egoístas que no ven latir sus ojos en los ojos de los otros. Y no te olvides de que aprender a ser libre es aprender a desobedecer los mandamientos secos, las falsas rutinas de las procesiones, las filas de los ejércitos y la gran estafa de los banqueros de la idiotez [53].
>
> And be careful of the princes who are princes without any merit. And watch out for those who fear too much, precisely because they are not curious. And watch out for the selfish that fail to see their eyes in the eyes of others. And do not forget that to learn to be free is to learn how to disobey the dry commandments, the false routines of processions, the ranks of the armies and the great scam of the bankers of idiocy.

The genderless messenger tells Cinderella to subvert and question all that has been given, making reference to the power maintained by just a few who have inherited it, which is clearly a commentary on the monarchy represented by the prince that Cinderella meets and marries in most versions of the tale. Cinderella is also encouraged to discard old ideas and to create her own, and to be brave and fearless about it. In other words, as the messenger of Cinderella's parents, the creature is invested with the authority to emphatically reassure and revitalize her. The protagonist is not wandering in the world alone, unshielded and confused anymore. Now she is strengthened not by magic or expensive clothes in which to appear to be a noble woman and attract the prince, but with strong moral values and codes that will make her reflect and will guide her and comfort her difficult path.

As it happens, this final adaptation of the "Cinderella" story encapsulates all of the concepts investigated over the previous nine chapters of this book. To create Cinderella as an enemy involves portraying her as a stranger and foreign, someone who, traversing countries, borders and regions, is rejected by the denizens and "owners" of the lands. As in "Estrellita de oro," Cinderella moves through the three stages of the creation of an enemy, as anonymous interlocutors engage her in dialogs in which they set out to rename her, displace her, and finally erase her.

The Spanish Civil War and its consequences, even during the period of transition to democratic government, is portrayed with reference to the hundreds of disappeared bodies murdered by Francoist ideologists. The photographs create a parallel narrative in dialog with the story. Text and images seem to recount dissimilar stories but connected by themes and tropes. One of the photographs shows the exhumed body of a woman wearing a ring. The decayed and corrupted remains are a shocking image which epitomizes the injustices and cruelty of this political moment in Spain. The second chapter is directly related to the attempt to erase any subversion or dissident discourse as displayed in Antoniorrobles' banned version of Cinderella.

The multiple masks and societal performances manifested in Chapter 3, are also a theme in *Te cuento ... Cenicienta*. Cenicienta, as Marisol in the musical version, is the leader of creative souls and the representation of strength and courage. Besides the adverse circumstances at a global scale in *Te cuento ...* and at a local scale in *La nueva Cenicienta*, the protagonists manage to rebuild themselves and convert the negativity in their surroundings to a positive and optimistic route to walk. Resilience is developed by the protagonist and she is enabled to face her difficulties with an open heart and good intentions.

Prominent literary devices as vehicles of meaning examined in Chapter 4 are also seen in *Te cuento ... Cenicienta*. Prosopopeia and synecdoche are the two signifying modes employed to represent the Otherness of Gabriela in *Solo un pie descalzo*. In *Te cuento ... Cenicienta*, hyperboles and synesthetic figures support the image of ubiquity and universality of the Cinderella character, as not only one woman in the world but all women in a disadvantaged position throughout history. The tropes indicate within the poetic realm the emblematic and symbolic charge in one character who embodies all disadvantaged women and anywhere in the world.

Superficiality and vainness is part of the world that Cinderella combats in this rewriting and it is the theme of Chapter 5. She walks a world of artificial values, where the worth of an individual is determined by the money he or she possess and not for their integrity and honor. The three women in *Cinderella Always Wanted a Wonderbra* are yearning for the prince, like the traditional story. In contrast, in *Te cuento ... Cenicienta*, the protagonist is not looking for a prince and does not even want to attend the ball. She is looking for an answer to make sense of what she experiences and encounters in her life's path. This protagonist creates a vivid and diametrical contrast with the main female characters in Chapter 5.

In Chapter 6, Cinderella is a lesbian and she encounters her princess at the ball in a gay discotheque. Gender is dislocated and reassigned to a homosexual couple contrasting the heterosexual normative encounter of all versions in the Spanish language. In *Te cuento ... Cenicienta*, the protagonist also finds a companion who is female. The rejection of the prince is as clearly visible as her objection to the hierarchical political power. When prohibited from going to the ball, Cenicienta dreams about a beautiful maid at the party carrying a jar of wine, who smiles and winks at her. "Cenicienta solo quiere bailar con la chica del flequillo que le recuerda a un lugar que sabe a fresas y a mar" (43) [Cinderella only wants to dance with the girl with bangs, who reminds her of a place that smells like strawberries and ocean]. Later this girl is the one that Cinderella finds and invites to join her at a ball.

In Chapter 7 the main theme is violence against women, which is represented in the first part of the narrative. The narrator mentions the many women abused, raped and brutally treated in many parts of the world. The victims of war in Kosovo, Jewish women in World War II, women burying their husbands in the Spanish Civil War, prostitutes forced to work on the streets for fear of hunger and need, and women rendered invisible by dictatorial and totalitarian regimes that see them as second-class citizens. This version encompasses the topic of women and violence from a bigger and historical scope.

Death and destruction is a topic in Chapter 8. *Cenicienta en Pensilvania* is the paradigm of sadness and despair in a world that has lost all empathy for those who are alone and in need. In *Te cuento ... Cenicienta*, death, pain and destruction is a recurrent topic surrounding the protagonist. The narrator constantly conveys the protagonist's preoccupation and obsession with mortality. "Pensó en el amor y en la muerte, en la vida que arrebató el fascismo, un ogro en pantalones bombachos..." (48) [She thought about love and death, about the life snatched away by fascism, an ogre in baggy trousers] "En todos los relojes las cinco en punto de la tarde y la muerte no volvería a recibir aplausos" (49) [In all clocks, it marked five o'clock in the afternoon and death would not receive applause again]. The desire for change is ingrained in the pain experienced by the character or by multiple Cinderellas in *Te cuento ... Cenicienta*. As in Mary, the protagonist of *Cenicienta en Pensilvania*, the pain is visible and on stage, which makes it a shocking truth.

In *Idiotizadas*, the gender double standard is the main theme along with the contrast between the city and the country. *Te cuento ... Cenicienta* reprises this idea by mentioning the various heroines in history treated unfairly because of their gender. Among fictional and historical characters of all times are: Frida Kahlo, the famous Mexican painter, who was until the seventies known only as the wife of Diego Rivera; Malinche, historically despised and unjustly designated a traitor to when she was only a captive woman given as a "gift" to Cortés; Scheherazade, who in spite of her disadvantages as a woman kept herself alive by recounting stories to the Sultan; Clara Campoamor fought for equality and the inclusion of female suffrage in the Spanish constitution of 1931; Hypatia, who was lynched by a mob of believers because she dared to yearn for knowledge; Rosa Luxemburg fought and died for the socialist cause but also for the equality of women within this cause. In her speech "The Proletariat Woman," she summarizes the sentiment of including women in the progress of humanity:

> As bourgeois wives, women are parasites in society, their function consists only in sharing the fruits of exploitation. As petty-bourgeois, they are seen as beasts of burden for the family. It is as modern proletarians that women first become human beings; for it is struggle that produces the human being—participation in their process of culture, in the history of humanity [410–11].[3]

At the end of the story, the narrator tells the protagonist that there is only a little bit more than four words remaining: "Escucha, me quedan poco más de cuatro palabras: casa, pan, madre, sílabas, lengua" (54) [Listen, there is only a bit more than four words left in me: house, bread, mother, syllables and language]. Symbolically, these language remnants will provide and fulfill the basic needs for the girl. A place to be safe, cared for, protected and live in a small or large scale is the house, or the home, as is the country or region that enables you to dwell there, and the minimum necessities are expressed and covered by a house and food to maintain health. The mother as nurturer and love provider for the child appears as one of the key words given by the narrator to Cinderella as well. Finally, the words "syllables and language" offer the capacity to have a voice and a language to utter a position in the world. At this moment, Cinderella is able to pronounce her name: "Y entonces pronunció para sí misma el nombre, aquellas palabras mágicas de su nombre" (53) [And then she pronounced for herself the name, those magic words of her name]. This act from Cinderella is a way to recuperate the words and the possibility of significance of these words. An act of resistance before the acts of violence, the words serve to amplify the vision of a destiny to build and not destroy. The poetic word with extreme delicacy offers the final resistance from within, since power besmirches the language in order to express lies and manipulation: "Cenicienta comenzó a hacerse amiga de las palabras, otras chicas como ella con las piernas sin medias" [Cinderella began to make friends with the words, who are also girls like her without stockings on their legs].

The tale has a positive ending. Cinderella has found a place for herself and an identity. Metaphorically, she has appeared as a human being with value, strength and bravery. She finally has a name or a notable self-value as a person and as a woman. Cinderella meets the girl in her dream as she invites her to another ball and welcomes her to their party. However, Cinderella has lost her shoe. Her new friend replies that she does not need shoes for this party, because everybody at this place is barefoot. Cinderella is extremely happy and says:

> Qué alegría. ¿puedo dejar que se vayan las lágrimas?
> Luego cuando me digas cuál es tu verdadero nombre [58].
>
> What a joy! Can I let my tears go away?
> Later, when you tell me what your real name is.

Te cuento ... Cenicienta is an ethical reflection on society. The story denounces the arrogance of the powerful with various humorous instances that diminish the solemnity of their idiocy. Cinderella incorporates the idea of common sense in a world lacking self-criticism and displays the importance of exposing societal and cultural wounds to make them palpable. *Te cuento ... Cenicienta* appeals to the union of all for a better world, and its revolution of words invites to a global conversation about intentions and compromises to make change. The story announces a language that accompanies the reality of stories, making words acquire value again as indestructible weapons of civility.

Cinderella as conceived in this version is depicted as a construction of one of the many toxic myths applied to women, as a space of lies and hatred. This adaptation is not a fairy tale for princesses, as Monedero affirms in the presentation of the book in Madrid. It is a tale of all Cinderellas that were/are killed and abused and the millions of anonymous women suffering in the world at this moment. In the story, barefoot and patiently, Cinderella advances as the emancipatory conscious of the future and exhorts the readers to create their own dictionary and definitions against the discursive imposition of power, whatever shape it takes. This poetic version of the tale inhabits realities and highlights and displays the current situation of our societies with the authority that words bestow. The story establishes and remarks what is not said about the metonymic value of Cinderella and reminds us of the power of words not only to lie and deceive but to convey the truth in this world of *cuentos*.

Chapter 11

Versions of Cinderella in Spain: A Survey of Primary Texts

The criteria to select the adaptations of "Cinderella" in Spain included in this project are twofold and paratextual: (a) versions that have the name of the protagonist in the title, and (b) versions that have one of the motifs of the story as a metaphor, allegory or allusion clearly within the title of the work. This list does not include the many hypertextual references such as for example, *Pretty Woman* (1990) mentioned and listed by Jack Zipes (399) as one of the Cinderella adaptations. In fact, and in agreement with Zipes' reading of Gary Marshall's story, this film and other works mentioned by Zipes in his list of "Cinderella Filmography" could be considered as having an intertextual reference with the tale. However, the name of neither the protagonist nor any of the motifs is stated clearly within the paratext of the work. This study is limited to those works that have a precise reference to the Cinderella story explicitly. Other type of references as those mentioned above would include without doubt thousands of works that have used the paradigmatic Cinderella in a figurative form; for this reason, it would be impossible to cover everything in this study. The limitations of the present examination of Cinderella are the possibility of overlooking some of the versions that have been published in Spain. Nevertheless, the study covers all adaptations encountered in the past eight years.

Among the many versions of Cinderella found in Spain, there are a variety of themes, formats or background topics surrounding the story's revalidations. The tale's rewritings come in different genres as versions written in verse, drama adaptations, essays, musicals, and, most commonly, short stories or novels. The themes vary from re-writings of the tale with slight variations from the canonical French and German versions of Perrault and the Grimms, feminist commentaries, detective stories, fractured fairytales, and stories based on Spanish folklore tradition, or contextualized by historical moments in Spain; for instance, the Spanish Civil War and/or La Movida Madrileña movement. Within these varieties, there are film and musical adaptations of the tale, picturebook versions, comics versions, illustrated versions, and/or romance novels. This study only covers the versions written in Spanish in Spain. Some of the adaptations in the other three languages spoken in Spain, Catalan, Galician and Basque are: *La Ventafocs* by Ada García (2013), the Catalan version of Cinderella and based on Perrault's recount of the story; in Galicia, *O prodixio dos zapatos de cristal* (2008) by Xosé Antonio Neira Cruz written in Galician; and the Basque version *Errauskiñe* (1964) written in Euskera by an anonymous author. There are motifs that recur more frequently than others in the rewritings found. For instance, the lost shoe is encountered in most adaptations with some exceptions as in "Estrellita de oro" examined in Chapter I. The shoe is substituted by a star on her forehead in this version. The ball is another distinctive motif in the various versions. There are many variations as the ball may be an event at a gay discoteque, a costume party, or a high school–like prom night, and in some adaptations the ball is the beginning of the story and not the end. Another motif is the fairy godmother that appears in many shapes and forms from a fish to a YouTube channel or a chat room. The transformation of the main character is present in all versions. In many retellings the metamorphosis is made through magic, in others through emotional states and in one version the change is lethal. The motifs and main characters comprise the elements of analyses and the points of relation among the works and the Cinderella mimetic continuum.

This study has found forty-four versions of the Cinderella story in Spain. The works have been classified by fourteen major themes. The findings are described as follows: six versions based on Perrault, one version based on the Grimms, one version based on both, four drama versions, two detective versions, three based on Spanish folktake, three fractured fairy tales, five versions on social, gender or feminist issues, three on social and political/Spanish Civil War issues, four romantic theme versions, four literary versions, five film versions (three of which are musicals), two comic versions and one version under other themes.

1. Adaptations Based on Perrault

Rewritings of Cinderella around the world frequently take either the French or the German recognized versions of the tale as a foundation. In the case of the Spanish rewritings, in many instances the story line follows either of these versions with some small variations. For example, *Cenicienta* by Isabel Díaz (2001) does not introduce new elements to the traditional story but dialogs with Disney's recounting of the tale. For instance, the stepmother and sisters tear apart Cinderella's dress to stop her attending the ball, and while Cinderella is locked up in the attic to prevent her trying the crystal shoe, the mice aid her and give Cinderella the key underneath the door. She is released, tries the shoe and marries the prince. Perrault's version is also the foundation of *La Cenicienta* by Miguel Calero (2002), in which no significant changes or local motifs are found. *La Cenicienta* by Belén Eizaguirre Alvear (2008) is similar to Perrault's version except that Cinderella's mother dies in the Black Plague. *La Cenicienta o el Zapatito de Cristal* by Federico Ribas (2010) departs from Perrault only by explicitly stating that the stepsisters are physically ugly and request fashion advice from Cinderella. In *La Cenicienta* by M. Eulalia Valeri (1981) the stepmother and stepsisters use vulgar language to refer to Cinderella, calling her "culo sucio" [dirty ass], for example, but it otherwise follows Perrault, as does the version by Miguel Calero Garmendia (2008).

2. Adaptation Based on Grimm

A unique version found with one of the Grimm adaptation's famous motifs is *Cenicienta y el mirlo mágico* by Luisa Villar Liébana (2007). The bird or "el mirlo mágico" [the magical bird] is the axis of the story. Even though a mirlo is a type of black bird, in this story it is white as in the Grimm version. The white bird is central to the story as it acts as the fairy godmother and helps Noemi, the protagonist, in her quest. Noemi is an orphan who lives with her stepmother and stepsister named Berta. Her father is a businessman who travels frequently. Noemi is the maid in the house and is constantly busy cleaning. At night, she converses with the white bird and tells him about her hardships. Cinderella's ultimate desire in this version is not to attend the ball, but to study and be a professional. The bird brings her books secretly. Cinderella obtains a computer and registers at a university to study engineering. With her engineering knowledge, she helps a group of motorcyclists by warning them about a bridge they are about to cross. At the end, one of the men she saves is the prince who falls in love with her, even though the only thing he knows and remembers about her is her name. In an attempt by Berta and her mother to deceive the prince, Berta impersonates Cinderella but to no avail. The mice, friends of Cinderella, help her and the white bird touches the prince to make him aware which of the women is Cinderella. The couple get together as Cinderella continues to work as an engineer. In this version, the bird does not pluck out Cinderella's sisters' eyes as punishment.

3. Adaptation Blending Perrault and Grimm

A version that combines Perrault and Grimm is *La Cenicienta* by A.M. Llandó (1960). Cinderella is an orphan who lives with her stepmother and sisters named Ramona and Romana. The stepsisters have the same name as in the censored "Cenicienta" by Antonio Robles. This adaptation is a mashup of Perrault—in the part of the story where the transformation occurs and a rat is turn into the driver—and Grimm, in that the sisters amputate their toes and heel to fit the crystal shoe. The end returns to Perrault's version, when Cinderella's stepsisters are forgiven and become benign and kind, trying to imitate Cinderella's character.

4. Drama Versions

Theatrical adaptations start with the early twentieth century, *La Cenicienta* by Jacinto Benavente (1920). Jacinto Benavente's account belongs to the drama genre composed of three acts. There are only a few innovations in the story. Cinderella's father marries for economic reasons to a new rich wife and allows her to mistreat his daughter. Cinderella is more articulate than in other versions and reacts to the ill treatment by protesting and questioning the abuse. The nobility depicted comprise the King, who is egoistic and the prince, who is chronically depressed. There are three magical characters: Fantasía, the Poet and the Old lady of the Forest. Cinderella is encouraged by these creatures to face her problems and confront them. There are members of the court like Count Fabio and two buffoons Bumbún and Bartolillo. This story criticizes individuals in power suggesting that they do not work for the people but for their own economic benefit; it talks about political corruption and the unjust state of poverty in which they keep the populace.

Another version in this genre is *Cenicienta: Aquél y Aquélla* by Mariano San Ildefonso (1972). All acts in this dramatic rewriting of the tale are written in verse. There are some variations from the traditional accounts of Cinderella. The prince is an artist who laments the growing materialism of the epoch. He is not excited about seeking a princess to marry, because he finds only superficiality and banality around him. Cinderella drops her silver shoe at the ball and turns into a beggar. The fairy godmother with this transformation is testing Cinderella's strength and valor. The prince finds her and she only turns into a princess when the fairy godmother intervenes and through magic converts her one more time. The version ends with the narrator saying, "Casó el príncipe Rolando con la Cenicienta enseguida; y fueron siempre felices, y tuvieron una niña, estando los tres contentos siempre, por toda la vida" (39) [Prince Rolando married Cinderella right away, and they were always happy, and had a daughter, the three of them always happy for the rest of their lives]. *La Cenicienta: un cuento de Perrault para leer y para representar* by Manuel Carcedo Sama (2007) is another version made to be performed on stage. In Lourdes Ortiz' *Los motivos de Circe* (1988), "Cenicienta: Parábola en dos actos" is also a drama version. Years have passed since the wedding between the prince and Cinderella. Cenicienta is now the queen. The king and his advisors think that the use of magic in the past surrounding the couples' encounter was the product of witchcraft. The Catholic church and the king with this argument conspire to kill Cinderella. The queen is killed and while the various characters appear and have a part in the conspiracy against Cinderella, the buffoon named Calabacillas (little pumpkin) sings verses. At the end of the story, the king is also assassinated by his own cabinet and advisors. Calabacillas sings the last verse: "Adivina quién te dio si no es uno, serán dos" (173) [Guess who hit you, if not one, probably two].

5. Detective Versions

El zapato desaparecido by Miguel A. Delgado Fernández (2011). The story belongs to a Detective Series. There are two professional detective characters: Sandra and Fo. They are hired by the prince to find the shoe and the owner under a threat that they will be decapitated if they fail. The detectives find out that Cinderella herself is the person who has hidden the shoe. She does not want to marry the prince, because he is a despot and an evil human being. Sandra and Fo devise a plan to give the shoe to

Cinderella's stepsister as she matches the prince's personality and character. The prince marries the stepsister and the detectives are not killed.

Maldita Cenicienta by Isabel Camblor (2005). María the protagonist of this detective story, s involved in a crime. Her best friend, Blanca, is her roommate and like María works as a high school teacher in Madrid. María suspects that Blanca is involved in some kind of illegal scheme as she sees a Moroccan man threatening to kill her. Amina, the maid in the house and also Muslim, helps María to look for Blanca who has disappeared. The search for her ends up at the police station where they find Blanca's good friend Bau giving information about Blanca's possible death. There is a digital robbery in Spain. María falls in love with Daniel, a stripper and student at the university. The story ends with a letter from Blanca to Maria a year after her disappearance. She confesses that she was the author of the cyber robbery, how she escaped from Spain, faked her own death and begs for her forgiveness. María (Cinderella) is secluded at home due to her hypochondriac personality until she finds a job. Unlike the typical story, María's conflicts are caused by her own demeanor. In some cases, as trying to solve the mystery of Blanca's disappearance, her tribulations are the product of her good character and empathetic heart. She finds a "disguised" prince (Daniel) and goes through many adventures with the help of her "fairy godmother" and maid, Amina.

6. Versions Based on Characters from Spanish Folklore

La Cenicienta by Cristina Soler Garmendia (1986). Cinderella's name is Blancaflor, a character from Spanish folk tradition. Her stepsisters are Mina and Muna and the King's name is Cirilo II. Cinderella encounters an old lady who is in need and asks for food and shelter. In recompense for Cinderella's kindness, she presents the girl with a dress and transportation, using magic, to attend the ball. The prince's name is Octavio. Cinderella's stepsisters are exiled and Cinderella later becomes the queen. Another version from Spanish folklore is "Estrellita de oro" by an anonymous author. This is the story of María who receives a star on her forehead from the fairy godmother and whose eyes and tongue are ripped off by her stepmother and stepsister (see Chapter 1). *La Señora del río* by Raquel Ilombé (1981) is a sanitized adaptation of the medieval version "Estrellita de oro." The story includes aspects of Equatorial Guinea culture and folklore, for instance, the ball is called the *balélé* dance, typical of the region.

Even though this version is not from a Spanish author, it is written in Spanish by an African writer.

7. Fractured Fairy Tales

Las desventuras de Cenicienta by Josep Lorman (2007). In this fractured fairy tale the narrator, after recounting the traditional tale, states that a reformed version of the story will be told. In this story within the tale, there are some new elements. For instance, the fairy godmother's magic wand fails to work. She, then, consults the queen of fairies, who advises her to prepare a spell. The fairy needs to gather a white hen, a crest of a black rooster washed in sulphate and a roasted rat's tail. Cinderella goes to the ball in a white cloud. One of the stepsisters on purpose crashes and destroys the crystal shoe and the prince cannot find it. Cinderella finds a job at the palace to escape the ill treatment in her house. The prince is depressed because he cannot find the girl who fled from the ball. Cinderella spreads the rumor that she is that girl. The prince glues the crystal shoe together and forces Cinderella to try it on menacing her that she will be killed if she has lied about it. The story ends happily.

Las tres mellizas y Cenicienta by M. Company and R. Capdevila (1988). This version is part of a collection of stories starring twins. The sisters are ruled by the Boring Witch (bruja aburrida), who gives them the duty to enter a folktale. Their punishment consists of the difficulties they must overcome in order to get out of the tale. The twins enter Cinderella's house through the chimney. They ask the fairy godmother not to give Cinderella a dress and shoes but a stove, a refrigerator, and a vacuum cleaner to help with her chores, and a Vespa motorcycle for transportation. Cinderella travels to the ball on the Vespa and pays for her own entrance ticket, since the kingdom has economic problems. The step sisters kidnap the twins who are helping Cinderella. When Cinderella is made aware of the situation, she helps and rescues the twins with the aid of the prince. Finally, Cinderella decides to see the world riding the Vespa, accompanied by the prince. *Las hermanastras de Cenicienta* by Fernando Lalana (1999). In this illustrated version, two sisters, Porunga and Turula, are both deeply enamored of a prince named Pío. The sisters move to a house close to the palace and try to get the prince's attention: they colored their hair with bright, shiny colors and played football in front of the palace, but only fail in their attempts. Their final scheme to catch the prince's attention is to entangle a kite on top of the prince's bedroom and ask for his help. He breaks his ribs and fingers trying to aid them. For this reason, the stepsisters are banished from the kingdom. They all move to another kingdom where Federico is the prince. The story concludes that from that point forward, it will begin another story, and closes with an account of the warning purposes of fairy tales as social indoctrination of children.

8. Versions Incorporating Social, Gender and Feminist Issues

Cenicienta tiene un mal sueño by Julia Massip and Chus Martínez (2002). Written by two psychologists, this version is part of a municipal program in Barcelona to educate women about domestic violence in this manual-like rewriting. Nunila López Salamero, the author of *La Cenicienta que no quería comer perdices*, a picturebook feminist version, is also a collaborator. In the prologue, written by three municipal authorities, it is stated: "El cuento que teneís en vuestras manos, queremos que sirva de ayuda a las personas que sufren estas situaciones de violencia. Es también un vehículo de información [...] la violencia es siempre un acto de cobardía y no tiene ninguna justificación. Cerrar los ojos ante esta lacra social también lo es" [We wish that the short story that you have in your hands will help women who suffer domestic violence. It is also an informative vehicle (...) violence is always an act of cowardice and it is never justifiable. Closing your eyes before this social illness replicates the cowardice] *Cenicienta tiene un mal sueño* erodes the familiar version of Perrault and discusses the abuse of women as a social issue. The story starts at the end. The prince turns into a violent man calling Cinderella ugly and abusing her on several levels. Cinderella asks rhetorically, ¿Sería culpa de ella el maltrato sexual? (20) [Was the sexual mistreatment that she endures her fault?] She is naive about her own sexuality and suffers from her husband's abuse. Finally, she finds help, gets a divorce and establishes a vegetarian restaurant employing many of the fairytale female characters escaping their "fairytale ending." The end of the story consists of final remarks and awareness on the issue of women's domestic abuse: "Y la Cenicienta lo consiguió. Dejó los tacones y las perdices y se hizo cocinera vegetariana. Y ahora está trabajando con otras mujeres como ella: Blancanieves y la Bella Durmiente que ya habían despertado, Caperucita, que había dejado al cazador por violento [...] Y entre todas decidieron cambiar sus papeles en los cuentos y empezar uno nuevo.... Érase una vez unas mujeres que no estaban solas..." (n/p) [And Cinderella finally escaped the prince, leaving the high heels, the partridges and becoming a vegetarian cook. She is now working with other women like her, that have woken up: Snow White and Sleeping Beauty and Little Red Riding Hood, who has left the violent hunter (...) Among them have decided to change their assigned roles in the tales and start new ones.... *Once upon a time there were women who were not alone...*].

La Cenicienta que no quería comer perdices by Nunila López Salamero (2009). A picture book adaptation that begins where the typical story ends. The plot is similar to *Cenicienta tiene un mal sueño*. The prince turns into an ogre, becoming abusive and violent (see Chapter 7).

In "Las cenicientas ya no son lo que eran" (1991) by Suárez Solís, Cenicienta is Beatriz and the prince, the engineer Pepín. They meet at the ball and Pepín insolently places his hand on Beatriz' derriere when helping her to enter the carriage. When they arrive at Beatriz' house, she takes off one of her shoes and throws it violently at Pepín's face making him tumble and fall on his back. The narrator ends the story stating: "Beatriz, antes de entrar a la pata coja en el portal, tuvo tiempo de verlo despatarrado en el suelo, los ojos estupefactos, la boca abierta, la estridente corbata floja y torcida. Entonces, sonriente, cerró con un sonoro portazo" (138) [Beatriz, before entering her home with only one shoe, had time to see him lying on the floor, his eyes stupefied, his mouth wide open, and his flashy tie all loose and crooked. Then, smiling, slammed the door].

Cenicienta en Chueca: mujeres que aman a mujeres by María Felicitas Jaime (2003) In this version Cinderella has no name and is a lesbian (see Chapter 5).

El zapato de Cenicienta: el cuento de hadas del discurso mediático by María Isabel Menéndez Menéndez (2006), a book essay on women's representation in mass media and popular culture discussing various stereotypes and preconceived myths about women. The author uses the shoe metaphor to describe the many constraints that women face and have faced historically in society. The shoe symbolizes the shackles concealed in this Cinderella motif and how it has been normalized and spread through the media and cultural representations affecting how women identify themselves and/or are identified in a highly sexist society. As the author states: "considero que el discurso mediático dirigido a las mujeres es un mensaje conservador, que consolida el orden político, social y religioso establecido y que implica un (pre) juicio [*sic*] moral que rechaza la libertad de obrar y actuar de las mujeres" (157) [I consider that the media discourse directed to women is conservative and as such consolidates the established political, social and religious order. It also implies a moral prejudice that obstructs women's liberty or action and agency in society].

9. Social Issues/Spanish Civil War Versions

"Cenicienta" by Elena Fortún (1928). Encarnación Aragoneses is the pseudonym of Elena Fortún. Her version of Cinderella is a short story in her book *Celia lo que dice* (1928). Solita plays the Cinderella character and is friends with the protagonist of the series, Celia. Solita is an orphan girl and works as a maid in Celia's home. She tells Celia about the dress she would wear to the ball. Celia doubts the credibility of Solita since she knows that the girl is poor. The story ends with Celia's question to the maid, Juana: "*¿Solita, tiene madrina?*" (Solita, does she have a fairy godmother?). (69) Celia's question implies the social differences and injustice hierarchies affecting Solita (Cinderella).

"Cenicienta" by Antonio Robles (1936). Cinderella refuses to be a princess and wears a pierrot dress to the ball (see Chapter 2).

"Cenicienta 39" by Sara Suárez Solís (1989). This story's social background is the end of the Spanish Civil War. Cinderella is Pili, a girl who loses a leg when her home town is bombed during the war. Her father is a soldier who fights for the Nationalists group. The story tells of the penury, lack of food and the angst in time of war. Pili's father is lost in the war and they do not know if he is still alive. Instead of the crystal shoe, Pili has a prosthetic leg and a shoe on it. The end of the war is announced and it is the cause of jubilee. Pili's family joins the populace on the streets. While Pili's stepmother and stepsisters are celebrating, they forget that Pili is alone in the house. Pili falls down the stairs and is injured, with no one to help.

10. Romantic Novels

Cenicienta siempre quiso un WonderBra, there are three Cinderellas in this chick version of the tale (see Chapter 6).

Cenicienta y el trovador by Azulplata (2011). Cinderella leaves her town to live in the Palace with the prince but misses his troubadour friend, who sings by her window every morning. *El despertar de Cenicienta* by José Mallorquí (1943). Romantic novel, optimistic, shows the economic struggle of a couple named Renna Barney and Fred Paine. They both live in New York and are low salaried employees who love each other. Fred Paine (the prince) inherits thirty million dollars as a consequence of a good deed made in the past. They live happily ever after. Isabel Gomariz is one of the characters who is called "la Cenicienta falsa" [The false Cinderella]. Isabel helps with arranging the mansion, clothes and wedding for Renna (Cinderella), because Renna does not know yet that Fred is a millionaire. Isabel thinks she will never be able to reach that status. At the end, she also finds her prince. Adapted to film in *Dos cuentos para dos* (1947) by Dir. Luis Lucia. *EL zapato de la cenicienta* by prolific author María Adela, Durango (1954), who wrote 300 romance novels with great success.

11. Literary Versions

Sólo un pie descalzo by Ana María Matute (1983). Gabriela is rejected by her family and looks for a world of empathy created by her (see Chapter 4). Cenicienta en Pensilvania by Cristina Cerrada. Mary is the protagonist and her transformation is by suicide (see Chapter 3). *Cenicienta en sangre* (2010) by Begoña Callejón is a collection of poems and short stories. In the first one-page story "Cenicienta expulsada en el país de las calabazas" [Cinderella Expelled from the Pumpkin Country], Cinderella is the narrator. She is at the entrance of Ildaboth, which is the name of the demiurge or "false god." She is talking about her feelings of abandonment, anger and deception. Her monologue is geared toward those who tricked her into believing that her mother was dead. She is in a state of limbo between the world that was given, a false world of fantasy and lies, and the world that she is about to enter. A voice says from inside Ildeboth: "-…pasa, aquí solo verás lo que quieras ver. Calabaza o zapatito de cristal" (22) [Come in, here you will only see what you want to see. Pumpkin or crystal shoe]. *Te cuento … La Cenicienta* (2015) by Juan Carlos Mestre and Juan Carlos Monedero. It is a modern and extremely poetic version of the tale, in which Cinderella traverses epochs, lands, climates and social situations. Cinderella is any person anywhere in the world and a reflection of our convoluted and unjust times (see Chapter 10).

12. Film Adaptations and/or Musicals

Dos cuentos para dos (1947) by Dir. Luis Lucia based on *El despertar de Cenicienta*, Mallorquí's romantic fable. Unlike the written version, the story is set in Spain. Both protagonists are employees in a prestigious business, Renna as a hairdresser and her fiancé Fred, as a jeweler. They struggle economically as their salaries are not enough to cover their minimum necessities. They want to get married but the financial situation prevents them from doing it. The story ends as Fred inherits 15 million dollars and is finally able to marry his fiancé. The film is a light comedy starring Spanish star Tony LeBlanc in his first leading role.

La nueva Cenicienta, musical version starring Spanish sweetheart Marisol and directed by George Sherman (1964) (see Chapter 3). *La Cenicienta y Ernesto* (1957) directed by Pedro Luis Ramírez. Spanish-Italian co-production in which Lieutenant Ernesto meets Julia, while looking for shoes. Julia is a seller at a store. A cunning lawyer tricks Julia into believing she has inherited 60 million pesetas and the nobility title of Marquesa. Felipe is the name of the lawyer who deceives Julia also by telling her that Ernesto is a millionaire. In the end, everyone involved finds out that Julia is not a marquesa and Ernesto is not a millionaire. Felipe says cynically: "¿Qué le esperaba siendo lo que era? Vender zapatos, ir al cine una vez por semana y casarse con un oficinista picado de viruelas. Ahora puede aspirar a todo: comodidad, lujo, confort, viajar en avión y 3 comidas al día. La gloria, la felicidad, el capitalismo" (93) [What do you think would be her future? Sell shoes, go to the movies once a week, and marry a blue collar man with acne. Now she can reach anything she wants: comfort, luxury, travel abroad and three meals a day. The glory, happiness, the capitalism]. Anselmo is Julia's father who requests an explanation from Felipe, who says: "Yo creé el sueño y ellos hicieron el negocio" (215) [I created the dream and they bought it]. The couple finds out the stratagem and start over again as they were at the beginning: poor but together.

La Cenicienta del Palace by Luis Escobar (1950) is a musical first performed in Teatro Eslava in Madrid on March 1st, 1950 starring famous Spanish actress Celia Gámez. As the original script found in the National Library in Madrid shows, this version is unique as it opens the adaptation with a political salute to the dictator of Spain: "¡Saludo a Franco y Arriba España!" (1) [A Salute to Franco and Viva Spain!].

La Cenicienta del Palace directed by Fernando García (1985) is a musical performed ten years after Franco's death. The story unfolds at a hotel (Hotel Palace) when twin sisters, Delia and Celia visit the city. One of the sisters in a millionaire and the other is poor. Schemes, plans and intrigues are plotted by the Baroness and others at the hotel where the sisters are staying to trick the millionaire girl into marrying one of two desperate suitors. Starring singer Paloma San Basilio, this musical version ends with the marriage of Delia/Celia with the man who is honest and kind to her. At the end, it is discovered that there are no twin sisters and there is only one millionaire lady, who, tired of all the ambitious, greedy and false suitors, fools all into thinking that one sister was poor and the other rich. It ends with Celia and Carlos' wedding and the last musical number, "Cenicienta, Cenicienta porque el sueño fue una verdad" (Cinderella, Cinderella, because the dream was true).

13. Comics Versions

Idiotizadas by Moderna de Pueblo. Zorricienta is a host in a radio show advising men and women about relationships (see Chapter 9).

La princesa que perdió el pie de su zapatilla (1979) [The princess Who Lost the Foot of Her Shoe] is a comics porn version of Cinderella by Nazario Luque-Vera. This Underground comic appeared in *El Víbora*, an adult comics magazine published from 1979 to 2005. Nazario, the author, is an emblem of the counterculture movement that surfaced in the eighties in Spain. His version *La princesa que perdió el pie de su zapatilla* depicts a sexually avid Cinderella. The shoe symbol is replaced by a penis, which she looks for by trying different ones in the search for it. There are explicit sex illustrations, incest and zoofilia.

14. Other Themes

"Bibicienta" (1991) by Suarez Solís, deals with the issue of rivalry between women. In this version, Cenicienta's "real name," claims the narrator, is Bibiana Fabiola Isabel de la Santísima Trinidad y Todos los Santos [Bibiana Fabiola Isabel of the Holy Trinity and All Saints]. She tells the fairy godmother that her shoe size is 34 (4) instead of 7. After the ball, the prince looks for the maid whose foot could fit the crystal shoe size 4. He finds a girl who is the baker's daughter and marries her. When Bibicienta finds out she resentfully says: -Pero ¿Habráse visto, tontorrón despistado? (144) [But, imagine that, what a scatterbrained idiot!].

Chapter Notes

Chapter 1

1. All translations from Spanish texts are mine, unless otherwise indicated.
2. Hayes' version was collected in New Mexico and Southern Colorado. These stories portray the colonial Spanish culture as in Juan B. Rael's *Cuentos españoles de Colorado y Nuevo México* (1936) and Lucero-White Lea's *Literary Folklore of the Hispanic Southwest* (1953).
3. All fairy godmothers are ladies, who the girls encounter by the river. In "Estrellita de oro," it is an elderly lady. In "La Señora del río," it is a young and elegant lady. In Sans-Souci's version it is a beautiful lady wearing a blue robe (as the Virgin Mary is traditionally depicted).
4. For example, South African *tokolosh* is a baboon. The *selkies* in Irish mythology are hybrid seals and humans. *Yoseis* in Japan appear as swans and/or cranes among other representations of fairies' animals or hybrids.
5. This resource is also used in the Academy Award Winner for Best Motion Picture 2016, The *Revenant* starring Leonardo Di Caprio. In the film, the protagonist's rebirth occurs after sheltering under the thorax of a dead horse.
6. In present-day society, social media through Twitter and Facebook are the means to enter the "Post Truth Era" (*The Economist*).
7. Inca's moral code was: "*Ama suwa, Ama llulla, Ama quella*," [do not steal, do not lie, do not be lazy]. Anybody breaking these laws was considered a criminal and punished with mutilation.

Chapter 2

1. This article was first translated into English by Michelle Giltner. A version of it was published in *International Research in Children's Literature* (IRCL) 7:1 (July 2014): 78–94.
2. In relation to the issue of class, José Antonio Primo de Rivera defines the sort of equality proposed by communism as: "[U]na versión infernal del afán hacia un mundo mejor" (xxi) [A hellish version looking for a better world]; regarding the issue of religion and Spanishness: "[L]a interpretación católica de la vida es, en primer lugar, la verdadera; pero además, históricamente, la española ... así pues toda reconstrucción de España ha de tener un sentido católico" (92) [the Catholic interpretation of life is, in the first place, the truth; but also, historically, the Spanish one ... therefore, any reconstruction of Spain should have a Catholic sense]; concerning gender: "[L]a ley de divorcio predica de modo

directo la inmoralidad familiar" (612) [the Divorce Law directly promotes family immorality] and in one of his discourses he asserts: "No entendemos que la manera de respetar a la mujer consista en sustraerla a su magnífico destino ... la mujer siempre casi acepta una vida de sumisión, de servicio, de ofrenda abnegada a una tarea" (Martín Gaite, *Los usos* 58). [It is not our view that the way to respect women is to prevent them from fulfilling their magnificent destiny ... women almost always accept a life of submission, of service, of selfless sacrifice to a task] (56).

    3. Martín Gaite dedicates Chapter 3 ("El legado de José Antonio) to this figure of the founder of the Spanish Falange and deepens the importance of his ideology within Franco's government (*Los usos* 55–72).

    4. This group parallels the one called the Generation of '27, which was formed by writers who were characterized by "el empeño en la renovación del humor" (Romera Castillo 241) [the struggle to renovate humor as a genre]. Together with Antoniorrobles, writers like Poncela, Neville, Mihura, Rubio, Lázaro, Bon and K-Hito, among others, formed part of this generation.

    5. Robles narrated various of his stories on the radio, which was an innovative medium for mass dissemination of information at the time. During the Spanish Civil War, Antoniorrobles moved to Valencia, "ciudad en pie de Guerra" [City ready for war] (Sanz 55), from there he would later go to the Republican government of Barcelona in October 1937. It was from here that he transmitted his stories on Unión Radio Valencia.

    6. The dictatorship of Miguel Primo de Rivera (1923–30) succeeded the reign of Alfono XIII (1902–30). The coup d'état of Miguel Primo de Rivera and his consequent government was supported by King Alfonso XIII. For this reason, the military dictatorship is often considered to be part of this monarchy.

    7. El Lyceum Club Femenino was the pioneer cultural association to be founded and created by women in Spain. The headquarters of this association could be found in the House of the Seven Chimneys in Madrid and it was founded in 1926. Currently, it is the headquarters of the Ministerio de Cultura de España.

    8. Jack Zipes and Xenia Mitrokhina study respectively the Czech film *Three Wishes for Cinderella* (1974) and the Russian film *Zolushka* (1940) finding similar principles such as the union helping Cinderella and the lack of magic in these versions.

    9. Julián Marías affirms that the Republican ideas resurge during the Kingdom of Alfonso XIII (1902–30) and its supporters grow: "Y, sin embargo, a pesar de esta experiencia negativa (de la primera república), el republicanismo sigue vivo entre parte de los intelectuales y en los movimientos obreros" (32). [In spite of the negative experience from the First Republic, republicanism was alive among the intellectuals and union movements].

    10. It was created in 1931 by Manuel Bartolmé Cossio at the beginning of the Republican government.

    11. According to Todorov, the fantastic occurs when a phenomenon cannot be explained using the laws of the natural world. In this version of "Cinderella," the exclusion of any element of the fantastic also eliminates the "doubt," that according to Todorov, one experiences in confronting the fantastic. In this version, all of the elements are tangible and material.

    12. Eugenio Paceli was elected as Pope with the name of Pius XII in April 1939; simultaneously, Francisco Franco, by order of the "Nationalists," assumed governing power in Spain after the fall of the Second Republic in the Civil War. The Pope called the Spain of the Francoist regime: "[L]a nación elegida por Dios como instrumento de evangelización del nuevo mundo" (Martín Gaite, *Los usos* 18). [The nation chosen by God as the main instrument of the evangelization of the New World] (20).

    13. For example, the prohibition of the use of languages such as Catalan, Basque and Galician during the Francoist regime was fundamental to the slogan "Habla la lengua del imperio" [Speak the language of the Empire], which tried to impose the obligation of the use of Castillian Spanish.

14. Elena Fortún together with Salvador Bartolozzi, Magda Donato and Antoniorrobles formed a group of writers of children's literature in this period. In her first works, Fortún responds to and questions the stereotype of the Spanish woman that is proposed by the regime. Following the triumph of Franco in the Civil War, although Fortún continues to write, in this second stage, the questioning nature of her previous works has been diluted. Caamaño Alegre refers to this in her study about the work of Fortún: "Cuando, en *Celia madrecita* (1939), la reencontramos, Celia es apenas reconocible. Toda rebeldía se ha esfumado ... Fortún parece recuperar algunas de las ideas tradicionales sobre la mujer, haciendo uso de un discurso similar al de la derecha" (15). [When we reencounter Celia, in Celia madrecita, she is unrecognizable. All her rebel spirit is gone ... Fortún seems to have acquired the traditional ideas about women, using a discourse very similar to that of the Franco followers].

15. *Raza* tells the story of the Churruca during the Civil War. It premiered in 1941 and was directed by José Luis Sáenz de Heredia, with a plot by Jaime de Andrade, although it is said that General Franco was the real creator of the story. *Raza* shows the characteristics of the Spanish "race" proposed by the regime just at the time following the Civil War. Alejandro Yarza emphasizes the heroic tone of the film as a representative of the Spanish "race" (65–88).

16. Marisol also interprets Cinderella in the film *La nueva Cenicienta* (1964). This movie is analyzed in Chapter 3.

17. Terdiman's study focuses on the French literature of the nineteenth century, but suggests continuities between the theory and practice of resistance then and theories of social semiotics today. His methodology has been applied to postcolonial studies and other counter discourses.

Chapter 3

1. The United States established the Marshall Plan to help western European countries economically after World War II. Spain benefited from this initiative in the fifties, even though the country was initially excluded from the Plan. Berlanga's film *Bienvenido Mr. Marshall* (1953) [Welcome Mr. Marshall] creates a satirical image of the political situation.

Chapter 5

1. Julie Law's version could be classified as slash fiction, or fiction that depicts popular heterosexual characters as homosexual, or even fan fiction. A comparable example of slash fiction is the Xena/Gabrielle relationship examined by Jeanne E. Hamming (2001). Law's adaptation of Cinderella as a lesbian is an online self-publication. The cover disguises the content of the novel, nevertheless, as there are no explicit sexual activities described in the relationship between Cinderella and Victoria (the prince's sister). This and other fan fiction texts are part of the queer representation of fairy tale characters discussed in this chapter. Although it is arguable that most of these works are not literary, I agree with Frederik Dhaenens et al. that because of their cultivation of "a fluidity of erotic identification" (Jenkins 189) some of these works could be studied in certain theoretical frameworks of queer studies.

Chapter 6

1. Postfeminist theory contends that chick lit constitutes a paradoxical discourse about women's sexuality and performance. On the one hand the raw description of women's sexuality is deemed progressive, on the other, the paradigm of women finding realization of their womanhood only through a prince charming is retrograde and stagnant, reinforcing patriarchal views. Some feminists argue that chick literature promotes

"raunch culture," "sexualisation of culture" and "pornification of the mainstream," among other representations of women's sexuality in fiction (Levy, Atwood, Mc Nair cited in Rowntree et al.).

2. Other female metaphors for the youthful flower, the bearer of life and the sage are the virgin, the mother and crone as studied by Livingstone, Wilshire and Caputi.

3. Even though Nicolaisen concludes: "Thus these tales, despite their unpromising beginnings, turn out to be painfully-glorious celebrations of the indomitable power and spirit of womanhood. Though the tales' endings may be formulaic, the storytellers make it quite clear that the marriages which are of the women's choosing and which permit them to stay away from home are predicted to be happy ones, with no signs of further persecution on the horizon" (70), the Cinderella protagonists of Chapters 7 and 9 in this volume contradict this notion as they become victims after the marriage.

4. A traditional discotheque named *Bocaccio* is situated in Madrid. At the same time, Paulina's chat name, Cibeles, is reminiscent of Madrid's main iconic symbol, the Cibeles plaza and fountain located in the center of the city.

Chapter 7

1. The origins of manga are a matter of controversy. Jaqueline Berndt argues that it involves "an intertwining of continuity and discontinuity" and whether critics argue for origins in 18th century Japanese pictorial art or in influence from American comics introduced during the occupation of Japan following World War II will depend on "what way critics have related modern manga to pictorial traditions and which artistic traditions they have had in mind" (309).

2. *Popol Vuh* means "the Book of Power" in the original K'iche language.

3. Coincidentally in Brazil, Maria Inês de Almeida observes the same practice in how indigenous texts from Brazil are classified in bookstores (95).

Chapter 9

1. These texts are considered precursors of "comics"; however, the taxonomy of iconic texts made by Andrés Romero-Jódar makes a distinction among the vast variety of them. Romero-Jódar classifies them as "narrative and non-narrative iconic" (125).

2. Part of this chapter was published as a Review of *Idiotizadas* in *Hispania* 102.3 (2019): pp. 434–35.

Chapter 10

1. "What form does the persecution take? (2) Where does it happen? (3) Who is the persecutor?" (63). In this variation the location, doer and shape of the persecution involve every abusive individual who has debased a woman anywhere in the world.

2. Clemente Bernard and Carolina Martínez' documentary *A sus muertos* [To Their Dead] has caused them to face legal prosecution. The two artists are being sued by the *Hermandad de Caballeros Voluntarios de la Cruz* [The Volunteer Knights Brotherhood of the Cross]. The members allege that their secret monthly meetings were filmed with hidden cameras. Nevertheless, the documentary does not show these gatherings. The purpose of the organization is to exalt the memory of Franco and all the "fallen for God and Spain" (Eldiario.es 14 Nov 2018).

3. The translation into English from the original quotation is mine. In German, it reads: "Als bürgerliche Frau ist das Weib ein Parasit des Gesellschaft, ihre Funktion besteht nur in Mitverzehren der Früchte der Ausbeutung; als Kleinbürgerin ist sie ein Lasttier der Familie. In der modernen Proletarierin wird das Weib erst zum Menschen; denn der Kampf macht erst den Menschen, der Anteil an der Kulturarbeit, an der Geschichte der Menschheit."

Bibliography

A sus muertos. Dir. Clemente Bernard and Carolina Martínez. Filmoteca de Navarra, 2018. Documentary.
Abuelo Made in Spain, Dir. Pedro Lazaga. Pedro Masó Producciones Cinematográficas, 1969. Film.
Aguilar, Claudia Carrasco, and Maria Julia Baltar de Andrade. "Chilean Public Policies on Female Labour and Sexual Education: Because One Day We Were Told That We Were Going to Be Princesses" *Revista de Psicología UVM* 3:5 (2013) 90–104.
Aguilar, José, and Losada, Miguel. *Marisol.* Madrid: Colección Portafolio, 2008.
Aladdin. Dir. Tad Stones. Disney Productions, 1996. Film.
Alexander, Sye. *Fairies: The Myths, Legends and Lore.* Avon, MA: Adams Media, 2014.
Almodóvar, A.R. *Cuentos al amor de la lumbre.* Madrid: Alianza Editorial, 1983.
Almodóvar, Pedro, director. *Entre tinieblas.* El Deseo Producciones, 1983.
_____. *Hable con ella.* El Deseo Producciones, 2003.
_____. *Kika.* El Deseo Producciones, 1993.
_____. *Pepi, Lucy y Bom.* El Deseo Producciones, 1980.
_____. *Tacones lejanos.* El Deseo Producciones, 1991.
Althusser, Louis. "Ideology and Ideological Apparatuses." *Lenin and Philosophy and Other Essays.* Trans. Ben Brewster. New York: Monthly Review Press, 1971.
Amago, Samuel. "Lesbian Desire and Related Matters in Carmen Laforet's *Nada.*" *Neophilologus* 86.1 (2002): 65–86.
Andersen, Hans Christian. "The Little Mermaid." Copenhagen, 1837.
_____. "The Nightingale." *Tales and Stories by Hans Christian Andersen.* Trans. Patricia Conroy. Seattle, 1844.
_____. "The Princess and the Pea." Copenhagen, 1835.
Anderson, Graham. *Fairytale in the Ancient World.* Oxford: Routledge, 2000.
ARAS (The Archive for Research in Archetypal Symbolism). *The Book of Symbols: Reflections on Archetypal Images.* Berlin: Taschen, 2010.
Aristegui, Miguel M. "Dos cineastas se enfrentan a penas de cárcel por rodar un documental sobre un monumento franquista de Pamplona" Eldiario.es [Navarra] November 13, 2018: n/p.
Ascarza, V.F. *La niña instruida.* Madrid: Magisterio, 1945.
Atwood, Margaret. *The Edible Woman.* Toronto: McClelland & Stewart, 1969.
Azevedo, Fernando José, Ângela Balça, Moisés Selfa Sastre and Judite Zamith Cruz. "Otherness in Contemporary Children's Literature Published in the Iberian Peninsula: Some Voices and Settings on the Construction of Gender." *ELOS. Revista de Literatura Infantil e Xuvenil* 2 (2015): 119–130.

Bibliography

Azulplata. *Cenicienta y el trovador.* El Ejido: Círculo Rojo, 2011.
Bacchilega, Cristina. *Fairy Tales Transformed? 21st-Century Adaptations and the Politics of Wonder.* Detroit: Wayne State University Press, 2013.
_____. "Foreword." *Cinderella Across Cultures: New Directions and Interdisciplinary Perspectives.* Edited by Marine Hennard Dutheil de la Rochère, Gillian Lathey and Monica Woźniak. Detroit: Wayne State University Press, 2016.
Baguñà, Josep. *Chiquitín.* Madrid: Imprenta de F.G. Pérez, 1886.
Bakhtin, M.M. *The Dialogic Imagination.* Trans. Caryl Emerson and Michael Holquist. Austin: University of Texas Press, 1981.
Banner, Lois. *Marilyn: The Passion and the Paradox.* New York: Bloomsbury, 2012.
Barker, Martin. *Comics, Ideology, Power and the Critics.* Manchester: Manchester University Press, 1989.
Barnish, Max, Heather May Morgan and Jean Barnish. "The 2016 High Heels: Health Effects and Psychosexual Benefits (HIGH HABITS) Study: Systematic Review of Reviews and Additional Primary Studies." *BMC Public Health* 18.37 (2018): 1–13.
Barreiro, Javier. *Marisol frente a Pepa Flores.* Barcelona: Plaza & Janés Editores, S.A, 1999.
Barrie, J.M. *Peter Pan.* New York: W.W Norton, 1911.
Basile, Giambatista. *Lo cunti de li cunti: "La gatta Cenerentola."* Bologna: Zanichelli Editori, 1634–1636.
Beauty and the Beast. Dir. Bill Condon. Disney Productions, 2017. Film.
Beauvoir, Simone. *The Second Sex.* Trans. Constance Borde and Sheila Malovany-Chevalier. New York: Random House, 1949.
Ben-Amos, Dan, ed. *Folklore of the Jews: Tales from Arab Lands.* Philadelphia: The Jewish Publication Society, 2011.
Benavente, Jacinto. *La Cenicienta, comedia de magia en un prólogo y tres actos dividida en quince cuadros.* Madrid: Librería de los sucesores de Hernando, 1920.
Berens, E.M. *The Myths and Legends of Ancient Greece and Rome.* Xist Publishing, 2015.
Berndt, Jaqueline. "Considering Manga Discourse: Location, Ambiguity, Historicity." *Japanese Visual Culture: Explorations in the World of Manga and Anime.* Edited by Mark W. MacWilliams. Armonk, NY: M.E. Sharpe, 2008.
Bernheimer, Kate. "This Rapturous Form." *Marvels & Tales* 20.1 (2006). Web. https://digitalcommons.wayne.edu/marvels/vol20/iss1/4.
Bettleheim, Bruno. *The Uses of Enchantment.* London: Thames and Hudson, 1976.
Bienvenido, Mr. Marshall. Dir. Luis García Berlanga. Unión Industrial Cinematográfica, 1953. Film.
Bishop, Elora, and Jennifer Diemer. *Sappho's Fables.* Create Space Independent Publishing Platform, 2012.
Borges, Jorge Luis. *Otras inquisiciones.* Buenos Aires: Sur, 1952.
Bottigheimer, Ruth. "Fertility Control and the Birth of the Modern European Fairy-Tale Heroine." *Fairy Tales and Feminism: New Approaches.* Edited by Donald Hasse. Detroit: Wayne State University Press, 2004, 37–51.
Boudieu, Pierre. "The Market of Symbolic Goods." *The Field of Cultural Production: Essays on Art and Literature.* New York: Columbia University Press, 1993.
Bourdieu, Pierre. *In Other Words: Essays Towards a Reflexive Sociology.* Cambridge: Polity Press, 1990.
_____. *Language and Symbolic Power.* Cambridge, MA: Harvard University Press, 1992.
_____. *A Social Critique of the Judgement of Taste.* London: Routledge, 1979.
_____. "Social Space and Symbolic Power." *Sociological Theory* 7:1 (1989): 14–25.
Boyd, Carolyn. "History, Politics and Culture, 1936–1975." *Modern Spanish Culture.* Edited by David Gies. Cambridge: Cambridge University Press, 1999.
Bridget Jones' Diary. Dir. Sharon Maguire. Miramax, 2011. Film.
Briggs, Raymond. *Fungus and the Bogeyman.* London: Puffin, 1977.
_____. *The Tin-Pot Foreign General and the Old Iron Woman.* London: Penguin Books, 1984.

_____. *When the Wind Blows.* London: Penguin Books, 1982.
Búsqueme a esa chica. Dir. Fernando Palacios and George Sherman. Guión Producciones Cinematográficas, 1964. Film.
Butler, Judith. *Excitable Speech: The Politics of the Performative.* New York: Routledge, 1997.
_____. *Gender Trouble: Feminism and the Subversion of Identity.* New York: Routledge, 1990.
_____. "Imitation and Gender Insubordination." *The Critical Tradition.* Edited by David H. Richter. Boston: Bedford/St. Martin, 2007.
Caamaño Alegre, Beatriz. "Cosas de niñas: La construcción de la feminiedad en la serie infantil de Celia, de Elena Fortún." *An Mal electrónica* 23 (2007): 33–57. Web. 10 August 2008.
Caballé, Ana. *El feminismo en España: La lenta conquista de un derecho.* Madrid: Ediciones Cátedra, 2013.
El Calentito. Dir. Chus Gutiérrez. Telespan 2000. Film.
Callejón, Begoña. *Cenicienta en sangre.* Almería: El Gaviero Ediciones, 2010.
Camblor, Isabel. *Maldita Cenicienta.* Sevilla: Algaida Editores, 2005.
Camporesi, V. "Spain: Bipolar Visions, Unified Realities: A General Overview." *European Cinemas in the Television Age.* Edited by Dorota Ostrowska and Graham Roberts. Edinburgh: Edinburgh University Press, 2007, 55–77.
Canova, Antonio. *The Three Graces.* 1814. Arlington House, The Robert E. Memorial. Arlington, Alabaster sculpture.
Caputi, Jane, *Goddesses and Monsters: Women, Myth, Power, and Popular Culture.* Madison: University of Wisconsin Press, 2004.
Carcedo Sama, Manuel. *La Cenicienta: Un cuento de Perrault para leer y para representar.* Madrid: Visión Libros, 2007.
Carola de día, Carola de noche. Dir. Jaime de Armiñán. Guión Producciones Cinematográficas, 1969. Film.
Carroll, Lewis. *Alice in Wonderland.* London: Macmillan, 1865.
Carter, Angela. *The Bloody Chamber.* Harlow: Longman, 1979.
Caspari, Elizabeth. *Animal Life in Nature, Myth and Dreams.* Wilmette: Chiron Publications, 2003.
Castellanos, Rosario. *Mujer que sabe latín.* México: Fondo de Cultura Económica, 1973.
La Cenicienta del Palace. Dir. Luis Escobar. Perf. Celia Gámez and Alfonso Godá. Teatro Eslava de Madrid, Madrid. 1 March. 1940. Performance.
Cenicienta y Ernesto. Dir. Pedro Luis Ramírez. Madrid: Prod. Cinematográfica S.A, 1957.
Cerrada, Cristina. *Cenicienta en Pensilvania.* Barcelona: DVD Ediciones, 2010.
Cerrillo, Pedro C. Torremocha, and Jesús María Martínez González. *Aleluyas.* La Mancha: Univ de Castilla La Mancha, 2012.
Cervera, Juan. *Teoría de la literatura infantil.* Bilbao: Mensajero, 1991.
Chisholm, Dianne. *Queer Constellations: Subcultural Space in the Wake of the City.* Minneapolis: University of Minnesota Press, 2005.
Cinderella. Dir. Clyde Geronimi. Walt Disney, 1950. Film.
Cinderella. Dir. Kenneth Branagh. Walt Disney, 2015. Film.
Cinderfella. Dir. Frank Tashlin. Jerry Lewis Productions, 1960. Film.
Claudín, Víctor. "Dejad a los niños ir a él." *Triunfo* 32 (1978): 50–51. Web. 12 ene. 2009.
Colomer, Teresa. "La evolución de la literatura infantil y juvenil en España." *Bookbird* 1.3 (2010): 1–5.
Company, M., and R. Capdevila. *Las tres mellizas y Cenicienta.* Barcelona: Editorial Ariel S.A., 1988.
Conquerwood, D. "Of Caravans and Carnivals: Performance Studies in Motion." *The Drama Review* 39.4 (1995): 137–141.
The Cop and the Anthem. Dir. Henry Hathaway. Twentieth Century–Fox. 1952. Film.
Cox, Marian Roalfe. *Cinderella.* London: David Nutt, 1893.

Cranach, Lucas the Elder. *The Three Graces.* 1535. The Nelson-Atkins Museum of Art, Kansas. Painting, oil on wood panel.
Las cuatro bodas de Marisol. Dir. Luis Lucía. Guión Producciones Cinematográficas, 1967. Film.
Daly, N. Kathleen. *Greek and Roman Mythology, A to Z.* New York: Chelsea House, 1992.
Dann, Kevin T. *Bright Colors Falsely Seen: Synaesthesia and the Search for Transcendental Knowledge.* New Haven, CT: Yale University Press, 1998.
De Almeida, Maria Inês. "Indigenous and Juvenile: When Books from Villages Arrive at Bookstores." *The Routledge Companion to International Children's Literature* Edited by John Stephens with Celia Abicalil Belmiro, Alice Curry, Li Lifang and Yasmine S. Motawy. London: Routledge, 2018.
De Certeau, Michel. *The Practice of Everyday Life.* Berkeley: University California Press, 1984.
Deleuze, Gilles, and Félix Guattari. *Kafka: Toward a Minor Literature.* Trans. Dana Polan. Minneapolis: University of Minnesota Press.
Delgado Fernandez, Miguel Angel. *El zapato desaparecido, basado en "La Cenicienta."* Barcelona: Imira Entertainment, 2011.
Della Mirandolla, Giovanni Pico, et al. *A Platonic Discourse Upon Love.* Edited by Edmund G. Gardner. Boston: The Merrymount Press, 1914.
Dentith, Simon. *Parody.* New York: Routledge, 2000.
De Pueblo, Moderna. *Idiotizadas.* Barcelona: Editorial Planeta, 2017.
Derrida, Jacques. *Limited Inc.* Trans. E. Weber. Paris: Éditions Galilée, 1990.
Dever, Carolyn M. "Broken Mirror, Broken Words: Autobiography, Prosopopeia and the Dead Mother in *Bleak House.*" *Studies in the Novel* 27:1 (1995): 42–62.
De Vos, Gail. "Storytelling, Folktales and the Comic Book Format." *Language & Literacy: A Canadian Educational E-Journal* (2001): n.p.
Dhaenens, Frederik, Sofie Van Bauwel and Daniel Biltereyst. "Slashing the Fiction Queer Reading and Transgressing the Boundaries of Screen Studies, Representations, and Audiences." *Journal of Communication Inquiry* 32.4 (2004): 335–347.
Díaz, Isabel. Cenicienta. Illustrated by Margarita Ruiz. Barcelona: Esin, S.A., 2001.
Díaz, Janet. *Ana María Matute.* New York: Twayne Publishers, 1971.
Díez Balda, María Antonia. "La imagen de la mujer en el cómic." *Ciencia Tecnología y género en Iberoamérica.* Edited by Norma Blázquez and Javier Flores. México: UNAM, 2005, 429–455.
Donoghue, Emma. *Kissing the Witch: Old Tales in New Skins.* Broadway: Harper Teen, 1999.
Dos cuentos para dos. Dir. Luis Lucia. Producciones Cifesa, 1947.
Douglas, Lord Alfred. "Two Loves." *The Chameleon.* London: Gay and Bird, 1894.
Downing, Collette. *The Cinderella Complex: Woman's Hidden Fear of Independence.* New York: Summit Books, 1981.
"Un drama desconocido." *Los Niños.* January 1875.
Dundes, Alan, ed. *Cinderella: A Casebook.* Madison: University of Wisconsin Press, 1982.
Durango, María Adela. *EL zapato de la cenicienta.* Barcelona: Bruguera, 1954.
Durkheim, Emile. *Suicide: A Study in Sociology.* New York: The Free Press, 1951.
Eco, Umberto. *Costruire il Nemico: E Altri Scritti Occasionali.* Milano: Bompiani Libri, 2011.
_____. "The Frames of Comic Freedom." *Carnival!* Edited by Thomas A. Sebeok. New York: Mouton, 1984.
_____. "Semantique de la metáphore" *Tel Quel* 55 (1973): 25–46.
Eisner, Will. *Comics and Sequential Art: Principles and Practices from the Legendary.* W.W. Norton: New York, 1985.
Eizaguirre Alvear, Belen, et al., illustrators. *La Cenicienta.* Leon: Editorial Everest, S.A., 2008.
Ellis, Brett Easton. *American Psycho:* New York: Vintage, 1991.

Encabo Fernández, Eduardo, and Isabel Jerez Martínez. *"The Cinderella Who Did Not Want to Eat Partridges:* Is Something Changing Culturally? The Importance of Classic Stories in Education." *Past, Present and Future of Popular Culture: Spaces and Contexts: Proceedings of the IV Congress of SELIC University Press.* Edited by Patricia Bastida Rodríguez, Caterina Calafat, Marta Fernández Morales, José Igor Prieto Arranz, Cristina Suárez Gómez. Palma: Universitat de les Illes Balears, 2011, 1–10.
Epps, Brad. "Virtual Sexuality: Lesbianism, Loss and Deliverance in Carmen Riera's Te deix, amor, la mar como a penyora." *¿Entiendes? Queer Readings, Hispanic Writings.* Edited by Emile L. Bergmann and Paul Julian Smith. Durham: Duke University Press, 1995.
Errauskiñe. Donostia: Edili argitaletxea, 1964.
Escobar, Luis. *La Cenicienta del palace.* Unpublished film script, 1940.
Escrivá, Vicente. *La Cenicienta y Ernesto.* Madrid: Copias Tudela, 1957.
Españolas en París. Dir. Roberto Bodegas. Ágata Films S.A, 1971. Film.
Espinosa, Aurelio Macedonio. *The Folklore of Spain in the American Southwest.* Oklahoma: University of Oklahoma Press, 1990.
Fernández-Babineaux, María. "Androginia e inversión de roles en *Nada* de Carmen Laforet." *Letras Peninsulares* 21.2 (2009): 331–45.
Fernández-Lamarque. María. "Antonio Robles' *La Ceniciento*: A 'Cinderella' Retelling Censored in Franco's Spain" (IRCL) *International Research in Children's Literature* 7.1 (2014): 78–94 with permission of *Hispania*, the American Association of Teachers of Spanish and Portuguese and John Hopkins UP.
Fernández-Lamarque. María. "El bosque, el baile, príncipes y princesas: 'La Bella Durmiente' en *Hable con ella." L'Érudit franco-espagnol* 11 (2017): 52–66.
Fernández-Rodríguez, Carolina. *La Bella Durmiente a través de la historia.* Oviedo: Universidad de Oviedo, 1998.
_____. *Las re-escrituras contemporáneas de Cenicienta.* Principado de Asturias. Consejería de Cultura. Oviedo: Universidad de Oviedo, 1997.
Flaubert, Gustave. *Madame Bovary.* Trans. Eleanor Marx-Aveling. London: W.W. Gibblings, 1856.
Folguera, Pilar. *El feminismo en España: dos siglos de historia.* Madrid: Editorial Pablo Iglesias, 2007.
Fortún, Elena. "Cenicienta." *Celia lo que dice.* Madrid: Alianza Editorial, 1928.
Foucault, Michel. *The History of Sexuality.* Trans. Robert Hurley. Paris: Éditions Gallimard, 1984.
Franco, Marie. "Para que lean los niños: II República y promoción de la literatura infantil." *Prensa, impresos, lectura en el mundo hispánico contemporáneo: homenaje a Jean-François Botrel.* Edited by Jean Michel Desvois. Bordeaux: PILAR, 2005, 251–272.
Freud, Sigmund. *Beyond the Pleasure Principle.* Trans. C.J.M. Hubback. New York: Bartleyby, 1922.
Gaite, Carmen Martín. *El cuarto de atrás.* Barcelona: Editorial Destino, 1978.
Garcia, Ada. *La Ventafocs.* Barcelona: Edicions Cadi, 2013.
García Padrino, Jaime. *Nuestro Antoniorrobles.* Madrid: Asociación Española del Libro Infantil y Juvenil, 1996.
Garlinger, Patrick Paul. *Confessions of the Letter Closet: Epistolary Fiction and Queer Desire in Modern Spain.* Minnesota: University of Minnesota Press, 2005.
Garmendia, Carmelo. *La Cenicienta.* Barcelona: Editors, D.L., 1986.
Genette, Gérard. *Palimpsests.* Trans. Channa Newman and Claude Doubinsky. Lincoln: University of Nebraska Press, 1982.
_____. *Paratexts: Thresholds of Interpretation.* Cambridge: Cambridge University Press, 1997.
Gimeno, Beatriz. *Su cuerpo era su gozo.* Madrid: Akal, 2005.
Goffman, Erving. *The Presentation of the Self in Everyday Life.* London: Allen Lane, 1969.
Graham, Susan Lochrie. "Some Day My Prince Will Come: Images of Salvation in the Gospel According to St Walt." *Culture, Entertainment and the Bible.* Edited by George Aichele. Sheffield: Sheffield Academic Press, 2000, 76–88.

Gramsci, Antonio. *The Prison Notebooks.* Trans. Quintin Hoare. New York: International, 1930.
Grimm, Jacob, and Wilhelm Grimm. *The Complete Fairy Tales of the Brothers Grimm.* Trans. Jack Zipes. New York: Bantam, 1812.
Haase, Donald, ed. *Fairy Tales and Feminism: New Approaches.* Detroit: Wayne State University Press, 2004.
Hable con ella. Dir. Pedro Almodóvar. El Deseo Producciones, 2002.
Hamming, E. Jeanne. "Whatever Turns You On: Becoming-Lesbian and the Production of Desire in the Xenaverse." *Genders* 34 (2001): para. 1–29.
Hartland, Sidney. "Notes on Cinderella." *Cinderella: A Casebook.* Edited by Alan Dundes. Madison: University of Wisconsin Press, 1982.
Haskell, Molly. "Golden Girl." *All the Available Light: A Marilyn Monroe Reader.* Edited by Yona Zeldis McDonough. New York: Touchstone Rockefeller Center, 2002, 113–119.
Hawthorne, Nathaniel. *The Scarlet Letter.* Boston: Ticknor, Reed and Fields, 1850.
Hayes, Joe. *Estrellita de oro.* Hong Kong: Morris Printing. 2000.
Hendrich, Joseph. *Komensky, Jan Amós (Comenius).* New York: Orbis Sensualium Pictus, 1948.
Hennard Dutheil de la Rochère, Marine, Gillian Lathey and Monica Woźniak, eds. *Cinderella Across Cultures: New Directions and Interdisciplinary Perspectives,* Detroit: Wayne State University Press, 2016.
Hertzberger, David. "Spanishness and Identity Formation from the Civil War to the Present: Exploring the Residue of Time." *Spanishness in the Spanish Novel and the Cinema of the 20th–21st Century.* Edited by Cristina Sánchez-Conejero. Cambridge: Cambridge Scholars, 2007, 11–21. Web. 23 January 2010.
Higonnet, Margaret R. "The Playground of the Peritext." *Children's Literature Association Quarterly* 15.2 (1990): 47–49.
Huberman, Edward. "Antoniorrobles' Stories for Children." *Books Abroad* 7.1 (1993): 18–20.
Hutcheon, Linda. *A Theory of Parody.* Urbana: University of Illinois Press, 2000.
Ilombé Raquel. *Leyendas Guineanas.* Andalucía: Doncel, 1981.
Jaime, María. *Cenicienta en Chueca.* Barcelona: Odisea Editorial, 2003.
Jaime, María Felicitas. *Cenicienta en Chueca: Mujeres que aman mujeres.* Madrid: Odisea Editorial S.L., 2003.
Jameson, R.D. "Cinderella in China." *Cinderella: A Casebook.* Edited by Alan Dundes. Madison: University of Wisconsin Press, 982.
Jenkins, Henry. *Textual Poachers: Television Fans and Participatory Culture,* 2d ed. New York: Routledge, 2013.
Jones, Margaret. *The Literary World of Ana Maria Matute.* Lexington: University Press of Kentucky, 1970.
Joosen, Vanessa. *Critical and Creative Perspectives on Fairy Tales: An Intertextual Dialogue from Fairy-Tale Scholarship and Postmodern Retellings.* Detroit: Wayne State University Press, 2011.
Jordan, Barry. "Shifting Generic Boundaries: The Role of Confession and Desire in Laforet's *Nada*." *Neophilologus* 77.3 (1993): 411–22.
K-Hito. *Macaco.* Madrid: Rivadeneyra, 1928.
Kakoudaki, Despina. "World Without Strangers: The Poetics of Coincidence in Pedro Almodóvar´s *Talk to Her.*" *Camera Obscura: A Journal of Feminism, Culture, and Media Studies* 68.2 (2008): 1–39. MLA International Bibliography. Web. 12 September 2013.
Kirkpatrick, Susan. *Mujer, modernismo y vanguardia en España (1898–1931).* Trans. Jacqueline Cruz. Barcelona: Ediciones Cátedra, 2003.
Kotecki, Kristine. "Approximating the Hypertextual, Replicating the Metafictional: Textual and Sociopolitical Authority in Guillermo del Toro's *Pan's Labyrinth.*" *Marvels & Tales: Journal of Fairy-Tale Studies* 24: 2 (2010): 235–254.

Kümmerling-Meibauer, Bettina. "Manga/Comics Hybrids in Picturebooks." *Manga's Cultural Crossroads*. Edited by Jacqueline Bernd and Bettina Kuemmerling-Meibauer. New York: Routledge, 2013.
La Cour, Erin. "Comics as a Minor Literature." *Image [&] Narrative* 17.4 (2016): 79–90.
Lacan, Jaques. *The Four Fundamental Concepts of Psycho-Analysis* Trans. Alan Sheridan. London: W.W. Norton & Norton, 1973.
_____. *On Feminine Sexuality: The Limits of Love and Knowledge*. Trans. Jacqueline Rose. New York: Norton, 1978.
Laforet, Carmen. *Nada*. Barcelona: Editorial Planeta, 1944.
Lalana, Fernando. *Las hermanastras de Cenicienta*. Illustrated by Violeta Monreal. Madrid: Editorial Bruño, 1999.
Lara, Antonio. *Tebeos: Los primeros 100 años*. Madrid: Biblioteca Nacional, 1996.
Lavilla Muñoz, Miriam. *Aceptamos marido como animal de compañía*. Barcelona: Editorial Esencia Planeta, 2009.
Law, Julie. *Cinderella*. Amazon Digital Services, 2016.
Leigh Beaman, Patricia. *World Dance Culture*. New York: Routledge, 2018.
Lévi-Strauss, Claude. *The Savage Mind*. Trans. George Weidenfeld. Chicago: University of Chicago Press, 1962.
The Little Mermaid. Dir. Jodi Benson. Disney Productions, 1989. Film.
Livi, Vincenzo. *The Three Graces*. 1840. Museo e Real Boco di Capodimonte, Napoli, Italy. Marble sculpture.
Livingstone, Glenys. "Re-Storying Goddess: Virgin/Maiden, Mother/Creator, Old One/Crone." *The Beltane Papers* 50 (2010): 18–21.
Llamas, Ricardo. *Teoría torcida: Prejuicios y discursos en torno a la "homosexualidad."* Madrid: Siglo XXI de España, 1998.
Llandó, A.M. *Colección Arco Iris*. Bilbao: Editorial Fher, 1960.
Íñigo. *Lola, el más gracioso personaje sexy del cómic*. Barcelona: Editorial Brugera, 1975.
Lo, Melinda. *Ash*. New York: Little, Brown Books for Young Readers, 2010.
López Salamero, Nunila, and Myriam Cameros Sierra. *La Cenicienta que no quería comer perdices*. Barcelona: Editorial Planeta, 2009.
Lorman, Josep. *Las desventuras de Cenicienta*. Illustrated by Lluiso. Barcelona: Marge Books, 2007.
Luce, Clare Boothe. "The 'Love Goddess' Who Never Found Any Love." *All the Available Light: A Marilyn Monroe Reader*. Edited by Yona Zeldis McDonough. New York: Touchstone Rockefeller Center, 2002, 83–102.
Lucero-White Lea, Aurora. *Literary Folklore of the Hispanic Southwest*. San Antonio: Naylor, 1953.
Luque-Vera, Nazario. "La princesa que perdió el pie de su zapatilla." *Comic El Víbora* No. 168. Barcelona: Ediciones La Cúpula, 1993.
Luxemburg, Rosa. "Die Proletalierin" Speech at the Women's Rote Woche (Red Week), Berlin. 8 March 1914. Published in *Ausgewählte Reden und Schriften* 2 (1951): 433–41.
Maas, Vera Sonja. *Cinderella Test: Would You Really Want the Shoe to Fit?* Santa Barbara: ABC-Clio, 2009.
Malinowski, Bronislaw. *Magic, Science and Religion*. Garden City, New York: Doubleday, 1948.
Mallorquí, José. *El despertar de cenicienta*. Barcelona: Editorial Molino, 1943.
Manet, Édouard. *Olympia*. Oil on canvas. Paris, Musée d'Orsay, 1865.
Marcantonio, Carla. "The Mute Female Body and Narrative Dispossession in Pedro Almodóvar's *Talk to Her*." *Women & Performance: A Journal of Feminist Theory* 17.1 (2007): 19–36.
Marías, Julián. *España ante la historia y ante sí misma*. Madrid: Espasa Calpe, 1996.
Marisol rumbo a Río. Dir. Fernando Palacios. Guión Producciones Cinematográficas, 1964. Film.

Martín, Antonio. *Historia del cómic español: 1875–1939.* Barcelona: Editorial Gustavo Gili, 1978.
Martín, Celia. "Defying Common Sense: Casting Pepa Flores/Marisol as Mariana Pineda." *Journal of Iberian and Latin American Studies.* 9:2 (2003): 149–61.
Martín Gaite, Carmen. *Courtship Customs in Postwar Spain.* Trans. Margaret Jones. London: Bucknell University Press, 2004.
_____. "Entrevista con Antoniorrobles." *La búsqueda de interlocutor y otras búsquedas.* Barcelona: Anagrama, 1973.
_____. *Los usos amorosos de la posguerra española.* Barcelona: Anagrama, 1986.
_____. *Usos amorosos de la posguerra española.* Trans. Margaret Jones. Lewisburg: Bucknell University Press, 1984.
Martínez, Noé. *Cenicienta siempre quiso un Wonderbra.* Barcelona: Grupo Zeta, 2009.
Marx, Karl. *The Essential Marx.* Trans. Anna Bostock. Edited by Ernst Fischer and Franz Marek. New York: Herder, 1970.
Massip, Julia, and Chus Martinez. *Cenicienta tiene un mal sueño.* Illustrated by Marisa Ordoñez. Barcelona: Ajuntament de Barcelona, 2002.
Matute, Ana María. *Caballito loco.* Barcelona: Lumen, 1970.
_____. *Fiesta al noroeste.* Barcelona: Editorial Destino, 1952.
_____. *Historias de la Artámila:* Barcelona: Editorial Destino, 1961.
_____. *Paulina.* Barcelona: Lumen, 1969.
_____. *Primera memoria.* Barcelona: Editorial Destino, 1959.
_____. *Sólo un pie descalzo.* Barcelona: Círculo de lectores, 1983.
Maxwell, Megan. *Los príncipes azules también destiñen.* Barcelona: Versátil, 2012.
May-Ron, Rona. "Rejecting the Glass Slipper: The Subversion of Cinderella in Margaret Atwood's The Edible Woman." *Cinderella Across Cultures: New Directions and Interdisciplinary Perspectives.* Edited by Martine Hennard Dutheil de la Rochère, Gillian Lathey and Monik Woźniak. Detroit: Wayne State University Press, 2016, 143–61.
McCloud, Scott. *Understanding Comics: The Invisible Art.* New York: Kitchen Sink Press, 1993.
McIntyre, Mel. *Ash: Not Just Another Cinderella Story*: Independently Published, 2018.
Mead, Herbert. *Mind, Self, and Society.* Chicago: University of Chicago Press, 1967.
Mecachis. "El día de la boda." *La Caricatura* No. 31 (May 25, 1885).
Medina, Celso. "Mesianismo militar en *Raza* de Francisco Franco." *Espéculo: Revista de Estudios Literarios* 30 (2005): n.p. Web. 15 May 2009.
Menéndez Menéndez, María Isabel. *El zapato de Cenicienta: el cuento de hadas del discurso mediático.* Oviedo: Trabe, 2006.
Merino, Ana. *El cómic hispánico.* Madrid: Ed. Cátedra, 2003.
_____. "Women in Comics: A Space for Recognizing Other Voices." *The Comic Journal* 237 (2001): 44–48.
Mestre, Juan Carlos, Monedero Juan Carlos. *Te cuento … Cenicienta.* Pamplona: Alkibla, 2015.
Mestres, Apeles. "Cuento lúgubre." *Granizada.* No. 11 (November 1880).
Miller, Henry. *Tropic of Cancer.* Paris: Obelisk Press, 1934.
Mills, Margaret A. "A Cinderella Variant in the Context of a Muslim Women's Ritual." *Cinderella: A Casebook.* Edited by Alan Dundes. Madison: University of Wisconsin Press, 1982.
Minakata. *Minakaga zuihitsu* (南方随筆). Kindai Digital Library Service. Higashiosaka, Osaka: The National Diet Library, 1911.
Mínguez-López, Xavier. "Subversión e intertextualidad en la saga Shrek." *Didáctica, Lengua y Literatura* 24 (2012): 249–262.
Mitrokhina, Xenia. "The Shining Path of Working Class Cinderella." *Cinderella Across Cultures: New Directions and Interdisciplinary Perspectives.* Edited by Martine Hennard Dutheil de la Rochère, Gillian Lathey and Monika Woźniak. Detroit: Wayne State University Press, 2016.

Moana. Dir. Ron Clements. Disney Productions, 2016. Film.
Moebius, William. "Introduction to Picture Book Codes." *Word and Image: A Journal of Verbal/Visual Enquiry.* 2.2 (1986): 141–158.
Moix, Ana María. *Julia.* Barcelona: Seix Barral, 1970.
_____. "Las virtudes peligrosas." *Las virtudes peligrosas.* Spain: Alfaguara, 1998, 11–51.
Molina Molina, Laura. "Un cuento de hadas en Educación Infantil." Diss. Universidad de Valladolid, 2016.
Morozzi, Cristina. "A Fitting Design." *Cinderella's Revenge.* Edited by Samuele Mazza. Madison: University of Wisconsin Press, 2010.
Mulan. Dir. Tony Bancroft. Disney Productions, 1998. Film.
Muntanyola, Antoni. *Patufet.* Barcelona: Publicaciones de l'Abadia de Montserrat, 1904.
Murayama, Wataru. *Fukigen Cinderella.* 15 October 2010. Tokyo: Dengeki Comics.
Naughten, Rebecca. "Comatose Women in El Bosque: Sleeping Beauty and Other Literary Motifs in Pedro Almodóvar's *Hable con ella.*" *Studies in Hispanic Cinema (Studies in Spanish and Latin American Cinema)* 3.2 (2007): 77–88.
Neira Cruz, Xosé A. *O prodixio dos zapatos de cristal.* Vigo: Galaxia, 2008.
Nerlich, Brigitte. "Synecdoche: A Trope, a Whole Trope, and Nothing but a Trope?" *Tropical Truths: The Epistemology of Metaphor and Other Tropes.* Edited by Armin Burkhardt and Brigitte Nerlich. Berlin: De Gruyter, 2010, 197–319.
Nichols, Geraldine. "Privation in Matute's Fiction for Children." *A Quarterly Journal in Modern Literatures* 39.2 (1985): 125–138.
Nicolaisen, W.F.H. "Why Tell Stories About Innocent, Persecuted Heroines?" *Western Folklore* 52.1 (1993): 61–71.
Nietzsche, Friedrich. *Thus Spoke Zarathustra: A Book for All and None.* Trans. Thomas Wayne. New York: Algora Publishing, 2003.
Nodelman, Perry. *Words About Pictures.* Athens: University of Georgia Press, 1990.
Novoa, Adriana. "Whose Talk Is It? Almodóvar and the Fairy Tale in *Talk to Her.*" *Marvels and Tales: Journal of Fairy-Tale Studies* 19.2 (2005): 224–48.
La nueva Cenicienta. Dir. George Sherman. Guión Producciones Cinematográficas, 1965. Film.
Ober de Baubeta, Patricia Anne. "Fairy-Tale Intertext in Iberian and Latin American Women's Writing." *Fairy Tale and Feminism: New Approaches.* Edited by Donald Hasse Detroit: Wayne University Press, 2004.
Odai, J. *Rehearsing the Revolution: Radical Performance, Radical Politics in the English Restoration.* Newark: University of Delaware Press, 2000.
Operación Cabaretera. Dir. Mariano Ozores. Îzaro Films, 1967. Film.
Ortiz, Lourdes. "Cenicienta: Parábola en dos actos." *Los motivos de Circe.* Madrid: Ediciones El Dragón, 1988.
Pan's Labyrinth (El laberinto del Fauno). Dir. Guillermo del Toro. Estudios Picasso, 2006. Film.
Payne, Stanley. *Franco y José Antonio: El extraño caso del fascismo español.* Trans. Joaquín Adsuar. Barcelona: Planeta, 1997.
_____. *El régimen de Franco: 1936–1975.* Trans. Belén Urrutia Domínguez and María Rosa López González. Madrid: Alianza, 1987.
Penmartín, José. *¿Qué es lo 'nuevo'?: Consideraciones sobre el momento español del presente.* Santander: Alsu, 1938.
Pennsylvania 6–5000. Glenn Miller Orchestra. Jazz.
Peppermint Frappé. Dir. Carlos Saura. Elías Querejeta Producciones Cinematográficas S.L, 1967. Film.
Pérez-Sánchez, Gema. *Queer Transitions in Contemporary Spanish Culture: From Franco to La Movida.* Albany: State University of New York Press, 2007.
Perrault, Charles. *The Fairy Tales of Charles Perrault.* London: Harrap, 1922.
Pertursa, Inmaculada. *La salida del armario: Lecturas desde la otra acera (Sylvia Molloey, Cristina Peri Rossi, Carmen Riera, Esther Tusquets).* Gijón: Libros del Pexe, 2005.

Piercy, Marge. "Looking Good." *All the Available Light: A Marilyn Monroe Reader.* Edited by Yona Zeldis McDonough. New York: Touchstone Rockefeller Center, 2002, 104–106.
Pinkola Estes, Clarissa. *Women Who Run with the Wolves: Myths and Stories of the Wild Women Archetype.* Random House: New York, 1992.
Pocholo. *El pueblo en armas.* Barcelona: Publicaciones Pocholo. 1936.
"Post Truth: The Art of the Lie." *The Economist.* September 10, 2016.
Primo de Rivera, José Antonio. *Textos de doctrina política.* Madrid: Sección Femenina del Movimiento, 1964.
The Prince and the Showgirl. Dir. Laurence Olivier. Warner Bros, 1957. Film.
The Princess and the Frog. Dir. Ron Clements. Disney Productions, 2009. Film.
Rael, Juan B. *Cuentos españoles de Colorado y Nuevo México.* Santa Fe: Museum of New Mexico Press, 1936.
Ramos, Máximo. *Las aventuras milicianas del terrible Paco Lara.* Madrid: Prensa del Movimiento, 1937.
Raphael, *The Three Graces.* 1515–27. The Metropolitan Museum of Art, New York. Print Engraving.
Raza. Dir. José Sánchez Heredia. CEA, 1941. DVD.
Reinhart, Coburn. *Domitíla.* Auburn, CA: Shen's Books, 2000.
The Revenant. Dir. Alejandro Iñárritu. Regency Enterprises, 2016. Film.
Reveter, Emma. *Citas en Manhattan.* Barcelona: Planeta, 2008.
Ribas, Federico (Illustrator). *La Cenicienta o el Zapatito de Cristal.* Madrid: Calleja, 1930.
Rich, Adrienne. "Compulsory Heterosexuality and Lesbian Existence." *Signs* 5: 4 (1980): 631–660. *JSTOR,* www.jstor.org/stable/3173834.
Riera, Carmen. *Te dejo, amor, en prenda el mar.* Trans. Luisa Cotoner. Madrid: Espasa Calpe, Colección Austral, 1975.
Rifaterre, Michael. *Fictional Truth.* Baltimore: Johns Hopkins University Press, 1990.
Robbins, Jill. *Crossing Through Chueca: Lesbian Literary Culture in Queer Madrid.* Minneapolis: University of Minnesota Press, 2011.
_____. "Cyberspace and the Cyberdildo: Dislocations in Cenicienta en Chueca." *Studies in Twentieth & Twenty-First Century Literature* 30.1 (2006): 107–28.
Robledo, Eduardo Tejero. "Nuestro Antoniorrobles." *Cuadernos de Literatura Infantil y Juvenil* 9 (1996): 346. Web. 10 August 2009.
Robles, Antonio. *La Cenicienta.* Madrid: Estrella, 1936.
Roman, Regina. *Del suelo al cielo.* Clessidra, 2011.
Romera Castillo, José. "Perfiles autobiográficos de la *Otra Generación del 27* (la del humor)." *Actas del XII Congreso de la Asociación Internacional de Hispanistas* 4 (1998): 241–47. Dialnet. Web. 21–26 August 2008.
Romero-Jódar, Andrés. "Comic Books and Graphic Novels in Their Generic Context. Towards a Definition and Classification of Narrative Iconical Texts." *Journal of the Spanish Association of Anglo-American Studies* 35.1 (2013): 117–35.
Ronnberg, Ami. *The Book of Symbols: Reflections on Archetypal Images.* Cologne: Taschen, 2010.
Rooth, Anna Birgitta. *The Cinderella Cycle.* Lund: C.W.K. Gleerup, 1951.
Rose, Margaret. *Parody: Ancient, Modern and Post-Modern.* Cambridge: Cambridge University Press, 1993.
Rowntree, Margaret, Nicole Moulding and Lia Bryant. "Feminine Sexuality in Chick Lit." *Australian Feminist Studies* 27:72 (2012): 121–136.
Rubens, Peter Paul. *The Three Graces.* 1636. Dulwich Picture Gallery. London, Oil painting.
Ruíz, Sofía. *Sexutopías.* Madrid: Editorial Egales, 2006.
Rus, Rebecca. *Ginebra para dos.* Barcelona: Editorial Esencia Planeta, 2013.
Said, Edward. *Orientalism.* Trans. Robert Hurley. New York: Pantheon Books, 1978.
Salmon Catherine, Symmons Don. "Slash Fiction and Human Mating Psychology." *The Journal of Sex Research* 41.1 (2004): 94–100.

San Ildefonso, Mariano. *Versión teatral de la Cenicienta en verso.* Madrid: Gráficas Sebastián, 1972.
San Souci, Robert. *Little Gold Star.* Singapore: Tien Wah Press. 2000.
Sánchez-Rodriguez, Virginia. *La banda sonora musical en el cine español y su empleo en la configuración de tipologías de mujer (1960-1969).* Salamanca: Editorial de la Universidad de Salamanca, 2014.
Santos, Juliá. *Historia de las dos Españas.* Madrid: Santillana, 2004.
Sanz, Carlos. "Antoniorrobles, Cuentacuentos radiofónico." *Cuadernos de Literatura Infantil y Juvenil* 147.15 (2002): 54–61.
Sartre, Jean-Paul. *Huis Clos.* Gallimard: Paris, 1944.
_____. *Nausea.* (French: *La Nausée*). Trans. Lloyd Alexander. New York: Penguin Book, 1938.
Savariego, Berta. "La correspondencia entre el personaje y la naturaleza en obras representativas de Ana María." *Explicación de textos literarios* 13:1 (1984): 59–67.
Scarry, Elaine. *The Body in Pain.* Oxford: Oxford University Press, 1985.
Schechner, R. *Between Theatre and Anthropology.* Philadelphia: Pennsylvania University Press, 1985.
Schofer, Peter, and Rice, Donald. "Metaphor, Metonyny and Synecdoche (Re) Visited." *Semiotica* 21: 1–2 (1977): 121–49.
Schwarcz, Joseph and Chava Schwarcz. *The Picture Book Comes of Age.* Chicago: American Library Association, 1991.
Sedgwick, Eve Kosofsky. *Epistemology of the Closet.* Berkeley: University of California Press, 1990.
Serrano, María Luisa. *La Cenicienta.* Madrid: Mestas Ediciones, 2002.
Seto, Ken-ichi. "On the Cognitive Triangle: The Relation Between Metaphor, Metonymy and Synecdoche." Unpublished manuscript, 1995.
Sex and the City. HBO New York. (1998–2004). Television.
Shawcross, Rebecca. *Shoes: An Illustrated History.* London: Bloomsbury, 2014.
Shrek. Dir. Andrew Adamson. Dreamworks Productions, 2001. Film.
Silva, Emilio, Juan Carlos Mestre and Juan Carlos Monedero. "Book Presentation: *Te cuento ... Cenicienta*." Bookstore Traficante de Sueños, Madrid. 22 December 2015. Lecture.
Simpatía: La vida de Marisol contada por ella misma en 25 capítulos. Bilbao: Editorial Fher, 1962.
Sipe, Lawrence R. "How Picturebooks Work: A Semiotically Framed Theory of Text-Picture Relationships." *Children's Literature in Education* 29: 2-1 (1998): 97–108.
Sleeping Beauty. Dir. Clyde Geronimi. Disney Productions, 1959. Film.
Smith, Paul Julian. *Laws of Desire: Questions of Homosexuality in Spanish Writing and Film, 1960–1990.* Oxford: Clarendon, 1992.
Snow White. Dir. William Cottrell. Disney Productions, 1937. Film.
Soler, Maria Cristina. *Cenicienta.* Illustrated by Garmendia, Barcelona: Editors S.A., 1986.
Soliño, María Elena. *Women and Children First: Spanish Women Writers and the Fairy Tale Tradition.* Potomac, MD: Scripta Humanística, 2002.
Spiegelman, Art. *The Complete Maus: The Survivor's Tale.* New York: Pantheon Books, 1996.
Stella, Gian Antonio. *Negri, Froci, Giudei: L'eterna guerra contro l'altro.* Studio Editoriale Littera: Milan, 2009.
Stephens, John. *From Picture Book to Literary Theory.* Sydney: Saint Claire Press, 1994.
_____. *Language and Ideology in Children's Fiction.* Harlow: Pearson, 1992.
_____. "Picture Books and Ideology." *The Routledge Companion to Picturebooks.* Edited by Bettina Kümmerling-Meibauer. London: Routledge, 2018.
_____. *Retelling Stories, Framing Cultures.* New York: Routledge, 2013.
Stephens, John, and Ruth Waterhouse. *Literature, Language and Change.* New York: Routledge, 1990.

Suárez Solís, Sara. "Bibicienta." *¡Mujer, mujer...! Artículos, charlas y cuentos*. Oviedo: Gráficas Summa, 1991, 139–145.
_____. *Cenicienta 39*. Ávaco, 1989. *CICEES*, http//www.jstor.org/stable/20795710. Accessed 11 Oct. 2017.
_____. "Las cenicientas ya no son lo que eran." *¡Mujer, mujer...! Artículos, charlas y cuentos*. Oviedo: Gráficas Summa, 1991, 135–138.
Tangled. Dir. Nathan Greno. Disney Productions, 2010. Film.
Taraborrelli, Randy. *The Secret Life of Marilyn Monroe*. New York: Hachette, 2008.
Tatar, Maria. *The Hard Facts of the Grimms' Fairy Tales*. Princeton: Princeton University Press, 1987.
TBO. Barcelona: Editorial Brugera, 1917.
Terdiman, Richard. *Discourse/Counter Discourse: The Theory and Practice of Symbolic Resistance in Nineteenth Century France*. Ithaca, NY: Cornell University Press, 1989.
Todorov, Tzvetan. *The Conquest of America or the Question of the Other*. New York: Harper Perennial, 1996.
_____. *The Fantastic*. Trans. R. Richard Howard. Cleveland: Case Western Reserve University Press, 1973.
_____. "Synecdoches." *Communications* 16 (1970): 25–35.
Tolan, Fiona. *Margaret Atwood: Feminism and Fiction*. Amsterdam: Rodopi, 2007.
Tómbola. Dir. Luis Lucia. Guion Producciones Cinematográficas, 1962.
Torres, Rosana. "Antoniorrobles, iniciador de la moderna literatura infantil española, falleció ayer en El Escorial." *El País* 24 January 1983. Web. 21 February 2008.
Towbin, Adessa et al. "Images of Gender, Race, Age, and Sexual Orientation in Disney Feature-Length Animated Films." *Journal of Feminist Family Therapy* 15:4 (2004): 19–44.
Trapeze. Dir. Carol Reed. Hill-Hecht-Lancaster Productions. 1956. Film.
Turner, V.W. *The Anthropology of Performance*. New York: PAJ Publications, 1988.
_____. *The Ritual Process*. New York: Cornell University Press, 1969.
Tusquets, Esther. *Siete miradas en un mismo paisaje*. Barcelona: Lumen, 1981.
Valis, Noël. "La literatura infantil de Ana María Matute." *Cuadernos hispanoamericanos* 382 (1982): 404–14.
Ventós, J. Massó. *La Rondalla del Dijous*. Barcelona: Editorial Catalana, 1924.
Villar Liébano, Luisa. *Cenicienta y el mirlo mágico*. Illustrated by Javier Olivares, Madrid: Ediciones S.M., 2007.
Vives-Falcó, Ramón. *Pocholo*. Madrid: Editorial Santiago Vives, 1931.
Weininger, Elliot B. "Pierre Bourdieu on Social Class and Symbolic Violence" *Alternative Foundations of Class Analysis*. Edited by Erik Olin. Cambridge: Cambridge University Press, 2005, 119–171.
Weinman, Jaime J., "Big Green Money Machine." *Maclean's* 120.19 (2007): n.p.
Weldt-Basson, Helene Carol. *Masquerade and Social Justice in Contemporary Latin American Fiction*. Albuquerque: University of New Mexico Press, 2017.
Wills, David, and Stephen Schmidt. *Marilyn Monroe: Metamorphosis*. New York: HarperCollins Publishers, 2011.
Wilshire, Donna. *Virgin, Mother, Crone: Myths and Mysteries of the Triple Goddess*. Rochester: Inner Traditions, 1993.
Wright, Sarah. *The Child in Spanish Cinema*. Oxford: Oxford University Press, 2015.
Yarza, Alejandro. "Las lágrimas petrificadas del general Franco: fascismo y *kitsch* en *Raza* de José Luis Sánez de Heredia." *Hispanismo y cine*. Edited by Javier Herrera and Cristina Martínez Carazo. Madrid: Iberoamericana, 2007, 65–88.
Zevallos. Zuleyka. "You Have to be Anglo and Not Look Like Me: Identity and Belonging Among Young Women of Turkish and Latin American Backgrounds in Melbourne." *Australian Geographer* 39.1 (2008): 21–43.
Zipes, Jack. *Don't Bet on the Prince*. New York: Methuen Inc. 1986.

_____. *Fairy Tales and the Art of Subversion: The Classical Genre for Children and the Process of Civilization.* New York: Wildman, 1983.

_____. "The Triumph of the Underdog: Cinderella's Legacy." *Cinderella Across Cultures: New Directions and Interdisciplinary Perspectives.* Edited by Hennard Dutheil de la Rochère, Gillian Lathey and Monika Woźniak. Detroit: Wayne State University Press, 2016.

Zolushka. Dir. Nadezhda Kosheverova and Mihail Shapiro. Lenfilms Studio, 1947. Film.

Index

adaptations 12–14, 19, 20, 27, 46, 57, 68, 82, 87–90, 100, 104, 110, 130, 138, 151–3, 161, 170
Almodóvar A.R. 9, 13
Almodóvar, Pedro 69, 177
American Psycho 81, 82, 172
Americanization 2, 14, 21, 27, 50, 52, 81, 104, 168, 172–3, 178–80
analepsis 70
Andersen, Hans Christian 120, 126, 140, 169
androgynous 10, 105
aporia 76, 80 19, 179
Arguedas, José María 6
ashes 5, 68, 82, 83, 90, 111, 175, 176
atheism 37
Atwood, Margaret 104, 111, 116, 168, 169, 176

Bacchilega 2, 3, 19, 55, 170
ball 1, 5, 7, 29, 33, 36, 38, 45, 46, 75, 86–8, 91, 93, 100, 101, 106, 107, 109, 121, 130, 133–5, 139, 144, 147, 148, 150, 152, 153, 155–7, 159, 160, 163
Basile, Giambatista 15, 26, 112, 170
Beauty and the Beast 61, 170
Beauvoir, Simone 48, 170
Bernard, Clemente 139, 169
Bernheimer, Kate 23, 170
Bettleheim, Bruno 81, 170
body 17, 18, 20, 34, 56, 63, 64, 69, 81–6, 91, 92, 115, 116, 120, 122, 127, 129, 147
The Body in Pain 113, 179
The Book of Symbols 24, 135–6, 169, 178
Borges, Jorge Luis 40, 170

Bottigheimer, Ruth 104, 170
Bourdieu, Pierre 57, 58, 170, 180
branding 13–21, 23, 25
Bridget Jones Diary 78, 170
Briggs, Raymond 94, 170
bullfighting 53
bullied 111, 131
Búsqueme a esa chica 43, 53, 171
Butler, Judith 7–11, 57, 73, 74, 77, 171

Caballé, Ana 129, 131, 171
El Calentito 66
camera 42, 29, 109, 112, 113, 122, 174
Campoamor, Clara 149
canonical 6, 27, 29, 33, 37, 97, 107, 152
Canova 87, 171
carnival 31, 34, 53, 86, 171, 172
Carter, Angela 15, 104, 171
Castilian, Castilian-Leonese 38–9
Catholicism 40, 52, 56, 86, 87, 126, 131, 155, 165
censorship 9, 26, 38, 154
chick lit 78, 79, 81, 85, 92, 93, 161, 167, 178
Chueca 10, 66–70, 72–7, 159, 174, 178
Cinderella Across Cultures 1, 4, 6, 19, 104, 170, 174, 176, 181
Cinderella Complex 11, 79, 85, 93, 108, 109, 172
Cinderfella 68, 171
Cohen, Leonard 141
Comenius, Jan Amos 95, 174
comics 12, 94, 96, 102, 124–8, 152, 163, 168, 170, 172, 174–7
communism 29, 37; *see also* Marx, Karl

183

Confessions of the Letter Closet 69, 173
Conrad, Bob 44, 49–53
conservative 55, 131, 160
The Cop and the Anthem 114, 171
cultural 13, 22, 24, 45, 79, 82, 108, 145, 159
cup 16, 61, 102

dance 10, 41, 44–52, 75, 76, 87, 107, 110, 133, 144–6, 148, 156, 175
Dann, Kevin 140
Deleuze and Guattari 125, 172
Dentith, Simon 132, 172
De Pueblo, Moderna 125, 134, 163, 172
Derrida, Jacques 42, 172
detective 12, 152, 155, 156
Di Caprio, Leonardo 165
dictatorship, dictator 8, 26, 28, 34, 141, 145, 148, 162, 166
Disney 1, 46, 51, 82, 84, 90, 91, 97, 153, 169, 170, 171, 175–180
doll 10, 41, 48, 49, 53, 58–60, 62, 115, 118
donkey 17, 18
Douglas, Lord Alfred 71
Downing, Collette 11, 79, 109, 172
drama 2, 11, 12, 28, 34, 97, 122, 126, 152, 154, 155, 171, 172
dress 1, 31–5, 38, 48, 50, 52, 75, 82, 83, 86, 91, 107, 135, 153, 156, 157, 160
Dundes, Alan 6, 18, 105, 172, 174, 176
Durkheim, Emile 121, 172

Eco, Umberto 8, 20, 172
economy 53
enemy 10, 21, 143
The Epistemology of the Closet 70, 177
erasing 21, 28, 69, 134, 143, 146, 147
Espinosa, M. Aurelio 13, 163
ethos 5, 97, 150

fairy godmother 5, 7, 14, 17, 20, 29, 33, 90, 100, 107, 132, 135, 145, 152, 153, 155, 156, 157, 160, 163, 165; *see also* godmother
Falange 26, 30, 35, 39, 166
feminism 2, 19, 3–5, 79, 90, 100, 103–5, 127, 152, 158, 168, 175, 178, 180
Fernández-Babineaux, María 67, 173
Fernández-Lamarque, Maia (Maria) 1–3, 69, 173
Fernández-Rodríguez, Carolina 105, 173
Flamenco 50–2

Folguera, Pilar 130, 136, 173
folklore 2–4, 13, 17, 152, 156, 165, 170, 175, 177
folktales 13, 18, 20, 23, 68, 69, 96, 100, 103–4, 124, 127, 129, 130, 172
Fortún, Elena 28, 36, 38–9, 160, 167, 171, 173
fractured fairy tales 12, 55, 152, 157
Francoism 3, 26–35, 37–40, 44, 47, 49, 50, 52–5, 66–7, 69, 127, 129, 130–1, 146, 162, 166–8, 173, 176–7, 180
Freud, Sigmund 10, 49, 173
Fukigen Cinderella 105, 177

Gaite, Carmen Martín 28, 30–2, 54, 69, 129–130, 166, 173, 176
García Lorca, Federico 141
García Padrino, Jaime 28, 173
gender 2, 8–10, 26, 28, 30, 34–5, 38, 40, 47, 58, 66–8, 73, 88, 96–8, 104–6, 144, 146–8, 152, 158, 165, 169, 171, 174, 180
Génette, Gerard 11, 97, 110, 113, 173
godmother 16, 25, 36–7, 100, 107, 152; *see also* fairy godmother
gods 36, 37, 86, 145, 166, 168
Goffmann, Erwing 42, 173
graces 86–7, 93, 171–2, 175, 178
Gramsci, Antonio 35, 173
grandmother 76, 108
Grimm 1–3, 5, 7, 12, 18, 27, 29–31, 33, 36–8, 44, 82–3, 104, 107–8, 112, 116, 130, 152–4, 174, 180

Hable con ella 69, 105
hell 25, 85, 141, 165
Homolumbú 60
Hutcheon, Linda 134, 174
Hypatia 149
hypertext 2, 11, 110–4, 125, 151, 174
hypotext 5, 72, 111–2, 117, 127

identity 8, 10, 20–1, 32, 34, 45, 48–9, 53, 58–9, 62–3, 66–9, 71–3, 76, 91, 96, 105, 136, 150, 171, 174, 180
ideology 26–7, 31–3, 35, 39, 47, 49, 61, 67, 96–8, 104, 126, 131
Inca 24, 145, 165
incarnation 14, 65, 88, 109, 140
intertextuality 9, 55, 69, 72, 96, 105, 151, 174, 176

Jaime, María Felícitas 159

Jones, Margaret 21, 55, 176
Jones, Swann Steven 2, 4

Kahlo, Frida 148
Kent, Victoria 32
Khmer Rouge 145
Kissing the Witch: Old Tales in New Skins 68, 172
Kümmerling-Meibauer, Betina 94, 174, 179

Lacan, Jacques 31, 32, 47, 175
La Cour, Erin 125, 175
Laforet, Carmen 54, 67, 69, 173–5
language 3, 6–7, 18, 24, 46, 54, 60, 73, 81, 93, 96, 98, 100–1, 125, 127, 146–7, 149–150, 152–3, 166, 168, 170, 172, 179
Latin America 2, 5, 14, 36, 66, 68, 71–2, 95, 105, 126, 175, 177, 180
law 24, 30, 34, 40, 66, 68, 124, 129, 162, 166, 179
Law, Julie 67–8, 174
lesbians 11, 67, 69, 70–1, 73–7, 147, 159, 167, 169, 173–4, 178
Lévi-Strauss, Claude 22, 175
liberal 30, 32, 53, 104, 132
literary 5, 10, 12, 14, 28, 40–1, 55–7, 61–5, 69–70, 76, 80, 95, 97, 110, 112, 125, 127, 140, 147, 152, 161, 165, 167
Little Red Riding Hood 28, 108, 127–8, 136, 159
Livi, Vincenzo 87, 175
lover 11, 68, 70–1, 73–6, 80, 87, 91, 112, 114–5, 118–9, 121, 130
Lucas Cranach 87, 172
Luque-Vera, Nazario 89, 163, 175
Luxemburgo, Rosa 149, 175

Madame Bovary 56, 173
magic 21, 25, 29, 33, 36, 41, 59, 60, 89–90, 103, 105, 107, 144–46, 149, 152–7, 166, 180
Malinche 148
Malinowski, Bronislaw 21, 175
manga 94, 96, 102, 105, 168, 170, 174
Marisol 10, 39, 41–53, 162, 167, 169, 170, 172, 175, 179
Martín, Antonio 126, 175
Marx, Karl 29, 30, 176
mask 32, 33, 34, 41, 47–9, 53, 61, 73–4, 86, 92–3, 147
Matute, Ana María 10, 54–5, 58–62, 64, 161, 172, 174, 176, 177, 180

McCloud, Scott 124, 176
Mead, Herbert 59, 176
meaning 3, 6, 11, 16, 18, 20, 23, 29, 38, 58, 61, 65, 76, 92, 98, 102, 108, 133, 134, 138, 147
Mecachis 126, 176
Merino, Ana 127, 176
Mesoamerica 95
Mestre, Juan Carlos 11, 126, 138, 161, 176, 179
Mestres, Apeles 126. 176
metamorphosis 7, 14, 17, 107–8, 120, 135, 152, 180
metaphor 11, 34, 60, 63–5, 70, 75, 78, 92, 95, 98, 113, 122, 139–141, 150–1, 159, 168, 172, 177, 179
metonymy 2, 6, 7, 9, 12, 63–4, 90, 141, 150, 179
Mills, A. Margaret 18, 19, 176
mimesis 46, 47, 50
minor 10, 57, 84, 124–5, 142, 144, 172, 175
mise en abyme 53
misery 2, 79, 86, 91, 99, 102
Mistral, Gabriela 126
Moebius, William 94–5, 176
monarchy 9, 28–30, 146, 166
Monedero, Juan Carlos 11, 138, 141, 161, 176, 179
Monroe, Marilyn 111, 113–4, 117, 119, 121–2, 174–5, 177, 180
Morozzi, Cristina 64, 177
mother 5, 10, 11, 13, 15, 17–18, 36, 38, 41, 43–4, 46, 49, 53, 55–6, 62, 90, 103–4, 106, 110–122, 129, 130–2, 142–3, 149, 153–4, 161, 168, 172, 175, 180
motherland 71
La Movida 66, 67, 152, 177
music 95, 97, 119, 122, 141, 145, 147, 152, 161–3, 179
mutilation 19, 23–4, 165

Nausea 115; *see also* Sartre, Jean Paul
Nelken, Margarita 32
Nerlich, Brigitte 63, 177
Nicolaisen, W.F.H 87, 138, 168, 177
Nietzsche, Frederick 107, 177
Nodelman, Perry 94, 95, 177
La nueva Cenicienta 10, 41–2, 45, 47, 49, 53, 147, 162, 167, 177

Olivier, Lawrence 114, 119, 178
otherness 10, 54–5, 57, 59, 61–5, 142, 147, 169

186 Index

pain 55, 82, 102, 109, 111, 113, 115, 116, 119, 123, 148, 179
El País del Pie Descalzo 59, 60
palimpsest 21
Pan's Labyrinth 60, 177
paratextual 11, 97, 98, 99, 151
parody 11, 125, 128, 134, 135, 137, 172, 174, 178
Pennsylvania 6-5000 114, 177
performance 10, 12, 34, 41–3, 45–51, 53, 74, 97, 113, 133, 135, 136, 147, 167, 171, 175, 177, 180
Perrault 1, 2, 5, 12, 15, 26, 27, 29, 30–1, 33, 36, 38, 90, 97, 104, 107, 116, 130, 152, 153–4, 158, 171, 177
persecuted girl 13, 138
Peruvian 6, 66, 70–2, 75
Peter Pan 10, 44, 170
pícara 10, 41–3, 49, 53
picture books 2, 11, 12, 94–98, 105–108, 124, 159, 176, 179
Pierrot 33–5, 38, 160
Pinkola, Estes, Clarissa 24–5, 84–5, 178; see also Women Who Run with the Wolves
Pinocchio 108, 128
poesis 46
Pope/Papa 35
Popol Vuh 95–6
porn 89, 128, 163
power 18, 21–5, 29, 34, 39, 40, 43, 53, 56–8, 62, 68, 88, 95, 107, 131, 142–6, 148–150, 154, 166, 168, 170, 171
Pretty Woman 38, 151
Primo de Rivera, José Antonio 26, 31, 165, 166, 178
prince 45, 49, 50–2, 55–7, 64, 75, 79, 81, 83–5, 90–3, 100, 102–5, 107–8, 112, 114, 119–120, 130, 133–5, 138, 144, 146–8, 153–6
The Prince and the Showgirl 114, 178
The Princess and the Frog 178
The Princess and the Pea 120, 169
principle pleasure/reality 173; see also Freud, Sigmund
progressive 9, 68, 137, 167
prosopopeia 10, 55, 61–2, 65, 147, 172

queer 66–71, 76, 161, 171–3, 177–8

race 9, 10, 20, 26, 28, 38, 39, 82, 96, 167, 180
rape 116

Raphael 87, 178
Rapunzel 82
raunchiness 3, 168
religion 9, 14, 20–1, 26, 28, 35–7, 165
renaming 8, 21–2, 29, 61, 89, 128, 143
replacing 8, 26, 28, 31–2, 55, 126, 166, 173
republic 8, 26, 28, 31–2, 55, 126, 166, 173
Rifaterre 61
ritual 7, 12, 13, 18, 20–3, 25, 36, 43, 145, 176, 180
Robbins, Jill 67–8, 70, 178
Robles Antonio. Antoniorrobles 9, 26–30, 32, 34–40, 147, 154, 160, 166,-7, 173–4, 176, 178–180
Rodophis 57
romanticism 51, 72–3, 90, 133, 152, 160–1
Rooth, Birgitta 6, 18, 50, 178
Rose, Margaret 134, 178
roses 16, 25, 50, 131, 141
Rubens 87, 178

Sans Souci, Robert D. 16, 20, 22
Santa Teresa Ávila de 5, 15, 16, 22
Sappho's Fable 68, 170
Sartre, Jean Paul 25, 115, 179
The Scarlet Letter 14, 174
schadenfreude 24
Scheherazade 149
Sección Femenina 30
Second Republic 31, 166
Sedgwick, Eve Kosofsky 70, 179
Sex and the City 80, 179
sexuality 17, 69, 73–5, 78, 81, 88–9, 93, 128, 131, 133, 135, 136, 158, 167, 168, 173, 175, 178
Sexutopías 67, 178
shoes 5, 50, 56–7, 81, 99, 100, 102, 106–8, 110, 135, 150, 157, 159, 162, 179
Shrek 84, 176, 179
slash fiction 74, 167, 178
Sleeping Beauty 69, 76, 82, 108, 120, 127–32, 134, 136, 159, 177, 179
Snow White 10, 44, 45, 46, 82, 83, 108, 128, 136, 159, 179
Soliño, María Elena 27, 179
Sonja Maas, Vera 89, 175
Spanish Civil War 9, 26, 28, 36, 52, 54–5, 146, 148, 152, 160, 166–7, 174
Spiegelman 126–7, 179
spiritualism 36, 86, 95, 145

stairs 7, 42, 42, 109, 160
star 9, 13, 14, 16–19, 21, 22, 50, 111, 113, 118–9, 152, 156, 162, 179
Stephens, John 1–4, 6, 95–6, 98, 172, 179
stepmother 1, 6, 15'16, 19, 20, 22, 24'5, 83, 87, 100, 112, 116–7, 138, 142–4, 153–4, 156, 160
struggle 43, 69, 75, 82, 90, 105, 112, 139, 149, 161, 162, 166
suicide 114, 116–7, 120–2, 161, 172
symbol 14, 18, 26, 29, 39, 56, 92, 114, 117, 119, 121, 125, 163, 168
symbolic power 58, 170
synecdoche 17, 54–6, 62–5, 147, 177, 179

Tatar, Maria 27, 180
tebeos 125, 128, 175
Terdiman, Richard 38, 39, 167, 180
Todorov, Tvetan 57, 63, 166, 180
Tómbola 44, 180
Trapeze 114, 180
Turner, Victor 10, 22, 24, 41, 46, 180

violence 14, 23, 102, 106, 124, 142, 148–9, 158, 180
virgin 11, 13, 14, 16–7, 20, 87, 89, 131–2, 165, 168, 180

womanhood 98, 167–8
Women Who Run with the Wolves 84, 178; *see also* Pinkola, Estes, Clarissa
wonderbra 60, 171
Wonderland 60, 171
word 6, 16, 22–4, 26, 36, 46–7, 58, 60, 65, 67, 74, 77, 80, 89, 92, 94, 100–1, 117, 120, 124–5, 128, 133–4, 138, 144, 146, 149, 150, 170, 172, 176, 177
Wright, Sarah 44, 48, 180

Ye Shian/Yeshian 57, 90

Zipes, Jack 27, 68, 104, 151, 166, 174, 180
Zolushka 112, 166, 181
Zorricienta 11, 132–7, 163

www.ingramcontent.com/pod-product-compliance
Ingram Content Group UK Ltd.
Pitfield, Milton Keynes, MK11 3LW, UK
UKHW042011140426
5217IPUK00015B/1109